I0761961

THE MYTHIC BONES DUOLOGY

BOOK ONE

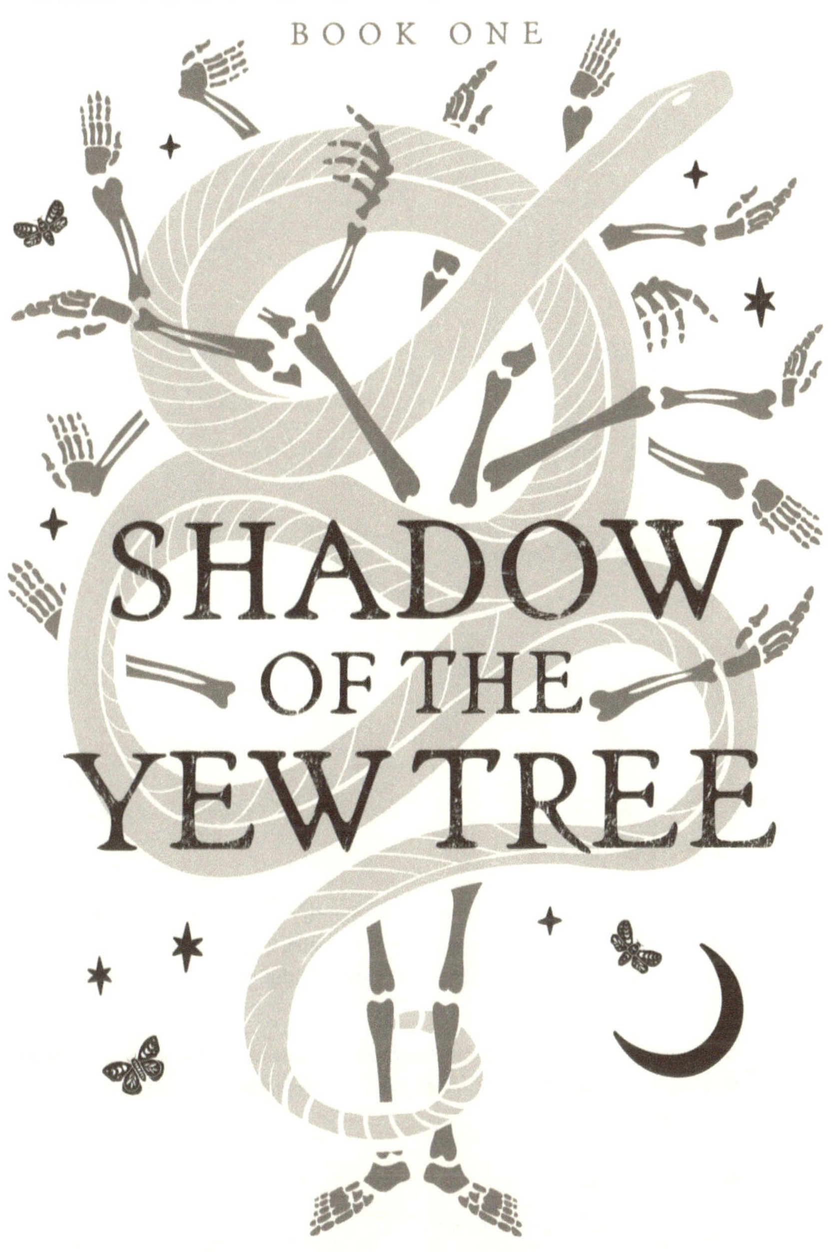

SHADOW OF THE YEW TREE

KATE GATELEY

First Edition—2025

ISBN

978-1-0694347-1-5 (Hardcover)

978-1-0694347-0-8 (Paperback)

978-1-0694347-2-2 (eBook)

Cover design: Covet Design

Author photo: Ashley Marston Photography

Edited by: Janet Layberry & M. Maryann

WWW.KATEGATELEY.COM

PRAISE FOR BOOK ONE OF THE MYTHIC BONES DUOLOGY

"This tale masterfully fuses worldbuilding (the "underground magic") with a burgeoning romance ... The many questions that linger and a smashing cliffhanger are more than enough incentive to keep eyes out for the next installment." —*Kirkus Reviews*

"The book's ability to incorporate the magical and the mundane, and to imagine reincarnated beings muddling through ordinary problems and seeking out therapy for help, makes for a refreshing, often surprising plot." — *Foreword* Clarion Reviews

"The seamless fusion of paranormal fantasy with Celtic folklore is an obvious plus, but the story's real power comes from the emotionally super-charged dynamic between Ronan and Phoebe. Their relationship is messy, confusing—and completely authentic." — BlueInk Review

To all of the neurodivergent kids lost in the shuffle:
May you find your peace and meet your people.

AUTHOR'S NOTE

Shadow of the Yew Tree is a contemporary fantasy and romance novel for adult readers. Throughout the story, readers will find explicit, on-page romance; mature language and themes; and violent imagery, including weapons and death. References to past trauma and abuse (including sexual abuse, forced confinement, and PTSD) are mentioned. Readers will also encounter on-page therapy and medical procedures, discussions of mental health and systemic violence (particularly against women), and references to drug and alcohol use. Found family, relational healing, and hopeful love balance themes of survival, loneliness, and mental illness. As always, please read with care.

PROLOGUE

Unmarked location, July 17, 2023, 4:15 a.m.

The lab attendant dropped her clipboard with a clatter and doubled over, her chest heaving from the sprint upstairs to the security office. "She's ... *escaped!*"

"What do you mean she's escaped? *Who's* escaped? From where?" the guard asked, barely fighting back the tremor in his voice. Cyril was too inexperienced to be left in charge of overnight security, let alone be held responsible for runaway test subjects. "That's supposed to be impossible ... right?"

"Apparently not! Patient Eighty-Seven has somehow unlocked her door, and she's on the loose!" The weary Wraith coughed violently, a thick, opaque liquid pouring from her cracked lips onto the linoleum floor. "You need to place the entire facility under lockdown!"

Cyril's eyes bugged out as he stared at the senior lab attendant. There was no way to know how old she was. Naturally aging human skin would be flushed after running so hard, but based on her ashy pallor—not to mention the oozing—she was much older than he was.

He slid his office chair back, its dirty wheels dragging a line of slime across the floor. "Uh ... so, why didn't you try to stop her? Patient Eighty-Seven, that is."

The lab attendant lifted her ghastly, dripping chin and gaped at him. "Are you honestly as stupid as you look? That door was not only locked from the outside but *heavily* spelled."

Cyril might be a newly minted Wraith and a novice in the vast world of underground magic, but even he knew this was bad. *Real bad.* Patient Eighty-Seven would have had to overcome several layers of precisely engineered enchantments to escape, not to mention force open the nearly three-hundred-pound double security doors—barred from the *outside*.

Cyril's heart pounded strangely in his chest—*beat, beat thump ... beat, beat ... thump ... beat, thump*—as something sour bubbled up in his throat with the (now) ever-present tang of dark magic slowly corrupting him from the inside out. It had only been six months, but he wondered how long it would be before *his* lungs would start to melt and his skin turn grey. His heart was certainly off-kilter already.

He gulped. "Look, I don't handle the magic bits around here, alright? *They* do. My job is to sit here and watch the cameras. That's it!"

"Lock it down," the lab attendant spat. "*Now!*" A primal growl clawed its way up from her gurgling lungs, startling Cyril into action.

He had absolutely no idea what he was doing but turned his attention to the large bank of monitors and filthy keyboard before him. His previous job at a grocery store had, on occasion, involved monitoring security—watching for shoplifters but nothing more. Mostly, it had been an excuse to skive off work and ogle juicy mamas bending over for pizza in the freezer aisle.

Now, though, the things he was forced to watch every day were *far* less titillating.

Keys clacked loudly under Cyril's clammy fingers as (miraculously) the main camera footage appeared on the centremost screen. A tall, bedraggled woman wearing a loose hospital gown was loping down a narrow hallway, dragging her hands lazily along the waist-high silver wall between her heavily guarded confines and the larger lab, occasionally chattering to someone or some*thing* off camera.

Cyril had never seen anything like it, and he'd witnessed some serious shit since starting this new job.

Hidden far above a locked and gated logging road on B.C.'s West Coast, the mountain facility comfortably housed anywhere between five and twenty-five human test subjects—all forcibly detained magic users—and approximately seven rotating lab staff, most of whom were either Wraiths or in the process of becoming Wraiths. There was also a handful of maintenance staff, including Cyril; he'd begun his employment as both lab porter and janitor. More than once, he'd been tasked with the disposal of bodies—both human and Wraith—whose causes of death had been indescribably horrific.

A lot of bodies had piled up over the past six months.

The fact was that few, if any, test subjects survived even their first weeks on-site, the majority of experiments being too brutal to endure. Yet, somehow, Patient Eighty-Seven had survived in captivity for almost a year, twice as long as Cyril had been a Wraith. Of course, she'd never be permitted to leave.

He peered closely at the monitor, slamming a sticky key and zooming in on the image with squinted eyes. Then he froze, his hands resting on the keys. "What's she *doing?*"

The lab attendant took a step back, slowly shaking her head. "I ... I don't know."

Together, they watched as the woman entered the lab and, forcing massive surges of lightning-white magic from her palms, began destroying equipment. Beakers, scanners, and work logs smashed and scattered like hail in a maelstrom of glass and paper onto the polished floors.

"Shit, shit, *shit!*" the lab attendant shouted, dancing anxiously in the slippery, oozing mess at her feet. There was nothing they could do but watch the destruction play out on the screen.

As far as Cyril knew, Patient Eighty-Seven had never done anything like this before. Although she'd always seemed different, the woman on the screen now looked ... *wrong*. Her movements were almost animalistic—wildly confident and undeniably feral. Demonic, perhaps, or so it would have seemed had Cyril been a man of faith. This was vastly different from the strange gait of the ancient, cloaked Wraiths, their joints popping and slipping inelegantly, a sign of their preternaturally extended lives on Earth.

Patient Eighty-Seven appeared entirely in control of her physical body.

And *full* of magic.

Cyril was petrified, his voice shaking as he asked, "W-what's happened to her?"

The lab attendant swallowed with a bubbling sort of sound but seemed at a loss for actual words.

While all their experimental test subjects had been abducted, no member of the facility staff had been forced into their role. Instead, they had all been lured in with promises of opulence and social clout within their new, darkly magical world.

Cyril had eagerly consented to become a Wraith, no questions asked. He'd survived the conversion ritual (barely), a month-long ancient rite in which the subject's physical body was infected with Wraith magic, which decelerated physical aging and decomposition, leading to an unnaturally long lifespan. It was different than the procedures and experiments performed on the test subjects in the facility, though. Those subjects had *not* been invited to become Wraiths; that choice, and all others, had been made for them.

On the monitor, the woman had left the main lab and was waltzing down a hallway towards the main patient-housing wing, lazily waving her hand towards each locked door she passed and spinning a few times in place, twirling easily as she continued chattering away, seemingly to herself. And though each door slid open in turn, none of the test subjects followed her out into the sparse hallway.

Were they afraid of her? Probably. Cyril sure as shit was.

"She's releasing the captives!" the lab attendant declared hoarsely.

Cyril stared at the screen, dumbstruck. Over the past six months at the facility, he'd reminded himself often that the Wraiths had promised him a life beyond his wildest dreams; he simply needed to put in his time. This promotion to security had seemed indicative of that future. Unfortunately, it seemed he was failing miserably at this new job.

Despite what he was seeing on the screens, according to his computer, the patient doors all remained locked, including Patient Eighty-Seven's, and no alarms had sounded.

"How, though?" Cyril asked. "How's she *doing* it?"

"I-I don't *know*," the lab attendant repeated.

Cyril pushed back in his chair, resting his hands on his faded baggy khakis. As a fifty-something man who'd lived off Hungry Man dinners and Friday Night Football for years, Cyril's odds of ever stumbling upon "something more" had been low. Sure, he'd always suspected that he was exceptional, with his ability to pick winning fantasy football teams a sure testament to an unusual prowess, but he'd been surprised to discover he had actual magical abilities—a requirement for becoming a Wraith.

When they'd cornered him in the parking lot behind his work one day, he'd counted his blessings that the Wraiths had deemed him worthy of joining their ranks. He should have known the entire proposition had been too good to be true.

Power and glory, my arse.

He was an underling, plain and simple—a vassal working for anonymous feudal (and rather homicidal) kings.

"Is she coming this way?" the lab attendant exclaimed, tying a swift knot in Cyril's unravelling focus. "Change the feed!"

On the screen, their escapee paused, as though carefully sensing every inch of her overly sterile surroundings. Then she turned her head from left to right and back again, sniffing the air like a wild animal.

Cyril clumsily switched the feed. "I don't think so."

The woman appeared to be headed towards the main hall, where the upper-level Wraiths routinely congregated, and where the "experimental fights" were held—spectacles reserved for days when powerful Wraiths from other factions were touring the facility.

And, *boy howdy*, had there been fights!

Cyril counted himself lucky not to have been forced to battle Patient Eighty-Seven; she'd grown vicious over the months he'd been watching her, and strangely, the Wraiths seemed to enjoy watching her kill the weaker members of their own kind.

A loud bang sounded from somewhere just beyond the security office.

"Just lock the fucking doors already!" the lab attendant shrieked, her eyes wide. "Do your damn job." She peered over her shoulder towards the brightly lit hallway, and then back at the screen. "They'll kill us both if she escapes!"

"You are correct," said a distorted voice behind them; the lab technician jerked, knocking her clipboard to the floor with a clatter.

The hair on the back of Cyril's neck stood up as he and the lab attendant turned slowly to face the powerful Wraith now looming in the doorway and considering their impending judgement.

Levi. Cyril recognized the Wraith's colossal frame, which dominated the tight quarters of the security office. He was now almost certain he would never leave this room alive again.

As Levi stepped towards them, a heavy hood concealing most of his face, his long black robes flowed like liquid night onto the polished floor. *"How many remain in captivity?"*

"C-currently, we're at over half capacity," the lab attendant stammered. Her hands shook as she reached feverishly for her discarded clipboard. Its papers were now soaked in her own pleural fluid, and her writing was completely illegible.

"A number," Levi pressed.

She closed her eyes. "I believe ... nine test subjects remain, including Patient Eighty-Seven."

"How many has she released?"

The lab attendant gulped noisily. "All of them, I think, though none seem to have left their rooms."

"How did she escape?" the massive Wraith asked, his voice rising, its magical reverberation agitating the monitor feed. Modern technology *hated* Wraith magic, especially the ancient stuff, and Levi was rumoured to be at least three hundred years old. Cyril, of course, had no idea what Levi's true name was, since his real moniker would have been discarded during the ritual, along with any other identity markers from his original life.

Cyril's own birth name (Kevin) had also been left behind after the ritual.

"I don't know!" the lab attendant said, looking frantically between Cyril and Levi. "One minute, her door was locked, and then next it just ... *clicked* open and she walked out."

Levi stalked towards the lab attendant and drew himself up to his full height, the top of his hood brushing against the ceiling. Then he cocked his head, his glamour flickering slightly to reveal the rotted flesh beneath. He might have even been giving them a sinister smile, though it was hard to tell with only blackened, pointed teeth showing where his lips should have been.

"Ambrosia, it was your responsibility to keep the patients sedated overnight."

Huh, Cyril thought, shaking his head. He hadn't expected the lab assistant to have such a pretty name. As he slid back in his chair, several things happened in quick succession: Levi lifted Ambrosia from the ground by her throat, a nearby phone rang dully from the mounted landline on the wall, and Patient Eighty-Seven disappeared from view on the security feed.

"It was *also* your responsibility to sound the alarm should something like this ever happen!" Levi growled as he squeezed Ambrosia's neck even tighter. *"Patient Eighty-Seven cannot be allowed to escape under any circumstance!"*

The Wraith clenched his fist and snapped Ambrosia's neck like a brittle bone left too long under a brutal desert sun. She collapsed to the floor, lying dead in a pool of her own sputum, and began deteriorating before Cyril's eyes.

Then Levi turned towards Cyril, who was already reaching for the computer, trying desperately to activate the alarms despite the clumsiness of his shaking fingers. Finally, it sounded, though Cyril still didn't know how to put the entire facility into full lockdown mode.

Hopefully, the alarm will be enough.

The massive Wraith reached for the still-ringing wall-mounted phone and hit the speaker button to answer it. *"Mal, your senses rang true,"* he said immediately. *"She has escaped her confines."*

"Then you must act quickly, Levi," a timeworn voice replied with a pompous air that made Cyril's teeth clench. That voice, and attitude, belonged to Malphas—Levi's main counterpart. He'd only met him once, but that had been more than enough for Cyril to know that he hoped *never* to encounter him again.

"I'm aware ..." Levi said slowly.

There was a long pause, before Malphas spoke again. *"Then why was there such a ... pregnant pause before sounding the alert?"*

Before replying, Levi flashed Cyril the same toothy "grin" he'd offered earlier, his glamour dropping altogether now. *"I've uncovered several ... errors in the facility's protocols."*

"Unacceptable!" Mal shouted. *"You must apprehend her. She carries within her too much of our magic to walk free."*

Looming beside Cyril now, the massive Wraith's voice took on a distinctly dangerous edge as he responded, *"Do you believe that is how she unlocked the doors?"*

"It is a possibility," his counterpart hissed, *"though we cannot know for sure until she is properly detained again and re-examined."*

"I will recapture her, and—"

"Bring her to me!"

The giant Wraith growled as he stared at the monitors. Cyril had brought up the latest feed of the main hall, where Patient Eighty-Seven was now facing off against seven or eight Wraiths. The alarms had finally alerted the resting legion of Wraiths on-site ... and yet, even as they watched, she began taking them down singlehandedly, one by one, as though they were just rooks on a chess board, and she, the grandmaster.

"And if she dies in the process?" Levi asked.

"If she dies, Leviathan, she dies. And whatever else might be destroyed in the process, I shall leave to your discretion." Mal's voice grew even more menacing then. *"But do NOT leave that facility without the files and removing any trace that you were there."*

The ancient Wraith hung up on Levi, who shifted his humungous frame towards Cyril, raising a heavily robed arm towards the monitors. "Is this being recorded?"

"All footage is recorded ... and automatically backs up onto those." Cyril nodded towards a bank of hard drives secured within a metal cabinet beside him.

"Stand up," Levi commanded.

Cyril did as he was told.

The Wraith seized the now unoccupied office chair, ripped off its base and castors, and exposed the blunt spindle below its well-worn seat. "You have heard and seen too much this morning. You will not survive another day."

Levi lunged forward, impaling Cyril with the bottom of the office chair like a hot fondue skewer through a chunk of meat. Cyril swayed on the spot, his own Wraith essence fighting (and failing) to keep him from the one true death. Slowly, he slumped to the floor, even as Levi returned his attention to the monitors, where Patient Eighty-Seven now appeared to be dying as well, writhing in agony as blood pooled around her broken body.

But the Wraiths she had been fighting had fallen first. Every single one of them.

As Cyril lay on the floor, the office chair jutting crookedly from his torso, his last breaths seeping from his lips along with whatever little dignity he'd managed to retain, he saw Levi reach into the cabinet and collect that day's security footage, now stored on the external hard drive.

The sound of alarms continued to blare all around him.

And then, everything went black.

CHAPTER 1

RONAN

Lake Cowichan, B.C., July 18, 2023, 10:07 a.m.

Simply put, the Druids had arrived too late. Where once a massive industrial building had stood, only a rugby-pitch-sized rectangle of destruction remained. Mounds of obliterated concrete blocks, shattered glass, burst pipes, and sparking electrical wires were intermingled with fragmented human remains—specifically, charred bones strewn pell-mell throughout the heaps of smoking rubble.

Records indicated that the facility had once been used as a Western Canadian telecommunications base before being abandoned many years earlier. Not even the foundation had endured what appeared to have been an *enormous* explosion.

What the hell had happened here?

And more importantly, who had been involved in it?

Dr. Ronan Gallagher stepped from his (now *very* dusty) black Range Rover onto gravel that crunched beneath his heavy boots.

Grimacing, he shielded his eyes from the blinding summer sun and took in the catastrophic sight before him. His comrades were climbing and searching through the rubble, investigating the damage and searching for victims, or clues.

It took several moments and some conscious breathing for Ronan to calm himself. *Air in ... Air out ...*

"Goddess help us," he muttered, running his hand back through his pepper-brown hair before returning to his vehicle to collect his black medical bag.

The bag, of course, contained the standard medical implements: headlamp, stethoscope, gloves, gauze and tape, hydrogen peroxide, Ambu bag and fluid line, saline and syringes, tourniquet, suture kit, lidocaine, and so on. Ronan had been a practising MD (and combat specialist) for nearly two decades.

However, this particular bag also housed a set of magical medicaments: enchanted pouches, potions, earthen tinctures, and closely guarded natural remedies, all specially curated to meet the needs of the Druid doctor when faced with magical injuries as well as civilian. He also carried several daggers of varying lengths and compositions, along with a handgun and silencer—not *all* adversaries were magic users, after all.

Ronan also carried an enchanted compass but preferred to keep that priceless item tucked safely away in his pocket.

"What do we think happened here?" he asked the twins, his Dublin accent disproportionately light as he sidled up next to them, looking past them at the grim sight.

Amos and Amelia Foster had arrived roughly ninety minutes before Ronan, pinging him their location at the ass-crack of dawn. He'd been blissfully off duty, sleeping in after a night spent celebrating his goddaughter's second birthday in Victoria—his reveries with the child's parents having kept him up long after the birthday girl had fallen sleep.

Domhnall—better known as Dom—and Julia O'Brien were Ronan's best friends and chosen family, so when a bottle of his favourite whisky had appeared after dinner ... well, who was he to resist? Besides, Ayla's birthday warranted that sort of merriment, even if she'd gone to bed at seven-thirty. She was the brightest toddler in the *entire* world. And as such, he surely owed it to her to celebrate the anniversary of her arrival.

In truth, Ronan had been frustrated by the timing of this callout. It had been ages since he'd enjoyed some time off with his friends. Not to mention he had a *raging* hangover. He was also acutely aware it was his unfortunate duty to clean up these messes whenever they presented themselves—no matter how much fun he might be having.

A disaster of this scale was truly a Ronan problem.

"It's definitely *their* handiwork," Amos said, picking at his teeth. He was the shorter of the pair, with thick, sandy blond hair and a sturdy disposition. "You can smell the stench of those fuckers all over this place."

Indeed, a distinctly sulphuric tang wafted through the air as the wind picked up around them, gusting through the building's smouldering remains. *Wraiths.* The burning was a more pressing concern than the evidence of their enemies, though. It was peak forest fire season on Vancouver Island, so being this far into the wild with only one road out made Ronan nervous.

They would need to act quickly.

"Any idea yet what the facility was used for?" he asked, kicking a smoldering piece of what appeared to be an office chair.

Amos smirked bleakly. "Take a *wild* guess."

Ronan closed his eyes and mentally stretched outside of his body, immediately sensing the presence of wild magics, free-floating and gradually returning to the earth. "There were Wielders here, and not a small number either ... Can you feel that too?"

Wielders were a type of magic user, like the Druids, who required an external source of power, typically borrowing the essence of magic from the natural world and returning it once spent. This created a gentle give and take between the Wielder and the environment, unless of course, the Wielder also happened to be a Wraith.

Amelia turned towards Ronan, her expression grim. "I can ... There are a lot of remains, Doc. Human *and* Wraith ... though the Wraiths are mostly dust now."

Wraiths stole earthen magic and kept it for themselves, trapping it within the confines of their physical bodies. And while it "gifted" them unnaturally long lives, by the time they *did* die—whether at the hand of an enemy or one of their own—their corpses were usually so degraded that they collapsed into heaps of dust. When the captured magic finally left them, there was quite literally nothing left.

Ronan knew a great deal about the physiological function of Wraiths, largely because he'd spent the last decade studying exactly how they "worked"—a curiosity that had once (quite literally) cost him his life.

"My best guess is ..." He paused and shook his head. "No, it couldn't be *that*, though ... *Could* it?"

Amos and Amelia waited in silence as Ronan worked to piece together what he was seeing and what he'd just felt. This wasn't an unusual dynamic. Based on the scale of this apparent disaster, though, he would need more time and information to process whatever they'd just uncovered.

But in the meantime, Ronan needed to act.

"Regardless of intent," he said finally, "we'll need to bag and tag any human remains we unearth. Ask Lennie to organize a forensics team if needed." He scratched his beard as he peered beyond the wreckage. "It looks like there's a helipad over there," he said, pointing his long index finger. "You might want to see if we can make use of that somehow to speed things up. If Lennie pushes back, tell him he owes me. I don't like the idea of being up here for too long."

"You got it," Amelia said, pulling out her satellite phone. She was the friendlier of the twins, though you'd never tell by the chronically serious expression she wore.

"Oh, and Amelia," Ronan added, "get him to route a waterbomber too. We need to put this fire out properly once we're finished."

She nodded before putting Ronan's directives into action.

He turned his attention to Amos. "How *exactly* did we find out about the explosion? I spoke to Lennie on the drive here, and he said some Witches called it in, but then his signal cut out before I could get any more information."

Amos rolled his eyes. "It's a bit of a long story, which is partly why it took us so long to get out here."

Through a series of underground connections, the Druids had been notified by a pair of local Witches about a strange disturbance they'd encountered while ambling through their favourite woods. More commonly referred to as "Bearers" in their hidden magical world, Witches were a rare type of magic user who not only could Wield external magic but also generate it from within.

"Apparently, a loud explosion had reverberated from high above them in the surrounding mountains. They suspect it originated from an abandoned logging area, that's where swaths of ancient rainforest had been *carelessly* clear-cut, *callously* replanted, and then *completely* abandoned, and then it travelled down to where they'd been peacefully trekking below."

There had apparently been little to no activity near this specific site or up this particular road for *decades* ... at least, beyond ambitious locals who climbed the heavily switch-backed road for fitness or, in the cooler months, to access coveted, top-secret mushroom-picking sites.

Except for that pair of Witches, apparently.

"What the hell were they doing hiking all the way out here at five o'clock in the morning?" Ronan snapped.

Amos smirked. "You know how they are."

Ronan chuckled. Oh, yes ... he knew *exactly* how Witches were.

Julia was a Witch—and an exceptionally powerful one at that—and though he was very fond of her, in his relatively lengthy experience as her friend, he'd discovered that her choices weren't always exactly logical.

Julia was, perhaps, just *slightly* cracked in the head.

"But now we know the explosion came from right here," Amos said, jabbing his index finger towards the ground.

In the end, almost everything about the Witches' report had been odd, from how their bodies had experienced the latent impact of the explosion like a hot, tingling sonic wave to the fact that no one else nearby had sensed it. It had certainly not been detected by any non-magic users in the area. Though, admittedly, the location *was* fairly remote.

There was no denying this disturbance had been distinctly magical in nature.

And so, as was protocol, a crack team had been dispatched immediately, following the orders of Lennie Crandall, who oversaw all central logistic and tactical directives for the Druidic Order. Most had come from Vancouver, which meant it had taken the team several hours to board a ferry, cross the strait towards the Island, and drive to the Lake Cowichan area. From there, they'd had to locate the actual source of the disturbance, which had cost them even *more* time.

It had ended up being nearly thirty-two hours after the initial explosion that the Druids had finally arrived on-site.

Ronan sighed. Though he'd been the last to arrive, he knew *he* would be the one dealing with the outcome of this mission for months. "This is a fucking disaster."

Amos nodded in agreement. "Do you want to take a look around?"

"Might as well."

Ronan gripped his medical bag and followed Amos into the debris, stepping carefully past a bundle of live wires, wondering how they'd powered such a large and remote building without detection. Then again, the bastards were (unfortunately) cleverer than they were generally given credit for.

"How do you think they managed to hide it for so long?" he asked, grimacing as he passed what he was pretty certain was a set of metatarsals blown free from the rest of someone's foot.

"Your guess is as good as mine."

Ronan dragged his boot through some broken beakers and knocked it against the remnants of an autoclave. "Looks like it was a fairly serious facility. A lab, perhaps?"

Though the Druids had been diligently tracking the Wraiths for years, the fiends had unfortunately done an exemplary job of concealing the existence of this latest depravity.

"If it was, the lab was still in active use at the time of the explosion," Amos said, stretching easily as he bit back a yawn.

For every member of the Order, there was a point in times like this when the scales shifted from reacting in horror to more of a down-regulated ease. Surviving this line of work would be impossible if every magic-induced calamity sent one into a tailspin.

But for anyone not in the fold, it was surely bizarre to witness.

Along with a rotating group of Druids who operated primarily from the Canadian West Coast, Ronan spent most of his waking days tracking and shutting down Wraith establishments—typically bars or nightclubs, though sometimes they grew bold and ran larger operations as well, as they'd discovered just this morning.

"We've uncovered viable rations and documents dated not even three days ago."

"Any computers?" Ronan asked.

"Some," Amelia said, returning to their group, "though Lennie doubts we'll be able to recover much. Still, we'll collect whatever we can find and see what's usable."

"Places like these usually have their data backed up. Any signs of an external storage unit? Hard drives and the like?" Ronan waved his hand at the destruction around them.

Amos nodded. "Yes, some. But what's interesting is that the most recent hard drives appear to be missing."

"For now," Ronan said, remaining cautiously optimistic. They couldn't be sure of anything until the entire site had been thoroughly searched. "Do we know who was heading the operations?"

Amelia shrugged. "Unclear. Hopefully, the recovered data will give us a direction to follow."

To their knowledge, there were at least two or three Wraith legions clamouring for supremacy at any given moment—and that was just in their neck of the woods. It was impossible to keep track of who was where, let alone how (or even if) they were connected globally. You could say what you wanted about the Child of Rome; he had at least kept the evil pricks *somewhat* organized.

"Thanks, you two. I'm going to keep poking around," Ronan said, wishing to continue his survey in silence. He needed room to think.

For almost two thousand years, Cassius—a.k.a. the Child of Rome—had acted as head Wraith, though he preferred to consider himself a Sorcerer, wholly differentiating himself from his underlings. That was until Ronan, Dom, Julia, Lennie, and their allies had finally defeated him.

It was hard to imagine that fated day had been only two years earlier.

Since then, the surviving Wraiths had been hell-bent on continuing Cassius's legacy of power by taking advantage of the demented, greed-fuelled power vacuum he'd left behind. And as a result, the Druids' job had devolved into a colossal game of whack-a-mole, with them and their Knave counterparts—another sect of positive Wielders—never *quite* able to get ahead of whatever it was the Wraiths were planning next.

This was because, in a post-Cassius world, the Druids faced not only the task of navigating their typical conflicts with the Wraiths—fighting for the rights and safety of magic users around the world (no big deal)—but now they also had to navigate any blowouts stemming from the infighting between warring Wraith factions.

Case in point: this obliterated building currently billowing hazardous smoke on the side of a sunbaked mountain during forest fire season. Had the explosion been a result of a lab accident or a Wraith-on-Wraith battle?

It was all fucking exhausting, truth be told.

At forty-seven, Ronan wasn't getting any younger. Of course, he took impeccable care of his health, considering himself a formidable adversary in combat and in bed (whenever he slowed down enough to *actually* date). He had a regular list of casual partners he'd wine and dine with in Vancouver—women who were just as busy as he was but appreciated a good rut as much as he did. There had been nothing serious, though. Ronan had no time for that these days. Besides, his true identity needed to remain as closely guarded a secret as their entire magical world.

Emily Coleman and Keegan Gill approached him as he stood in the very centre of the lab's remains. Both were Druids from the Lower Mainland and regularly crossed paths with him, though he didn't know them nearly as well as the twins did.

"Do we have any idea yet of the layout?" Ronan asked them. "I assume the Wraiths would have retrofitted themselves into the existing building."

"We've come up with a rough idea, I think, though some of it still needs confirmation," Emily said. "Did you want to see it?"

"Of course," Ronan said, grateful that he really was working with the best.

Emily procured a tablet and stylus from her backpack, opening an original map of the building on the screen overlaid with their hypothesized plans for the destroyed facility. She'd drawn in the details of where they suspected test subjects had likely been held, along with the main-lab area, security station, and a potential mess hall—not that Wraiths really *ate* anything.

"Did you come up with all of this just now?"

She nodded. "Don't be too impressed. It's kind of my other job. I'm an architect."

Ronan conceded with a grin but quickly sobered once more. "Will the record eventually show where all of the remains were found?"

"Definitely."

Keegan spoke up then. "Most of the remains seem to be concentrated in this area." He pointed to yet another layer Emily had added to the map. "But there's possibly one or two outliers over here too." He gestured to the area labelled Mess Hall.

"Amelia has a better sense of that than us, though," Emily added.

"Speak of the devil," Ronan said, watching the approach of the twins, who soon crowded around Emily's map with the others.

Amelia brushed a strand of sweaty hair off her face. An hour had already passed since Ronan's arrival, and temperatures were rising. "Since the bones seem to belong only to Wielders, we should be able to make sure all of them are accounted for."

Ronan arched an eyebrow at her. "You're not thinking about trying bone magic, are you?"

"We're going to have to attempt *some sort* of bone magic if we want to make this right," Amos said a little too calmly.

Though he'd never met them, Ronan knew that the twins' parents had been career Druids themselves and were rumoured to have dabbled in dark Druidics on occasion. *Bone magic.*

He also knew that their parents had died suspiciously while on active duty.

Bone magic was something rarely put to use in the modern era. It was not only extremely dangerous but also quite unethical, often being referred to as "dark Druidics." Although it was still firmly seated in the oral tradition, the practice had been out of use for so long that anyone attempting to use it would likely die right along with their target.

His best friend, Dom, had dabbled in bone magic once long ago, back in eleventh-century Ireland, enlisting the assistance of ancient Druids to help him follow Julia—the love of his life and present-day wife—from one life to the next for generations. The Druids had successfully tied Dom (a non-magic user) to Julia using the bones of her recently dead mother, but it had been a huge gamble for all involved. It was no small thing to mess with bone magic of that nature, and Dom could very well have been cursed into some otherworldly limbo (or worse) rather than returning with her as he had. Over and over again.

Dark magic indeed.

The great Celt *always* had shit horseshoes, though.

Regardless, very few Druids in the modern era even contemplated its use. There was simply not enough knowledge remaining on how to use it safely, and used incorrectly, the consequences could be grave.

"Right," Ronan said thoughtfully as he measured the odds of disaster. "Well, use it if you must, but ... please be careful. I don't need any more of a mess on my hands than I've already got."

"Not to worry, Doc," Amelia said. "We won't take any chances that aren't absolutely necessary." Amos nodded.

Ronan stepped away from the group to consider his next steps. He'd need to check in with Lennie soon. While it was Ronan who was usually on the ground for these sorts of things, they typically worked as a team. At least remotely. The Brit worked primarily from England, though he visited Canada and the United States with some regularity. Ronan also needed to affirm that their immediate action plan, whatever it was, would ensure his people were off this mountainside as soon as possible.

He wiped a bead of sweat from his temple as his satellite phone rang. He answered it quickly but calmly. "I was just about to call you."

"I have an update."

"No surprise there," Ronan said with a snort. Lennie was predisposed to info-dumping on occasions such as this, relaying whatever new information he'd gathered while Ronan and the other Druids were out in the field. "But first—"

"No. You need to listen to me." Lennie's voice was serious. "I think there was a survivor."

Apparently, Ronan's intuition had been correct after all. He was, indeed, about to spend *many months* trying to clean up this mess.

For fuck's sake.

CHAPTER 2

RONAN

Six months later.

Dr. Ronan Gallagher took a steadying breath as he eyed the woman seated alone across the nightclub. In another realm, he supposed his magnifying gaze might have scorched the exposed skin between her shoulder blades. In this reality, however, she didn't seem to detect the heat of his attention or have any awareness of the danger lurking only steps away from where she was perched. Instead, his target sat absently chewing on a short, green cocktail straw.

Ronan drummed his fingers impatiently on the sticky tabletop, watching ... *waiting*.

To stave off boredom, he'd fallen into a pattern of visually tracing the ridges of her semi-exposed spine. From the top of the zipper of her short, summery floral romper, which stuck out like a sore thumb in the dim nightclub, right through to the nape of her neck, where her straw-coloured hair was pulled into a high messy ponytail. Ronan shuddered involuntarily as he dragged his eyes from her bottom thoracic vertebrae to her cervical spine and back again, utterly tormented by what an *enigma* this woman had become over the preceding months.

He also suspected that she had mild scoliosis, though he'd need to take a closer look to be certain.

At this thought, Ronan shifted uncomfortably in his seat, and his comrade immediately barked into his earpiece, *"Don't make your move until her motive for being here is crystal clear."*

"I'm not *moving* anywhere, Lennie. My arse is just falling asleep," he muttered, glaring towards the camera in the corner of the nightclub. Ronan didn't need reminding; one wrong move, and she would disappear on them yet again.

Lennie snorted. *"You're not getting too old for this, are you, Ronan?"*

"Fuck off."

This woman had apparently walked away from the catastrophic laboratory explosion, made her way down the mountain, and somehow disappeared for several months before reappearing again. And since discovering her existence, she'd slipped from their grasp so many times that Ronan had nearly lost track. She'd kept crossing paths with him while he was performing his usual duties, infiltrating the Wraith underground, but each time they'd come close to rustling her from whatever operation she was on, she would disappear again.

At this point, the Druidic Order simply wanted to question her, as she'd technically done nothing wrong. Afterwards, they would let her go. Maybe. Of course, they still had no clue if she was acting independently or under the directives of some other entity, though Ronan highly doubted the latter. This woman had "lone wolf" written all over her.

More than once, Ronan's ruminations around the woman's unusual existence had threatened to take over his daily work, thanks to a proclivity for obsession that had once nearly cost him everything he held dear. But the Druid just couldn't figure out *why* it'd been so hard to track her down before today.

Before *now*.

A pair of well-worn women—there was no other way to describe them—stole Ronan's attention momentarily as they slithered arm-in-arm through the club's heavy entrance door, wobbling precariously on too-high heels before skittering into a group of low-level Wraiths.

Beyond the narrowing crack in the entrance door, Ronan noted the silvery light of dusk fading into darkness. Soon, the club would fill up, bursting at the seams with magic and non-magic patrons alike. Though the club was already crowded with what he assumed were regular patrons, many of them sipping cocktails or perhaps looking to score something harder before their night took off in earnest.

His target, however, seemed to be looking for something else.

Ronan reached for his glass then remembered his ice had long since melted, leaving his whisky watery and disappointing. But what else was new? The Druid's life had become a series of elaborate disenchantments as of late, punctuated by moments of only moderate success. Life in the Druidic Order rarely offered thanks, but for Ronan—who had not only died and come back to life but had played a crucial role in the final defeat of Cassius, the evillest Sorcerer in known history—he'd found little in the way of job satisfaction since.

Instead, he'd spent most of the last two-and-a-half years cleaning up messes.

"*Fuck me*," Ronan growled as he ran his hands through his hair. He really *was* getting too old for this shit. Not that he'd admit that to Lennie.

Fidgeting, he reached into his pocket and procured his compass, setting it on the table. The needle spun, wobbled, and then settled ... pointing directly at his target, just as it had been doing all night.

In the name of the Goddess, what is she waiting for?

This question was (miraculously) answered as a surly, stupid-looking man approached her. Ronan's heart pounded as he watched the woman draw her shoulders back, stiffening uncomfortably in her seat, as the man whispered something in her ear and then slumped away. Ronan watched her reach back and remove her hair tie, letting her long blonde hair tumble down her crooked back in roguish waves. He'd always had a thing for blondes.

His eyes flicked to the back of the club, where the messenger had disappeared through a set of double doors. The woman exhaled a slow shaking breath.

Enough is enough. Lennie's caution be damned.

Ronan silently rose from his seat even as he heard Lennie scoffing loudly through his earpiece, *"She's obviously preparing for something—or someone. Don't fuck this up by playing the Prince Charming card, Ronan. You're not Domhnall! I don't get the sense that would work on her anyway."*

Domhnall was known for being extraordinarily charismatic and for his uncanny ability to make everyone he met swoon.

Ronan rolled his eyes. "Fuck you very much, Lennie."

"You know I'm right," the Brit replied, his light tone reflecting their kinship and deep history; Lennie rarely joked with anyone. *"And besides, you've been drooling over her for over an hour now. It's embarrassing."*

"Christ, Lennie," Ronan moaned. It was worth noting that Lennie had retained his knack for mindreading, even from afar. *The smug bastard.* "It's not like that."

Still, as he drew air in quickly through his teeth, Ronan had to admit she was undoubtedly beautiful and *unmistakably* dangerous, making it hard to look away.

She still had her back turned to him as he stalked towards her like a starved cat hunting a songbird. Ideally, he would catch her off guard, getting the upper hand right away, and pounce on her just in time to allow them both to get the hell out of there before anything significant happened with the Wraiths.

He'd estimated there were eleven paces between him and his target. He was now down to six ... *five* ... *four* ...

Ronan collided with a crash into a harried-looking server and took a step back to avoid further damage. *Too late.* Several ounces of greenish liquid slopped down onto Ronan's freshly polished boots. He could smell a sickening, syrupy sweetness—likely sucrose-laden lime cordial or something just as repulsive.

"*Shit*, man!" barked the server, who appeared to be unfamiliar with the basics of hospitality. "You came out of nowhere!"

"My apologies," Ronan said, smiling good-naturedly and feigning casual ease when tonight's mission was anything but.

Still visibly perturbed by Ronan's abrupt appearance, the server gawked at him for several moments before righting the glasses on his tray and bustling off, completely disregarding the broken glass on the floor. Ronan awaited a snide remark from Lennie about his clumsiness but (shockingly) received nothing through his earpiece—not even a derisive snort.

Shit! He'd lost the earpiece in the commotion.

Ronan groaned internally. He knew better than to risk precious time searching for the earpiece in the broken glass at his feet. Instead, his eyes remained trained on his target: *Phoebe Ashburn.*

Up close, her sunny visage contrasted wildly with the walls of the dimly lit nightclub. Called *The Devil's Details*, it was the kind of hell-hole one entered at their own risk—a perilous sort of establishment that screamed of organized crime. Too many people, too many drugs, and too much dancing. It was also the middle of December, so unless Phoebe was simply quirky in her choice of personal attire—or confused about what month it was—she'd outfitted herself tonight hoping to get attention. And really, it was hard to miss her long, muscular, and fully exposed legs punctuated by those black strappy heels.

He doubted it was *his* attention she was trying to get, though. This nightclub was owned and operated by one of the most notorious Wraiths in the Pacific Northwest: Andrew "Nyx" Fairburn. This particular son-of-a-bitch was known for many things in the magical underground, not least of which was the illegal production and transport of illicit drugs within both magical and non-magical communities alike.

In the years following the demise of the Sorcerer Cassius, the Wraiths—his former minions—had been busy, and Ronan was genuinely worried for Phoebe's safety.

And for his own safety as well if he were being honest.

He now stood close enough to smell Phoebe's alluring perfume, which to him smelled of vanilla and patchouli. He could feel the increasingly heated, carnivorous stares she was getting from the men behind him. Of course, he'd been staring at her too, but at least *he'd* had good reason.

As he stepped forward in his now-sticky military boots, Ronan could feel the immense weight of this mission on his broad shoulders. When he was exactly one pace behind the woman, he cleared his throat.

She didn't appear to have heard him.

"Care if I join you?" he asked, leaning hard into his Dublin lilt as he slid onto the seat beside her.

Without turning towards him, she let out the tiniest puff of air through her nose before speaking. "Would you leave me alone if I said no?"

The honeyed tones of her voice threw him off momentarily, reminding him of a late-summer evening full of delicious, forbidden promises.

"*Ehm* ... of course, I would," he said in a choked voice.

She took a long sip of her drink—mostly ice now, by the looks of it—before turning to face him head-on. Her green eyes were piercing. "Are you going to introduce yourself, Druid? Or will you let me get on with my evening? You've been staring at me for over an hour now. It's rude."

How did she know? Ronan wondered as he steeled himself for whatever came next. He'd been cautious, even using one of his priceless magical pouches to keep any unwanted attention from him until he'd gotten the lay of the land. Come to think of it, the pouch magic was likely why the server hadn't seen him coming in time to avoid their collision. He could hear the broken glass being swept up behind him now, as well as the oaf's murmurs of frustration.

"That depends," Ronan said, pleased to find his voice sounded more normal now and hoping to appear nonchalant even as his mind was racing a mile a minute.

Phoebe reached for her drink, only to discover that she'd already finished it. Looking aggravated, she slammed her glass down and slid it towards the bartender. "Another whisky sour."

Ronan redirected his attention to the barkeep, smiling kindly. "I'll take another whisky too. No ice this time, please." Perhaps his arrival had indeed angered the woman.

The pair waited in prickly silence for their next round to arrive.

Ronan discreetly eyed Phoebe's profile as he placed his palms on the bar top, which was also sticky. Her expression was serious, with a slight wrinkle in her brow. He watched as she pulled out her cell phone, tilted the screen away from him, and checked something. Then she tucked it back into a small black clutch on her lap, looking around the nightclub as though searching for someone. She fidgeted in her seat for a few more moments before pulling out a tube of bright-red lipstick and smearing it expertly across her lips.

Something had her spooked, and Ronan suspected it wasn't him. Not entirely at least. Had she received some sort of message? He couldn't glance directly at her phone screen without her noticing. However, he could feel strange magic radiating from her at increasingly short intervals, even though he had not yet touched her.

Yes, this was *definitely* the woman he was looking for. But what could she be after in this hellhole that was making her so afraid?

The murky, greenish drink she'd ordered suddenly appeared before her.

"You don't actually like that stuff, do you?" Ronan asked lightly, sticking and unsticking his boots from the bar rail below them.

Phoebe and the bartender both glared at him. Seconds later, his whisky arrived, this time filled nearly to the brim with ice.

I guess I deserved that.

Ronan cleared his throat, angling himself towards Phoebe once more. "Can I ask what brings you to a place like this? You're not exactly dressed for the season." He, on the other hand, was wearing black jeans and a thick, rather expensive, wool overshirt. It was the dead of winter here in Seattle, after all.

Phoebe laughed darkly. "If you were *anything* else, I'd think you were trying to pick me up."

"And how do you know I'm not?" Ronan said, eyes twinkling. "And hold on now, darling, what do you mean by *thing?* I take offence to that."

"Wouldn't you like to know?" Her tone was so clipped he expected her to leave in a huff. Instead, she sighed and continued in a familiarly Canadian accent. "I'm Phoebe, by the way."

"Dr. Ronan Gallagher," he said, sipping his drink casually.

"*Fancy*." She gave him an unimpressed look then, chewing on the end of her straw for a moment before taking a hard sip.

Ronan thought she was about to start flirting with him, but when she shifted to face him with a skeptical look in her eyes, he quickly dismissed that expectation.

"I bet all the lassies love that, don't they?" she said a bit haughtily. "A Scottish doctor—"

"Irish."

"Fine. An *Irish* doctor approaching them? ... *How charming!*" She rolled her eyes. "What can I do for you, *Dr. Gallagher?* Because I'm actually quite busy at the moment."

"You don't seem very busy," he said smoothly, leaning in closer. He was suddenly finding her combativeness intriguing.

She leaned away from him. "Well, I am."

"I think we might actually be here for similar reasons," Ronan said, adding just enough nuance to signal he knew more than he was letting on. When Phoebe suddenly stood up and started gathering her things, he quickly realized he'd missed the mark.

"We most certainly are *not*." She checked her phone again with a hint of panic. "Now leave me alone."

"Wait." Ronan reached reflexively towards Phoebe but caught himself as his fingers lightly grazed her arm. He could feel jagged magic radiating from her now, and in that moment, she exposed a wildness that threatened to derail him completely and make him forget his mission altogether.

He suddenly found himself craving her. Desperately. *What the fuck is happening?*

"You'd be wise to step back, Druid," she said, her words dripping with menace. "If you value your life."

Ronan felt an unexpected heat claw up his neck; it had to be the whisky, combined with the inherent danger of the mission.

He dropped all pretence now. "I can't explain here, but I've been tasked to find you. In fact, I've been tracking you for months. I know *who* you are." Her eyes flashed violently towards him. "And if you're about to do what I *think* you're about to do, it's you who won't be leaving here alive. There are too many of them."

Behind them, the club was steadily filling with beasts, both Wraith and human alike. Ronan watched as Phoebe processed what he'd just said. Her look of shock and anger from moments before seemed to melt away, quickly replaced with a mask of absolute calm, showcasing a mental resolve he would have found impressive under any other circumstance.

"You know nothing," she said dismissively, raising her hands to muss her hair up a bit, then adjusting her breasts beneath the soft material of her summer outfit to expose more soft flesh. She tucked her clutch purse under her arm. "Don't get in my way, Druid."

"Jesus, Mary, and Joseph," Ronan muttered. Was she legitimately planning to seduce someone here of all places?

She has a bloody death wish!

He started to panic then. "Look, we actually *do* know a bit about what happened to you—not much, but the part about you being held captive and experimented on by Wraiths." Anger and something else ignited in her expression. Was that fear? "You escaped before we could speak to you, though."

"Shut your mouth right now!" Her eyes flickered to the double doors that led to the back room—the same doors through which the brute who'd recently whispered something into her ear had disappeared.

"There's no one nearby," Ronan said soothingly, getting up from the bar stool to face her. Although, at six foot two, he wasn't exactly short, with the heels Phoebe was wearing, she was almost taller. "I've also used one of my pouches to—"

"We're being watched," she whispered as if this wasn't entirely obvious. Wraith establishments like this one always came complete with surveillance of those in attendance. And unbeknownst to her, this time, Lennie was *also* watching from afar.

"My people are watching too," Ronan said evenly. The statement was meaningless, though, as with his earpiece lost, Lennie would be unable to communicate with him regardless of what he was seeing from his distant vantage point.

I might as well be dead in the water.

"Your *people*," she snorted. "Where were *your people* when I was—" She fell abruptly silent then, her mouth snapping shut as an impossibly tall and roguishly handsome man waltzed into the room, dressed from head to toe in unmistakably European couture. Even his hair was perfect, without a single strand out of place.

Phoebe froze on the spot. Without warning, Ronan reached and grasped her forearm.

"*What the fuck are you doing?*" she hissed, digging her nails into his hand, attempting to pry herself free.

"Getting you out of here," he said, wincing. Ronan's grip held firm as his voice dropped to a whisper, "Trust me, you do *not* want to do this. Not tonight."

"You don't know anything about me! Or what I *want* to do," she growled. She was quickly growing frantic in his grasp, her magic—whatever that might be—pulsating dangerously now. "This might be my only shot!"

If he didn't know any better, he'd say she was having a tantrum. "Please, Phoebe," he said soothingly, as though he were trying to coax a skittish cat down from a tree. "I'm here to *help* you."

"*Fuck off*," she hissed.

There was no point in hiding his desperation any longer. So, it was time to change tactics. "And perhaps, in exchange, *you* can help *us*."

"Ah, yes! There it is!" she said, her voice suddenly dripping with cynicism. "You want something from me. Just like everyone else."

"We have to go now! But I *promise* that you'll be safe."

He knew this statement was technically a lie; he couldn't possibly keep a promise like that. But her leaving with him right now would be infinitely less dangerous than handing herself over to the Wraiths.

Her chest rose and fell hard as she considered his words. "If this is some sort of trap—"

"It's not," Ronan said firmly, though he couldn't guarantee this woman hadn't just captured *him* instead of the other way around.

What is she?

He held his breath, and for a split second, thought she might actually concede. But without warning, Phoebe shoved him away and, turning towards the looming figure behind her, popped a hip enticingly to the side.

Nyx glared momentarily at the dumbstruck Ronan before refocusing on the gorgeous and volatile magic-user standing between them.

"Sorry to keep you waiting, *Sasha*," Nyx said, his voice low and menacing. "I had important business to attend to before I could give you my *full attention*."

Ronan absolutely abhorred the way Nyx began to eye Phoebe from toes to tits ... the way the Wraith bastard's eyes lingered on her mouth for far too long. And then, without any hesitation (and to Ronan's abject horror), Phoebe moved directly towards one of the vilest Wraiths this side of the Rockies.

As Ronan stood frozen, Nyx wrapped his arm around her waist and led her to the back of the club, through its double doors, and into his back-room lair.

"Fuck, fuck, *fuck!*" Ronan said once he'd managed to shake himself free of his temporary paralysis and pulled out his cell phone. Only a few seconds had passed since Phoebe had disappeared, but his phone was already blowing up with messages from Lennie:

> Do NOT follow her in there until you have backup.
>
> Backup, ETA thirty minutes.

Amos and Amelia were somewhere between the Canadian border and Seattle, rushing towards his location. But Phoebe didn't have ten minutes to wait, let alone thirty. The expression on the Wraith's face had said only one thing: he was out for blood. The way Nyx had called her "*Sasha*" had caused the hair on the back of Ronan's neck to stand up. It was highly probable that the Wraith knew who Phoebe really was and had arranged to bring her back into captivity. Or worse.

> Don't even think about it, Ronan.
>
> Nyx is beyond dangerous.
>
> There are at least four other high-ranking Wraiths on-site, as well as their minions.

Ronan already knew there were Wraiths present in the nightclub. He'd done his research.

Don't be a fool!

He looked to the security camera in the corner of the room, through which Lennie was still watching, and shook his head. A moment later, another text came through.

On your head be it then … asshole.

Ronan rocked once on his heels before striding towards the back room, simultaneously pulling out a full vial of Bloodsbane from his breast pocket, uncorking it, and tossing it back. His heart pounded as the magical "speed" surged through his system.

"She'd better be worth it," he muttered, knowing damn well already that she was.

As he shouldered his way through the swinging double doors, in his wake, the now-discarded empty vial rolled across the sticky floor.

CHAPTER 3

RONAN

RONAN CHECKED HIS COMPASS, WHICH STILL POINTED IN PHOEBE'S general direction somewhere beyond the double doors. He pocketed it and, drawing a short dagger, entered the nightclub's back-of-house, naively hoping to arrive where he was needed undetected.

"I saw you watching her," a lumbering figure said from the shadows before lunging clumsily into the light. It was the same surly man from before, who'd *clearly* been expecting him. He attempted to pull Ronan into his meaty grasp, presumably to pummel him into submission. "Tonight, she belongs to *Nyx*."

"Oh, does she now?" Ronan quipped, ducking swiftly in the other direction before realizing he'd let himself be cornered.

"Sometimes, Nyx lets us play with his leftovers." The figure laughed then, a harsh, reedy sound that grated on Ronan's nerves. "Maybe I'll get lucky tonight. She looked ready for it—"

"Go fuck yourself."

"You're done for!" the oaf yelled. In the next instant, his two oversized hands were reaching for Ronan's neck.

"Weird choice," Ronan observed. "I would have gone for a sucker punch."

Far quicker than his opponent, and considerably more skilled, Ronan expertly stabbed the bastard deep in the eye with his short dagger, the force of it causing blood and vitreous fluid to gush out in all directions. Ronan then grabbed him by the shoulders, and with a great shove, sent the large man tumbling backwards into a nearby storage room and its bank of shelves. Cocktail straws sprinkled down as several bottles of grenadine smashed loudly on the linoleum.

Ronan's boots were sticky enough already, so he opted to leave his dagger behind, embedded in his opponent's head. His attacker appeared to be human, rather than Wraith, so Ronan didn't feel called to finish the job and "kill him dead," as they described it in the Order. Instead, he left the man jerking and writhing in agony on the floor.

Judging by where he'd been stabbed, the oaf would likely succumb to his injury long before anyone else would find him. As much as he hated it, Ronan knew that there was a time and place for inflicting harm, and this had definitely been one of those times.

Leaving the storage room, he carried on into a primarily unused central kitchen where an acne-scarred youth was loading a tray of used glasses into a sanitizing dishwasher. Ronan had to hand it to the Wraiths; at least they attempted to avoid health-code violations in their various establishments. The worker spotted Ronan, looking momentarily confused, but then quickly resumed scrubbing plates. Evidently, staff members knew it was best to keep their heads down.

Ronan passed by, hurtling towards the doorway at the far end of the galley kitchen. As far as he could tell, it was the only direction Phoebe—a.k.a. *Sasha*—and Nyx could have gone. As the Bloodsbane took hold of his adrenal glands, he could feel a deep surge of adrenaline rocketing through his veins, even as his pupils dilated, sharpening his vision for combat.

On the far side of the doorway, he immediately came to a dimly lit staircase that curved steeply upward. He squinted, noting that the walls were decorated with black velvet and damask wallpaper (which he found *incredibly tacky*) marred by long gouges that had clearly been made by human fingernails scratching and scrabbling to survive.

Creepy.

He was definitely headed in the right direction.

Ronan felt a slight vibration coming from his left breast pocket as he ascended the stairs. Lennie was no doubt following his progress through the nightclub's security cameras. He ignored the nudge as he reached the second floor, where his footsteps swiftly became muffled by dense carpet.

Perfect.

He stalked towards the last room on the right, the only one from which any light was emanating, surprised not to encounter more Wraiths along the way. Their earlier recon had indicated that as many as ten high-ranking Wraith generals could be present at Nyx's establishment at any given time, even above and beyond the four they'd already detected.

So, where are they now?

What made it all the more ridiculous was that fucking Phoebe Ashburn thought she could come here tonight, all alone no less, and just do whatever the hell it was she was trying to do. It had been challenging to parse her true objectives over the past several months, as she'd been infiltrating various Wraith establishments. Even more perplexing to him was that they had been the very same Wraith businesses *he'd* been profiling and infiltrating. So, what was in it for her?

It was a serious red flag, if nothing else, and yet another reason they needed to bring her in for questioning.

Ronan crouched low until he spotted the poorly hidden hallway security camera suddenly flash red and then green again. As usual, Ronan was grateful to have Lennie keeping watch over him, though he would never tell him that.

Silent as a cat, he finally approached the only lit office in the corridor and froze as he took in the scene before him. Nyx's office looked surprisingly standard, complete with a desktop computer and general office supplies. Several large black filing cabinets lined the far wall, along with a well-stocked bar cart and a low chaise lounge for after-hours entertaining. The only thing clearly unusual about the space was Phoebe, who was perched far too prettily on Nyx's lap beside his desk ... all long limbs and sunshine as the Wraith's hand snaked its way greedily between her legs. Phoebe simultaneously coiled her arms behind his neck and whispered something into the bastard's ear.

Ronan's heart thumped strangely, which he attributed to the Bloodsbane, although he couldn't be sure that was to blame. Phoebe clearly knew what she was after. Taking advantage of their distracted state, Ronan silently entered Nyx's office unnoticed and locked the door behind him, not wanting any additional Wraith company before his backup could arrive.

"Wow, you work fast," Ronan remarked coolly.

Phoebe's head snapped up in his direction just as Nyx's grip tightened around her thigh like a vice. If his grasp hurt her, though, she didn't let it show on her face. Instead, her mouth just opened and closed several times like a beautiful goldfish with widened eyes, unable to speak.

Was that fear he saw in her eyes?

Nyx stood up, growling even as his prey was pitched from his lap to fall headlong to the floor. "Druid scum! How the fuck did *you* get up here?"

A dark laugh escaped from deep within Ronan's chest. "Druid scum? Is that *really* the best you've got?" he asked sarcastically. Then he frowned, wondering what had gotten into him. Obnoxious banter before a fight was Dom's thing. It had never been his.

Phoebe gingerly pushed herself up from the floor. "Good question."

For a brief second, Ronan wondered whether she was remarking on his question or Nyx's. He didn't have time to consider further implications though. In the next instant, the Wraith's massive frame was hurdling over the desk, feet first, sending surplus office supplies clattering to the floor. On the far side of his leap, the Wraith's feet landed on several fallen pens, and he stumbled slightly before righting himself, giving Ronan a momentary reprieve.

In truth, he hadn't expected the fucker to be quite so agile under all that bulk. But then again, Wraiths were known to modify their physical bodies far more than Druids. The Wraith likely *would* have had the upper hand if not for the Bloodsbane still surging through Ronan's veins. Ronan reacted like a man possessed.

One glimpse of Phoebe in Nyx's clutches had sent him raging to a whole other dimension; instead of seeing red in his fury, he saw only pure and blinding white. He launched himself into Nyx, colliding with the great bastard mid-stride, the clash between magic Wielders emitting a deep and resounding *"thud"* that seemed to go well beyond the physical.

Whenever the Wraiths donned their traditional cloaks, discerning how many weapons they had hidden beneath the billowing, stinking layers of linen was always a challenge. However, Nyx seemed more worried about his image than his ability to "pack heat." Indeed, the nightclub kingpin was far lighter on weapons than Ronan's usual opponents.

Ronan, meanwhile, was indeed packing.

"What? No sickle?" he asked. His Dublin accent was thick now, reminding him of the brawling days of his youth. He ripped open his wool overshirt and reached for the two long curved blades he wore beneath in a leather harness.

"I'm going to crush you," Nyx snarled, wrapping himself around Ronan so tightly that it was difficult for the Druid to fully extract his blades.

Ronan cursed inwardly, knowing he'd been too flashy in his approach, allowing the Wraith to fully anticipate his move.

The pair of entangled Wielders shifted and grunted for several strenuous moments.

Ronan tightened his grip on the hilts of his blades. "I've still got ..." he grunted, "a few ... tricks up my sleeve." Silently cursing himself for the cheesy joke, he moved swiftly, releasing the literal daggers he was wearing up his sleeves, which had been designed precisely for this type of skirmish, and spinning their blades inward.

Feeling him shifting in his grasp, Nyx shouted, *"I'll fucking kill—"*

Ronan's dual daggers drove into the soft flesh of his adversary's kidneys, silencing him in an instant.

Bingo.

Once properly positioned, it had been easy to take out the Wraith ... if not a little anticlimactic.

Ronan hugged his arms around the hulking Wraith for several moments as he waited for the wounds to do him in and take him down, hoping to avoid being crushed beneath the creature in the process. Staggering, he shifted the still groaning Nyx onto the floor to his left, away from where Phoebe had fallen.

Ronan looked over, expecting Phoebe to say something pithy or perhaps start to scream, but she wasn't there. Looking back up quickly, he spotted her perched in the room's only window, clutching her purse and holding a stack of files tucked neatly beneath one arm.

She was preparing herself to jump.

"Don't you fucking dare!" he shouted ... even as she slipped from view.

Ronan let out a measured breath as he prepared to pull a three-inch shard of metal from the pale buttock now presented before him. It had been far from a clean entry, leaving the surrounding tissue jagged and raw, but thankfully, it didn't seem to have nicked any major arteries. He wondered if she'd ever had a tetanus shot, but the truth was that he knew next to nothing about Phoebe, let alone the sordid details of her medical history.

What he did know, however, was that she had likely been through much worse than this.

"*Fuck*," she complained through gritted teeth. "Just get it over with!"

Despite the nastiness of the injury, the extraction should have been easy and would have been but for the location where this impromptu medical procedure was taking place: the back seat of a rental car in a Seattle alleyway. Far from the ideal clinical conditions. His medical bag sat on the floor beside her exposed right butt cheek; he'd covered the left cheek with a small disposable surgical drape.

Ronan shifted slightly to get a better view ... of the injury. The lighting was dim here, and unfortunately, he'd forgotten to charge his headlamp before departing on tonight's mission.

"Perhaps," he said evenly, "you shouldn't have jumped from a second-floor window into a waste bin then." He clamped his forceps around the protruding metal, having to bend his arm a bit awkwardly in the small, enclosed space.

"*I was trying to escape!*" she hissed, twisting to look over her shoulder at him. While Phoebe's expression was hostile, her trembling hands told a different story.

She was shaking like a leaf; shock, no doubt.

"Stay still," Ronan said tersely. His hands remained steady. "And you should have known better. That stunt shite they pull in the movies never works in real life!"

"Don't get all condescending, Druid, like you're so much older and wiser!"

Ronan scoffed. He *was* older and wiser, though she was no spring chicken herself, at only about ten years his junior (according to Lennie).

Phoebe continued crossly, pushing through her shock and madder than a wet hen. "You only have yourself to blame, you know! It's not *my* fault you rolled in and sullied my plans and—*Argh!*"

Ronan had chosen that precise moment to remove the fragment with a quick yank. "Got it!" he said, wincing a little. He'd perhaps not given quite enough time for the local anesthetic to fully take effect.

Phoebe let out a quick burst of air, even as her prone form visibly relaxed on the upholstery. "You're lucky I'm still indisposed, asshole. Otherwise ..."

Ronan resisted the urge to remind her that it wasn't *his* asshole that had been in danger tonight, as hers had clearly been. Two or three inches to the left, and the damage could have been *far* worse and even more problematic. Instead, he adopted the clinical tone he reserved for his more difficult patients. "I just need to clean the wound, stitch you up, and then we can be on our way. Please stay still."

"Will I have a scar?" she asked with a surprising vulnerability. His hands faltered slightly in their work.

Phoebe was tough, especially considering that (as far as he knew) she had no background in combat. Despite that though, she'd still attempted to infiltrate Nyx's headquarters, presumably with *some* sort of escape plan. She'd been foolish to tackle something this big alone, though. He sighed, realizing she was still waiting for an answer. "No scar really," he said quickly. "At least, not if I have anything to say about it."

Several beats of silence passed between them as he flushed out the wound and readied the sutures, still able to sense some unfamiliar magic thrumming deep within her.

"Thanks," she said finally.

Ronan nodded but quickly realized she couldn't see him. "*Ehm* ... you're welcome."

The evening's adrenaline and the shot of Bloodsbane were both starting to wane as he got to work, methodically closing the wound. Phoebe's floral outfit was still bunched up near her waist, with the crotch of the garment pushed out of the way, wedged up between her ass cheeks—one perfect, and the other marred by grievous injury but wonderfully shapely all the same.

This was going to be a problem.

"So, what's next?" she asked, bringing Ronan back to the present as he gently laid a piece of soft fabric on her right glute to complete his job. "Are you going to kidnap me?"

"I've been tasked with getting you somewhere safe. So, we're heading north to Canada—to Vancouver, specifically—as soon as my backup arrives. The Druids want to ask you some questions."

She pushed herself up. "I have none of my things."

Ronan couldn't help but notice how quickly she rose from her prone position. "Where were you staying?"

"Nowhere ... specifically," she said, climbing out of the vehicle and into the dim alleyway.

Ronan tried (and failed) not to look concerned as he slid across the back seat and out the door. "Oh, is that right?"

After a momentary stare-down, Phoebe let out a resigned sigh. "Fine! My bag is just behind there." She pointed towards a grease-disposal bin. "And like I said, if you hadn't been such a pain in my ass"

—she gestured wildly at her backside—"I would have just taken what I needed, grabbed my things, and already been *gone* by now."

"Got it." Ronan watched her warily before casually flicking through the files she'd taken from Nyx's office. Then his heart started pounding. These were the exact files that he and the Druids had been after for months!

"Hey! Those are mine! Give them back!"

"We'll talk about the files in a moment," he said curtly, quickly pouring through the pages and relying on his hyperlexia to help him process a great deal of information very quickly. He didn't see his name among the printed words or any reference to his involvement in the birth of the recent Wraith bout of experimentation. *Thank the Goddess.*

For the time being, the rest was irrelevant.

"Asshole." She stomped a high-heeled foot on the shoddy pavement to get his attention.

He took a step back to study her from head-to-toe. She was wearing the most impractical shoes possible, especially for someone with obvious back problems. "How exactly did you expect to incapacitate Nyx and escape with these files, Phoebe?"

"Who said I was going to incapacitate him?"

"Come on. One look at you in his clutches told me everything I needed to know."

Her eyes grew wide. "You're a judgemental piece of—"

"No, no, Phoebe, wait!" Ronan interrupted quickly, suddenly more concerned with her opinion of him than anything else. "I only meant that you seemed to know what you were doing. Or was I mistaken in that assessment?"

She stared coldly at him. "You're not mistaken."

"So, what *was* your plan?"

A rat streaked out from behind a dumpster, causing them both to jump. Ronan quickly returned his gaze to hers and raised his eyebrows. She wasn't getting out of answering his question.

"It's my secret," she said stubbornly.

"Fine." His tone was clipped. He might barely know her, but he was already getting tired of her antics. He would eventually get the information out of her ... one way or another.

Phoebe rolled her eyes.

Ronan watched as she dug into her purse and pulled out the same tube of lipstick that he'd seen earlier. While he expected her to start reapplying it—though only the goddess knew why she would feel the need to do so at this moment—instead she chucked it into the grease-disposal bin beside her before reaching gingerly behind the bin for her backpack.

Aha!

"You're kidding ... the lipstick?" He studied her expression carefully. "So ... would I die if you kissed me right now?"

She blushed.

His guess had evidently been correct. "Well now ... Aren't you full of surprises? First jumping out a window with the files and now *poison lipstick*." He couldn't help but laugh. "Where did you even get something like that? And how—"

"Ronan!"

Before he could finish his question, Amos and Amelia pulled up in a nondescript gold sedan, which had no doubt been fed their location by Lennie. The twins jumped out of the vehicle, leaving their doors wide open as they approached Phoebe with obvious caution, their arms outstretched.

"Who are *they?*" Phoebe asked, pursing her lips as she looked back and forth between Ronan and this new pair of Druids.

Ronan couldn't tell if she was surprised, nervous, or annoyed.

Maybe all of the above?

"She's going to come quietly," Ronan said, looking at her, "right, Phoebe?"

Realistically, she had no chance of escape. Amos and Amelia's car now blocked the only entrance to the alleyway, and behind Phoebe, the only way out would entail climbing up a drainpipe back into Nyx's office.

Resigning herself to her fate, she nodded. "For now."

"Good." Ronan swept his arm invitingly towards the newly arrived vehicle. "Now, I've got a quick phone call to make."

"We'll need to bind your hands for the trip," he heard Amelia say to Phoebe as he walked out of earshot. "Just as a precaution." He smirked at Phoebe's groan of annoyance and dialled Lennie's number, speaking as soon as he heard the call connect.

"Hello, I—"

"You have a bloody death wish, Ronan!"

"*What?* We got the files! And Nyx is dead."

"*We* got the files?" Lennie's tone sounded incredulous. "*We* as in the Druidic Order or *we* as in you and Phoebe, you know, your *actual* target for the evening?" Evidently, there had been no security cameras in Nyx's office, and he'd been left in the dark for some time now.

"Well, you must have assumed she's with me since neither of us came back out the front door."

"I know she's *with* you, idiot! But I also *assumed* you were apprehending her!"

"I did."

"No, you didn't! Amos and Amelia did! From what I saw, what *you* just did was spend the better part of fifteen minutes perched proudly above her magnificently exposed ass."

Ah ... Ronan looked over at a security camera affixed to one of the walls high above the alley and grinned. "You saw that, did you?"

"I saw the whole bloody thing, Ronan! So, I stand by my earlier statement. You're an—"

"*Idiot*. Yes, I got that, thank you. Anyways, the files, Lennie, she's been working to gather up the same files that we've been looking for from the facility ... or at least, very similar ones." Ronan was finding it hard to keep the worry from his voice.

Lennie didn't say anything, and the silence stretched on long enough for Ronan to wonder about their connection. "Did you hear me?"

"Yes." Lennie sounded distracted. Then Ronan heard him typing away at his distant keyboard. "Well ... that explains things."

"What's that?"

"I've been trying to figure out who else has been accessing certain Wraith computer systems for some time now. There's been an unfamiliar digital signature on the lower security servers. At first, I thought nothing of it, but now ..."

"I see." Ronan's best guess was that Phoebe wanted more information about the time she'd spent in captivity, which made him feel oddly sick to his stomach, imagining what they might have put her through.

He reined his thoughts back in, knowing that he couldn't afford to go there. Not now.

"Oh, fuck me." Lennie started typing even more loudly from his end of the line.

"What is it?"

After a moment, the typing stopped. "I don't know how I missed it, but ... it seems she's been relieving the Wraiths of certain classified documents for quite some time now, both digitally and in person. However, from what I can see, it's just been pretty basic stuff so far. Nothing as in-depth as those documents with your actual signature ... Though I suppose it's possible that she—"

"Let's talk about this later," Ronan said firmly, not wanting to risk spiralling at present, mentally or emotionally.

The timing of Lennie's discovery was terrible, coinciding as it did with the sudden onset of his Bloodsbane crash; it was making his stomach start to churn and hot bile to rise up in his throat. He gritted his teeth and swallowed it back.

"Alright. Now, what about Nyx's body?" Lennie asked, either oblivious to Ronan's current emotional plight or dismissing it as irrelevant.

"Left it on the floor."

Eventually, the body would be discovered, of course. Wraiths lived to an unnatural age only by stealing magic, so when they were killed, depending on how old they were, their bodies effectively disintegrated. Nyx hadn't appeared as aged as most, though, so there would likely be some remains still needing disposal.

"I'll have someone pick up your rental car," Lennie said. "Leave the keys under the hood."

"Cheers, Lennie." Ronan nodded and promptly hung up.

Quickly hiding the keys as instructed, he took a steadying breath before slipping into the back seat of Amos and Amelia's sedan next to Phoebe. Through the rear-view mirror, he nodded to Amelia in the driver's seat, and she took off without further instruction.

As he settled back in his seat, Ronan was again met by Phoebe's intoxicating scent, now mixed with the sweat of their shared exertion, her blood, and his antiseptic.

Ronan cleared his throat. "I'm not giving up on the lipstick, Phoebe," he said to her quietly from across the back seat. They'd been driving for fifteen minutes of cool quiet already, and he felt the foolish need to break the silence. "How were you going to do it?"

Her laugh sounded cruel for a moment before she leaned over with widened eyes and whispered in a tantalizing voice, "Kiss of death."

"Pardon me?"

She smiled with her teeth, showing off what remained of her now cracking lipstick. A streak of red marred the bright enamel of one front teeth, which she mischievously licked away.

Ronan was silent for several beats. "I assume you have the antidote?"

Her strange smile faded.

"I'm serious, Phoebe. I'm no expert on poisons, especially when I don't know what they are, but—"

"Are you going to give me back the files?" Her tone was venomous now.

Ronan thought about Lennie's comment regarding the digital signature he'd been encountering lately and shifted in his seat. "That depends."

"Typical," she muttered, shaking her head in disgust and looking out the window.

He let out a small puff of air and settled his attention on the view from his window, which wasn't much to look at—the I-5 was even more bland at night than during the daytime. "Get some rest."

Phoebe didn't respond.

As they sped down the highway, Ronan began running his usual marathon of rumination, which now included a delightful concern that Phoebe might up and die from her own poison during transport.

Minutes passed as the low hum of the highway soothed his frayed nerves. Drowsiness crept in, so Ronan rested his eyes, though he knew he wouldn't sleep until they arrived at their final destination.

"I'm not going to die, okay?" Phoebe eventually whispered from her side of the back seat.

Ronan's eyes shot open, and he held his breath for a moment before closing them once more. One thing was certain, apprehending Phoebe Ashburn had just thrown a significant wrench in the gears of everything that mattered to him.

Shit.

CHAPTER 4
PHOEBE

PHOEBE JOLTED AWAKE, HEART POUNDING AND LIMBS SLICK WITH sweat. Even in the Druids' safe house, she was plagued by her usual nightmares. She blinked away the bodies ... the blood ... the rubble. She could feel the forcibly entrenched magic reverberating through her weakened frame as she attempted to settle the turmoil. Nighttime was always the worst.

She sat up and gazed at the glowing blue numbers on the digital alarm clock: 5:15 a.m.

Still too fucking early to get up for the day.

She stretched her hands above her head, sniffed her armpits, and cringed. When was the last time she'd showered? She'd lost her deodorant somewhere back in Seattle. It was probably on the ground behind that alley dumpster where she'd prepared to infiltrate Nyx's lair. Hopefully, someone in need could use the brand-new deodorant stick; she sure as shit wasn't going back for it.

Phoebe sighed and rubbed her face, which felt like an oil slick. In her life before, she'd taken great care of her acne-prone skin, all the way down to fuzzy absorbent wristbands to prevent water from dripping down her arms while doing her skincare routine ... what a luxury.

All things considered, the Druids' safe house was comfortable enough. Her sheets were clean, and the room was relatively tidy. However, they'd placed her on the topmost floor, where the air was sticky and hot despite the freezing rain outside. Oppressive, really. Phoebe dragged her feet towards the tiny dormer window in search of relief, pausing to run her long fingers along the dusty windowsill before noticing that the window was painted shut.

It was also rigged with an alarm system.

"Well, *that* feels a bit redundant," she muttered, though her outer calm belied her inner fear. The last thing she wanted was to be trapped again. She already knew the Druids saw her as a flight risk; that had become obvious when Amos and Amelia had met them behind Nyx's bar. In her opinion, binding her hands had been entirely over the top.

But at least it had made their transit from Seattle to Vancouver delightfully awkward.

Though Phoebe hadn't *technically* been taken against her will, she hadn't been about to come easily either. She sensed that Ronan had expected some modicum of gratitude from her or, at the very least, some cordiality, but she'd had other plans.

She was nothing if not a brat.

"Can you please pass me my drink?" she'd asked Ronan the night before, her voice saccharine. They'd stopped for late-night sustenance at a roadside Arby's—much to Ronan's dismay. Something about him screamed health nut ... he was a doctor, after all. She'd wondered then if he was a distance runner or a cyclist; no one his age was that fit without putting real effort into it.

"What's stopping you from grabbing it?" he'd asked, barely looking up from his phone.

Phoebe had raised her bound hands with a shrug. *"I guess I'm just afraid I'll spill."*

Following that, she'd "required" Ronan's help for every step of their late-night meal—including drizzling a packet of horseradish on several burger bites. He'd finally broken when she'd asked him to fish out any "bonus" curly fries that might have fallen to the bottom of the bag, shoving it forcibly onto her lap. *"Enough!"*

She'd snorted out a laugh. *"Worth it."* She could have sworn she saw Amelia smirk through the rear-view mirror.

Phoebe had no idea why she'd felt compelled to rile Ronan up, other than that it felt good at the time. The more she pushed, the more aggravated he became, all the while giving her exactly what she wanted. It had been a surefire way to get the true make of him. She'd learned that Ronan did not like it when someone else dictated his circumstances.

In essence, he was a control freak.

He was also laughably exasperated by her, but the fact he'd still done precisely as she'd asked—down to drizzling horseradish on her burger—said a lot about him. Phoebe knew precisely how to deal with people like Ronan if she really needed something. But that could wait. Everything could wait.

She'd navigated the rest of her meal with little difficulty as the miles dragged on. And then at the border, with little grace, they'd finally removed her bindings.

"Don't even think about giving the border guards trouble," Amos had instructed her as they waited in line at the Peace Arch. He was an incredibly serious human.

It was boring.

"You do realize I'm a Canadian citizen."

"With a stolen ID," Ronan had mumbled.

Phoebe, naturally, had rolled her eyes at the paranoid Druids. *"It worked just fine coming down."*

"That doesn't mean it'll work in reverse," Amos had replied coolly. *"Behave yourself."*

Amelia had smiled apologetically. She was clearly the nicer of the two.

Meanwhile, Ronan had ignored their discussion entirely, too busy almost frantically texting on his phone. Phoebe hadn't had the chance to wonder who or what had drawn him in with such ferocity, though, as they'd been next in line for screening.

Thankfully, their passage through the border had been smooth as grease, and they slid right through, mercifully reaching the Druids' safe house at just after two a.m. Everyone had gone straight to bed, saying that they would "reconnect in the morning," presumably to interrogate her. Phoebe had been deposited on the top floor, where she'd passed out almost immediately.

At least for a time.

She could feel the volatile forces vibrating within her as her thoughts spiralled. Three hours was not nearly enough sleep to keep the trapped magic at bay, let alone her emotions. She was clammy, shaky, and rather weepy.

Not to mention that the wound on her butt hurt like hell.

Sinking carefully to the floor, Phoebe knelt down in front of the small window, placing one hand on her heart and the other on her womb. She let her soft belly relax, which only made room for more aching. Salty tears tracked down her cheeks as she rocked back and forth, groaning from her throat all the way to her sit bones as they ground into her heels. She moaned through her pain—both the old and the new.

She didn't give a flying fuck if she woke the entire house up.

What did any of it matter?

Memories of her time in Wraith captivity were foggy. Not only had she spent most days sedated (by both pharmaceutical and magical means), but she'd also been so dissociative that she'd logged very few memories. For the most part, she could reconcile the absence of any concrete recollection as being "for the best."

She knew the gist of what they did to her over the twelve-month period she'd been held in captivity and experimented on, and didn't particularly wish to re-live any of the grislier bits. However, the memory that quite literally ran through her veins was impossible to forget: being forcibly injected with their own disgusting dark magic—usually with syringes but sometimes, over longer periods of confinement, with an IV drip.

And now it was trapped inside of her. Forever.

Initially, she'd been an experimental vessel to them, just like everyone else they captured. At the onset of the trials, they'd informed her that she was a "Wielder," whatever that had meant. The truth was she'd never touched a lick of magic in her life. Didn't even believe in it.

Not until the Wraiths had captured her.

Once the experiments had begun—and they had inflicted an unhuman, unearthly pain upon her body and mind—she had no choice but to believe in magic. She remembered little else, other than that they'd quickly discovered Phoebe didn't fit into any exact magical taxonomy, and that was when their real fun began ...

Suddenly, her mouth was *unbearably* dry. And of course, she'd passed out without a glass of water at her bedside. She'd have to descend to the kitchen ... assuming it was allowed.

Phoebe rose gingerly to her feet, stretching her sore back and bending to press her palms to the hardwood floor. Then she straightened, feeling light-headed, and took several steps forward to grip the door handle, relieved to discover no one had locked it from the outside. *Thank fuck.*

But alas, stepping into the hallway offered no relief.

It was equally stuffy out there, the heat now combined with a nearly suffocating floral scent of rose and ... honeysuckle? Bile rose to the back of her throat as she suddenly recalled the sulphurous yet similarly earthen smell of the Wraiths.

She'd always had an overly sensitive olfactory system.

If the Druids smelled like vibrant living things, then the Wraith smelled like their composted, rotting counterparts, and both scents completely overwhelmed her. However, while the Wraiths' stench elicited fear, she sensed the Druids' herbal essence might be calming should they reduce it by half (at *least*).

It was almost tranquilizing ...

She rolled her eyes. Did they think she required sedating?

Her trapped magic was far from soothed; it roiled and churned in response. She knew little of the hidden magical world—and even less of the Druids, who guarded their secrets even more closely than the Wraiths, though she sensed they weren't nearly as righteous as they appeared. No one was. And if they thought containing her here was remotely ethical or that everything would be coming up roses (and honeysuckle, apparently), they had another thing coming.

Phoebe padded barefoot down the narrow third-floor stairwell, hunching slightly under the low ceiling as she took a sharp turn towards the second-floor landing. This house had to be at least one hundred years old and had apparently been built for people far shorter than she was.

No wonder Ronan didn't sleep on the top floor.

Phoebe was wondering vaguely which room he occupied, when the magic inside her suddenly clawed so violently for its freedom that she nearly collapsed on the spot. Woozy, she sank back down to the floor as the memory of her first (official) meeting with Ronan nearly engulfed her.

At first glance, he was intelligent, strong, and brutally handsome; nothing went unnoticed by his sharp blue eyes. He smelled subtly of cedar and strangely of ... *lime cordial?* Ronan was also a bit of an asshole, which she wasn't entirely sure she hated. The Druid's introduction had been confident and held a hint of danger, as though he was full of juicy secrets just waiting to be exposed.

Once a journalist, always a journalist, she supposed.

Naturally, Phoebe had been keenly aware of his surveillance from behind all evening. He was no stranger to her, even though they'd never formally met. Once she'd reoriented herself to the world after (somehow) escaping the lab, she'd done as much research as she could about her captors, and who their adversaries might be. As it turned out, that was Druids.

The bad guys always had challengers—often sanctimonious people who deemed themselves "above" the antics of whatever group was currently in low standing, even though they were more often than not just as dastardly. All that was required was someone like Phoebe to expose their lies. In the past, she'd investigated competing corporations and, on several occasions, organized crime syndicates as well. Both had landed her in hot water more than once. So, comparatively speaking, the Druids didn't seem all that bad.

Yet their ability to hide nearly everything about their operation was a red flag. She'd spent several weeks trying to dig up *anything* about them, and besides profiling some of their main members (Ronan included), the most she'd managed to dig up was that wherever she would find Wraiths gathering, the Druids were likely to show up as well.

They'd been crossing paths for months, but Phoebe had been vigilant at all times, not wanting to be caught. And though she'd nearly exposed herself digitally several times, she was fairly certain she'd never before let them get as close to her as they had last night.

In a small way, the feeling of playing cat and mouse with the Druids had been a thrill, but she'd also had zero interest in ever meeting them, and specifically Ronan, face to face. But when he'd slid from his bar stool to stop her from pursuing Nyx, wrapping his arms around her waist and begging her to think twice about what she was about to do ... *everything* had changed.

The trapped magic inside her, which had never been anything but a tumultuous force within the frail container of her body, had responded to him in kind ... taking on a vibration that had matched his pleading timbre. Almost soothing—and undeniably familiar, like she'd met him somewhere in another lifetime perhaps. A recognition. His touch had brought both respite and warning ... and she'd had to fight every fucking urge in her body in order to push away from him and pursue Nyx.

She'd been (stupidly) ambitious in thinking that she could infiltrate Nyx's office, as evidenced by Ronan's arrival on-site. She'd been sloppy. But, after months of tracking and tracing information, she'd finally confirmed that the Wraith "boss" was part of a greater network and had pertinent data in his possession.

Though, she didn't think he'd been there at the lab when they had ... when she ...

Phoebe's eyes snapped open.

She had no idea how long she'd been slumped on the floor in the dark hallway. A soft light was emanating from downstairs like a beacon. *The kitchen, perhaps?* Phoebe just needed some water and maybe a snack. The Arby's sandwich wasn't sticking to her ribs like she'd hoped. After eating something, she hoped she could sleep, allowing her to better contain the magic until tomorrow.

Phoebe rose slowly, gaining her bearings with some effort.

"So far, so good," she muttered, treading carefully down the final flight of stairs. And indeed, a dim light *was* coming from the kitchen doorway.

She gently pushed open the door. "Hello?"

Ronan sat at the small kitchen table, wide awake, sipping a large mug of something, and reading the newspaper like some kind of nocturnal freak.

"Oh," she said, pausing. The last thing she wanted right now was to chit-chat. Frustration flared in tandem with her walls rising; it would be a cold day in hell before she let him witness her unmasked vulnerability. "Uh ... sorry."

He cleared his throat, evidently surprised to see her too. "It's alright. I was just leaving." The Druid neatly folded his paper, plainly diverting his eyes from Phoebe's sleep-rumpled body as he got up from the small kitchen table. "A strange noise woke me earlier, and I couldn't fall back asleep. An owl, maybe—"

"I'm just grabbing some water and then heading back upstairs." She turned from Ronan and started fumbling through the unknown cupboards in search of a glass.

Her hands trembled; she'd stupidly turned her back to him ... again. Of course, she'd had little choice when he'd been stitching her ass back together following her spectacular two-story dumpster dive (she at least deserved marks for creativity). However, there was no good reason to place herself in such a vulnerable position now.

Least of all with *him*.

"Let me help," he said. A shiver ran up Phoebe's spine as Ronan reached over her shoulder, almost making physical contact as he began aiding in her search. Again, the trapped magics simmered. She swayed on the spot as he handed her a cup.

When she turned around, they were face to face.

She couldn't breathe.

"Are you alright, Phoebe?" His tone was disarming. He drew in his lower lip slightly, evidently concerned.

She was surely a hot mess, her hair askew and her face flushed. And for the briefest moment, she considered telling Ronan the truth—that she'd awoken in a nightmare-induced panic and, terrified that she'd been trapped upstairs, had spiralled spectacularly, nearly fallen down the stairs, and just now stumbled into the kitchen looking like an unmade bed, only to find herself trapped by him, instead.

"Yup! Totally fine." She gasped. A lie was infinitely better than the truth in this situation.

"Alright. Well, you're welcome to some of this herbal tea, and ..." He paused, as though debating whether or not to say more. Finally, he gestured at the table. "I've had my fill. So, it's all yours if you want it."

"Oh, thanks," Phoebe said. She hated tea.

Ronan turned to leave but paused again on the threshold with his back to her. "I'm told this particular brew helps with nightmares." With that, he let the kitchen door swing shut behind him.

"Goodnight, Dr. Gallagher," she whispered, far too physically aware of his exit than she'd care to admit.

Phoebe sat alone in the kitchen until midwinter's late dawn, growing bleary-eyed as she mulled things over. While she'd been held in captivity, during periods of lucidity, she had gleaned that the birth of the experiments, and the foundation of her torture, had stemmed from an estate in Gloucestershire, England, once owned by an evil Sorcerer named Cassius—this fact, alone, had taken her weeks to reconcile. At this estate, a turncoat Druid had implemented the initial exploration into how Wraith magic worked—a turncoat Druid named *Dr. R. Gallagher*.

Ronan.

The way the Wraiths had spoken of him had been consistently belittling, calling him a "quack" or worse. She'd repeatedly heard them say that *"The bastard nearly let himself run out."* Since then, Phoebe had learned that "running out" referred to the process of being exposed to (a.k.a., receiving) Wraith magic and starting to transform into one of them, even while denying the process of letting it actually take over one's body.

This was different than her experience, but it still sounded pretty uncomfortable.

She'd listened to their descriptions of Ronan directly from their lips—assuming they *had* lips, since their Wraith flesh was constantly rotting away as they aged. They'd made Ronan sound pathetic, chronically pushed around by his superiors and forced to undertake endlessly gruesome experiments. To her, though, resisting the Wraiths' magic as he had apparently done sounded incredibly difficult, and meeting Ronan had disproved their opinions of him.

The Druid doctor didn't appear weak to her. In fact, he was nothing like they'd described. But then again, some people were *very* good actors.

Phoebe eyed the cold tea before her with disgust before rising to her feet. It wasn't just that she felt an aversion to the drink (she *really* hated tea), but the fact that Ronan had offered it to her in some bullshit attempt to reduce her unease in the house—*"I'm told this particular brew helps with nightmares"*—left her feeling annoyed and overexposed ... He must have heard her moaning in pain earlier.

Slowly, she padded from the kitchen towards the narrow stairway. Somewhere in the back of her mind, she could feel her stitches stinging from the movement as she ascended the stairs, this time of her own free will. It was strange the things people took for granted. At least the Druids were allowing her to move freely within the house. She would attempt to get a few winks before they (inevitably) began to question her within an inch of her sanity.

Deep breaths.

She could bend this circumstance to her advantage. Being a journalist for most of her adult life had transformed her into a truth-seeking missile; justice was in her bones, even if she could no longer focus her attention the way she used to.

Perhaps with time, she would heal ... though, she had her doubts.

Phoebe reached the second-floor landing and started examining the four closed doors in the dimly lit hallway belonging (she assumed) to Ronan, Amos, Amelia, and some unknown. She'd noticed a large pair of beat-up Vans sneakers beside the front door on their arrival and wondered who they belonged to. They were too large for anyone she'd met so far.

She pushed up the final flight, the old steps creaking as she swayed a bit on her feet, feeling faint with exhaustion.

To her knowledge, following Ronan's experiments (and *after* he'd allegedly escaped), Cassius had elevated Ronan's existing work to even more gruesome heights if such a thing were possible.

And then roughly two-and-half years ago, Cassius had been vanquished in what had been (according to the Wraiths) a thousand-year-long battle to the death. When the Wraiths didn't think she was listening, she'd often heard the words *"curse," "prophecy,"* and *"rebirth"* being tossed around.

Following Cassius's defeat, her captors—newly free and (in her opinion) arrogantly industrious—were eager to capitalize on an already existing framework to assure Wraith "dominion." Her captors weren't the only Wraiths, or Wraith groups, out there, but unfortunately, they were some of the worst.

And every bit of it would have been impossible for her to believe if not for the evidence reverberating through her tortured body even now ... the magic she still felt even as she collapsed onto her third-floor bed. She tried to fall back asleep, but the dark magic was swirling violently, an ever-constant reminder of her stolen freedom.

It was an ache so deep that she felt it in her bones.

She couldn't help but remember how it had all begun. She'd been chasing a lead about a steadily growing shadow conglomerate on Canada's West Coast but had pushed her nose too far into somewhere it hadn't belonged. She should have clued in that something wasn't right when the CEO of Spectre Fidelities Corp had agreed to meet with her in person following only one inquiry email.

It was never that easy.

Little did Phoebe know, this company dealt with nosy reporters by either exploiting them—the outcome she'd anticipated as soon as she arrived—or if they happened to be a magic user, capturing, torturing, and experimenting on them.

She'd reached the Downtown Vancouver office just after four p.m. on a Friday. Realistically, this should have been another red flag. What shitty CEO took a meeting with an independent reporter on a Friday afternoon and *didn't* intend to take advantage of them in one way or another? Phoebe's hunger for the truth—one of the many pitfalls of a good lead—had blinded her rationality and sense of self-preservation far too often throughout her career.

And on that day, she'd definitely pushed it too far.

Jordan Cole had met her in reception as soon as she'd stepped off the elevator. *"I've sent my admin staff home early. They've worked so hard this week."*

His voice had been strange, as though something was wrong with his vocal cords, making the hairs on her neck stand on end. His words had echoed strangely through the overly modern office, lending an aura to the space that had practically screamed "danger."

"Ah, okay," she'd said, clutching her bag and backing towards the elevator. *"Honestly, I can come back another day."*

Jordan Cole hadn't liked that.

He'd raised his hand in a strangely measured gesture that she realized far too late was pointing to three goons who were now standing between her and escape. *"You're not going anywhere."*

By all rights, Phoebe should have died that day.

The CEO had lunged forward with seemingly superhuman speed and dragged her screaming into his office. He'd barred the door, though this wasn't strictly necessary as the three other men (whom she later learned were also Wraiths) now stood outside. She'd kicked and punched to no avail, managing to carve out a few deep scratches on his face, before he'd shoved her face-first onto his desk and struck her so hard she'd seen stars.

Phoebe blinked hard at the memory as she nibbled at her brittle, chewed-down nails in the dark of the Druid safe house. She could still remember how Jordan Cole's deteriorating flesh had felt under her well-manicured claws, as though she'd been scraping a hundred years of thick dust from equally ancient upholstery.

This had been Phoebe's first interaction with a Wraith but would be far from her last.

His strength had gone beyond anything she'd ever experienced as he held her down and forced himself inside. The pain might have been excruciating if she'd managed to stay conscious for longer than a few moments. But perhaps luckily, he'd given her a severe concussion.

Small evil favours, she supposed.

When she woke up, she'd found herself tied up in the back of a van.

She learned later that, while the unholy piece of shit had assaulted her, something unexpected had occurred, and he'd been wholly stripped of his dark magic ... as though she'd drawn the entirety of his essence within herself. This had not gone over well, of course, since somehow, Phoebe had also managed to kill him in the process.

That was how she'd ended up tied up in the back a van, being taken to the test facility. It would be almost a full year before she was free again.

And now *Dr. R. Gallagher* had clearly mistaken her for someone who would stay caged.

Rolling onto her side and scrunching up her pillow, Phoebe curled her wrists under her chin like a T-rex. Her nervous system might be shot, but she decided to meet with Ronan in the morning and face their line of questioning. Willingly. But if the Druids thought she would stay with them any longer than was necessary, they would soon learn otherwise.

She didn't trust *any* of them.

If they couldn't help her find a way to remove the magic trapped within her, which had been her singular motivation for the past six months, she would be forced to look elsewhere for solutions. As each week passed, Phoebe felt the "infection" more frequently and intensely—creating an escalating sense of panic and urgency. Time was of the essence. The problem, however, was the new yet somehow familiar pull she'd felt to the Druid doctor since they met—a fact she was actively denying. It would make it challenging to leave abruptly, though she couldn't quite pinpoint why.

With this thought still echoing through her mind, Phoebe finally drifted into a fitful sleep.

CHAPTER 5

RONAN

"ARE WE ALL SET ON YOUR END, RONAN?" LENNIE ASKED FROM HIS side of the world.

Ronan's laptop was set up on the safe house's dining-room table, the screen open to an encrypted video call. The light of his screen lit up Lennie's face, but any details beyond that were unclear.

They'd initially arranged the inquiry call for the first thing that morning, but Ronan had elected to reschedule it for the afternoon once Phoebe had rested. He'd heard her climbing back to bed at dawn as he also struggled to sleep following their encounter in the kitchen.

"Nearly," he said breathily, fussing with the wires around Phoebe's waist and chest. Placing the chair against the wall—an effort to put her at ease—now added a layer of difficulty to the process.

Contrary to how she'd presented at the nightclub, Phoebe was now notably dishevelled in a loose t-shirt and crinkled jeans. It was hard for Ronan to ignore his appreciation for her physical body as he wrapped the sensors around her ... he also tried not to think about it when she'd appeared in front of him wearing pyjama shorts earlier that morning. There was no denying how attractive Phoebe Ashburn was—or that she knew how to use it to her advantage—but he would be keeping things strictly professional.

"Is this absolutely necessary?" she asked, irritably. She was already onto her second cup of coffee.

"I recognize this process is going to be somewhat uncomfortable for you, Phoebe," Ronan said, not dispassionately. "But it's standard protocol."

"You still haven't told me the exact purpose of today's ... *examination*," she said, picking at her nails.

Ronan couldn't help but notice how collected she seemed, despite what he knew had been a terrible night of sleep for her.

"If you're going to reside in the Druids' safe house and if you want allowance for movement within the community while doing so, we need to ask you some standard questions," Lennie said firmly.

"Then why do I get the sense that this"—Phoebe wiggled her fingers as Ronan attempted to attach sensors to their tips—"is non-standard? I can't help but feel like I'm being held against my will. Is this how you treat all of your guests?"

Ronan rolled his eyes. "You're not being held against your will."

In theory.

As it stood, the Druids had no intention of holding her captive, and she could technically leave if she wanted to—not that they wouldn't just track her down all over again. However, should they uncover something today that signalled any danger to the greater magical world, they might have to consider a different route.

Phoebe snorted. "The restraints you used last night would beg to differ."

"That wasn't my call," Ronan said, which was true. He'd privately advocated against the use of any cuffs or bindings (Phoebe's year-long Wraith confinement a guaranteed recipe for post-traumatic stress) but was overruled by Lennie and Amos. Amelia, meanwhile, had remained neutral.

Lennie grumbled, "Amos tends to be a tad overzealous when bringing in—"

"Suspects?" she suggested.

"Wayfaring magic users and Wraiths," Lennie finished, giving her a haughty look.

"I'm not a Wraith."

Ronan sighed. "We're not saying that you are, Phoebe."

"Then why all of this? I honestly can't believe you're using a lie detector. These things don't actually work, you know. Not to mention how discriminatory they are—"

"It's not a polygraph," Lennie said before she could argue further. "Not in the traditional sense. It's more of a magic sensor, if you will, though it is based on the same fundamentals as a lie detector. It may even detect lies as well, depending on how the data is interpreted."

Phoebe rolled her eyes.

"Lennie invented it," Ronan said under his breath so only she would hear. He'd woken up determined to play the good cop today, especially after how exhausted she'd looked in the kitchen that morning; he was legitimately worried about her mental state. "I'm sure he'd tell you *all* about it if you asked him."

"I heard that," Lennie said, ignoring the barb and carrying on. "It was initially developed to detect magic levels within a Wielder at any given time. Moreover, we were curious to see what happened to Wielding magic under significant stress. You can imagine how useful that is to study."

"And what, pray tell, happens to magic when under stress?" Phoebe asked, mocking his pretentious tone. Ronan could sense her anger and distress rising. "And how the *fuck* does any of this apply to me?"

The sensors went off then. At the very least, they'd just proven the legitimacy of the machine for detecting a state of emotional arousal. The connection to Lennie also froze momentarily—magic and technology were a terrible mix.

Ronan sat beside her at the table, rather than across from her, in another effort to make the whole ordeal feel less formal and encourage her to trust him. "Well, when I touched your arm at the nightclub, I felt a lot of magic inside you."

Phoebe swallowed hard. "And?"

"And essentially, Phoebe," Lennie said, enunciating carefully and staring at her through the laptop screen, "we need you to tell us *everything* you know." She was either getting under his skin or he'd caught on to Ronan's ploy and was playing the bad cop in today's interrogation. "The good, the bad, and the ugly. Especially the ugly if you're willing."

Phoebe wasn't a usual suspect and wouldn't be treated as such. "Fine. I'll tell you what I can, but there's a lot I don't remember."

The Brit nodded mildly. "That's fine. Let's begin."

"But first, I need a different bedroom," Phoebe said unexpectedly, crossing her arms over her chest, which pulled out several wires from where they were attached to the sensor. Ronan tried not to bark at her as she shifted. "The room you've given me is fucking with my sleep. It's way too hot. Plus, the window has a security thingy. I'm guessing that's your doing?" she asked Lennie pointedly; she'd already pegged him as the eye in the sky. "I don't like it."

Ronan felt his chest tighten. He hadn't considered what psychological effect the third-floor bedroom might have on Phoebe (or more accurately, he'd avoided the discomfort of the thought entirely). To their knowledge, the Wraiths had held Phoebe entirely against her will. So, of course, even a simple security sensor on the upstairs bedroom window would leave her feeling squirrelly.

It was a feeling Ronan understood all too well.

He'd avoided the topmost bedroom like the plague since his return to Vancouver, as the space unearthed repressed memories of his own time with the Wraiths spent on the top floor of Cassius's Gloucestershire estate. Not to mention that Dom had repeatedly complained about how hot it was up there, even in the dead of winter.

Phoebe needed to feel safe. And he wanted that for her.

"Of course." Ronan nodded vigorously. "Amos and Amelia leave tomorrow, so you can take your pick of their rooms." The Druid twins didn't live anywhere permanently. None of them did really. Only that asshole Ian would linger longer than he should, apparently missing the memo that the house was intended as a *temporary* residence for Druids working locally.

Phoebe's eyes flashed to Ronan. "Great. Thanks."

On-screen, Lennie furrowed his brow.

"Is something wrong, Lennie?" Ronan asked pointedly.

"Nothing," the Brit said, shifting his keyboard closer to himself.

Ronan knew that it was definitely *not* nothing. He would press the nosy bastard about it later.

"Now, that we have that sorted," Lennie said, "I'd like to proceed with some questions."

Phoebe let out a slow breath. "Alright. Give me your worst."

After they'd reattached the loose wires to the sensor, Lennie began with a series of perfunctory questions: name, age, date of birth, nationality, and the like. However, as soon as it came to things like her family history and profession, it became clear that the Druid's standard questioning procedure was far more forceful than it first appeared. Despite Phoebe's insistence that she was an only child and that her parents had died when she was in her twenties—it really was true—Lennie continued to press her for any knowledge about her family lineage.

"You are aware that I have the means to look into them fully, correct?" he asked with more than a hint of a threat in his tone.

"Obviously." Phoebe rolled her eyes dramatically. "Why would I bother lying?"

She was similarly grilled about her professional and various personal connections prior to the Wraiths' abduction—not that she couldn't handle it.

"Why have you been infiltrating Wraith establishments over the past several months?" Lennie asked, tenting his fingertips; his stamina and professionalism in the face of her verbal jousting was admirable.

Phoebe smirked. "I could ask you the same."

Ronan cleared his throat. "We're upholding our duty as ethical magic users and keepers of the peace. It's our responsibility to protect the world from Wraiths." Which was a fucking farce if he was honest, as in his darkest hours, he'd nearly become a Wraith himself.

She rolled her eyes again. "Is this a self-appointed role? Or—"

"Please answer the question, Phoebe," Lennie said. "You'll have plenty of time to question us afterward."

She shrugged. "I'm missing large swaths of my memory from my time with them in captivity, so I'd like to find out what happened to me, I guess."

Ronan eyed the magically sensitive polygraph, which remained relatively calm. He assumed there would be a certain level of continuous frequency when it came to Phoebe.

Lennie's expression was unreadable. "You have been singularly motivated, it seems ... unless you're working with someone else?"

"No."

"Alright. Where are you keeping the files?"

"What files?"

"The ones you lifted from"—Lennie checked his notes—"at least *seven* different Wraith establishments over the past three months."

"Any documentation I've collected is either upstairs in my bag or backed up on an external hard drive. You're welcome to it. My laptop broke a few weeks ago though, so it's been difficult to properly manage the data."

Ronan didn't imagine she had a hidden storage locker. "If you don't mind me asking, what do you do with the paper files or documents you take?"

"If useful, I scan them to my phone and then burn the paperwork."

So, she had a system.

"Right," said Lennie, his interest piqued. "And the digital signature I picked up? Are you using a unique virtual private network or—"

"Yes, I have several non-P2P double-layered VPNs."

Lennie looked impressed.

Meanwhile, Ronan was becoming more curious about Phoebe by the second; she was incredibly tech-savvy.

"We have a questionnaire for you to fill out once this meeting wraps," Lennie said, "about your previous employment and skills."

"I don't have any of my personal identification anymore. And as you so rudely reminded me when we were on our way here, my passport's a fake."

Lennie scratched his short-cropped hair. "I've already set plans into motion to replace your passport and any other relevant identification. You should receive them sometime in the coming weeks."

Phoebe leaned forward in her chair slightly. "*Really?*"

"Really," Lennie said. "Should you decide to stick around and work with us, rather than continuing your rogue solo missions, the Druids would endeavour to support you as needed. At least until we can determine next steps."

While Ronan had expected Lennie to dangle this carrot in front of her, which they'd agreed would provide an excellent precedent to keep her around, buying time to observe her further, he hadn't expected this response. She'd been combative but now seemed so ... vulnerable.

"Next steps?"

Lennie ignored this. "Are you seeking any sort of retribution?"

"If that's what it takes, then yes, I am." Phoebe's face grew hard.

"To date, and according to our records, you've eliminated at least five Wraiths in your path."

"Is that a problem?" She raised her chin in defiance.

A laugh slipped from Ronan. "Absolutely not, however—"

Lennie cut him off. "Moving forward, we will need to be more coordinated on such ... efforts. That is, assuming you'd like to consider working with us."

Phoebe's face was unreadable. And she neither agreed nor disagreed. It left Ronan feeling uneasy.

Lennie, meanwhile, forged ahead like a battering ram. "Can you tell us more about what happened in Kelowna?"

"At the biker bar?"

"The very same."

Ronan and Lennie questioned Phoebe for over three hours before the internet finally gave out, whether from the increasing deluge of rain outside, which was standard fare for Vancouver in the wintertime, or Phoebe's roiling inner magic. The harder they'd pushed her, the more Ronan had been able to feel it. Pulsing ... slashing ... raging.

He hated putting her through this so soon, but as she was obviously a flight risk, they needed to glean as much information as possible while they had her in their midst. At one point, however, Ronan had feared they'd pushed her too far.

"And you don't remember any extractions from your lungs, specifically?" Lennie had asked, meticulously working through the curated questions he and Ronan had compiled weeks before finally bringing her in. "Or any moments where something was taken from you?"

"Beyond the usual bloodwork, that is," Ronan added, his blood pressure rising as Lennie's questions circled closer to his own dark past and betrayal to all that was good. He took several deep breaths, willing his well-trained surgeon's hands not to tremble. He was barely successful.

"No ... no, nothing extracted from me," she said, shaking her head and growing paler by the second. "Not while I was awake, at least, but ... I could be wrong."

Most of the early experiments seemed to have occurred while she was unconscious. Small mercies, perhaps. But it was also possible (and more believable) that she was (quite justifiably) repressing a significant amount of her experience.

Phoebe continued speaking, growing less steady by the moment. "It was ... well, from what I recall, it was more like—"

Suddenly, her eyes slammed shut, every attached sensor went off, and Lennie's screen cut out. The magical polygraph was going wild.

Ronan's hand instinctively shot out to hers. "Are you okay?" Her vitals, while elevated, remained within the acceptable range.

Phoebe started to shake then, her chest rising in fits and starts as she wrapped an arm around her ribs in an attempt to steady herself. Several long moments passed before, ever so slowly, her eyes opened once more. She immediately found Ronan's eyes, locking onto them like a lifeline, and he could feel magic pulsing through their connection, dark and ragged.

Guilt welled in his chest as he witnessed yet another outcome of his poor decisions. Shoving the feeling down, he focused instead on how solid Phoebe's hand felt in his, gripping tight as he stared back at her, desperate to communicate the promise now beating rapidly in his heart: he would help her, should she let him.

Ronan willed the magic to settle, sending a silent prayer to the Goddess for Phoebe ... and himself.

"Please continue when you're ready," Lennie said calmly; Ronan's attention snapped back. He had no idea when he'd restored the connection, let alone how long he and Phoebe had been sitting silently like this.

Phoebe's green eyes flickered to the screen and then back to Ronan before she spoke again. "They planted their magic inside of me ..."

She did not relinquish Ronan's hand as she relayed her tale.

While in captivity, the Wraiths had discovered that Phoebe was unlike any test subject they'd ever encountered. She had the unique ability to hold magic and keep it within her without becoming a Wraith, and without any logical (or magical) explanation. They'd suspected that she was a Bearer, though she had no idea what that was, and accused her of Wielding magic, though she didn't know what that meant either at the time. Unsurprisingly, her claims hadn't mattered to them. They had no intention of believing her.

Nor had they planned on *ever* releasing her.

Much of her experience had been a blur. She remembered very little of her actual capture and the days that followed, and as such, she was unable to provide the Druids with any useful details.

Allegedly. It was hard to tell the truth from fiction with her, and Lennie's sensors had proved utterly useless.

Phoebe was all magical chaos, all the time.

At the end of her story, she gently released Ronan's hand, blinking as if she almost didn't remember what had just happened, or the fact that she'd been clinging to him so hard his fingers had gone numb.

The shame hidden within Ronan threatened to creep up his neck as he spoke. "Thank you for sharing that with us, Phoebe," he said kindly, wearing a false mask to hide the anguish he felt growing within him. *What else did they do to her?*

Well, he had a hunch, of course ... but he desperately hoped it wasn't what he suspected.

Regardless, she'd been traumatized.

Lennie just barged ahead. "Are you now clear on what Bearers are, as opposed to Wielders?"

At this, Ronan's eyes widened at Lennie's image on the screen. The Brit was relentless.

Phoebe shook her head, her voice shaky as she replied, "*No. Not entirely*."

"Wielders are magic users who can take and hold magic within themselves, at least temporarily. This includes Druids, Wraiths, and another sect you've likely never heard of called Knaves. We Druids draw it from trees, nature, and other natural sources."

"Where are your trees?" Phoebe asked then, gesturing to the screen at the bank of servers and monitors that was barely visible behind Lennie. Ronan assumed she meant this question to be cheeky, but she still sounded *very* uncomfortable.

Lennie ignored her question again. "Bearers, also known as Witches, can not only Wield—i.e., bring magic into themselves from the outside—but also generate it naturally within themselves. It's an innate ability one is born with."

"Which is likely why they wondered if you were a Bearer," Ronan offered sympathetically, "since you held their magic differently."

Phoebe shrugged. She either didn't want to know or didn't care to understand how the magical world worked.

And that had been that.

Following the interview's closure, Ronan had swiftly shut his laptop, thanked Phoebe for her time, and exited the room, leaving her to remove the sensors wrapped around her by herself. It was a coward's move, when really, he should have checked in with her to see how she was feeling, and whether or not she needed anything. He knew damn well that they'd pushed her with their approach, not letting it be properly informed by her trauma. Lennie had led with the big questions, and there had been several instances when he'd wondered if she'd actually break.

Yet somehow, she'd held it together, which was more than he could say for himself.

Ronan barely made it to his bedroom before succumbing to a near-catastrophic panic attack—the worst he'd had in years. The way Phoebe had described what was done to her by the Wraiths without her consent—all stemming from his own initial, obsessive research, hoping to understand exactly "how" Wraiths worked—had triggered his darkest memories and deepest shame.

It wasn't supposed to be like this anymore.

He'd reconciled his choices with the Otherworld. He had (quite literally) died for his sins and returned to make things right, first with his best friends and chosen family, and then with the broader magical world. But now, confronted with the fruits of his most significant and egregious errors, he wasn't sure if it would ever be possible to feel whole again.

When he regained control of himself nearly two hours later, lying in the fetal position on the hardwood floor of his bedroom, he forced himself to stand.

He had to carry on.

Running had always helped him feel somewhat human again, so Ronan quickly gathered his gear, pulling on a pair of shorts and a tight quick-dry t-shirt that highlighted his firm physique (something he'd poured considerable effort into over the past two-and-a-half years) and descended to the main floor of the safe house.

Ronan ran his hands through his hair as he prepared to push open the kitchen door. He knew he'd find Phoebe inside; he'd heard her laughter coming from the kitchen all the way from the second floor. It sounded like *she'd* recovered from today's ordeal just fine.

He let out a slow breath and pushed the door open. "Phoebe—"

She was indeed laughing, tucked up close in the breakfast nook beside none other than Ian *fucking* Braithwaite.

Though they'd known each other for years, having moved through the same West Coast Druidic circles and even going on several missions together, Ian—the heavily tattooed (and indisputably "attractive") Druid—had never "got on" with Ronan, for no other reason than their being complete opposites. Ian was easygoing yet quick to start a fight over mundane things, which exhausted the overly calculated and even-keeled Ronan immensely.

In Ronan's opinion, Ian was a freeloader who took advantage of the Druid network's hospitality, and his work ethic was piss-poor unless adrenaline was involved. Meanwhile, Ian accused Ronan of being a stuck-up jerk who never had fun unless his hero, "Donny O," was around, which was patently untrue. Dom was most certainly *not* his hero … though he was his best friend.

For his part, Dom generally tolerated Ian, though admittedly, the lesser Druid seemed intimidated by the hulking Celt and usually avoided him. Wise, perhaps, since if Ian had put any moves on Julia while she'd visited, Dom would have knocked his teeth in.

For all his modern learnings, Domhnall O'Brien was still a bit … primal.

Now, Ian was resting his arm just behind Phoebe, which made Ronan's blood boil. Maybe Dom had a point about primal protectiveness—not that he had any claim on Phoebe's time or attention, of course.

"Oh, hey, Ronan!" Phoebe said.

Ronan waited to see if she would shift away from Ian, but she didn't flinch.

"Hello," he said coolly.

"Want to join us? We've ordered pizza, and Ian rustled up some whisky." She waggled her eyebrows excitedly.

Ian grinned at him, the smug bastard. "*Pheebs* was just telling me how much she hates tea."

Ronan fought back a primal growl. What had gotten into him?

Phoebe scoffed, waving her hand as she shifted away from Ian. The knot in Ronan's stomach loosened slightly. "That's not what I said. I just said I'd rather drink week-old coffee abandoned in a work truck than a cup of tea."

Ian barked out an utterly obnoxious laugh. "As I said."

She giggled before sobering suddenly as she took in Ronan's outfit. "Going somewhere?"

It was pretty obvious. "I'm going for a run."

"Ooh, no thanks." She laughed, then as an afterthought added, "But good for you."

Ronan gritted his teeth. He hadn't invited her to join him.

"I'll make sure she doesn't go anywhere," Ian said, pouring a slog of whisky into her coffee.

"They've already set an alarm in my room for that," she said cheerfully. For the briefest moment, Ronan detected a darkness behind Phoebe's sunny demeanour. But then she smiled brightly. "Have fun!"

He grunted, exiting the kitchen without looking back.

Ronan took off at a sprint. Usually, he would have taken time to stretch, but the anxiety and unexpected anger coiling through his body felt almost irrepressible. He *had* to run. Some proprioceptive feedback on his joints would surely soothe his troubled mind ... and keep his proverbial "demons" at bay.

Running until he vomited was a tonic to an otherwise uncomfortable life.

His and Lennie's interrogation of Phoebe had been gruelling, but it was nothing out of the norm. Through his many years with the Druidic Order, and before that with the military, he'd sat through countless interrogations. Not to mention his own med-school-admission interviews, which had been the worst of all. However, pressing Phoebe for details had brought him closer to his darkness and sordid past than he'd cared for, which made him deeply uneasy.

Ronan rounded the corner, turning towards UBC, where he'd made one of the most ruinous decisions of his life—he had turned on his closest friends and allies to climb into a waiting helicopter with the Sorcerer Cassius.

Julia had offered to kill him then and there, upholding her end of an unorthodox magical pact between them, which was more than he'd deserved. Dom, meanwhile, had looked like he'd been struck a death blow. Then Ronan had turned away, shutting down his humanity and descending into darkness.

There had been a time, following his "rescue," when Ronan could barely look at his hands—the hands of a surgeon and a skilled lover—without recoiling as he recalled the countless things they'd done under Cassius's rule. For over seven months, Ronan had willingly been in the Sorcerer's employ.

Well, *employ* was perhaps not the correct term.

His breath came fast and heavy now as he nearly sprinted towards the campus. Perhaps today would be the day he actually crossed the threshold and approached the monument of his treachery. He didn't know why, but he'd charged the campus at a dead sprint nearly every day he'd been stationed at the Druids' Kitsilano safe house, and each time he'd come up short, panting and gasping for breath—sometimes even drooling and vomiting as his body revolted against this self-inflicted abuse.

Thankfully, today, the contents of his stomach stayed put.

Ronan slowed to a canter, breathing heavily through a stitch in his side. Then he pressed his smart watch, which had already sent him several warning notifications about over-exertion, and began dictating an email to his therapist:

Good evening, Eunice,

I'm sorry to bother you, but I'm sensing a need to reconnect. The problem is that I'm on the move again, so we'll have to meet virtually. Do you have any time available in the coming weeks?

Thanks, Ronan.

Eunice wasn't a magic user, though she knew Ronan partook in work that he couldn't always be open about. Luckily, she'd been fine with his vagaries from the start and was somehow able to see through his bullshit without being offered any more details than were absolutely necessary.

Ronan placed his hands on his hips as he turned back towards the safe house, desperately hoping that by the time he returned from his run, the kitchen party would have dissolved. He was famished and would prefer to eat in silence without jabs from Ian or giggles from Phoebe.

He walked for a time, his head clearer than it had been in days. Running was a miracle for his mind, and he hoped like hell his body would hold up for many years to come.

Thinking better of his chances, he ducked into one of his favourite local sushi restaurants. He slid into his usual booth as a pot of

Genmaicha tea was placed before him. He started with some miso, followed by some tuna tataki. Just as he drizzled fresh lemon juice onto his dish, an email notification vibrated from his watch:

Hello Ronan - Thanks for reaching out.

It sounds like you are in the process of peeling off several more layers. Unfortunately, I don't have availability for at least three weeks. However, I think it might be prudent to dig out that handbook I sent you awhile back - the one about the parts of yourself that would join you around a campfire.

I can accommodate you on the following dates ...

Ronan scrolled through the openings in Eunice's schedule. Realistically, he couldn't promise that any of them would work, not now that Phoebe was in the picture. In fact, he had the distinct sense that three weeks from now might as well be a year away.

CHAPTER 6

PHOEBE

Sleeping with Ian probably hadn't been her wisest decision. But she hadn't wanted to sleep alone either, not after Ronan and Lennie had interrogated her for *hours* that afternoon. She knew the nightmares would be worse than ever following that and preferred to fuck the pain away over tossing and turning through an entire night of fighting nameless demons.

Instead, she could blame any discomfort today on her raging hangover. And bonus: it might piss Ronan off too, which made her feel slightly better. He was fun to tease. So much so that the delight she'd uncovered while forcing him to dig around for french fries at the bottom of a takeout bag had almost reminded Phoebe of her past self ... of the woman who existed before captivity; she'd been authentically playful once, if not a bit of a mischief-maker.

By the time the Druid doctor had returned from his run the night before, Phoebe was three sheets to the wind and shout-singing "Sweet

Caroline" by Neil Diamond at the top of her lungs, right along with Ian, Amos, and Amelia, whom she'd convinced to join in their fun. They weren't so bad with a few drinks in them and had also provided the perfect vehicle for Phoebe to seduce her way into a different bedroom.

Not that it had taken much.

She knew how to get noticed by guys like Ian—the kind of guy who pretended to be unaware of his good looks and in denial about his "kooky fashion sense" but was secretly just as shallow as everyone else (and, in fact, gave *many* shits about his laidback outfit choices each day). With guys like him, one simply had to ignore them.

Well, not entirely. The trick was to ignore them just enough that they'd fear having lost their chance at something good. She opened with a *neg*, "a term used by pickup artists (PUAs) to describe using a backhanded compliment to trigger validation-seeking behaviour." She'd once profiled the misogynistic online community in an in-depth article that had explored the ethics behind their various tactics—particularly when it came to the application of hypnosis and neuro-linguistic programing.

In the case of Ian, she'd teased him about his tattoos—two full sleeves depicting a West Coast forest motif. Objectively, the tattoos were a work of art, but Ian didn't have to know she felt that way.

"So, tell me," she'd said, gesturing at his exposed arms with a cheeky grin. *"If a cancerous mole develops in the forest, does anybody hear?"*

Ian had blinked slowly at her with his mouth gaping, unsure whether to laugh or be offended.

"No, seriously," she'd insisted. *"I have weird moles. How would you know if you had them too?"*

His face had split into a stupid grin then. He had nice teeth; she had to give him that. *"You know what, I've never actually thought of that."*

Next, you show them how much fun you are—in Phoebe's case, she'd convinced the others to play Ride the Bus, a relatively simple drinking game that involved guessing colours, suits, number range, etc., from a deck of fifty-two cards. There were varying stages, which of course, grew more difficult the more you drank. They had all (naturally) delighted in Phoebe's playful antics and her ability to direct the fun ... which she used to her advantage to direct extra attention to Amos, instead of Ian.

Like clockwork, Ian had grown jealous and started vying for her attention—so much so that, by the time Phoebe was ready to go to bed, Ian was wrapped so tightly around her finger that she simply had to blink at him and he'd come running.

Phoebe's article on the PUAs had concluded that their methods were, indeed, unethical. But deeper than that, the community represented a group of (largely cis-het male) individuals who had lost touch with the magic of spontaneity and, more importantly, authentic human connection. If you select every social action from a "rolodex" of behaviours, are you really connecting to your inner self? Further, was it respectful of others to control what they think of you to that degree?

Surely, folks like herself knew what "masking" was all about. The world was not inherently designed to be inclusive of diverse neurotypes. However, these "seduction tactics" took this to another level with the conscious manipulation of the behaviour of others, ranging from simple emotional-climate control to harmful manipulation.

Her choice to bunk with Ian had been made more from necessity than anything else, though the fact that he was good in bed had been a surprising perk.

Phoebe rolled over, assessing the situation. The naked and deliciously tattooed Druid beside her was fast asleep and snoring quietly in the early morning. He was certainly attractive, but as soon as she'd slid down onto his cock, it had been plain that he was just another good time—a perfect (and rather girthy) distraction.

She wasn't capable of, or open to, deeper intimacy any longer—not after what had happened—and she didn't get the sense that Ian was looking for anything more either. He'd even told her as much after they'd finished their sloppy session, to which she'd replied by slapping his ass and saying, *"I'm glad we're on the same page!"*

Indeed, seduction tactics weren't a skillset Phoebe liked to employ unless it was really necessary. She knew damn well it was fucking toxic. But her brain was also so naturally wired for patterning (specifically scripting) that she'd fallen into it quickly, especially through the latter part of her career. She'd often used it to her advantage while chasing leads to reach juicy conclusions—typically taking down powerful men in the process. Sometimes, it was simply appealing to take the easier route. Men did it, after all. So, why couldn't she?

And yet, she was regularly reminded of the double standards women faced daily.

Ronan's reaction to her cozying up with Ian in the kitchen had been humorous initially, but how he avoided her gaze when he'd returned from his run had been surprisingly unnerving. What did he think she owed him?

The answer was: fucking nothing.

Phoebe sat on the edge of Ian's bed, gathering her clothes from the floor and dressing quietly before slipping from his room without another word. Breathing a sigh of relief, she turned towards the bathroom, only to walk directly into Ronan.

"*Ouch!*"

"You should watch where you're going," he said a little *too* coldly.

Peering past him, she could see the open door to what must have been Ronan's room, located directly beside Ian's with a shared wall. She could easily picture how pristine it must be, everything in its rightful place; between her exhaustion and the hangover, she found it difficult not to sass back at *His Highness*.

"Apologies, *sir*," she said sarcastically, lowering into a mock bow and immediately regretting it as the contents of her stomach threatened to exit with a vengeance. She choked down bile as she straightened to face the clearly disgruntled Druid.

Ronan stiffened, avoiding her gaze. "I need to speak with you this morning as soon as you've sorted yourself out."

"About what?" She was unprepared for another three-hour interrogation.

"Lennie has a directive for us based on the information you provided. If you're still interested in ... *reciprocating* our help."

Phoebe's eyes wandered towards Ian's closed door. What would she give to return to his bed and sleep off her hangover ... hidden away from Ronan.

But was that entirely true?

"Oh ... oh, okay."

"Ian won't be joining us."

"What does Ian have to do—"

"I'll see you downstairs."

Again, Phoebe somehow felt Ronan's exit as he stomped away from her and down the narrow staircase; while his presence seemed wrought with judgement, she strangely preferred it over his absence—at least when it came to her physical body. He'd provided her with real comfort during the interview when the flashbacks had set in ...

Somewhere, deep within her psyche, alarm bells screamed.

"So, what's the mission?" Phoebe asked, plunking herself down across from Ronan at the kitchen table. He was eating a bowl of stew or hamburger soup or something. The sight turned her tender stomach.

Ronan didn't reply initially but instead slurped loudly, as though each spoonful of soup was directed her way. When at last he'd completed his meal, he looked up. "Lennie sent your interview transcript."

She stared at him. "That's good, but—"

"I've printed it off for you," he continued, patently ignoring her potential questions and nodding at a duotang at his side. "That way you can keep it for your records in case you forget anything you said. We want to be transparent with you, as we hope you've been with us."

Was that a threat?

Phoebe had divulged to him and Lennie that while she maintained a clearer picture of her life before captivity (though she felt decidedly numb and avoidant about her past life), she was missing large swaths of memory both from her time in the Wraith lab and the months that followed. To this end, she felt like her working memory was still barely functional some days, depending on stress and fatigue. She was also significantly (and unpredictably) affected by the endlessly drumming magic inside of her.

Which was the *truth*.

Why, then, was he being so passive-aggressive about the transcripts?

"Ronan, with all due respect ... What the fuck is your problem?"

He let out an audible puff of air through his nose. "What makes you think I have a problem?"

She rolled her eyes, pulling the transcripts towards herself. "Is it because I spent the night with Ian? What I do with my time and my body is none of your business."

Ronan was clearly not expecting the pushback and stiffened. "You're correct, Phoebe. What you do with your body and your free time is *none* of my business. But Ian Braithwaite is an asshole. And so far, at least, you seem better than that."

Phoebe laughed darkly. "Do you really think that you actually know me after *one* interview? During which I was pretty much under duress, I might I add."

She watched as his Adam's apple bobbed once before he muttered something that sounded like *"I know you better than you think."*

"What?"

"I know you don't care what I think."

She narrowed her eyes at him before flipping open the duotang containing the transcript from their interview and the supplementary questionnaire she had filled out. The first page in the binder was part of the questionnaire:

Name: *Phoebe Marie Ashburn*
Age: *36*
Birthday: *March 23, 1988*
Gender: *Cis-female*
Pronouns: *She/her*
Nationality: *Canadian*
Next of kin: *Parents: Deceased, Siblings: N/A, Dependents: N/A*
Address: *Druid jail :P*
Driver's licence: *Lost, but I can drive*
Social insurance number (SIN): *Also lost/unknown*
Personal health number (PHN): *BC – lost/unknown*
Passport: *Canadian – Lost*

Phoebe had been relieved when Lennie promised her a new passport and other identifying documents. At least something in this Druidic capture process would be to her benefit. She continued reading:

> Education: *BA Communication (Journalism), SFU*
> Previous employment (most recent to least):
> *Journalist/podcaster, Junior editor, independent student paper, Sandwich artist (actually though, why do you care about this?)*

The next fifty-two pages of the report contained a detailed transcript of their discussions. Phoebe flipped through the pages, one after another, until she landed on the portion where she'd almost given too much away:

> LC: *So that it's on the record … You cannot, or will not, answer that question?*
> PA: *I can't … I don't remember anything from that period. I remember little from my capture other than being tied up in the back of a van. And then the first few months were a blur to begin with, but I do remember (clears throat) … I think, eventually, they'd put so much magic in me that—*
> RG: *Hold on, the detector is doing something strange …*
> LC: *You don't have to disclose, Phoebe. But we will detect any abnormalities in your response.*
> PA: *I'm not lying to you.*
> RG: *I don't think it's that … Whenever we touch on more difficult subjects, the sensors go off. Very likely it's the trapped magic, perhaps combined with the emotional response.*
> LC: *Okay, different question …*

Phoebe had absolutely no intention of telling them how she'd ended up at Spectre Fidelities Corp or about her assault, or what she did remember from those early days. It was none of their fucking business.

She looked up at Ronan, who was now leaning against the counter, scooping up the last of his soup. "You must think I'm extremely untrustworthy."

"What makes you say that?" he asked.

"Well, since I'm unable to remember so much of my time there, I might as well be a sleeper agent for the Wraiths, right? As far as you're concerned, I mean."

Ronan stiffened. "You said you don't remember, so you don't remember." She couldn't tell if he was lying. His face was turned towards the sink, and his body language was unreadable. "Flip to the next page."

LC: *We're curious if you have affiliations with organized crime or underground operations. That can include anything from cults and gangs to groups from the dark web.*
PA: *I have no shady affiliations if that's what you're asking. But I probably have a few enemies.*
RG: *Can you elaborate?*
PA: *(Laughter) Besides the Wraiths?*
LC: *My apologies, Phoebe. I should have been more specific. Enemies who are non-magic users, please.*
PA: *I don't have a list off the top of my head, and I have no idea if any of them would consider me an enemy, per se. But during the years before my capture, I was an investigative journalist. You know how people feel about journalists ...*
LC: *I do, but please enlighten us. For the record.*

Phoebe recalled that this was when the sensors had gone off again.

RG: *Is this important right now, Lennie?*
LC: *Yes, it is.*
PA: *Can't you search my published works? Surely, you've searched almost everything else about me.*
RG: *We can.*

Phoebe's cheeks grew hot. Seeing the interview transcripts laid bare before her, in writing that wasn't her own, suddenly felt incredibly private and *personal*. She genuinely didn't recall every single person she'd pressed for information in the past. It hadn't always been honourable work, and on more than one occasion, she'd done whatever had been necessary to "get the story."

Anger rose in her throat as the implanted magic churned below it. "Why, exactly, do the Druids feel it's their place to pry around in my personal and professional life from *before* my capture? Clearly, my life isn't even remotely the same as it used to be."

"If you're going to be integrated into the Druidic network, we need to know as much about you and your past as we can. It's all important, especially in consideration of keeping you safe—"

"Wait," she said, interrupting him. "Who says I intend to integrate?"

Ronan sighed. "Well, we've already expressed that we'd like to help you find your answers. I would assume that to be motivation enough."

Phoebe suddenly felt woozy. The trapped magic was always more brutal after a night of heavy drinking, even without arguing with stuffy Druid doctors. She gripped the table, swaying slightly.

Practically right before her eyes, Ronan's icy demeanour thawed.

Then she blacked out entirely.

When she came to, Ronan was kneeling before her, taking her pulse, his expression full of authentic concern. "Can you hear me, Phoebe?"

She'd apparently fainted and was currently slumped over in her chair. "Yes, I'm fine," she replied blearily as his concerned (and annoyingly handsome) face came into view just six inches from her own. He smelled like soup.

"You're clearly not fine."

She forced her grimace into a tight smile. "I said I'm fine. I just faint sometimes when I'm hungover. I'm dehydrated. I'll drink some water."

"Oh, *please*, Phoebe. I'm a doctor."

Just then, Ian slid into the room, followed by Amos and Amelia. The twins were dressed in sturdy boots and weatherproof jackets in preparation for their next mission; Ian was barefoot in sweatshorts and a sloppy, oversized t-shirt. She noticed then just how big his feet were.

Ian let out a righteous snort. "Still trying that line, eh, Ronan?"

"Fuck off, Ian. She's not well."

"I actually *am* fine," Phoebe said, laughing this off.

She wasn't fine at all, but she didn't want Ronan or anyone else to know that. She also had absolutely no patience for any sort of dude dispute between the two of them.

Ronan pushed back, frustrated. "We leave at ten p.m. sharp for tonight's mission. Meet me outside. Dress for the club."

"For the club? How am I supposed to ..." She let her voice trail off then as he had already stormed from the kitchen without another word.

Amelia looked just as confused as she was. "I have no idea what he means by 'dress for the club.'" She chuckled then. "But there's a trunk of extra clothes in the crawl space in my old room that might help you out. Things left behind by various Druids over the years."

"Awesome. Thanks, Amelia." Phoebe didn't ask whether the clothes had been left behind by dead or living Druids, as she didn't want to know.

Sweating and cursing, Phoebe grabbed hold of the Druids' "tickle trunk" and pulled. It was a shiny, if somewhat dented, blue beast of a thing, with brass embellishments and creaky latches. Someone had affixed a strip of green painter's tape, upon which was written EXTRA CLOTHES in bold black letters. She dragged the beast just over the crawl space's threshold and let go, worried she'd scratch the floor or hurt herself further in the attempt; she'd already scraped the shit out of her back on the low beams.

This old house was going to kill her.

Phoebe flipped up the brass latches and lifted the lid, unsure what to expect. To her surprise, she found all sorts of clothes that didn't even smell too bad. A small pouch of herbs with a scent of lavender lay nestled in one of the corners.

"These earthy assholes think of everything," she muttered.

Phoebe didn't trust Ronan or any of the Druids entirely. And so, if she were to obtain the information she needed, nurturing this budding relationship would mean constantly walking a very fine line. She had to admit, to herself at least, that she'd cut it too close the other night with Nyx, though she'd never admit that to Ronan. Operating alone—particularly in establishments as big as that club—had become far too risky.

Maybe it wouldn't be such a bad thing to work with the Druids ... for now.

In fact, in another life, she might have elected to join their shadowy league, or at least research the shit out of them to craft a juicy story. However, exposing the magical world like that was obviously a big no-no.

Her efforts now weren't all that different from what she'd done before her capture. She liked intelligence work and didn't even mind working with a team. Sometimes, at least. Some of her favourite projects had been working with others, hot on the trail of some great story.

Her most impactful work, however, had always come when she worked her leads alone.

CHAPTER 7
RONAN

RONAN PUSHED THE RANGE ROVER'S IGNITION AT PRECISELY TEN p.m. sharp. He was pleasantly surprised to see Phoebe leave the Druids' safe house at 10:02.

Acceptable. Though only just.

He could scarcely make out her tall figure as she zipped her knee-length raincoat and stepped out into the West Coast winter; it was already dark out and absolutely pissing rain. Seconds later, Phoebe slid into the front passenger seat without a word, splattering heavy rain droplets on the console and across the leather upholstery.

She didn't seem to notice, much less care.

Ronan immediately shifted gears and reversed the vehicle down the driveway, gravel crunching under its tires, and then kicked it into drive. They took off down the road.

"I assume you found something suitable to wear," he said evenly, side-eyeing her black combat boots and long, exposed legs. It was impossible to discern what she was actually wearing under the raincoat.

"Amelia pointed me towards the tickle trunk upstairs," she said, buckling herself in.

Ronan raised his eyebrow. "Tickle trunk?"

"Yes. You know, like from *Mr. Dressup?*"

Ronan continued to look puzzled.

"That old-school Canadian show on CBC?"

He stared at her. "I'm Irish."

"Never mind. Some old clothing was stored in the crawl space in my bedroom. Unfortunately, I couldn't find anything suitable for my height or shoe size."

"What size are your feet?" Ronan frowned. Why the fuck had he just asked her that?

She smirked. "People would pay me a lot for that information, Druid."

Ronan wondered if she'd ever capitalized on making money posting videos of her feet. Honestly, she seemed the type. "Right. Well ..."

"Don't worry. I've made do."

That statement made him nervous. Ronan's nostrils flared as he pictured Phoebe flippantly unzipping her raincoat and exposing her naked body for all the world to see ... simply to spite him for his earlier rudeness.

He cleared his throat. "I see."

She loudly shifted in her seat. "So, what are we doing tonight?"

"We're going to a club."

"Yes, I'm aware of that." She turned to face him. "But why? What type of club?"

He ran his left hand through his thick salt-and-pepper hair. Since interrogating Phoebe, he and Lennie had argued about how best to apply her "usefulness" to their cause and whether or not to initiate her into the Order.

"I suppose, more accurately, it's a rave."

"Cool."

"Part of tonight's mission is to retrieve further information about your time in captivity." Ronan flipped on his signal light as they changed lanes, heading south towards Surrey.

"Right, thanks. And the other part?"

"Well, if you are truly considering joining the Druidic Order, or at least working with us, we need to test you in certain circumstances, assessing your ability to take direction, work as part of a team, etcetera."

"Did you just use 'etcetera' in a sentence?" Phoebe asked, smirking again.

Ronan felt mildly affronted; he wasn't used to having his language choices commented on. "Is there something wrong with that?"

"No, it's just quirky."

He sighed. She was focusing too much attention on him. "Tonight's mission is moderately high risk, though hopefully with an even higher reward. You've made plain your desire to uncover exactly what happened to you in captivity and, ideally, to find a way to remove the magic. Correct?"

"*Correct.*"

Long term, they'd also need to look into why she wasn't turning into a Wraith—or dying, for that matter—but Ronan wasn't particularly eager to point her in that direction.

"So," he continued, "we hope that you'll be able to demonstrate your eagerness around our ... *shared* incentives." He sounded like Lennie now, formal and never getting down to the brass tacks. "Basically, tonight is your first test."

"Haven't I already demonstrated my skills? I mean, I did track and locate the Wraith establishments by myself." This skill would definitely benefit them; there was no denying that. "Plus, I thought sitting through that nearly four-hour interview was my first test."

Ronan had no doubt she would be challenging every step of the way. "Let me rephrase it then. Your first test in the field."

"Right ... but are you forgetting that you also need my help?"

It was Ronan's turn to smirk. "Do we?"

"Oh, I think you do. In fact, I'm guessing I know much more about their experiments than you do." She shifted her whole body towards him then, her raincoat straining audibly against the motion.

Is she admitting to not telling us the whole truth about her experience? he wondered, suddenly feeling like she was testing him.

Phoebe undoubtedly held priceless insider knowledge of the Wraiths' research activities, even if she claimed the remembered details were patchy due to the rigorous torture she'd undergone. Another reason she was adept at hunting down the Wraiths was likely because of her own curiosity about how their minds worked.

Ronan knew this phenomenon all too well.

"Correct," he said, surprising himself with the icy chill in his tone. "Your experiential knowledge is an asset, one which we hope to take advantage of at least for the time being. With your consent, of course," he added, warming his tone only slightly.

Phoebe leaned back wordlessly and stared out the window.

Conversation over.

They drove silently for a time, travelling further south into the Lower Mainland. Passing under the Massey Tunnel, the electric lights pulsed through the windows, intermittently highlighting Phoebe's beautiful face.

Mercifully, the lateness of the hour meant there were no delays through the tunnel.

Phoebe's partnership with Ronan was as much one of necessity as calculation. She required a senior Druid to train her, and he was the best local candidate for the job. It also didn't hurt that he had full understanding of the dangers of having an untrained Wielder walking around with trapped Wraith magic inside them. Not that she fully understood that second bit.

In truth, she also needed someone who wasn't afraid to "keep an eye on her." The woman was a flight risk, an enigma, and a ticking time bomb all in one. To Ronan's surprise, however, it had taken Lennie far *less* convincing than he'd anticipated to get on board with Ronan volunteering for the job.

"Don't you think it's a conflict of interest?" Lennie had asked earlier that afternoon. *"You're way too close to this whole mess, and you bloody well know it. Perhaps we could send her to the Knaves."*

"Absolutely not. The last thing we need is for her to accidentally—or worse, intentionally—channel whatever magic is trapped inside her through their

weaponry and out. She's like lightning in a bottle. I can feel it whenever I'm around her."

The Knaves were a kindred sect of Wielders who primarily trapped their magic inside their weaponry, which made them a bit *squirrelly*, even though it made for interesting results in combat.

"Interesting ..." Lennie had said.

"What's interesting?"

"Your sense of her magic." He was more curious than Ronan would have preferred. *"We didn't need that machine in the interview at all. You detected it just fine all on your own."*

"I'm sure you'd feel it too if you were here in person."

"Perhaps. But that also remains to be seen."

"You'll be here soon enough," Ronan had said, knowing he was scheduled to visit in early February. *"What did Amos and Amelia report to you about her?"*

"Mostly that she was unusual. They liked her, though."

"How definitive," Ronan had grumbled through gritted teeth.

In the end, Lennie had agreed that Phoebe needed to remain under the care of the Druids, at least until they discovered what was going on with the magic inside of her and why it remained trapped there.

Lennie had cleared his throat then. *"After that interview, though ... Well, I have to say that my instinct is practically screaming at me that there's far more to Miss Ashburn than meets the eye."*

"I agree entirely."

After a long moment of consideration, Lennie had said, *"Alright, hear me out, Ronan. Amos and Amelia are away for the next month on a mission. What if we partner her with Ian—"*

"No."

"It would be interesting to see—"

"Absolutely not," Ronan had growled into the receiver.

Lennie had barked out a laugh, correctly assuming that Phoebe had already interreacted with Ian in the house, for better or worse. *"I'm just taking the piss, Ronan. Ian's a moron."*

That tattooed bastard was incapable of remaining quiet, which was a trait Lennie didn't value at all. And so, it had been decided that, at least for the time being, Ronan would take Phoebe along on his missions to their mutual benefit.

Though *that* remained to be seen.

"Are you going to brief me or is this all going to be one big surprise?" Phoebe asked then, yanking Ronan from his thoughts as she released her long, sandy blonde hair from a creaky black claw clip. It tumbled messily around her shoulders.

Ronan tried not to stare, but once again, she looked like an unmade bed ... in the best possible way.

He gritted his teeth. *She's not for you.*

Ronan cleared his throat a bit awkwardly. "As I said, we're continuing to locate and gather any documentation from the lab that might be associated with the Wraiths' legacy experiments, as well as seeking *additional* information pertaining to your case files and those of any other patients. I'm sure you can agree to that?"

Phoebe nodded before fussing with her hair again; several hairpins pinched expertly between her pursed lips as she worked. They were nearing their location now, which it seemed she'd sensed somehow.

"Excellent. So, tonight we're going to infiltrate a storage room in a new Wraith establishment—a pop-up club they've been using as a front for raves and shipping."

"Weird combo."

"Well, and likely also for trafficking."

She frowned but stayed silent.

"When I said that this is a moderate-risk level mission," Ronan said, "it's because there *will* be Wraiths present throughout the establishment. However, the chaos of the night and the nature of the event being held there will hopefully allow us fairly easy access to the storage room."

"Alright ..."

"Lennie has collected a lot of intel, and the lead Wraith there, named Oslo—"

"Okay, sorry, but are those, like, their real names? I've always wondered about that."

Though she'd interrupted him again, a trait that was beginning to aggravate him immensely, Ronan found himself chuckling. "You know what? I've never really thought about it, though I assume they take on a new moniker once they're transformed. Hard to know for sure, though ... *Sasha*."

"Hey! That was the best I could come up with at the time," she said, laughing at herself, which Ronan liked.

"One time," he said, "I came across a Wraith named Jeremy, and it felt very off-brand when compared to names like Alastair and Rubeus." He bit his tongue then. Recalling the names of the many Wraiths he'd experimented on, and killed, sent a chill up his spine. But just like their decaying bodies, their names had all been somewhat antiquated. He forced the memories down.

"Jeremy," she said, chuckling.

He shrugged. "I'd like to come across, like, a Chad or Dale ... You know, normal fellas."

Phoebe snorted. "*Dale? Can you imagine?*"

In person, as was standard to most Wraith establishments, the club was both physically and magically hidden. Ronan supposed its industrial location was meant to offer a sort of mystique to its patrons. To him, though, it seemed more like an excuse for folks to be assaulted while attempting to get home from a night of euphoric dancing and illicit substances. Assuming they didn't tragically overdose on B.C.'s toxic drug supply first. He'd seen far too much of that in the ER as of late.

On paper (and according to the building plans Lennie had shared with Ronan only hours earlier), their target location was a standard (if fairly large) storage facility, complete with six loading-bay doors.

"I think it was originally built as a drop-ship location," Lennie had told him. *"But the builder went into foreclosure before they could lease the space for what it was worth."*

"And who owns it now?"

"A numbered company bought it in 2022, which doesn't offer us much information."

"But you did some digging."

"Yes, I did some digging, and the company is owned by the same expanding conglomerate that owned the property: Spectre Fidelities Corp."

"How delightful," Ronan had replied, scratching his beard.

"I've no doubt there will be something to uncover there—hopefully more documentation from Phoebe's time in custody." Their intelligence had spent the past six months tracking and locating remnants of the destroyed research facility—the one Phoebe had emerged from covered in rubble, only to somehow disappear moments later. *"I think you'll agree we need to obtain her intake health records in particular."*

Lennie was correct. Ronan was desperate to learn more about the mysterious woman beside him.

He parked the Range Rover and turned to face her. "Are you ready?"

Phoebe took him in for a moment. Ronan was wearing his standard dark-green, button-down wool jacket, black jeans, and military boots.

"I am, but ... have you never been to a rave before?" She smirked as she fought the zipper on her raincoat. "You won't want anything burdening you."

Ronan resisted the urge to tell her that it was, in fact, she who'd become the burden in his life. Instead, he flashed the interior of his jacket to her, exposing several weapons, as well as Druidic implements: several odd-looking pouches and murky vials. "I'll take my chances."

"Suit yourself," she said, continuing the fight with her jacket.

Ronan had been in his partying prime during the Celtic Tiger, a period in the late 1990s and early 2000s when Ireland had been experiencing its first economic boom, making spending money and wild excesses the norm. Unlike the rest of the global West, which had experienced a boom following WWII, Ireland was a latecomer to economic prosperity in the modern era. One time, he'd even arrived at a party by helicopter simply because one of his friends had wanted to do so.

"You keep forgetting how old I am," he said, slipping from his seat and closing the door behind him. He walked around the front of the SUV and met her standing at her door. "Of course, I've been to a—"

He fell abruptly silent as his jaw dropped.

Phoebe had finally removed her raincoat to reveal ... well, he wasn't entirely sure what the garment's official origins might have been. It appeared she'd repurposed some sort of plaid shirt or jacket into a jagged, layered miniskirt. On top, she wore a cropped black bandeau top, which was held together with safety pins at the centre of her cleavage.

Somehow, the outfit all made sense, from her hair now twisted into half-up "space buns" to her combat boots, and Ronan found himself shocked and impressed in equal measure. He also found it suddenly difficult to string together a coherent thought. "*Ehm* ... You found all of that in the trunk upstairs?"

It was no secret that Phoebe was tall and curvy in all the best ways, but this particular outfit did *everything* it could to emphasize that point —rather redundantly.

"Not exactly," she said, twirling once, her ass cheeks nearly hanging out of the makeshift garment. "I may or may not have altered a few things to suit my needs. I'm decent with a sewing needle—"

"And apparently with scissors and safety pins."

She snorted. "You didn't exactly offer to take me shopping after you stormed out of the kitchen this morning." Her eyes glimmered dangerously as she added punishingly, "And I didn't exactly get the impression I was allowed to leave the house without a *chaperone*."

Ronan felt his hackles rise at the word "chaperone." He might be older than her, but he wasn't an old man. And it wasn't like she was twenty-one either. Phoebe was thirty-six and had lived an entire adult existence before being taken captive.

"Chaperone? Really ..." His eyes darkened.

Phoebe's breath hitched at this subtle shift in dominance, which pleased him. "You *just* said you were old, like ... two seconds ago."

"That outfit is going to draw attention," he said simply, not altogether sure he meant this as a compliment. The truth was that, between the magnetism of her trapped magic and how she *looked* tonight, the Wraiths would be clamouring for her. "Not exactly our objective tonight."

"Fuck you very much. It's not like you gave me any information ahead of time." She procured a silver tube of dark lipstick from the pocket of her raincoat and smeared it onto her lips, smiling mischievously as Ronan watched. "*Dress for the club*," she said, shaking her head while mocking his accent and tone of voice perfectly.

He ignored her barb and gestured to the tube of lipstick in her hand. "More poison?"

"Nope, just Clinique Black Honey," she said with a wink. "If you must know, it's what Liv Tyler wore as Arwen in *The Lord of the Rings*." Liv Tyler was about as gorgeous as they came, as far as Ronan was concerned. "You really should leave your jacket behind; you're going to absolutely melt. And you look ... *stiff*."

"*Fine*," he said as offence rose like bile in the back of his throat.

Phoebe was an absolute brat, but he knew how to handle her. Ronan removed his jacket, revealing a leather harness over his dress shirt that held two short daggers at his lean sides. The harness had been commissioned by the Knaves several years earlier and was made from buttery brown leather with brushed brass fixings. It framed his broad shoulders perfectly. In fact, more than one woman had swooned over this particular get-up before submitting to his advances.

And as for the daggers, they only revealed themselves to magic users and allies, which worked in his favour in more ways than one.

"Ooh, those are fancy ..." Phoebe's eyes flickered across his chest, between the straps holstering the golden blades, and back again. Then she nodded in approval. "This look is *much* better."

To his surprise, Ronan's ego was thoroughly stroked.

Then Phoebe placed her hand in the middle of his chest, effortlessly shifting the power dynamic back towards herself. "If you want, I can shove some of your pouches in my top."

He rolled his eyes; this push and pull was wearying. "I don't think I'm quite that desperate."

"What's that supposed to mean?"

"Let's go!"

CHAPTER 8

RONAN

RONAN AND PHOEBE APPROACHED THE WAREHOUSE, THEIR COMBAT boots—Ronan's, military issue, and Phoebe's, a heavy-looking pair of Doc Martins—crunching loudly on the gravel. Phoebe followed behind Ronan about half a pace and to his left. She was brave, but there was no question that walking into a Wraith nest came with reservations.

Hell, he'd prefer to be somewhere else as well. He was simply better at hiding his fear.

Ronan relegated several Druidic vials and pouches to the front pockets of his pants. Should things go sideways, he would use them to ensure their admittance to the club.

And things *always* went sideways.

He patted them, and Phoebe laughed. "It looks like you've been stuffing your pants. Is that a rocket in your pocket or are you just excited to see me?"

He simply rolled his eyes and continued towards the entranceway.

The Wraiths might not identify Ronan as a Druid—he was good at hiding who and what he was—but he suspected that the magic trapped inside Phoebe would draw the eye of even the daftest Wraith. They'd never been particularly brilliant, even during Cassius's rule, but they were nothing if not industrious. Especially now that they were running (nearly) unchecked across the globe. And the Druids and Knaves could only do so much with their limited resources.

At the door, and standing several paces back from them, a clipboard-wielding Wraith leered at Ronan, looking him up and down. Next, he studied Phoebe from top to bottom with a long-savouring glance. Finally, he stepped forward, sniffing in her direction. Phoebe gripped Ronan's shirt sleeve.

"Are you both on the list?" the Wraith asked, tilting his head strangely and ogling them now as a pair.

Ronan's instincts and long experience told him that the bouncer was young by Wraith standards—for certain less than a hundred and fifty. However, to the casual observer, he'd likely appear in his mid-thirties. The slight waxiness of his skin was a dead giveaway for Ronan, though.

The bastard was *full* of stolen magic.

"We are," Ronan said clearly. "Rory Seal and Sasha Hayes."

The Wraith flipped loudly to the next page of the guest list. *You'd think they'd use a tablet of sorts,* Ronan thought, as the paper, pen, and clipboard felt archaic.

"Give me a minute," the Wraith said, shuffling towards two colleagues who were flanking the door's interior.

Ronan noticed that the Wraith's gait was slightly off-kilter, confirming that he was getting up in age, though he was still quite a new recruit by recent Wraith standards. Their ability to appear outwardly "normal" tipped at around two hundred years old, at which point, they could no longer get by without a cloak, their original skin becoming too grey and rotted for public appearance.

The Wraith with the clipboard also didn't smell too terribly. Not *yet*.

Phoebe shifted uncomfortably beside him. "We *are* on the list, right?"

Of course, they were on the guest list. Lennie had ensured that. However, fuckers like this one made it their business to have men like Ronan jump through hoops at any opportunity. He was certain they wouldn't have even checked the list if Phoebe had arrived there alone.

"We are," he said calmly.

Ronan noted that the Wraith's voice had started to change, another indicator of age. Along with epidermal decay, the magic inside them eventually rotted their vocal cords, which gave older Wraiths their signature echoing tones. Admittedly, the cloaks and vocal transformations really *did* make the bastards appear formidable. If only their age were a clearer indicator of skill and threat level. Unfortunately, some of the newest Wraiths could be the deadliest, and vice versa. It all depended on what skills they brought to the fight.

However, tonight, Ronan preferred not to find out where these three assholes landed on that scale. So, he slid his hand into his front pocket and procured a small, white leather pouch—the first of many options to help get them through the door if needed.

"They're just checking if we're magic users," he told Phoebe quietly.

"*How can they know that?*" she hissed.

"The same way *I* know they're Wraiths."

With as much subtlety as he could, Ronan released the pouch's sandy, magical contents onto the gravel in front of them. This particular blend had been designed to create a sense of ease for anyone in close proximity—particularly those with stolen magic.

And the more stolen magic they had, the greater its effect.

Ronan guessed too late that the pouch might have a similarly pronounced effect on Phoebe since she also held an unknown volume of Wraith magic inside of her. However, *nothing* could have prepared him for the severity of her reaction.

Following the magic's release, Phoebe let out a moan of low dissent, like a heavily sedated cat heading into a medical procedure, and then slumped into him from behind. Thank the Goddess she was still standing. Otherwise, they would have had to abort the mission altogether. Either that, or he'd be forced to stuff her in the trunk of his Range Rover and enter the club alone.

He didn't think anyone in the Order would take kindly to that, least of all Phoebe.

"What ... the fuck ... was in ..."

The Wraith bouncer lurched towards them again before she could finish her thought. Thinking fast, Ronan pulled her close and whispered in her ear. "It will wear off in a few minutes. Hold still and don't speak."

It was more than likely the bouncer would assume that whatever drugs she'd taken in advance of the party were just now kicking in, but they couldn't be too careful.

"So?" Ronan said cockily, eying the Wraith.

"So, I just noticed you were added to the guest list earlier this afternoon," the Wraith said gruffly. He looked at Phoebe, who was clearly growing more intoxicated by the second, and gave Ronan a sinister grin. "*Go ahead*."

Ronan didn't want to imagine what sort of fucked-up approval the Wraith had just given him for dragging a half-conscious woman into a rave.

Passing through the blacked-out double doors, Phoebe and Ronan found themselves in a large ... entryway, for lack of a better term. During daylight hours, this area would likely serve as a receiving office, but at night, it appeared more like a makeshift lobby area—a central hub connecting the three separate, massive warehouse bays beyond.

Immediately, Ronan's nostrils were assaulted by the heavy scent of artificial smoke and stale human sweat. Nondescript music washed over them, pulsing in a muffled thrum all around them, an odd blending of rhythms from three different "dance floors" with three separate themes. Bright strobe lights flickered intermittently through the three doors whenever they opened briefly. Several Wraith bouncers guarded each door, standing on either side with their arms crossed.

The warehouse was packed. But who were all of these people? And why were they *here*, specifically ... aside from the obvious human need to lose oneself to the fever of the night. Ronan sniffed deeply, focusing his sense of smell beyond the expected, and (thankfully) failed to detect anything too sinister floating through the hazy atmosphere.

Blessed be the Goddess.

And it truly was a blessing. Cassius's killing smoke, a mechanism that Ronan had (shamefully) had a hand in creating, was still routinely posing problems for the Wielders. The smoke, produced through a complicated magical process that only a few of Cassius's past minions, including himself, knew about, could essentially "choke out" and kill any Wielders that came in contact with it.

It was a horrific weapon.

However, the Wraiths were also susceptible to its effects, so following Cassius's demise, the frequency and scope of its use had been reduced—another blessing.

Of course, he'd brought protection with them just in case in the form of an invention he'd developed himself: magically and herbily infused, double-layered face masks that could be affixed over the wearer's nose and mouth for short-term protection against the smoke, allowing them time to escape. He had a pair of these masks shoved in his pocket, but he would prefer not to use them. If it came down to that, he knew it meant they'd have bigger problems than getting caught stealing illicit documents from the storage room of a warehouse rave.

He did, however, smell something abnormally rich and earthen—a scent utterly out of place in a repurposed shipping warehouse. He caught particularly strong whiffs of it whenever the furthest door opened and shut. It reminded him of the forest floor in late fall, with its distinct tang of decomposing leaf mulch, mushrooms and moss, dead things, and sleeping bugs and beetles.

More organic than the Wraiths' usual putrid stench, this odour reminded Ronan distinctly of *natural* death.

"Can you smell that?" he asked, turning towards Phoebe.

She didn't reply. Her eyes were glazed over as she slumped down onto a narrow bench set along one wall, her head lolling to one side. Beyond her, a dark hallway led to what Ronan presumed were offices and bathrooms based on the number of people coming and going from the dim corridor, though he couldn't be entirely sure.

He strode over to Phoebe's side and sat down beside her.

"Seriously though," she slurred, the Druidic magic still impacting her significantly, "what's happening to me? I feel like I've been roofied …"

Ronan felt a sudden, protective anger start to burn within him. Did she have first-hand experience with such abuses? With effort, he brushed that thought away as it wasn't relevant to their current mission.

"Don't worry," he said, perhaps more tersely than was necessary. "It will wear off in a few minutes. Be patient."

Ronan leaned against the black, sloppily painted cinder-block wall and mentally considered the building's layout, which he realized with a jolt he'd wholly neglected to share with Phoebe; they'd been too busy fighting over outfits.

His "ops partner" had apparently just come to the same realization.

"That's just it … I'm not worried about *anything*. Like … I just realized you didn't really brief me on logistics for tonight, and … well, I don't even care …" Phoebe swallowed visibly then. *Excess drool,* he assumed. "What was *in* that pouch?"

"The pouches are complicated to explain and not something I'm willing to discuss in present company," he hissed as a large, cloaked Wraith walked past them from the darkened hallway. "And as for the layout, we're currently in the lobby. Beyond us, are three different dance floors, each with its own theme—"

"What are the themes?" Phoebe interrupted loudly.

"Different exoplanets or something." He scratched his beard in annoyance. He really didn't give a shit about that sort of thing. "The first is a desert planet. Do you see the people dressed like they've just walked off the set of *Mad Max?*" Just then, a group of women wearing eyepatches, bodysuits, and army boots passed by. "And then there's the dark planet, which looks to be the most guarded of the three—probably where they're selling the drugs. And then there's a rainforest one or something …"

His voice trailed off as a mental lightbulb went off. That had to be the smell he'd been detecting when they'd first arrived. But what could be giving off such a potent, earthy odour?

"I see." Phoebe squinted feebly as if trying to spot the difference between the three doorways. "You could have told me that, you know ... I would have dressed for a theme."

"Does it really matter?"

"Normally, I would care quite a bit actually. I love a good theme. But right now, I just ... don't."

Ronan felt unexpectedly guilty. "I *am* sorry, Phoebe. I didn't consider the impact the pouch might have on you. Give it a few more minutes, and you'll return to normal. Or at least, normal enough to move forward."

"Whatever you say, boss," she said, still slurring significantly, though slightly less than before.

Together, they waited out her accidental high.

Apart from the trapped magic inside her, Ronan surmised that this might also be a matter of first exposure—she'd likely never come across Druidic implements before. Whatever the Wraiths had used to control and subdue her in captivity would have had an entirely different makeup than anything the Druids created.

Wielders guarded their trade secrets with their lives.

"Alright," Phoebe said suddenly, reaching for his hand, a move that took him far too long to notice. "You'll have to lead the way, or I'm dead in the water."

He received her hand awkwardly, the connection sending an unexpected shudder through his body. Ronan wondered if he would ever get used to the constant thrum of her trapped magic.

"Sorry, Phoebe. I really should have shown you a map."

He realized that he was saying "sorry" a lot all of a sudden.

In his defence, it had been a long time since he'd mentored another Druid—let alone taken someone this green with him on a mission. She'd also clearly put her best efforts forward this evening, hoping to throw Ronan off before they'd even gotten started. And it had worked. He was definitely off his game, and Phoebe was still higher than a kite.

Neither of which would do at all. What would Lennie say? Or Dom?

He sighed. Dom would probably laugh and call him an idiot. Meanwhile, Lennie would save his assessment for the perfect moment, when he could use it to highlight Ronan's imperfections ... likely when they were arguing about the best methods or approach to a mission.

"It's fine. I'm fine," Phoebe said, sounding unconvinced by her own words. "Just ... how long again until this wears off?"

"I've already answered that question. *Soon.* You may feel a slight sense of euphoria before the effects are fully released from you, though. That can happen sometimes."

Phoebe rested her head against his shoulder for several moments, breathing deeply. Ronan pretended to assess their surroundings. In truth, he was grateful for the electronic beats shaking the warehouse to its foundation as they masked his heart rate increasing at the warmth of her touch. It had been a while since a woman had leaned on him for comfort. Not high on Druidic magics, of course, but with ... *intimacy*.

He needed to get a fucking hold of himself.

"Let's go," she said finally, straightening. He wondered if, perhaps, she was feeling the same but quickly dismissed the thought.

Together, they stood up and headed for the belly of the beast.

Phoebe slowed down before the last door to the right, allowing Ronan to draw her close and whisper hoarsely into her right ear from behind, "Lennie says we'll find what we're after in a private room near the back of the third warehouse floor, near the receiving bays."

"So, into the rainforest?"

"*Yes.*"

She nodded, resolute. "Lead the way."

Her willingness to follow his lead surprised him ... but he should have known better. As soon as they walked into the pulsing room, she spun them both on the spot and stepped quickly backwards, dragging him out onto the dance floor and then turning to lead him onward. "There's no reason we can't dance our way over there!"

It would appear she was now deeply into the euphoria portion of the evening.

Just fucking perfect.

Ronan had intended to skirt the dance floor entirely, drawing as little attention as possible to themselves and their mission. Instead, Phoebe's ass was now rubbing against him intermittently as they moved deeper into the pulsing crowd. Thoroughly enjoying herself (and torturing him), she threw her hands high in the air and turned briefly to look at him before reaching out to him and dragging her nails seductively down the sides of his neck.

He realized he'd likely lose her in the crowd if he didn't play along.

And admittedly, they might have been forced to cut through the centre of the dance floor in any case, as every wall in this large warehouse room was covered from floor to ceiling in dense, leafy vines. This explained the strange smell from earlier, but Ronan remained unclear on what exactly this foliage was, not to mention how it was managing to thrive in this utterly windowless box of an environment. And it clearly was.

Wraith magic, to be sure. And not so different from whatever was currently surging through Phoebe's body.

She had to be chock-full of dark magic, judging by how strongly she'd reacted to the magic in his pouch, which had been fairly tame compared to some of the other concoctions he knew how to make. He knew that they had to have forced that dark magic into her somehow, and imagining her being taken advantage of like that and what they had done to her ...

Well, it wasn't good.

Ronan struggled to calm his body, his fight response escalating far too quickly to keep a clear head. He would never dream of using Druidic magic to harm her. And the notion of others having done so brought forth a side of him that might actually take *great* pleasure in a Wraith kill.

Many Wraith kills.

He did not suffer those who hurt innocents well at all.

And then a different sort of darkness floated into his mind. Perhaps Phoebe was actually faking the intoxication and the euphoria ... and actually taking advantage of *him*. She wasn't exactly innocent after all.

Not *entirely*.

Ronan growled in her ear. "Phoebe, we're here for one thing. Stop fucking around."

She didn't appear to even hear him, much less care about his warning, which was problematic on several levels. First, she was making him fucking frenzied—at least in his physical body—grinding up against him like she was ... writhing and laughing like a bloody maniac.

And second, she was drawing countless eyes her way—and not just those of the Wraiths.

Lights flashed, and music pounded as a hungry-looking woman with colourful hair approached. Phoebe welcomed her advance. The pair danced erratically to the music for a bit, heads back and limbs flying, before Phoebe pulled Ronan onward once more—though not before sharing a passionate kiss with her fleeting dance partner, biting her lip, and then looking at Ronan mischievously. This happened several more times with several different club-goers, with Phoebe luring in dance partner after dance partner and being naughty each time before catching Ronan's eye and daring him to act like a chaperone.

Or worse, to claim her for himself.

Ronan's nostrils flared; this was not the moment for teasing. They had a mission to complete.

Finally—agonizingly—they reached their destination. Ronan was dizzy from overstimulation and dazed by Phoebe's universal allure. She, however, appeared to be absolutely thriving ... the euphoria still burning hot through her system.

"I'm glad to see you can still let loose, old man," she said seductively, dragging her hands down his sides now.

A shiver ran up his spine as he fought back a moan. "Your instructions, Phoebe, are to go in there and search for the files. In and out fast. I'll guard the door."

She gave him a quick squeeze before releasing him to unlock the door using an enchanted pen knife, which had been a gift from the Knaves. She slid past him, reached a hand down and unlatched the door, then slipped into the darkness with a wink.

At her sudden absence, Ronan felt a smothering sense of foreboding that had nothing to do with the almost claustrophobic nature of the club. He knew they likely wouldn't escape the rave without encountering at least a few more Wraiths; he just hoped that Phoebe would be able to gather what they needed before things started to get messy.

Why didn't I make sure that she was armed?

He sighed. Then a thought occurred to him. Patting his weapon's harness, a wry grin crept over his face as he realized that, while he'd been distracted by her grinding on him, she had taken the opportunity to arm herself.

Ten minutes later, Ronan was still idly guarding the door. There wasn't much else for him to do really. They didn't appear to have been followed across the dance floor. Perhaps Phoebe's more overt approach had been wise after all. Meanwhile, he was entirely alone in a dark alcove near the door. He checked his phone for any new messages from Lennie warning him of danger, but there was nothing.

So, he tried to busy himself with examining the foliage that was growing wildly throughout the warehouse. The roots of the strange plants seemed to be deep within the darkened corners, from which the plant itself had spread and expanded, climbing up the walls and appearing to be moving still, right before his eyes. It reminded him of the Kudzu vine—a trailing and rapidly growing plant known for outcompeting anything that grew near it, only more ... alive. And that was saying something, knowing what he did about such plants.

Ronan crouched and collected a small sample of the vine, which had been slowly creeping towards him across the floor for several minutes. *Are these vines sentient somehow?* He frowned. *That's not possible ... Is it?* Still, its approach *had* seemed almost purposeful. As he collected his sample, he noticed that small white buds were forming along the vine's length, which almost seemed to glow when he began handling it.

Suddenly, the three Wraiths from the front door were standing before him, their sickles in hand.

"What exactly are you doing back here ... *Druid*."

Ronan had been found out. Taking a deep breath, he shrugged.

"Cutting trimmings from these rabid plants of yours was a dead give-away, wasn't it?"

CHAPTER 9

PHOEBE

Ten minutes earlier.

Phoebe entered the dimly lit storage room alone. It smelled like damp earth and ... *fish?* Ahead of her, massive, opaque white vats of some sort of brownish-green liquid were bubbling away. *Fertilizer for the plants, maybe?* Phoebe didn't care to find out.

While she felt relatively safe with Ronan keeping watch outside—despite the fact that he was a lying asshole—Phoebe still wasn't eager to linger for too long.

Okay, she thought, realizing the unfairness of her assessment. She supposed that Ronan hadn't technically lied to her outright. It had been more like a lie of omission. And it wasn't like she'd just straight up asked him, *"So, are you that same Druid who partnered with the big daddy Wraith to begin a series of experiments that completely robbed me of everything that's ever made me who I am? You are? Cool."*

Yeah. Not happening.

No matter how hard—or more realistically, how little—Ronan had tried to connect with her over the past few days, a deep chasm still existed between them. She hadn't trusted him when she first arrived at the safe house, but what had changed since then that meant she could? Nothing. He and the Druids had "insisted" she join their cause but were clearly omitting meaningful information she might need to stay safe. And Ronan was worst of all. The most recent issue she had, of course, was his failure to brief her properly for tonight's mission. Not to mention that he'd fucking drugged her!

Sure, it had been an accident, but she wished she could have just faked the whole thing—that would have been one hell of a way to get back at Ronan for his lack of proper care and concern. She couldn't deny, however, that he hadn't exactly pushed her away when she'd needed him most. But really, that was the bare minimum, given the circumstances.

And sure, she might have even felt bad for stealing one of his daggers without his consent, but he did have two of them after all. She'd snagged it shortly after they'd landed on the dance floor—Ronan was surprisingly easy to distract, despite his obvious experience with these sorts of missions. At first, Phoebe had suspected that using her body would be the best route to diverting his awareness from the weight of his cloaked, enchanted blades. But it seemed he'd actually been the most agitated when she was interacting with other club-goers: club-goers who weren't *him*.

So, she'd stolen it during a moment of push-and-pull when she knew Ronan was feeling frustrated with her. It was his own fault for not arming her from the start, especially since she knew *exactly* how to use weapons like his.

Phoebe reached into her boot, pulled out a pen-sized flashlight, and placed it between her teeth before starting to rifle through a series of boxes that had been piled in a darkened corner. What they'd expected to be an office—or at the very least, a storage facility—actually more closely resembled a utility room and dumping ground, housing not only the vats of that strange stinky liquid but also unmarked wooden crates and simple garbage.

She'd had to step over several bags of trash and empty bottles before even approaching the only logical place in the room for storing information: a gathering of three very dented, very rusty filing cabinets. Perhaps the Wraiths thought that hiding the documents in plain sight was the best plan for some reason. She doubted it though. The evil bastards were cleverer than they let on. So, she had a hunch that whatever was in there would hold little value to anyone.

Still ... she had to check.

It took her little time to track down a small stack of mildewed logbooks. She quickly dug through the first box but found nearly everything ruined or illegible. She shuffled around through a few more files, fearing this mission would be an utter failure, then pulled out a couple of black, leather-bound books that looked different from the rest.

They were also miraculously untouched by the surrounding moisture and humidity. "Strange ..."

She opened the final box and screamed, causing her slim flashlight to drop from her mouth and onto the ground with a clatter. Then it skittered out of reach, along with the brown, fuzzy rat whose roof she'd just lifted away.

"*Fuck!*"

The last thing she wanted was to get down on all fours in rat-piss paradise and search for her lost flashlight. Then she thought of Ronan keeping watch outside, risking his own life too, and sighed. She needed to be absolutely certain that the final box didn't contain anything valuable to them—or more accurately, to *her*.

A loud, metallic sound filled the room as a bay door at the far end began to open. The red glow of taillights shone into the large room as a delivery truck backed up towards the storage bay.

Fortunately, this provided just enough illumination to let her see into the final box. *Unfortunately*, she found nothing of value there, only more boggy, fishy-smelling papers.

Phoebe knew she would have only seconds to slip back out of the room before someone exited the truck and climbed up into the bay. So, she tucked the few intact logbooks she'd found into the back of her skirt's waistband, kicking herself for her earlier stubbornness in her choice of attire. As it turned out, a good costume was *not* more important than practicality in situations like these.

The logbooks immediately slipped from her waistband and fell out the bottom of her skirt. She caught them just as another door flew open, and Ronan came flying through. "Phoebe! We have company!"

"What do you want me to do?" she hollered back. Shit was getting messy fast.

"We need to get out of here!"

"Well, we can't go this way," she said, pointing towards the open bay doors, where several hooded Wraiths now stood, unsheathing their sickled blades.

"*Fuck!*" he shouted as a large, balding Wraith charged into the room after him.

Phoebe set the books down in the driest place she could find—on top of a discarded microwave—and braced herself. She knew that Ronan's opponents were likely younger than the ones she was facing, simply because his were unrobed. This meant they would be stronger in combat yet less magically powerful than the trio approaching her from the loading bay. If she could just get her knife into the cloaked Wraiths before they could Wield any magic in her direction, she knew they would disintegrate into piles of dust on the floor. If not ...

The three cloaked Wraiths ambled slowly towards her, their decaying bodies twitching and creaking as she braced for their magical attack. She assumed the two flanking her would come at her first, as this was a common formation of theirs.

So predictable.

She'd gained plenty of experience fighting the Wraiths while in captivity. In fact, that was one of the few things from her time with them that she remembered with any clarity. The Wraiths had delighted in her ability to deflect magic, both by conventional means, ducking and rolling, and by her own mysterious nature.

Now, though, the trapped magic inside of her gave her a distinct edge.

As the middle Wraith spread his cloak wide, Phoebe laughed. "Have we met before? Or are you assholes *really* all the same?" She was positively vibrating at the chance to exact violence on those who'd hurt her at the facility—and, in the end, a Wraith is a Wraith.

She grinned dangerously, baring her teeth.

The rightmost Wraith raised his arms and released a burst of molten power in her direction, the heat of it scorching her shoulder as she hurled herself to the right. She knew they only had so much stolen magic within their wretched frames at any one time, so if she could make them chase her for long enough, they'd eventually be forced to use their physical weapons instead.

Then *she'd* have the advantage.

Phoebe danced through the messy storage room, hiding behind the tanks, crates, and slumping stacks of wet boxes. An errant burst of energy struck one of the tanks beside her, causing its opaque plastic to explode, releasing a loud gush of liquid to spill across the floor.

It smelled *disgusting*.

Phoebe could hear Ronan partaking in a battle far more physical than her own, with the sound of crunching bones and splattering blood rending the air behind her.

"Are you alright, Ronan?" she shouted as she dodged another burst of magic from the cloaked Wraiths. They were growing weaker now, but she was also growing tired.

"I'm fine!" he hollered, followed by a loud grunt, a thud, and a splash.

The Druid could clearly hold his own, which was a relief, considering he was her only way out of here.

Phoebe realized with a groan that she should have stolen his keys along with his dagger just in case he was slain before a retreat to their vehicle could be accomplished. She had no idea what the Druid protocols were for leaving bodies behind.

Hopefully, it wouldn't come to that.

Her adversaries were now closing in on her from all sides. Usually, she'd pick the weakest-looking one and attempt to roll past him across the floor, but as she was standing in several inches of fish guts and water—with a literal fish head floating past her feet—she was desperately searching for an alternative.

She looked towards the most slumping of the three, its shoulders utterly lopsided as it staggered towards her. Then she whirled to the right, pumping her legs as she charged towards it from an odd angle. She'd learned that the old ones didn't have great eyesight and relied more heavily on their magic to detect those around them.

Gripping Ronan's dagger tightly in her right hand, which strangely seemed to be vibrating to its own subtle rhythms, she connected *hard* with the Wraith, thrusting the dagger into its ribs. It collapsed to the floor almost immediately, its dusty, disintegrating mass quickly dissolving in the scummy water.

Phoebe struck down the next Wraith using a similar method, though the bastard managed to use some of its remaining magic on her, the force of it smashing into her chest and causing her to stagger back, though not for long. Recovering fast, she twisted, ducked low, and rammed into the Wraith.

Killing it dead.

"Behind you!" Ronan shouted.

Phoebe whirled, shanking the third Wraith mere seconds before it could wrap its grubby claws around her throat. "Thanks," she said, panting as it fell to the floor.

Ronan wiped his brow. "No problem. Did you find what we're after?"

"I think so." She nodded towards the small stack of logbooks on the microwave. "There honestly wasn't much here ... and most of it seems to have been damaged by whatever is in those tanks. Boxes and boxes of soggy paper."

Ronan sniffed loudly. His nose was quite a prominent feature on his face, but she kind of liked it. "It smells like fish fertilizer."

Phoebe shifted impatiently in her boots as a pair of dead-fish eyes looked up at her from the water. "Great job, Sherlock. Can we leave now?"

"Yes," he said, but he seemed distracted by the strange, bubbling tanks. There were several pipes extending from each vat, pumping (or collecting) the liquid from (or to) who knows where. There were also bags and bags of compost stacked against the far wall, presumably to be mixed with the fish guts.

Ronan blinked several times before (apparently) remembering the precarious nature of their current position. Then he stepped back to look at her. Assessing. "Are you alright?"

Phoebe took several deep breaths, suddenly lost in the overt concern that had spread across his face. "Yes, I think so. Though I don't know if I'll ever get this smell out of my boots."

He reached forward, as though to right her dishevelled clothing but, instead of doing so, walked past her towards the logbooks.

"Hey!" she shouted.

Gathering them up, Ronan turned and started moving towards the open bay door. "If you're going to work for the Druids," he said, "then you'll need to learn that anything you confiscate has to go through your senior first."

"See? You *are* old," she said, pointing at him with his own dagger as she jogged to catch up.

He ignored her. "We're also going to need to discuss how you learned to fight like that. You said you were decent in combat but ... what I just saw was something quite different."

Phoebe raised her chin. "You never asked if I knew how to fight."

If Ronan was going to lead with omissions, then so would she.

CHAPTER 10

RONAN

RONAN STOOD SHOULDER TO SHOULDER WITH DR. IMOGEN SCOTT, distantly surveying the surging crop of Wraith vines that were creeping aggressively from the back of the warehouse and across the gravel parking lot.

"And you said they're growing these vines without any real light source?" she asked, perplexed.

Ronan had only known the Canadian botanist-turned-Druid for a few short years, but how her mind worked always put him at ease. She was clever and, more importantly, concise.

"Unclear. When I first encountered them, they were growing inside a makeshift warehouse rave." Ronan gestured up ahead of them. "So, I suppose there were lights, just not grow lights."

"Interesting." She stepped forward to get a better view.

He held out his arm. "We can't move in closer until Amos gives us the signal."

Up ahead of them, about thirty metres away, stood the recently targeted Wraith warehouse. It looked rather unassuming in the daylight, with the last of its clubgoers still trickling out.

Ronan, of course, hadn't slept a wink either.

Imogen crossed her arms. "I don't anticipate they'll give us access inside."

He shook his head. "And I certainly won't be able to join you. They'll recognize me after last night. But if Amos and Amelia play their cards right, you should be able to at least get close enough to gather a bigger sample."

Ronan had phoned the twins immediately after he'd deposited Phoebe at the safe house. She'd been eager to sleep, her body spent from her shockingly adept combat with the Wraiths—another subject he would have to address with her today and another omission from her interview. She obviously knew more about Wraith composition than she'd let on. Even from afar, Ronan could see that she'd entered the fight with a strategy.

This morning, though, he didn't need her help—or her *distraction*.

Once Phoebe had been secured inside the safe house—with Ian on guard, unfortunately—Ronan had reversed his Range Rover from the driveway and driven straight back to the warehouse. They needed boots on the ground and fast. He'd dropped a pin to Imogen, requesting that she join him this morning before work, and she'd obliged without asking any questions.

"So, what exactly *is* the plan? If you don't mind me asking."

"Sorry. I haven't been clear on anything," Ronan said, scrubbing his face. He was exhausted. "Amos and Amelia have secured a delivery truck—one that can carry commercial-sized tubs of fish—and will approach the loading bay from the south." He checked his watch. "In five minutes."

He ignored the fact that his smartwatch was giving him shit for not sleeping enough. *Fucking robots.*

"Right," Imogen replied, eying the contents of the small Ziploc bag Ronan had handed her. He hadn't been able to gather anything more than a few leaves for a sample thanks to his being so rudely interrupted by the Wraiths. "What sort of substrate were they growing it in?"

"No clue. The floor I walked across was poured concrete."

"Walked across or *danced?*"

Ronan gave her a sidelong look and smirked. "I'm not telling."

"You must have been *very* focused on your target."

"What makes you say that?"

"Oh, it's nothing really ... It's just not like you to miss important details like that."

"It wasn't part of the mission."

Imogen tilted her head, clearly not buying it. "I see ..."

"I didn't exactly expect the walls to be covered from floor to ceiling in thick vines."

She laughed. "No, I suppose not."

Imogen was in her early forties. She was attractive in the nonconventional sense, with thick, straw-coloured hair that pooled heavily around her shoulders, small blue eyes, and big horn-rimmed glasses. She was also only about five feet tall. In her youth, she'd probably contended with being perceived as meek and cute at first glance. But in Ronan's adult experience at least, he knew that Imogen was whip-smart and extraordinarily perceptive, which made her a formidable ally to the Druids. Cuteness didn't even factor into the equation.

"Our intention was to collect some sensitive documents that we believed had been moved to the warehouse for temporary storage. However, by the time we got in, most of the files were soaked."

"So, they are watering the plants somehow ..."

"I think it was fish fertilizer."

"Fish *emulsion*," she corrected. "If it was the liquid."

Ronan didn't get the sense that the Wraiths were being particularly technical about how they were feeding the rapidly growing plants. The storage room was disorganized, clearly indicating that no professional had been involved in the setup. In fact, everything in the room had seemed like an afterthought. Were the plants growing faster than the Wraiths had expected? And more importantly, why were they even growing them in the first place? They'd definitely lent a very specific ambiance to one of the rave themes, but there had to be more to it.

That was one of the reasons they needed Imogen. She would be able to at least see through some of the mess and help them gather useful insights.

"I'm not clear on their methodology," he said. "I actually don't think there really was any. But as soon as I entered the room, it reeked of fish. And then, during combat, several of the tanks burst, and the proof came pouring out. Or ... well ... more accurately, it floated past and looked me in the eye."

Ronan made a silly face.

Imogen laughed. "And let me guess. Amos and Amelia are delivering more fish this morning?"

Indeed, Lennie had hacked the Wraith warehouse's delivery charter and found out that they had a delivery scheduled for eight a.m. It was up to Amos and Amelia to beat that truck with a false delivery of their own instead.

"You don't miss a beat," Ronan said grinning.

She returned his smile and stood quietly beside him.

Ronan rocked on his heels, stretching his calves. "While we're waiting, can I ask you a question?"

"Of course."

He reached into the pocket of his jeans, pulled out the emptied pouch from the night before, and held it out on his palm. "I used this last night."

Imogen sniffed. "I see. Valerian root and ... skullcap?"

"Yes, and lavender, along with some of the other usuals. It was a mild batch."

"I can tell. You can barely smell the chrysanthemum."

"Right, so ... My usual protocol in these situations is to start small, especially when the mission's intent involves infiltration rather than combat."

"Makes sense to me."

"Agreed. So, I had Phoebe with me—"

"The girl from the experiments?" Imogen's eyes grew wide.

Ronan schooled his features into a stoic façade. "The very same."

"Bold of you. And her too, for that matter."

Ronan waved this away with one hand. Their decision to bring Phoebe along on the mission wasn't up for discussion; he'd had his reasons. “Regardless, when I dropped the pouch, it elicited the desired effect from the Wraiths, who let us into the club.”

She nodded, listening intently. “And what about you?”

“I felt minimal effects, as usual. I’m exposed to it with such frequency that this particular dosage really doesn’t do much apart from improve my mood.”

“And Phoebe?”

“Seriously adverse effects.” Ronan grimaced, running his hands through his hair. “I’m talking full-on inebriation, followed by a massive spike in euphoria. I’ve never seen anything like it.”

“That sounds highly unusual. Are you sure she wasn’t faking it?”

This was precisely why he’d come to Imogen, appreciating her no-bullshit approach.

“Fairly certain, though I suppose we can’t rule it out. While she has consented to working alongside us, she’s still keeping plenty of secrets.”

Ronan again thought about how clever she’d been in going against those three ancient Wraiths.

Imogen pursed her lips and scrunched up her nose, an expression that made her greatly resemble a bespectacled rabbit. “I know little of her beyond the initial reports you shared after that lab exploded ... An untrained Wielder on the loose with trapped Wraith magic, yada-yada.” Imogen waved her hand dismissively.

“Unfortunately, we still know very little about her.”

Which was true. Even after the hours of interrogation that he and Lennie had put her through, they were no closer to understanding why Phoebe had been selected for the Wraith trials nor why, out of all their “participants,” she seemed to have handled the trapped magic so much differently than the others. Not to mention that they had no idea how to get it out of her.

Ronan was growing increasingly concerned with how the trapped magic might be affecting Phoebe, particularly when she was stressed or being exposed to high quantities of free magic.

Imogen nodded. “Well, if she’s willing, you should conduct more tests.”

"I highly doubt she'll be okay with that after her time in captivity. Even the interview we put her through was hard on her."

"The tests don't have to be wholly clinical. There are plenty of Druidic tests you could administer ... Gentler applications. This whole thing"—she waved her hand again with a bit of flare—"her heightened sensitivity to the Druid pouches ... It's fascinating."

"Is that something *you'd* be comfortable doing?"

"Me? Certainly. But it'll cost you." She winked.

Ronan smirked. "Cost me *what?*"

"What about ... dinner? We haven't gone out for a while."

Ronan raised his eyebrows. He knew it wouldn't be a date, as their relationship wasn't like that, but she did have expensive taste. This *was* going to cost him.

"You've got yourself a deal."

Just then, Ronan's phone pinged. Amos's signal.

In the distance, a nondescript white delivery truck approached the warehouse. Ronan could scarcely make out the twins in its cab as they popped the vehicle into reverse and headed towards the loading bay. Amelia hopped out first, clipboard in hand, and pressed the buzzer.

After several moments, the bay door opened. Ronan could see Amelia drop her own pouch to the ground, though he had no idea what it might contain. Druidic pouches were specific to the user more often than not. But whatever it was, it worked. Soon, Amos was hopping from the driver's seat and opening the vehicle's back door.

"That's your cue," Ronan said.

Imogen nodded. Then he watched as she stealthily skirted the parking lot, sticking close to the blackberry brambles and scotch broom lining the ditch between her and the road. This wasn't a bustling area in the Lower Mainland, and the fact that the exhausted ravers were still scattered about, awaiting Ubers and the like, was definitely to their advantage. Amos and Amelia were expecting Imogen, and so she joined them seamlessly by the large loading doors.

Amelia handed her the clipboard, which she began inspecting closely.

It was a familiar routine: the old delivery van arriving on-site, followed by an inspector, who interrupted the process and created a diversion by making the delivery driver appear to be the main focus, thereby easing any Wraith's suspicions about the often-unexpected deliveries they received.

Imogen needed no coaching in this bit; she was as seasoned as the rest of them. As expected, the Wraiths were annoyed by Imogen delaying the unloading process, crossing their arms and looking disgruntled. Amos also carefully displayed physical distress at the interruption, providing the perfect cover for Amelia to slip inside the warehouse.

Ronan waited, hidden far enough away to avoid drawing attention to himself. A few moments later, a young woman broke from a group of ravers and approached him directly.

"Are you selling?" she asked, looking at him with pupils the size of dinner plates.

He chuckled. "No. But can I ask what it is about my appearance that gave you that impression?"

She shrugged. "You just look the type."

Of all of the masks he'd worn in his life, and the shoes he'd filled, "drug dealer" had never been one of them. Not even when he'd been working undercover.

"Sorry," he said.

Without another word, the woman returned to her group, and they shuffled on.

Instinctively, he pulled out his compass, which was currently pointing directly at the warehouse. Then he checked his watch. Again. It was 7:17 a.m. They'd clocked this mission at about forty-five minutes assuming all things went according to plan, meaning that (ideally) he'd be back in his vehicle by eight and tucked into his bed by nine. Though, whether or not he'd be able to actually sleep was a whole other question.

His mind was fucking racing, bringing him back to watching Phoebe work in that Seattle nightclub where they'd finally connected with her. She was still just as much of an enigma as she was then. In fact, it seemed that for every answer he uncovered about her, ten more questions popped up.

And then there was how she'd fought the night before ...

She'd somehow developed her own combat skills, and though she lacked finesse, from what he'd seen, she had impeccable "twitch" reaction-time when it came to anticipating the Wraiths' movements. When he'd hollered to her that there was a Wraith attacking from behind, she'd reacted immediately with both precision and strength.

In many respects, it should not have been possible. Ronan knew that Phoebe's physique—while impressive—didn't have the power or agility to strike at the Wraiths like she had. That would mean that she sourced it through magic, which was either her own innate Wielding abilities or the trapped Wraith darkness within her. Even if it was the latter magic that wasn't "her own"—and which was both unpredictable and potentially harmful to her—it still spoke to a natural aptitude within Phoebe.

Frankly, this was a requirement for Ronan when it came to any Druids with whom he might enter combat. Still, there needed to be a sort of symbiosis between partners, and he'd initially doubted if Phoebe would have those kinds of skills, which meant that their time working together would always have an end date. Now that he knew she could fight, though ...

Ronan was jostled from his thoughts as Amelia swiftly exited the warehouse. He refocused his attention sharply, but it appeared that they were still having no issues. He watched as she worked with Amos to start unloading the delivery truck, using a manual forklift to transport several grey tanks of chum from the back of it and into the loading bay. It was awkward work, and Ronan was reminded again why he was grateful for his elevated (though hard-earned) station in the Order. Amos and Amelia were still being tasked with a lot of grunt work.

He was also grateful that their Druid network had been established so close to the coast, as coming up with several barrels of dead fish on short notice might have been impossible otherwise, though it still hadn't been exactly easy.

Ronan left his hiding spot finally and walked casually towards his Range Rover parked several metres away between a dumpster and a blue minivan, partly to avoid another illicit encounter but also to get a closer look.

In the distance, Imogen was standing with her arms crossed, intense boredom clear in her posture. Of course, Ronan knew that she was anything but bored. As he watched, she pulled her cell phone from her pocket and brought it up to her ear.

Seconds later, Ronan's phone rang.

"Hello," she said.

"Go ahead."

"I'm calling regarding report AG5383, regarding procuring, storing, and transporting aquatic matter to industrial sites. It is approximately seven-thirty a.m., on Tuesday, December 22nd."

Ronan groaned, realizing that he'd missed Dom's birthday yesterday, which was on the winter solstice, though this hadn't been the point of her call.

Imogen continued, either unaware of Ronan's groan or ignoring it as she worked to buy Amos and Amelia some more time. "The chum in question is being added to a rudimentary fertilizer system housed in Langley. It was picked up this morning and transported from Richmond."

Several Wraiths milled around inside the large bay door, mere steps above where Imogen was standing. The bay access was about five feet from the ground—as evidenced by Imogen's head barely reaching its top edge. Ronan could see Amos's body tense as water and fish guts suddenly poured from that same edge, covering Imogen in water and rotted fish guts. She leaped back and out of the splash zone.

The Wraiths were apparently growing impatient with the delivery delay.

Amos and Amelia swiftly delivered the last pallet of chum and closed the loading door of their truck, just as another delivery truck approached—a delivery truck marked with a faded logo of an open-mouthed lingcod.

Within seconds, the twins had started their engine and were driving away.

Imogen, meanwhile, was nowhere to be seen.

"Imogen, are you still there?" he said into his cell phone, which had been silent for too long.

It was several more moments before he heard her whispered voice. "I'm inside."

Somehow, in all the commotion, she'd managed to climb the short ladder up into the loading bay and had stowed herself away in the warehouse.

"What? Why?!"

"If they catch me, I'll just say that I needed to wash off the fish guts before I left." Ronan could hear the sound of running water. It seemed she'd found a tap. "But what I *really* need is to inspect those plants more closely."

"Imogen—"

"Didn't you see them growing towards me outside?"

In truth, Ronan had been too busy watching the delivery activity to notice the plants doing anything but continuing to be inconceivably robust as they grew outwards from the loading bay. Now that she mentioned it, though, the plants over there had now reached the warehouse roof.

Alright, he thought. *That's new.*

Imogen wasn't done. "I don't think it's the fertilizer feeding them."

Ronan's jaw ticked. "What do you mean?"

"I think that the plants are feeding on Wielding magic."

CHAPTER 11
RONAN

"WE NEED TO TALK ABOUT THE MAGIC TRAPPED INSIDE OF YOU," Ronan said, carrying a stack of brown folders into the living room of the safe house.

"Hello to you too," Phoebe said from where she was curled up on one of the house's many plush couches like a satisfied cat in the afternoon sun.

"Sorry ... *ehm* ... Good afternoon ... Phoebe," he said, adding her name as an afterthought, then realizing how stupid he sounded.

"Whoa!" she said, perking up. "You look like shit."

Ronan had only returned two hours earlier from his morning stakeout with Imogen. Of course, even if he hadn't arranged to meet the botanist at the crack of dawn, he doubted he'd have slept a wink anyway. He'd become utterly engrossed in figuring out Phoebe's unusual reaction to the pouch.

He knew it wasn't a good pattern for him to fall into, but there he was.

He cleared his throat. "I didn't sleep last night."

"I can tell. Are you okay?"

"I was briefly detained this morning by a ... pressing matter."

Following Imogen's entry into the warehouse, he and the botanist had spoken at length about her findings and what they might mean for this branch of Wraiths who were trying to fill the power void that had been left behind after Cassius's death. They already knew about the now-demolished facility that had been experimenting on magic users, with other similar labs undoubtedly popping up even as they spoke. They knew at least some of the details surrounding the "smoke production" in the south, where select Wraiths were being "recycled" into their lung-choking weapon of biological warfare. But what exactly was this particular branch hoping to achieve? What was the purpose of growing those strange plants?

Whatever the answers to those questions might be, they knew that it was surely aligned with the common drive among all the Wraith groups: to claim progressively more power in the vacuum left by Cassius, whether through dark magical means, the conversion of more Wielders to their cause, or the hostile takeover of competing groups.

Ronan sat down in his favourite armchair right across from her. The chair's arms were worn perfectly for reading or sipping scotch, though less for clinical discussion. He shifted awkwardly and began to speak. "More important than that matter, however, is that I've come to realize that I'm not putting nearly enough of my focus on your health. I have concerns about the longevity of your physical body on several levels with ... well, with their magic trapped inside of you as it is. Not to mention how you reacted to my pouch last night."

"Is this standard protocol?"

Ronan put on his round tortoiseshell reading glasses then, which he knew made him look both sexy and intelligent, and ignored the part of himself that hoped she'd notice. "What do you mean?"

Phoebe quietly closed the book she was reading and clutched it on her lap. "I mean ... Do you take a personal interest in the medical status of all the Druids, or just mine?"

It seemed she either didn't notice his glasses or didn't care.

He sighed impatiently. "None of the other Druids have Wraith magic trapped inside of them."

"Still ..."

Ronan removed his glasses and looked her dead in the eyes. "As you're aware, the Druids don't make a practice of keeping magic within them long term, which is what differentiates us from the Wraiths. We routinely return magic to the earth after its use."

"I would do that too if I could," she said, shrugging.

Ronan started thinking aloud. "I find it perplexing that you never noticed that you were a Wielder in any way before they captured you ... Though, I suppose that not all of them know they're capable of magic."

"Well, I mean, I can maybe think of a handful of moments in my life where I was a little luckier than I should have been. But nothing that particularly stands out."

"*Hmm* ..."

"Apparently, I'm 'force sensitive' rather than a full-blown Jedi."

Ronan smirked. "Didn't take you as a *Star Wars* fan."

"There are many things you don't know about me, Druid," she said playfully.

Ronan wasn't about to take the bait. He returned to his stack of files, flipping through them for several moments before sighing heavily. "Alright, I'm going to let you in on some of our ... trade secrets."

She sat up at this, cocking her head and once again reminding him of a sun-warmed cat. "Oh?"

"While we Druids return our magic to the earth, the Knaves don't. Instead, they store the magic in their weapons, which I'll admit has caused some friction between our two factions."

"Why?"

"Because it's risky."

Phoebe remained attentive as Ronan set the files down on a side table, crossed one leg over the other, and started nibbling on one of the arms of his glasses. He needed to tread carefully. She wouldn't trust any of them if she were to ever become privy to the truth of his early involvement in those grandfathered experiments at the facility.

"What you may or may not understand, Phoebe, is that when Wraiths collect magic, they do not *allow* it to leave their bodies." He cupped his hands in front of him then. "Think of our bodies as containers. We can only hold so much magic in them at any one time and for only so long before that container starts to crack."

She nodded, following along easily. So far, at least.

"As Druids," he continued, "whatever we don't use up in combat or creation is returned to the earth in a give-and-take process that maintains the balance of the natural and magical worlds. The Knaves share a similar story. Much of their magic is returned to the earth, but some is also put into their weapons permanently, creating their magically imbued blades and the like."

"Like that dagger I *borrowed* from you at the warehouse?"

She was far too cheeky for her own good. "Yes," he said, clearing his throat. "You've noticed, I'm sure, that the Wraiths don't have an unlimited supply of magic available to them in battle. That's the same as it is for us as Druids, which makes sense since we share the same ancient origins."

She nodded, looking briefly like she was about to ask another question before stopping herself.

When she remained silent, Ronan continued. "So, what happens to their bodies, do you think, should the Wraiths not return the magic but also not actually *use* it?"

She pondered this momentarily. "Well, if I were to guess, I'd say that they decay, like a gross office fridge when no one clears out their lunches."

"Exactly," he said, chuckling approvingly. "While allowing the magic to fester might gift them an unnaturally long life, over time, the containers—that is, their *physical* bodies—become unstable and, eventually, unusable."

"Hence that Wraith smell," she said, scrunching her nose. "Gotta throw those containers out."

They did indeed smell terrible. Through his extended experimentation on Wraiths under Cassius's rule, Ronan had also learned that most of their festering magic would eventually end up in their lungs—as pleural fluid specifically, which was the same fluid that the industrious Wraiths to the south still used to create their killing smoke.

"While they might gain something not too far from immortality," he said, "their bodies simultaneously rot away until they are basically walking corpses. It's a dark trade indeed. Even though the Sorcerer Cassius was once the 'big daddy' Wraith of them all, his body had rotted so severely that he needed to maintain a constant glamour to hide his disgusting, putrefied form."

"Did you ever see him? Cassius, I mean—"

"I did. Yes," he said shortly. They weren't here to discuss his relationship with the evil Sorcerer. He leaned forward then, with both feet flat on the floor and his elbows on his knees. "As you can imagine, it only stands to reason that it's highly unusual that this magic is not degrading you as well ... at least in some way."

"Who's to say it isn't?"

"Hence my concern about your health."

As Phoebe pondered this for a moment, biting her lip, Ronan tried and failed to keep from savouring her subtle and (hopefully) unconscious nibbling.

"How do they *become* Wraiths, though?" she asked then. "I don't think I'm becoming one ... or at least, I hope not." She sounded scared.

Ronan was reminded of the dark, painful, and profoundly secretive process of Wraith transformation going on while he had worked at the Gloucestershire estate. He'd never seen it in action, as it really was an extremely highly guarded process, but he'd heard the screams it had elicited.

"You're *not* becoming a Wraith."

"How do you know?"

He steeled himself. She didn't need to know how he knew this, but she did deserve some reassurance on the matter. "To my knowledge, the mechanism to complete the change requires the presence of other Wraiths. While exposure to Wraith magic can degrade our systems—or most people's systems anyway—there is an element of acceptance that is also essential to a successful transformation. That's actually part of the ancient ritual, or so I understand."

"So, you can't *accidentally* become a Wraith?"

"No, not that I'm aware of." She looked immensely relieved, which improved his mood if only slightly. "However, that doesn't mean the dark magic doesn't affect Wielders. It's still degenerative. Wholly unnatural and—"

"Are you calling me a degenerate?" she asked teasingly, though the humour didn't reach her eyes.

"It's *degenerative*," he repeated, choosing not to take the bait. "And over time, it *kills* us."

"So, how do we stop it?" Her voice sounded suddenly thin, like glass about to shatter.

"Reducing exposure is the only sure-fire way. Over time, the dark magic, which is inherently ... *sticky*, for lack of a better word, seeps into our systems."

"Do you know anyone who's died from it?"

Although the "stickiness" of Wraith magic had been the precise reason for Ronan's death several years earlier, he wasn't ready for her to know that. Not *yet*.

But perhaps it *was* time to tell her about Julia.

"I do." Ronan swallowed hard. "A friend of mine, Malcolm, died when such magic was stripped from him several years ago—during a battle against the Sorcerer Cassius. I assume the Wraiths talked about him?"

Phoebe's eyes widened. "They did, but ... What do you mean by *stripped?*"

It seemed strange that she seemed more alarmed by the idea of magic being stripped away than of the evil Sorcerer. He sighed. "It's complicated to explain. A bit of a long story, really."

"Try me. I've got time," she said, leaning back.

"Well, my best friend, Domhnall ... His wife, Julia, was the one who eventually defeated Cassius." He frowned slightly. "Julia's actually one of my best friends too, so I don't know why I said it like that. Anyway, Julia is a Witch—a Bearer—and one with a special power that lets her forcibly remove Wraith magic from their decaying bodies."

Phoebe's brow furrowed at this. She was clearly getting agitated.

Ronan could feel her magic churning even from where he was sitting several feet away. "Then why are there still Wraiths walking the earth?"

"Because it's a rare occurrence for Julia to actually manage to *harness* that ability. It's not something that can be done on a broader scale without the involvement of higher powers."

Ronan's thoughts returned to that day on the ramparts years earlier, with Julia rising high above the battle and violently casting her magic down below. That had been one of the most spectacular and life-changing events he'd ever witnessed, as well as being the actual birthplace of his obsession with the inner workings of the Wraiths—something he definitely wasn't about to share with Phoebe.

"Unfortunately," he continued, "when this dark magic is stripped from someone who has *not* undergone the whole process of actually becoming a Wraith ... it kills them."

"Oh," Phoebe said, and he thought he could actually see her deflating.

Uncomfortable with her reaction, Ronan cleared his throat awkwardly. "Which is what happened to my friend Malcolm, though he knew the risks. He'd chosen to use darker magic to create more *explosive* pouches in his desperation to help us put an end to Cassius once and for all. In doing so, however, he was required to hold onto magic for longer than was safe."

"Did Julia know what would happen to him?"

"She did not."

"Wow, that's ... really sad."

"It is."

Several long quiet moments ticked by. As Phoebe considered what he'd just told her, Ronan listened to the nearby grandfather clock, breathing along with its tempo, and waited to follow her lead.

Finally, she shook her head. "Shit. You've been living a *literal* fantasy life."

"In many ways, I suppose I have. But this is your world too now, Phoebe, whether you like it or not."

Phoebe stared at him as she tried to process this, which made him nervous.

"So, what exactly is it that you want from me?" she asked finally.

"I'd like to run some medical diagnostics."

"Didn't you recover the Wraiths' records after the explosion?"

"Many of them but not all, and definitely not enough of them to understand why you seem to be an exception to every magical rule."

"The Wraiths did always say that I wasn't *like the other girls*." There was no humour in her tone now. Only bitterness.

"I don't doubt it," he said, scratching his head.

It seemed it would be more complicated than he thought to get her to agree to further testing without either triggering the trauma of the experiments they'd performed on her or exposing more of his own complicity in their beginnings. But he still had to find a way. "What I'm wondering is whether you'd be opposed to visiting the hospital with me so I could run some tests? It would be a lot easier—"

"No!" she exclaimed, her eyes wide. "No hospitals."

"Of course." He had worried this would be her response, which is why he hadn't proposed any test of her Wielding abilities, though he had his own theories. He wouldn't be able to run even half of the medical tests he wanted to at the safe house without bringing in a ton of equipment. "I understand. But would you be comfortable with me running a few tests here? Just in the living room maybe?"

She bit her lip for a moment but eventually conceded. "I think so."

"Excellent!" This would be better than nothing and far more than he'd dared hope for. He quickly shifted gears. "We can operate on a paradigm of strong consent throughout. I can also bring in a chaperone if you want one. We can see if any of the local Druids might come by—"

"I don't want anyone else here."

Ronan shifted in his seat, consciously adjusting his body language to appear more open and in no way dangerous. "Are you sure? A friend of mine, Imogen, has offered to join us."

"Is she also a doctor?"

"Imogen has a PhD, but she's a botanist. More importantly, though, she's also a Druid who specializes in the sorts of magic we use in our pouches and various other medicaments. You'll like her. I promise."

"I ... no, yeah. Not yet. Just ... just you."

Ronan smiled softly and nodded. "The way you Canadians combine 'no-yeah-no's' into yours sentences has always been very amusing to me."

"What do you mean?"

"Never mind. It's just cute."

"You think I'm cute?" Phoebe cocked her head and grinned mischievously at him, her expression cat-like once more. "Are you flirting with me, Dr. Gallagher?"

"Maybe I just have a good bedside manner when it's worth my time," he said, giving her an exaggerated and overtly smarmy grin.

She laughed heartily at that, surprised at his playfulness. "Feels like a bit of an ethical issue to me."

He knew that it had been risky to shift gears like that when Phoebe was so obviously uncomfortable, but thankfully, it had led to a notable relaxation in her posture.

"Let's give your preliminary tests a shot," she said at last, "and then we can see how I feel."

"Thank you, Phoebe. That's perfect. And all I can ask for."

He stood up and stretched his tired back, turning from Phoebe even as she picked up her book once more and leaned back into the cushions. "Hey, Ronan?"

"Yes, Phoebe?"

"Can I have the rest of today off? Or are you going to keep working me to the bone?"

"Of course." He chuckled. "I need to sleep anyway. We can reconnect tomorrow afternoon."

Ronan woke up in a cold sweat with the Sorcerer's voice still oozing in his ears, pulsing thickly with the heavy threat it carried.

"Let me be clear, Druid. You are only allowed access to the Codex by my good graces ..."

He shook himself the rest of the way to consciousness as best he could.

Two-and-a-half years after the defeat of Cassius, Ronan was still suffering from recurring nightmares and panic attacks. Cassius's voice haunted him still, especially at night. Even more problematically ridiculous was that the contents of the *Codex Druidicus*—an ancient tome so dark and dangerous that it should never have been created—still lived "rent free" inside of him ... even without the continuing physical existence of either Cassius or the book itself.

If anything, the real threat was the knowledge now trapped within him ... what he could do with that knowledge should he ever choose to try.

The copy-Codex—a replica that he'd created to prove to Julia and Dom that he truly meant to aid them in the war against Cassius—now resided with the Bearers (and far away from him), just as it should. It felt right that the group of people who'd been most violently targeted, hunted, and killed by Cassius, using the very same instructions now contained within the copy-Codex alone, should be left firmly in charge of its care. If it had been up to him, of course, he'd have destroyed it altogether, but instead, he'd chosen to leave it up to Julia and her kin to determine the best path forward.

As for Ronan—and the Codex knowledge, which was very much alive within him—he now knew that he would truly do no harm with it. Such was the deal he'd struck with the Otherworld upon his return to the land of the living. Still, for all intents and purposes, he now *was* the Codex—magic and all.

Ronan lay in bed, staring at the ceiling for what felt like hours. He knew that he was developing an obsession with Phoebe, and that his excessive focus on her was more than likely what was provoking his current round of nightmares. She remained an "unknown" in a world where he had grown fully accustomed to solid truths. He realized that he still craved such truths, even after his thirst for them, and his earlier obsession with the Codex, had quite literally killed him.

He found himself longing to understand how she worked ... which was a dangerous path to wander alone. So, he reached for his cell phone and dialled his best friend's number. And, as usual, it took him far too long to answer.

"Ronan?" Dom grumbled finally in a gravelly voice. "Why're you calling at this ungodly fucking hour?"

Ronan looked at the clock. It was 3:15 a.m. "Maybe I'm feeling poorly about having missed your birthday."

Dom snorted. "I didn't even notice." In the background of the call, Ronan could hear a child crying. "Ayla's been right miserable for the past few days. Running a fever. And before you ask, we've already been to the doctor. She's got an ear infection. We're just waiting for the drops to start working. She's also madder than hell whenever we put them in, which doesn't help matters."

"Ouch! Poor girl," Ronan said, feeling farther away from them than ever. He'd grown truly fond of Dom and Julia's firstborn. She was tenacious like Julia and tender like Dom, with a mop of wispy, reddish-blonde hair and a keen knack for convincing Ronan to break all the rules. "Tell her that Uncle Ronan will come to care for her properly if she doesn't get better soon."

Dom snorted. "I can't tell her that! She'll fake being even sicker than she already is!"

"True enough ..." Ronan fell silent then, feeling guilty for bothering Dom about something as trivial as this when the man clearly had his hands full with fatherhood.

"Seriously though, Ronan. What do you need? It's not like you to call at this hour."

"I *did* want to wish you a belated happy birthday."

"Thanks ... and?"

Ronan's mind drifted to where Phoebe was sleeping, in the room just across the hall from his. Having her so close definitely beat her sharing a room with Ian, but he didn't love that she might be able to hear him speaking on the phone.

"*Ehm* ... Well, I need some advice about ..." He paused uncertainly, then lowered his voice to a near whisper. "About handling Phoebe."

"Let me guess: Your brain and your cock have different ideas on what 'handling her' might mean at this—"

"Have you been talking to Lennie?!" Ronan snapped, cutting Dom off.

The big Celt laughed. "No. But ... I know you. What could have you been dialling me in the middle of the night about if not a woman? Is she interested in you?"

Ronan considered. While he was surely attracted to the woman (what person with eyes in their head *wouldn't* be?), bedding Phoebe was not in the cards for him. Remembered words from the Otherworld rippled through his consciousness then.

"... And the promise of who you'll meet in what comes after."

He swallowed hard. The fact was that Phoebe simply didn't fit into that timeline. The Otherworld had tasked him with cleaning up the mess he'd made, and since he was still a far cry from completing *that* mission, he knew that "what comes after" had yet to even begin ... assuming it ever would.

"As far as I can tell, she's not interested at all," he answered at last, knowing better than to read more into her flirty banter than was warranted. "Or at least, I don't think so ... which is for the best."

Dom let out a nearly inaudible *"Hmm ..."*

Ronan gritted his teeth then and continued speaking in a hurried whisper. "She actually fucked Ian the other night, though."

"Already?"

"*Already?!*" Ronan was beginning to regret making this phone call. "What do you— Actually, you know what? Never mind."

"Calm yourself, Ronan," Dom said in a carefully measured tone, as though Ronan were some spooked horse he was trying to ride.

Bastard.

"It sounds to me like Phoebe's a bit lonely, Ronan, which is unsurprising, considering all she's been through. And remember, you did pluck her out of nowhere just a few days ago, dragging her off to an unfamiliar house full of strange Druids."

"I have a feeling you don't mean 'strange' in the sense of them being unknown."

"No, I don't," Dom said, laughing. "What can I say? You Druids are a weird bunch. In any case, maybe she just wanted someone to warm her bed. Surely, you can empathize with such a feeling."

Ronan said nothing.

"What exactly are you worried about?" Dom asked more seriously then as his previous mirth finally melted away.

"She has secrets," Ronan whispered. "I can tell."

"Of course, she does. So, do you ... *Codex boy*."

Ronan couldn't help but laugh. "No! I don't mean the usual kind of secrets. I mean, she's keeping something from us. From *me*. I just have this sense that she knows something important or has done something, maybe, but isn't willing to tell anyone about it."

"And again, I say, *so do you*."

Ronan groaned, even as Dom muttered something indiscernible, seemingly turned away from the receiver. He then heard Julia's voice in reply, speaking in the same unmistakably concerned tone that she used almost constantly when it came to Ronan.

"Yes, he's fine," Dom said, then turned his attention back to the phone. "Sorry about that."

"I can go if you're needed," Ronan said, feeling slightly (and surprisingly) spurned. *I must be even more tired than I thought.* He sighed. *It was silly to call him at this hour.*

Dom ignored his deflection. "Are you jealous of Ian?"

"Fuck off."

Dom laughed. "All I'm saying is that you *could* bed her—if she's keen, that is. It actually might not be a bad idea to get a good rut out of your system," he said, pondering aloud as only the great Celtic beast could. "But I think you should probably befriend her, instead. Or at least *first*."

Typical Dom: fight, fuck, and make merry. Life really was that simple for Domhnall O'Brien, the time-bending dynastic son of the ancient Celtic ruler *Brian Boru*.

Ronan sighed loudly. "Okay, for the sake of discussion, let's say that I did ... 'bed her,' as you so aptly put it ... Wouldn't that compromise things?" The question felt ridiculous as soon as it left his mouth. Of course, it would compromise things.

Dom barked with laughter. "You're a grown-arse man, Ronan. You know the answer to that."

Sex always complicated things. *Though it can also relieve a hell of a lot of tension.* He shook his head to dismiss the mental addendum. "Right ... Can I ask you something else?"

"Always."

"I guess it's more of a statement than a question, actually." Ronan was waffling now. "I suppose ... Well, I'm concerned ... that Phoebe might ignite something else in me ... you know?"

"An obsession, you mean? You're concerned she might trigger a new obsession?"

"Correct."

Dom cleared his throat. "I can certainly see that being a potential issue for you ... assuming it isn't one already. After all, she's a problem that has yet to be solved, not to mention one that's mighty close to the core of who you are. It only makes sense that you'd be hyper-focused on her like this. But still ..."

"I'm being careful," Ronan said reassuringly. "And I've asked for Imogen's help."

"That botanist you sometimes work with?"

"That's right. And I'm also trying to reconnect with my therapist, which has been tricky lately because of our busy schedules."

"Isn't that just how it always goes?" Dom said, yawning.

Ronan grimaced slightly. "Sorry. I'm blathering on here. I think I just wanted to check in with you about it all. Keep me honest, you know?"

"You're doing the right thing ... And you know you can call me anytime."

"I know, brother ... Again, happy belated."

With that, Ronan hung up the phone and closed his eyes as he considered his next steps. Sure, he'd felt intense chemistry with Phoebe during the warehouse mission, especially on the dance floor; he couldn't deny that he'd been equally turned on as he was frustrated by her at that moment. He'd also liked discovering that she was a competent fighter and could actually imagine them making a great team, once they were on the same page.

While they hadn't formally tested Phoebe's Wielding abilities yet, Ronan had the distinct impression she would be an asset in the field once trained (even without the influence of the Wraith magic within, which he suspected had falsely bolstered her at the warehouse).

This was all assuming, of course, that she didn't turn apoplectic when she eventually learned his connection to her current predicament—she would find out one way or another about his work with

Cassius and the Wraiths if they got close enough. It would continue to eat him alive in the meantime.

But he also knew that it was a quintessentially bad idea for him to romantically pursue Phoebe in any way. Not anytime soon at least. Not without her first knowing the truth, and not while his larger task remained unfinished. He knew the stakes; nothing good would come from it.

He would just have to get used to his cock stirring every time he watched her stab a Wraith.

CHAPTER 12

PHOEBE

PHOEBE SHOVED ANOTHER ORANGE WEDGE INTO HER MOUTH, relishing the tart juice as it dripped down her chin. Her tongue was sore from the excess of citrus, but she couldn't help herself; she'd only rarely been given fresh fruit in captivity. Perhaps she was just trying to make up for lost time, but either way, the stinging sensation on her tongue was nothing compared to even the slightest of discomforts she'd suffered at their hands.

Most of her meals in Wraith captivity had consisted of beans straight from the can, tinned spaghetti served cold, and expired military rations. If she were lucky, she'd be served oatmeal—bland, yes, but at least one could choke it back without getting a stomach ache. Or worse.

She and the other prisoners were fed twice daily, at sunrise and sundown, or at least, that's what she surmised since their allotted feeding times shifted gradually as the weeks wore on—they were rarely, if ever, given access to any windows to the outside world.

They'd looked through plenty of interior windows, though.

Most of each day was spent either strapped to a bed or being tested against other magic users as the Wraiths and their "scientists" scribbled away in their notebooks. Initially, the tests with other captives had been passive. She'd even found some sort of fucked-up solace in interacting with others who were undergoing the same torture as she was. However, the faces rarely remained the same for long, and Phoebe learned quickly not to become attached.

She seemed to be the only constant ... and the Wraiths' most perplexing guinea pig.

Eventually, the interactions with other magic users became more violent. Or more accurately, the captives were now provoked into violence against one another—something she worked to block from her memory with every ounce of her being.

She couldn't allow herself to remember. It was too much ...

Eventually, they were pitted against the Wraiths themselves. This was when Phoebe had first learned how to fight them—something Ronan hadn't anticipated at the warehouse when she'd snatched his second dagger and helped take down the three Wraiths, enabling their escape.

Despite the Wraiths' attempts to develop a program for trapping and storing their deteriorating magic in the bodies of Wielders—trying to modernize the Wraith world as they knew it—they remained technologically cautious and arcane in their methods.

Phoebe knew little of the lore of the Wraiths but was aware that their longstanding instinct for oral traditions lingered even still. Which explained why the Druids, who allegedly shared similar origins, as Ronan had so kindly alluded to during their discussion in the living room yesterday, were also prone to overt secrecy and strictly guarded paper trails.

As a journalist, trying to get to the bottom of the "Story of the Druids" would have been a nightmare. As things stood now though ... it was even worse.

Still, the peace of the Druids' safe house was growing on her.

Phoebe stretched her legs out under the simple cotton bedsheet. She felt as lazy as a cat and was absolutely relishing it. It was nearing midday, but as far as she knew, there were no objectives today. Or, at least, Ronan hadn't told her of any when they'd parted ways yesterday afternoon, with him heading for the kitchen and her, upstairs to her new bedroom.

Directly across from his.

Phoebe knew that she *should* really find out what was in the notebooks Ronan had practically shoved down his pants back in the warehouse, but there was still time for that. So, she leaned back, settling in for the next dog-show group on TV: the terriers, her favourite.

There was a soft knock on her door then, and she jumped a bit, hastily attempting to finish her citrus wedge, though in the end, she simply suctioned it against the front of her teeth behind her lips.

"Come in," she mumbled. When the door opened, she offered Ronan a beatific, orange-rind smile.

"*Ehm*, hello." His expression oscillated between awkwardness, surprise, and then laughter. "What are *you* up to?"

"Watching re-runs of last year's *Westminster Dog Show*," she said, extracting the wedge from her mouth with gusto. "And eating *all* of your oranges."

Ronan had brought home the bag of Buck Brand oranges the day before, and she was dead curious to learn if he would be one of those roommates who was protective of his groceries. So far, he didn't seem to care.

Instead, he shifted awkwardly on the balls of his feet before taking a step into the room and gesturing towards the small TV in the corner. "You remind me of Dom. He loves that shit."

"You know, I've realized I actually have a vague memory of the Wraiths talking about him."

It was true. Phoebe had considered telling Ronan this detail the day before but had preferred to reveal what she knew on her own terms.

"*Really!?*" Ronan's voice rose a full octave.

She nodded. "The Wraiths would talk about them both sometimes. About her, specifically."

His eyebrows rose and fell in quick succession. "I suppose that makes sense."

"*Does it!?*" she asked, unable to help mimicking his shocked tone from moments earlier.

Ronan plainly resisted the urge to roll his eyes, which resulted in his eyes bugging out briefly. He released a long, slow breath and perched on the very edge of her mattress. "Well, we know the Wraiths attempted to trap magic within you. And that's the same thing they tried to do with Julia. Anyway, I—"

"It wasn't an attempt, Ronan. They managed it."

He gulped audibly. "Yes, of course. Can you feel the magic—*their* magic—inside you even now?"

"Yes." The Druid doctor certainly had an uncanny knack for rolling in and absolutely ruining her mood.

"I know I've already asked this, Phoebe, but are you certain there's no way for it to leave your body safely? As far as you know, I mean?"

"Correct. They tried, I think, to understand how it—how *I*—worked in the first place ... but no. They failed. That's why I ..." Phoebe paused then, thinking of her disappointment the day before when, after briefly thinking Ronan's friend Julia might be able to remove her magic after all, she'd concluded that stripping the magic from her in that way would mean certain death. "That's why I need your help," she finished somewhat lamely, shrugging one shoulder.

He shifted to face her directly and took her hand reassuringly in his. "While we might still not technically know what's happening to you, I think it's something we *both* desperately want to get to the bottom of. It's also something I'd like to promise to see through to the end with you. It's become ... *personal*."

Looking away then, seemingly uncomfortable, he released her hand and quickly started checking his cell phone for messages, absentmindedly reaching down and fiddling with his wool sock with his free hand.

Phoebe understood his apparent eagerness to distance himself from his last statement and hopefully change the subject entirely. She actually understood it all too well unfortunately, but she wasn't ready to expose her knowledge of Ronan's personal contribution to her experiences in captivity. Not yet. She needed his help.

And she needed leverage.

Ronan ran a hand through his thick hair as he lowered his cell phone again. "So ... anyways, I wanted to say thank you for the other night at the warehouse. You ... well, I appreciated that you stayed to fight."

"Did you think I was going abandon you?" Although she'd meant her tone to be playful, his back immediately went up.

"Well, I know you're a Wielder, trained or not, but—"

"I'm *teasing* you," she said quickly, sliding the plate of orange peels onto the bedside table. "I was glad to help. And anyway, I *told* you I could hold my own."

"That's another thing I'd like to speak to you about."

Phoebe chuckled a bit stiffly, trying to make light of a conversation she'd known was coming. "Oh ... *I bet*."

Ronan shifted back towards her. "I'll admit I had my doubts about your ability to fight the Wraiths, but clearly you've had some experience."

"They used to make us fight each other, and then we were also forced ... or mainly, *I* was also forced into situations where we fought *them* too ... the Wraiths."

Ronan ran his tongue over his bottom lip, then quietly said, "But you only killed the Wraiths ... right?"

Phoebe truly remembered little of the fights. Honestly, even right after they happened, she'd been unable to remember much. It had almost felt like, when her body was flooded with adrenaline, she'd operated on some sort of autopilot. Realistically, she knew this was almost classic dissociation. Either that, or perhaps just her own natural reaction to the free magics they'd infused her with.

"Wait! I just remembered something else!"

Ronan stiffened slightly. "*Oh?*"

"When we were fighting, sometimes they would release substances into the room with us ... like you do with your pouches."

"You didn't mention that in your interview."

Phoebe let out a loud huff. "Didn't I *just* say, 'I *just* remembered something else?'"

"Sorry, yes. Please continue."

Phoebe considered what might happen should she choose to just end the conversation there—if she were to look him dead in the eye and kindly ask him to "get the fuck out" of her room. Ronan would likely see that as proof she was every bit the lying piece of shit he already suspected her to be.

But she wasn't lying.

Though she'd fought often in captivity, her recollections really were blurry at best. Interestingly, though, she remembered everything about having fought alongside Ronan at the warehouse.

"Try to keep up, Ronan. You already know that my memories of fighting in captivity are blurry, probably because of how the magic works inside of me. But ..."

"But?"

"But when I fought with you ... my thoughts were clear."

"Despite the effects of my pouch."

"Or perhaps *because* of its effects?"

Ronan pondered this for a moment. "I'd really like for you to meet with Imogen."

For deeply personal reasons, Phoebe had resisted his initial request for this, the idea of being poked and prodded at again seeming like an absolute nightmare. That said, it couldn't be denied that she'd experienced "wild" or "free magics" much differently than the rest of the Wielders at the facility.

She nodded, still somewhat hesitant. "Alright."

Suddenly, a voice blared from her TV. "Let's welcome the Terrier Group into the ring!"

Phoebe clapped her hands together, soothed as always by an afternoon spent watching a show from Westminster. "These are my favourite! Let's watch."

Ronan shook his head with a wry smile. "You really do remind me of Dom."

Phoebe decided to take that as a compliment as Ronan settled down beside her. She even handed him an orange wedge, which he accepted gratefully.

Another week passed without much movement, yet Phoebe's days with the Druids were far from wasted. Christmas and New Year's arrived with little fanfare, though she enjoyed a delicious homecooked dinner on December 31 with Ronan, Amos, and Amelia, with the twins back at "home" briefly before setting out on another mission. She had a feeling that the overwhelmingly positive atmosphere—particularly from the normally brooding Druid doctor—had as much to do with the absence of Ian as with the holiday itself. He'd been sent on a mission south of the border along with several other local Druids she'd yet to meet.

"The Washington Knaves needed backup," Amelia had explained to Phoebe. "Usually, Amos and I go, but we're pretty burnt out and needed a few days off."

Phoebe was quickly learning that life in the Druidic Order came with little balance. She didn't mind this. Her journalism career had certainly been anything but balanced.

"I don't care much for resolutions," Amos said heartily, "but I think one of mine is to take more vacations."

"How does the Order handle scheduling? Like, for missions," Phoebe asked, sipping some very excellent red wine. Allegedly, it was Ronan's favourite low-budget pick. She guessed it was still an expensive bottle, far from accessible to the general populace.

"It depends on where each Druid is working from, whether it's with a regional group or if there's more movement. International espionage and such," Ronan said a little too casually, as though he knew this was fucking cool.

"Fancy," Phoebe said, uncorking a second bottle of his wine.

"And then each group will also have their own internal structure," he continued. "Members higher up in the Order are more likely to set their own schedules based on need."

"Meanwhile, plebs like us are still regularly told what to do," Amos said with a wink, gesturing towards Ronan.

Amos was definitely on the fuzzier side of drunk and far more outgoing than his naturally stoic demeanour. This was in stark contrast to his twin sister, who was bubblier and more approachable on the whole.

"Oh, come on, Amos," Amelia said. "You and I both know we need to do our time, just like everyone else." She looked at Phoebe then. "We mostly report to Lennie and sometimes Ronan."

"But Lennie isn't here," Phoebe said, quickly surmising that there really wasn't a strict organizational structure to the Order. It seemed like they worked intuitively more than anything else.

"Like I said earlier," Ronan said. "It depends on the dynamic and the need. As in, whatever's required of a Druid with their specific skillset. Because of my shared history with Lennie, working closely to help defeat Cassius, we still work together both logistically and as a team. Neither of us has worked with regional partners for quite some time, so we fill that role for each other."

Phoebe wondered if Ronan was hinting at something else. Was he actively looking for another partner or just the opposite? She couldn't quite tell.

"Do all Druids work with partners?" she asked. She'd always been someone with lots of questions, which was why journalism was such a natural fit, but she was also desperate to get her head around exactly how the Order worked so she could use it to her advantage.

Amos piped up then. "Not always. Ian, for example, prefers to join in on larger group missions, while Amelia and I like working together as a unit. It's what our parents did as well."

Phoebe had learned that Amos and Amelia's parents had been Druids, and they'd died in the line of duty. But their specific cause of death had never been shared. The mortality rate didn't seem particularly high within the Order, all things considered.

Phoebe shifted in her seat, offering her best listening stance to the three Druids across from her. "So, if you don't mind me asking, what's the average lifespan of members of the Order?" She knew this was a big question, but it was one she *needed* answered.

Ronan took a long breath.

"Well, it depends ..." he said, in near perfect unison with a sarcastic Phoebe, who'd even mirrored his tone—much to the amusement of the others. The group shared several breaths of laughter, sipping on wine and clearing empty plates to the side.

"Honestly, it seems to come down to the Druid," Amelia offered.

"Our parents were very keen to stick their noses into places they shouldn't."

Amos laughed. "Which is the same as us."

Amelia smiled wistfully. "I think Amos and I come from the kind of stock that thrives on the adrenaline of the mission ... the thrill of the hunt."

Ronan nodded. "Other Druids fulfill a more theoretical, spiritual role. My friend Peggy—the widow of Malcolm, whom I've already told you about—has made it her life's mission to bring as many new Druids into the Order as possible before she passes. And she's training a friend of mine, Thomas, to take over that role once she's gone. She found him as a 'Wielder in the wild,' as it were, and has been training him ever since."

Phoebe thought about how nice it might have been to be "found" by a grandmotherly Druid like that, rather than only discovering she could carry (and theoretically use) earth magic while being tortured by Wraiths. The magic within her began roiling angrily at this thought, and her head started to pound. Perhaps it was the red wine, though she suspected it was something else.

She feigned a yawn. "Ooh ... Will you look at the time. I think I'm going to bed."

The last thing Phoebe wanted was for her headache to escalate into a full-blown migraine or, worse, a nosebleed in front of everyone, drawing unwanted attention. She didn't feel like she could stomach much more of the conversation anyway ... let alone their pity.

The others bid her goodnight with a smile before returning to their conversation, though she couldn't help but sense Ronan's eyes on her back as she exited the kitchen.

South Surrey, B.C., 4:37 a.m.

In the early hours of the morning, two sleepless Wraiths stared perplexedly at the dead body they'd uncovered at the edge of the dance floor, which was currently dangling several inches from the ground, held tight against the wall by several thick tendrils. Beyond the now-barricaded doors, the last few drunken or drugged stragglers continued stumbling their way home from the warehouse, feeling even more bedraggled and depleted than was to be expected after a good night raving and ringing in the new year.

"Still warm," the first Wraith said, reaching out to touch the corpse; the temperature of the woman's exposed skin was a shock against his ancient fingertips. "What do you think happened to her?"

The second Wraith took a nervous step back. "What does it look like? The vines strangled her to death!"

And indeed, it appeared the rapidly growing plants had wrapped themselves around the woman's neck, ankles, and wrists, sucking her dry of magic ... and life. Purplish-blue bruises were already blossoming from where the vines had coiled around her pulse points like starved boa constrictors.

"Are the vines supposed to do that?"

Before the second Wraith could answer, a loud, magically enchanted voice boomed from somewhere across the warehouse, followed by scattered footsteps as the clean-up crew scurried from the scene like rats. *"Nigel! Arlo! Show me the body."*

News had travelled quickly through their ranks, up to their on-site superior. The pair turned slowly to face their caller, a Wraith named Arcturus. He was as gigantic as his name depicted—they hadn't called him the Bear for nothing.

The pair bowed low as he strode across the filthy dance floor.

"It's here," Nigel said, gesturing towards the wall of robust vines. "We were sweeping the floor when we found her."

Arlo blinked nervously between Nigel and Arcturus; Arlo was one of the many Wraiths tasked with cultivating and feeding the swiftly growing vines, though he had yet to be read in on their true purpose. As far as he knew, they were merely running an experiment to see if the plants could passively steal stored magic from unsuspecting Wielders; what they planned to do with the stolen magic had not yet been revealed.

"Is this ... an expected outcome?" he asked tentatively.

"Silence."

The Bear was by far the oldest Wraith on-site—and until recently, the most commanding—and rarely appeared on the main floor unless absolutely necessary.

That was until *he* had arrived ...

A little over one week ago, following a botched fish fertilizer delivery the morning after one of their biggest collection nights to date, their new leadership had arrived in a flurry of armoured vans and one slick black Mercedes Benz sedan. Soon, they were introduced to one of the most wrathful Wraiths in existence: *Malphas*. While he wasn't physically formidable, he bore such terrifying darkness that even the senior-most Wraiths cowered at the hem of his robes.

Allegedly, Malphas—who sometimes went by Mal to be discreet—had once worked under the late Sorcerer Cassius and, up until recently, had taken residence primarily in Europe. However, with the warring (and ever-growing) factions of Wraiths on the West Coast of North America, he'd relocated to be closer to the action ... and to take over every Wraith power centre he could find, along with his ginormous counterpart, Leviathan.

They were a terrifying duo who had long ago dubbed themselves *The Hounds of Hell*.

Their takeover targets had included everything from high-powered executives leading shadow corporations to hidden test facilities and, in one case, an offshore human trafficking operation that posed as a fishing company. The Hounds had taken each of them one by one with little pushback.

And those who had pushed back were long dead ...

Arcturus finally broke the silence. *"Are these flowers new?"*

Surrounding the body, white bell-shaped blossoms appeared to be slowly opening and closing in response to the magic they'd just siphoned from the raver's body. "We've seen the buds but have never seen the blossoms actually open before, and—"

Arcturus stilled Arlo with a gloved hand, his robes hanging limply around him.

Time passed slowly as the blossoms winked and unfurled in a sort of demented halo around the freshly dead woman.

And then, after several agonizing moments during which neither Arlo nor Nigel knew their fate at the hands of the notoriously tempestuous Wraith, the Bear slowly shook his head before procuring a cell phone from within his robes. His gloved hands shook as he prepared to deliver the unexpected news to his new boss.

It was remarkable to witness someone as formidable as Arcturus cower to anyone. Malphas and Leviathan had risen as kings among peasants.

CHAPTER 13

RONAN

AFTER A WEEK OF RELATIVE CALM FOLLOWING THE HOLIDAYS, Ronan and Phoebe found themselves embarking on another impromptu mission. Alone. It was uncommon to pull a new (and not fully approved) Druidic recruit into the field so early in their training, but with Ronan as senior as he was, and Phoebe being the exception to practically every rule, no one had even batted an eye when the suggestion that the pair accept the recon mission had arisen.

And in any case, Phoebe had (mostly) proven that she could hold her own in combat.

The mission's aim was to identify and confirm the movement of some of Cassius's old guard, who'd recently fallen off their radar. A small group of Canadian Druids, supported by Lennie's network, kept tabs on every Wraith establishment on the coast, with a special focus on those deemed the most "industrious."

And it was those particular bastards that had just gone AWOL.

The Wraiths in question had previously been stationed at Cassius's Vancouver mansion. Ronan knew this because he'd visited the locale on more than one occasion in memories he would have preferred to bury. The senior Wraiths had disappeared weeks ago, but Lennie's intelligence had finally detected movement from them on Vancouver Island, seemingly working out of Port Alberni and the remote coastal community of Bamfield.

An overly secretive Wraith was a dangerous Wraith.

The only trouble was that travelling to the Island would bring them into proximity of the facility where Phoebe had been held captive—or more precisely, the ruins that were left. Ronan had assured her they would steer well clear of the site, even showing her the exact route they would take (much to her annoyance). She assured him it would be fine and so, with Phoebe in tow, Ronan travelled to the Island.

"I realize I know very little about you," he said as they disembarked from the ferry.

"Join the club." She laughed awkwardly for a moment, then sighed. "Sometimes, I feel like I don't even know who I am anymore, let alone what I like. Is that weird?"

It wasn't weird at all. In fact, on more than one occasion, Ronan had wondered the same thing. How much of "before Phoebe" still existed—and if those parts would (or could) even return? And what might he have thought of her? He'd read some of her articles, forwarded to him by Lennie, but knew that her *journalistic* personality didn't necessarily reflect the person she'd been back then.

Everyone had work personas.

Besides, Ronan knew all too well what it was like to return from the brink of darkness with only a splintered sense of who you were. Not that he was about to share that with her.

"It's not weird at all," he said a little too easily. "You've been to hell and back. But what I was trying to say is that I hope we can, perhaps, get to know each other a little bit better over the course of this trip."

She snorted. "So, you want me as your permanent partner then?"

He bit back a smirk. "That remains to be seen."

Phoebe smiled, sipping her coffee and gazing out the window.

In truth, Ronan wasn't sure he even wanted to return to working in the field as he'd once done so often. Over the past two and a half years, his work had focused solely on tracking down any residual traces of his own mistakes. And for a time, he'd thought he was actually making some progress fulfilling the Otherworld's mission for him. Ronan had found and destroyed much of his remaining research records, and he, Lennie, and the Druids had otherwise been keeping the Wraiths in check. Or so they thought; unfortunately, discovering the exploded lab had definitely thrown a wrench into the gears.

Or rather ... *Phoebe* had.

He cleared his throat. "I should ask, though ... Are you feeling alright? Now that we're on Vancouver Island? I don't know how much time you actually spent outside of the facility once you—"

"I'm fine," she said quickly. "Don't worry about me ... *Please*."

"Grand," Ronan said, relieved. He activated his turn signal to merge his Range Rover onto the Island Highway, which would eventually lead them east to Port Alberni and then southwest to Bamfield. "I hope you're able to enjoy this excursion. The best missions usually involve a road trip and some time away from the city. You know?"

"Uh, no ... but I believe you."

"You don't like the outdoors?"

Phoebe set her coffee down absently in the console's cupholder, splattering several large drops of milky liquid near the gear shift. She wiped it with her sleeve, but her efforts only widened the spread. "Well, I certainly wouldn't classify myself as 'outdoorsy.' I've always preferred the city. Though I do like to escape to the woods occasionally and rent a cabin or something." Her reply arrived with quick but assured conviction, as though it was something that had always been true for her.

Ronan tried to ignore the mess she was making of the vehicle. "What about a smaller community? Or perhaps somewhere more rural?"

"Hmm ... maybe a smaller city, sure. But, honestly, it's one of my worst nightmares to live somewhere super isolated."

He realized he'd likely just misspoken and sighed. *For fuck's sake ... Of course, feeling trapped somewhere isolated would be unattractive to her after all she's been through.*

"I felt this way before captivity too if you're wondering," she said then, seemingly reading his mind. "I like to be able to just walk for my groceries, go to the pub, and visit the thrift shops, you know?"

Just then, the croissant Phoebe was eating crumbled all over the upholstery and tumbled down to the floor. She was starting to wear on Ronan's nerves. "Well," he said a bit tersely, "I hope you find this trip tolerable, at the very least."

"Relax, Druid. I'll vacuum everything up when we've finished our mission."

Ronan wasn't certain if he was imagining things, but the farther they drove into the wilderness, the more agitated Phoebe seemed to become, even though they were nowhere near the facility. He knew it must be difficult for her to return to the Island, despite his assurances. Or perhaps she was just growing increasingly uneasy after being trapped in a vehicle with him for hours on end.

Both seemed equally plausible.

They'd been bumping along a poorly kept gravel road for about thirty minutes when he asked her a question, and she finally snapped. "I'm not sure what more you want from me, Ronan! I've already told you! I don't remember almost *anything* from that day!"

He had been gently prodding to see if any memories were returning, and he'd merely asked her if she'd managed to recall anything else from the day of the explosion, specifically since their interview. This had been a colossal mistake.

What the fuck had he been thinking ...

Now, Phoebe was virtually vibrating in the seat next to him. He could feel the steady reverberation of her trapped magics lashing against the inexplicably magical container of her body. Ronan watched as Phoebe pulled her arms around herself as if doing so would be enough to keep the magic steady.

Then she started rocking ever so slightly in place, her eyes distant.

Instead of extending her any compassion or expressing thoughtful curiosity, Ronan fell back on habits he'd sworn long ago to shed: he grew immediately defensive in response to her explicit discomfort and clung to his own "rightness" like a lifeline.

He'd been triggered as well. "I'm allowed to have feelings about this, Phoebe," he retorted, nostrils flaring. "And I can just tell that you're keeping something from us about that day."

"You know what, Ronan? Fuck you! It wasn't you who was experimented on for months on end! Tortured! And then—"

He slammed on the brakes in the middle of the logging road as a burst of anger overtook him; he simply could not help himself. The Range Rover slipped and slid for several feet before coming to a stop dangerously close to the edge of the road. "You have no idea what I've been through, Phoebe! No clue what I've done to get to where I am today!"

When he looked over at her, she looked equally frightened of his erratic driving and sudden aggression. For several long moments, they just stared at each other, excess emotion making their breathing fast and unsteady.

Ronan put all his efforts into calming himself, breathing deeply and counting the sides of a square in his mind, just as Eunice had recommended that he do in circumstances such as this.

It never really worked.

Before he could compose himself, Phoebe began to speak again through gritted teeth. "So sorry to disappoint you, *Druid*, but I don't *care* about you ... *or* whatever bullshit you *think* you've been through."

Ronan hated when she called him "Druid" like that, as though it were a dirty word. He released a loud sigh and shifted the vehicle into drive once more.

They drove in silence for the remainder of the journey.

Ronan pulled his Range Rover into the motel's gravel parking lot just as dusk gave way to night. Across from him in the passenger seat, Phoebe was seemingly asleep, her arms crossed tightly over her chest and her jaw firmly set. How she'd ever managed to doze off like that on the rough logging roads, even if they hadn't argued so badly earlier, was a mystery to him. But what else was new?

The woman was infuriating on *so* many levels.

Still, not wanting to wake her, Ronan exited the vehicle as quietly as he could, gently closing his door before taking in his surroundings. The parking lot was quiet but for the audible buzz of a flickering fluorescent light from high above them on a nearby lamppost. He removed his compass from his pocket and found its arrow completely still. He was on the right path, though nothing about their current location felt extraordinary to him in any way—at least not in terms of any Wraith magic.

Ronan could still feel Phoebe's trapped magic pulsing nearby, though ... just as he could hear his own heartbeat.

Shaking off the increasingly concerning connection developing between them—and how easily he could detect the dark magic she carried inside—he moved confidently across the gravel, boots crunching loudly as he approached what he assumed to be the motel's main office, immediately noting that the lights inside were off. Taped to the door, he found a white paper envelope addressed to him:

Ronan G. & Guest – Room 13 (second floor, stairs to the left)

He removed the envelope from the door and ripped it open. Inside, he discovered a single key for Room 13 and groaned. Whoever worked the office had obviously taken off for the evening. So, how was he supposed to rectify the issue of there being only one guest room for the pair of them?

Ronan dialled Lennie using the satellite phone he'd been provided for the mission due to spotty cell service in coastal outposts like Bamfield.

"What's wrong?" Lennie asked groggily from England, where it was *very* early in the morning.

"The motel office is closed," Ronan said.

Lennie yawned. "Yes, but I asked them to leave you the key outside if you were later than closing. Is it not there? She assured me they would leave it—"

"Yes, they left it, Lennie! *One* key. As in *singular*."

"I know that, *Ronan*," Lennie said, a grouchy edge in his tone as he tried to rouse himself more fully. "There was only one room available. So, that's what I booked."

"What do you mean there was *only one room available?*" Ronan hissed. He could see Phoebe stirring in the passenger seat even as an inexplicable panic bloomed inside his chest. "Lennie, no ... *Please?*"

"I'm sorry, mate. It's all they had. Of course, you're always welcome to sleep in your vehicle." Lennie spoke to him slowly but firmly as though he were a petulant child.

Ronan and Phoebe had been driving for hours already, a trip that had culminated in a heated argument, followed by chilly silence that had continued until she'd eventually (and allegedly) fallen asleep. He was exhausted, and the last thing he wanted to do now was spend the night curled up uncomfortably in his vehicle. He wasn't like Domhnall, who could sleep practically anywhere. Ronan liked his comfort and always had ... but he also needed some space from Phoebe.

All he wanted now was to shut off some lights and close his eyes for a few hours, putting their argument firmly in the rear view.

The Druid doctor again ran his hand through his hair, which was now standing messily on end. "Are you absolutely certain, Lennie? It's just that—"

"Look, Ronan, you've said yourself that you're tired of keeping track of her between missions. I didn't think sharing the room would be an issue. There are two beds, and you're just there to sleep anyway, *aren't you?* ... And you'll be on your way again in the morning."

Ronan groaned, knowing that Lennie was insinuating something between him and Phoebe that he knew he could *never* let happen.

"*Fine*," he conceded at last, sounding sulky even to his own ears.

"Wonderful. Goodbye." Lennie hung up on Ronan without further ado.

On the one hand, the last thing Ronan wanted for this mission was to draw attention to themselves, and sharing a room with Phoebe could help mitigate that risk, at least in theory. But on the other hand—

"Were you able to get the keys before they closed?" Phoebe asked through a deep yawn.

Her voice immediately sent shivers up Ronan's spine. It was lower than usual ... rough with sleep.

"*Key*," he said, not bothering to hide his discomfort as he turned towards where she was now standing, illuminated ethereally in the flickering fluorescence overhead. "And yes, I did."

"Oh, okay ... Lead the way then." She'd already slung her sunflower-patterned backpack over her shoulder, clearly eager to get back to her slumber as soon as possible.

Ronan hastily grabbed his own bag before locking the SUV and directing her to the exterior stairwell at the left side of the building. Approaching the door of Room 13, Ronan's boots caught unexpectedly on the grippy mat in front of it, and somehow, the abrupt movement dislodged his glasses, which fell to the ground.

"For fuck's sake," he muttered, embarrassed.

Phoebe bent to reach for the glasses, but Ronan grabbed them first, keeping his eyes on the door handle and carefully avoiding her gaze. Straightening, he inserted the key and jiggled it several times before the door opened at last, revealing a simple corner suite.

With a single bed.

"You can't be serious," Ronan groaned. He was going to *kill* Lennie the next time he saw the bastard.

"That disgusted by me, are you?" Phoebe said a little *too* breezily. The way she'd kept her face hidden as she'd pushed past him into the room was likely cause for concern.

Had he offended her even more now? In that moment, at least, it certainly felt likely.

Ronan watched as she walked confidently across the motel room to its far side, where a chair had been placed beside the bed. She looked exhausted as she dropped her backpack unceremoniously to the floor, then sat down with a groan and started removing her boots.

He opened his mouth ineffectively several times before finally finding his voice, worried he'd inadvertently start another argument, which was the last thing they needed before trying to sleep.

"No, that's not it, Phoebe. The single bed's just ... sort of—"

"Inappropriate?" she said as she pulled her sweater over her head, momentarily revealing her soft stomach and bra before pulling her t-shirt back down.

Was she baiting him? If so, the woman was a goddamn menace.

"No. Just ... unprofessional," he said with narrowed eyes.

She snorted. "Has *anything* we've done together over the past two weeks been professional? Anyway, it'll be fine. I promise not to steal all the covers."

His cheeks flushed.

This sort of barbed and cleverly pointed banter was nothing new between them. However, at least for Ronan, something about sharing a bed with her following a heated argument was bringing an unexpectedly erotic edge to their situation.

Which was another tendency of his that he was trying to shake.

Phoebe didn't know this about him—and *never* would—but he'd always been partial to intense make-up sex following an argument. The more carnal, the better. His therapist had once suggested that he actually used that sort of sex as a way to sidestep difficult conversations and avoid accountability. If he could make his partner come multiple times in a row, they'd often forget all about his various fuck-ups.

At least for a time.

"Right. Well, it's been a long day for both of us," he said quickly before she could say anything else that might spark even more inappropriate thoughts and urges. "I'm going to have a shower before bed. If you leave me a pillow and blanket, I can sleep on the floor. Does that sound—"

"Always such a hero, our Dr. Gallagher," she said wryly, the fire from earlier still smouldering behind her sleepy gaze.

"No, it's just—"

"We both know *I'm* sure as shit not sleeping on the floor. You're right about that. But neither are you. We can both just sleep on the bed like grown-ups." Her fire receded slightly then, only to be replaced by an almost chilling grin. "Unless you think I'd actually want something *else* from you tonight?"

The harsh laugh she let out following her statement nettled Ronan far more than it should have. Was imagining being intimate with him really *so* laughable to her? He stared at her for a moment—unsure whether to be offended, hurt, or relieved—but he was careful to school his features, remaining impassive.

She didn't seem to notice his discomfort though, or perhaps, she simply didn't care. "I want to go pee before you shower, but I'll be super quick. Then you can take as long as you need ..."

His eyebrows raised sharply at whatever she was insinuating.

"Pardon me?" he demanded, offended now and fully ready to defend himself. Then his attention was diverted as his betraying cock began to stir, awoken from its slumber by the slightest grazing of her hand against his thigh as she passed him by, carrying her pyjama shorts with her into the washroom.

Ronan shook his head and told himself to get his shit together before Phoebe came back out. This entire scenario was ludicrous. They were there for work ... to track down the missing elder-Wraiths and find out what they were up to.

That was *it*.

Yes, Phoebe was gorgeous, but he knew that she was *not* for him. And besides, she'd basically just told him as much straight to his face.

"I'm too old for this," he muttered, busying himself with plugging in his various devices for the night.

True to her word, Phoebe was in and out of the bathroom within minutes. Ronan passed her with a simple nod before stepping into the bathroom himself, taking extra care *not* to make any physical contact.

Once inside, he unzipped his jeans to take a much-needed piss before his shower.

In truth, it'd been *far* too long since he'd been with a woman, which explained why he was so stirred up by the mere idea of sharing a room, let alone a bed, with Phoebe ... who just so happened to *be* a woman.

A gorgeous woman with the most incredible legs and ass I've ever seen ...

He made a mental note to amend this disparity as soon as they were back in Vancouver. He could ring up any one of *many* interested parties who would gladly spend a night with him. He knew his ego was saying this mostly to protect him, of course, but strangely, the idea of fucking some other woman—any woman *but* Phoebe—didn't seem to excite him as much as it should.

He groaned as he finished pissing, then looked down to the floor. Kicked into the corner beside the shower were the pants (and underwear, it seemed) that Phoebe had worn that day. He blew out a loud breath, exasperated with her messiness.

And yet, his balls still ached.

How on earth (or hell) was he going to be able to sleep soundly beside her if even her discarded underwear was turning him on? Had he become some sort of deranged animal? No. It *had* to be whatever strange magic was trapped within her. She was like a Siren, gorgeous and dangerous in equal measure.

The temptation she offered was clearly unnatural.

Ronan turned on the shower tap and tested the temperature. He was unsure whether a smoking-hot shower or an icy one would be best, given the circumstances. In the end, he opted for normal temperatures. He was fine. *This* was fine. He just needed to focus on the mission ahead.

Ronan stripped down and stepped carefully into the shower.

As the warm water streamed down his back, intrusive thoughts flooded in with it. Thoughts about Phoebe's naked body. And these weren't images he called up from the glimpses he'd had of her exposed body since meeting her, like when she'd been injured and under his care. No, these were imaginings based solely on the way she moved throughout the day, having seen her in combat against the Wraiths, and how badly he'd like to see her moving like that while riding his cock.

Giving in to that feeling for the moment, Ronan started rigorously pleasuring himself, frustrated with how hard she'd made him simply by existing. He justified what he was doing (and imagining) as something that would likely help him sleep better that night, even as he rested his free forearm on the wall above his head, locked his jaw for focus, and gave in to the pleasure.

Then there was a series of quick knocks at the door.

Fuck!

Was Phoebe *determined* to leave him in chronic *"sexistential"* agony? What could possibly be so important that she couldn't have waited another five minutes?

"Is it an emergency?" he asked, struggling to hide the heaviness of his breath as he shouted over the running water.

"Kind of ... I need back in. I have a nosebleed."

Looking down, Ronan was unsure how he'd be able to hide his

prodigious erection beneath the thin towels the motel provided. "*Ehm* ... One second!"

"Please, Ronan? I just need to grab a towel ... and you've locked the door."

Of course, I fucking locked the door! he thought to himself but resisted saying out loud as she actually sounded upset. For real.

Tossing back the shower curtain, he scrambled for a towel, leaving his embarrassment behind as he wrenched open the bathroom door to discover Phoebe standing there, drenched in her own blood from chin to chest.

"What *happened?*" he asked, alarmed at the sight of the bright red fluid pouring from her nose, which she was attempting to catch in a cupped hand and several sodden napkins from the motel room's poor excuse for a coffee bar.

She nearly retched into the extra towel that he held out to her, shoulders drooping as she hurried past him into the bathroom, gagging, and spat blood from the back of her throat into the sink. "I don't know, actually. I've been getting them more and more often over the past six months ... especially at night. Usually, I'm alone and can just sit in the shower until it stops ... But I'll just take the extra towels, and then you can carry on in here."

Ronan resisted scolding her for not seeking help for this sooner. Help from *him*. He knew then that he'd been wrong to put off more testing—physical and magical—before embarking on another mission with her.

He was an *idiot*.

He shook his head. "No. Come here. We'll stem the flow, and then we can get you all cleaned up. I have some things in my bag that will help." His towel slipped slightly to expose his upper pubic area as he helped her to sit down on the closed toilet seat. He hoped to the goddess she was too distracted by her nosebleed to notice his slowly ebbing erection beneath his thin towel. He was still considerably swollen. "Are you okay to wait here for a second?"

"I think so," she replied, her voice muffled as she tilted her head back.

The look of sheer relief on her face as he began caring for her was staggering. And bolstered by this, Ronan hustled to his medical bag and started rifling through its contents as quickly as he could, looking for his tincture of yarrow and witch hazel, before returning to the bathroom, towel still wrapped loosely around his waist.

"You can put some underwear on." She laughed. "I'm not dying."

Ronan chuckled, low and deep. "I know."

She closed her eyes for a fraction of a second before opening them and looking directly into his. "Thank you."

Between the Druidic herbs and modern medical implements, Phoebe's nosebleed slowed quickly, and they were soon tucked into bed ... side by side.

"I'm impressed you managed to keep the blood mostly to the bathroom," Ronan said.

"I wish I could say I've always been so adept at keeping blood off the carpet. In the past, I've made quite a mess."

He hated that this had become a regular occurrence for her. He knew all too well about chronic nosebleeds; he'd suffered from them himself through his youth. "How long has this been going on for?"

"Since I left the lab."

Ronan's body stiffened. "So, you didn't have them before?"

"Not really." She turned quietly to her side to face him. "Not like this, anyway. Not as far as I can remember. But I've been trying to figure out what causes them. I think ... It's nothing ..."

"You don't have to tell me if you don't want to," he said, surprised at both his patience and compassion in that moment. Usually, for him, his need to unearth answers trumped everything else. "But I do want to help you if you'll let me."

"I think they're linked to days when I'm forced to engage with the trapped magic more intensely. When my emotions—"

"Wait," Ronan said, puzzled. "We didn't fight anyone today. We were just in the car all ..." His voice trailed off as he looked into her eyes and felt a dawning realization sweep over him. "Oh ... fuck. I'm so sorry, Phoebe."

To Ronan's shock, she reached out and placed her hand gently on his cheek. "It's not your fault."

"But you just said—"

"*Shh* ..." she said, placing one long, warm finger over his lips.

His entire body shuddered, which did not go unnoticed. Even in the dim light, he could see her blush at his response.

"Phoebe ..." he rasped, his lips moving beneath the warm pads of her finger.

When she sighed and drew her hand back, Ronan instantly noticed the startling absence of her touch.

Her warmth.

"I don't think it has anything to do with the cause of the conflict," she said quietly then. "It's just ... whatever magic is trapped inside me seems to stir when I feel anything intensely, and then my physical body seems to suffer because of it. It's not always nosebleeds. Sometimes its migraines or dizzy spells. I never really know ... Coming out here, deeper into isolation, has been a bit of an adjustment for me."

Ronan's heart sank. What kind of life must it be to suffer (not so) minor medical crises whenever you felt extreme stress or emotion? "We'll get to the bottom of this, Phoebe. I promise."

What was it about this woman that caused him to make promises that he (likely) couldn't keep?

"Maybe," she said, smiling sadly.

Knowingly.

They lay in silence for a time, just close enough to feel the electricity passing between them. The *magic*. Ronan decided to let it slide. She didn't seem so dangerous at the moment.

"You're tired."

"Maybe ..." he grunted, guilty of having nearly drifted off.

She laughed then, sweet and low. "Goodnight, Ronan."

Despite his drowsiness, Ronan anticipated her unspoken need. "What's going to help you fall asleep?"

"What do you mean?"

He cleared his throat. "Well, the nosebleeds have to be pretty upsetting for you, even if you're used to handling them alone. And then having me witness it? That can't have been easy."

He thought back to his own frequent nosebleeds as a youth, knowing all too well the loneliness that went hand in hand with waiting for the bleeding to stop.

"Oh, yes. Well ... I don't need anything ... Your care has been more than enough."

Ronan's voice softened even more. "What's going to settle your soul enough to let you rest?"

Phoebe let out the smallest sigh. "It's silly."

"Nothing is too silly," he said, genuinely wishing to comfort her. He also liked that she seemed to be allowing him to do so.

After another long moment, she quietly said, "Could you rub my back?"

Those five words were possibly the most vulnerable thing anyone had ever said to him. "Of course, I can," he said in a choked whisper as his eyes grew unexpectedly damp. Thankfully, she was already turning away.

He placed his hand on her lower back and traced her vertebrae to her nape, then across the rest of her back. She stiffened. He paused for several beats before continuing. Ronan could feel her magic ... the chaos within her and the darkness that had been used to trap it inside her. He knew it all too well, having grown familiar with it while studying and experimenting on the Wraiths. It broke his heart that he knew of nothing that could yet fix her—whether from his vast medical and Druidic knowledge or even the *Codex Druidicus* and his time with Cassius.

Ronan spent an indiscernible amount of time gently rubbing her back—continuing with the soft motions and somehow soothing himself in turn. He watched as she shivered from his touch at first, trembling perhaps from the strangeness of it all. He might never fully know what happened to her in captivity, but he was confident that the Wraiths were not gentle. Eventually, she stilled though, her muscles relaxing as she drifted off into a soundless slumber. Finally, he slowed his movements, allowing his hand to come to rest briefly between her shoulder blades, enjoying her radiating warmth, before drawing it back towards himself and promptly falling asleep too.

CHAPTER 14
PHOEBE

PHOEBE AWOKE IN THEIR OCEANSIDE MOTEL ROOM ALONE, WITH THE clock reading 8:57 a.m.

Following her ill-timed nosebleed the night before, she'd drifted into a dreamless sleep with Ronan tenderly rubbing her back. At his initial touch, she'd battled the fear of having someone so close. She probably would have resisted his touch altogether if not for the rawness emanating from the typically stoic Druid and how it soothed her deep yearning for connection. He seemed to genuinely want to look after her ... just as she was. For the briefest instant, she allowed herself to imagine what it might be like going to bed beside Ronan every night.

To be cared for ... to be loved even.

It was hard to imagine that the same hands that had led the experiments responsible for her turmoil were also capable of delivering such tender, loving care. She thought of how his fingertips had felt, trailing along her back as he'd gently caressed her, and wondered what it might be like to allow him—or anyone, really—that sort of closeness again ...

But sadly, it seemed more of an impossibility the worse her symptoms became, even if (on occasion) his presence was as soothing as aloe to a sunburn. She couldn't let her warming feelings for the man—or the fledgling sense of physical safety she felt around him—cause either of them further distraction, coming between her and any chance of finding a cure.

Even if the Druids *were* keen to support her in removing the trapped magic, the fact was that Phoebe didn't trust them, or Ronan for that matter, as far as she could throw them. Who was to say they wouldn't turn on her as well? And where would that leave Ronan—someone who couldn't even be fully transparent with her about his involvement with Cassius?

She could *not* afford to get too close, no matter how nice it might have been.

Phoebe sat up and stretched. She was braless and wearing only minimal clothing, and she wondered if she should put more on. She'd seen Ronan's very noticeable erection when he'd opened the bathroom door last night and guessed he'd been just as physically bothered by her presence in their shared room as she was by his. Of course, that wasn't surprising. He was so deliciously reactive when it came to her, which was made all the better by the fact that he legitimately thought he was being smooth most of the time.

She could see right through him, though, which was *hilarious*.

No. The intimacy of falling asleep together now had Phoebe doubling down on her determination to protect herself from any deeper connection; it would only lead to further pain and heartache.

It was far better to focus on the job at hand. They were currently hours down a logging road beside the mighty Pacific Ocean. The Wraiths they were tracking were supposedly arriving any minute now, which led Phoebe to start questioning where Ronan had gotten off to.

A soft knock at the door announced his return from wherever that had been. Strangely, she hadn't worried even once about his absence. Instead, she'd just assumed he'd stepped out on some errand or perhaps had needed to make some phone calls. And she'd been correct.

He opened the door and stepped inside. “Oh, good! You’re up. When I left, you were dead to the world.” He juggled two coffees and several oily bags of what looked to be baked goods as he attempted to close the door behind him with his hip.

Phoebe sat up, not bothering to help the fumbling Druid, and instead just enjoying the sight of his struggle from across the motel room.

“I’ve grabbed us coffee and breakfast,” he said as the door finally latched. “I’m not sure what’s going to be open on the other side of the water.” He strode across the room and handed her a large coffee and a sausage roll.

“I’m sorry for sleeping in,” she said, though she wasn’t.

“You needed the rest.” He caught her gaze, and she noted a strange shadow behind his eyes. Was that sadness?

Phoebe’s stomach growled loudly then, and they both laughed. “And now I need food, apparently. Thanks for thinking of me.”

Ronan blinked as if he’d just remembered something and reached into his pocket, procuring a tired-looking naval orange. “It was slim pickings for fruit,” he said, suddenly busying himself with his phone, keeping his head down.

Touched (and surprised) that he remembered her love for oranges, Phoebe tucked into her breakfast, noticing that Ronan’s hair had slightly more curl than usual. The result of going to bed with wet hair, perhaps? He had been somewhat preoccupied with her care after all.

Suddenly overwhelmed by the pressure of their upcoming mission and their need to work together as a team, Phoebe couldn’t bear the thought of them harbouring any lingering tension before they even got underway. “Look, Ronan. About yesterday—”

“I shouldn’t have yelled at you on the drive yesterday,” he said simply. “That was inappropriate and disrespectful.” He cleared his throat. “We’re good. That is … if that’s what you were about to ask.”

In her mind, Ronan had already apologized to her with his tender actions the night before. Still, she appreciated his taking accountability; it was an attractive quality in a man.

“Thanks,” Phoebe said, her voice suddenly feeling small and shaky.

"It's been a long time since anyone touched me or ... or cared for me like that. What I'm trying to say is ... it helped."

Several beats passed before a seemingly awkward Ronan shifted and walked somewhat jerkily to her side of the bed. Then he crouched down, reaching for her hand even as she dropped her sausage roll onto the bed cover. She expected him to say something about how many germs were on that top sheet, but instead, he just drew her gaze to his.

"We may have our differences, Phoebe. But as long as ... well, as long as we're working together, I'll be here to care for you. No matter what."

The look in his eye reminded her of something familiar but just out of reach. Regardless, she felt her walls go up in response to his vulnerability. "Don't make promises you can't keep, Druid."

He looked like he was about to fight back, to defend his honour if nothing else, but instead, he slowly stood up, releasing a long breath from his nose. "We'll need to leave soon. Once you're done eating and getting dressed."

The sky outside was overcast and threatening to rain at any moment. Ronan wore a small grey hiking backpack, hiking boots, and a deep-green Gore-Tex raincoat, making him look like a West Coast nature enthusiast more than anything else. Meanwhile, Phoebe wore her Docs, black jeans, and a long black raincoat. She was leaving the rest of her things in the SUV, knowing that anything she might need, mission-wise, was already in Ronan's backpack.

This time, though, *she* was going to be properly armed as well.

"What's your preference for weapons?" he asked as they threw her things in the RV's back hatch.

"I've only ever really worked with short-range blades," she said. "Daggers and short swords. The Wraiths didn't use guns or anything. And they certainly didn't share their sickles with anyone."

"They hardly ever use guns. Their magic erodes the properties of gunpowder," he said knowingly. "It makes firearms too unpredictable." Ronan handed her a sheathed blade approximately seven inches long.

Phoebe looked curiously at the hilt, which was wrapped in dark black leather, and its pommel, which sported an esoteric-looking silver-sun detail.

It was *gorgeous*.

"Is this yours?" she asked curiously. It felt weighty in her hands, vibrating slightly.

"It's *yours*," he said, avoiding her gaze. "I called in a favour from someone I know. A Knave forge master in Washington State named Shereen."

Phoebe's heart skipped a beat. "Really? And she was able to make it this quickly!?"

"Yes. As I said, she's a master. And a friend. But after you stole my dagger—

"*Borrowed*—"

"After you *stole* my dagger at the warehouse," he continued, not letting her sidetrack him, "I figured you could probably use a blade of your own. More often than not, the Knaves create blades specific to the user ... You might have noticed that my dagger felt strange in your hands that night. Sort of ... *off?*"

Phoebe had, indeed, noticed that, though at the time, she'd chalked it up to the strangeness of the situation rather than the dagger itself. "So, then what's special about *this* blade that makes it fit *me* specifically?"

"Usually, Knave blades draw a certain awareness from the user ... a connection if you will. The stronger the connection, the more the blades sing."

"*Sing?*"

He waved this off. "I'll have one of the Knaves explain their process better to you someday. But when I explained to Shereen that you have volatile magics trapped inside of you, she had a different suggestion for how she might tailor a blade to your use."

Phoebe could sense that Ronan thought it might be a bad idea—read: *terrible*—to allow such a blade to connect to those volatile magics. And she didn't entirely disagree. "Oh?"

"Shereen figured that you needed a blade specific to your unique situation. I suspect it works as an external focal point, capable of discerning between the magic trapped within you and your own Wielding abilities, which you're still only just learning about. But it's also got something a bit ... *ehm* ... extra."

Phoebe was damn curious now. "Shall I assume you can't tell me exactly how she managed it? ... Trade secrets?"

Ronan had said the words "trade secrets" right along with her, though not as a question. They seemed to be getting in the habit of anticipating each other's words and rhythms.

Phoebe unsheathed the blade then and was immediately awestruck by the black swirling lines that coiled through the brilliantly silver metal. The central edge was slightly indented, with the blade's impossibly sharp edges gradually tapering to a smooth tip. "It's ..." She slowly shook her head, unsure of how to describe it.

"Powerful?" he offered, but Phoebe remained speechless.

Ronan pulled out his compass then and looked at it, his lips drawing upwards into a self-satisfied smirk as he shook his head. It was pointing *directly* at Phoebe and her blade. "If I were to guess, I'd say that she forged Wraith bits right into it."

Phoebe's jaw dropped. "How do you ... Wait. What *is* that?" She pointed the tip of her blade at his compass.

Ronan stiffened and checked his watch. "I'll tell you about it another time. Now, sheath your dagger. We need to go."

Despite his unprecedented thoughtfulness last night, it had taken very little time for Ronan to revert to his familiar rigid stoicism. As they walked downhill towards the commercial dock, he received a series of messages—from Lennie, she presumed—which had suddenly demanded his attention.

"So, you're at their beck and call twenty-four hours a day? Sounds a little ... *culty*."

Ronan grumbled, clearly not in the mood for playfulness now that they'd left the safe cocoon of their motel room. "More like they're at mine. I missed a bunch of stuff last night, and now this morning, they're practically crawling up my arse. I'll be done in a moment."

Apparently, he'd ignored his phone throughout the night.

She *almost* felt guilty about that. Her sudden-onset nosebleed and neediness had occupied his focus and kept him from his work. But then again, neither his time management skills nor his relationship with the other Druids was her problem.

"So, you're the cult *leader* then," she said teasingly.

He ignored her momentarily, but then one side of his mouth curved wickedly upwards. "If I'm a cult leader, then that makes you one of my disciples."

She snorted. "I haven't joined any cult."

"Not yet," he said knowingly.

"Not willingly," she huffed.

Phoebe had yet to determine if she even wanted to be a Druid, let alone whether she *should* be one. This weekend's mission was part of an ongoing decision-making process for her. It was hard to imagine what life would be like within the Order when she could barely imagine what tomorrow might look like. Until the trapped magic was released, she could think of little else, let alone start planning for it.

As if on cue, the magic started to churn violently in her belly, making her lurch slightly.

Thankfully, Ronan didn't notice. He was walking several steps ahead of her on the rather steep ramp down to the water. She'd learned this morning that they'd need to board a water taxi to cross to the far side of this inlet. There were no cars over there, which made her nervous about their ability to make a rapid escape if needed. But it also gave them a distinct advantage as they could be sneakier on foot and less likely to be noticed. This was only supposed to be a reconnaissance mission anyway.

Famous last words, she thought.

"You'd be a terrible cult leader," she said, verbally poking him as they boarded the small vessel: a small pontoon-style boat with beige plastic seats curving along its back, giving the impression of an empty hot tub floating on the water.

"What makes you say that?" Ronan followed her to the back and seated himself beside her. She could tell that he wanted to place his arm along the back of the seat behind her but was restraining himself.

Phoebe laughed. "What? Are you offended by that?"

"Not exactly," he said, running his hands through his salt-and-pepper hair, the action scattering tiny raindrops onto both his coat and hers as rain had recently begun to fall in a light mist. "I'm just curious what makes you so sure I wouldn't be an *excellent* cult leader."

Phoebe considered this question as the boat took off across the calm water. A few minutes later, they picked up another two travellers at a second dock along the way—research scientists if their red Helly Hansen one-piece rain suits were any indication. They chatted familiarly with the driver, paying no mind at all to Ronan and Phoebe, tucked into the back.

"I suppose I just don't think you're delusional enough," she said, watching as her flattery flickered across his face. "Though ... you've certainly got the ego for it."

"Really," he said evenly, his tone perfectly deadpan.

"*Really*. You're very self-assured. Not everyone sees that as a strength, but I do. Even if you *do* sometimes come across as stern or cold."

She meant this sincerely. Phoebe found his self-confidence appealing, if not exactly attractive, even if he *could* be a bit of a dick sometimes.

Ronan considered her for a moment. "Thanks, Phoebe."

They completed the crossing to the opposite shore without attracting any unwanted notice. Phoebe played the part of an uncomfortable, city-slicking girlfriend very well, because minus the girlfriend part, it was simply true. She hadn't been lying yesterday when she'd told Ronan that she preferred city life. Isolation set her teeth on edge. And the further they got from civilization, the more nervous she felt.

Ronan told the boat's operator that he'd surprised her with a getaway weekend on the coast but had not accounted for the fact one couldn't *drive* to their cabin rental. His girlfriend had not expected to be crossing the inlet in the rain, but they were "making the best of it," yada, yada, yada ...

Phoebe noted that the Druids routinely stretched the truth almost as much as (bad) journalists did.

"So, why *did* you join the Order?" Phoebe asked just before they stepped off the water taxi and onto the dry dock. Ronan handed the operator a crisp, red fifty-dollar bill and then followed her.

"I didn't think it was going to be *that* expensive," Phoebe whispered.

"It wasn't. I gave him a tip," Ronan said coolly. He waited until the boat took off before continuing. "Now, to answer your question, unlike you, I've known that I was able to Wield magic for most of my life."

Ronan shared the brass tacks of his childhood with her then. He'd been raised by his grandmother Sheila, a closeted Druid who had mostly used her magic to grow prize-winning tomatoes.

"Isn't that cheating?" Phoebe asked with a smirk.

He smiled fondly. "Depends who you ask. Though there was one particularly cool summer when nearly everyone was suspicious of her beefsteaks. It caused quite a stir."

Phoebe chuckled.

Ronan also shared that, when he was a teenager, he'd gotten into trouble using "bad magic" with some of his pals. They would routinely sneak off into the forest to do spells they found in his dead-beat grandfather's notebooks. Of course, that had only been until Sheila had found out and put an end to it, making him enlist in the military.

"How long were you in the army for?"

"Long enough to learn that it wasn't for me," he said sagely. "I applied to med school after that. A bit of a later start than some of my peers. I actually met Dom while I was at university in Cork, but I was already involved with the Druids again by then."

"You've lived a lot of life."

"That's not even the half it," he said. "What about you—"

"Look!" Phoebe said suddenly, pointing out an eagle circling high overhead.

It was good timing. She had no interest in unpacking her own backstory with Ronan. And thankfully, he seemed willing to oblige her.

Together, they walked in amicable silence down the strange car-less streets, occasionally pointing out interesting properties or other things of note to each other. She realized that this place wasn't actually *entirely* free of cars. Broken-down ones could be seen parked in a few places, in varying stages of disrepair. It had likely taken considerable effort to bring them over to this side of the inlet in the first place, let alone having to haul them back off once they died. As such, this had basically become an auto graveyard—though there seemed to be plenty of ATVs kicking around.

She realized then that she was enjoying herself. It was easy being with Ronan like this, focused on a mission while wandering new territory.

After about fifteen minutes of walking, Ronan announced that they'd reached their destination. They staked out the area under the cover of an unoccupied house with a large deck. This would give anyone watching the impression that they were supposed to be there, even while offering Phoebe and Ronan a perfect vantage point from which to watch the large dock beyond, which was allegedly where their targets were set to soon appear.

Lennie had done his research.

They sat down together in two unassuming and well-hidden Adirondack chairs as the magic in Phoebe began to roil. Though their conversation had soothed her for a time, she felt her anxiety start rising again as an acute awareness of just how isolated they were entered the foreground of her thoughts.

When she felt anxious, she needed control—something she assumed the Druid seated beside her was quite familiar with.

And so, much to her shame, Phoebe felt herself slipping (or more accurately, catapulting) back into old habits to keep herself safe. She had been in survival mode for many years even before her capture. In fact, she had first lost herself (and much of her integrity) to her work in order to cope with her own hyperactive brain and a penchant for problematic ruminations.

In her research on pick-up artists, she'd come across a tactic that used physical touch (or a specific movement) to program a particular (and often illicit) emotion into someone else's mind. An emotion they would learn to associate with the programmer. It had worked well for Phoebe on countless occasions, altering someone's behaviours or perceptions to her favour, and she suddenly found herself intensely curious to learn if Ronan would be susceptible to it too.

This was taking seduction to a whole other level.

"So, you've told me about the later years of your life back in Ireland," Phoebe said, shifting to face him. She kept her body soft and open, her hand brushing ever so slightly against the side of his arm as though she were just brushing away a piece of lint. "But what about before that mischief in the forest, when you were just a little boy? What did you want to be when you grew up?"

It took several seconds for Ronan to process this question, the brush of her fingers against his skin having elicited the desired effect. He put down his binoculars and looked at her strangely. "Why do you ask?"

She casually removed her hand. "Oh, I'm just curious. I think childhood dreams can tell you a lot about a person."

He remained skeptical. "You answer first."

"I wanted to be a novelist," she said, which was the truth. "Fantasy novels specifically ... stories you could escape into and forget daily life. And the more romantic, the better."

"But instead, you ended up in journalism," he said, with one eyebrow raised.

She laughed easily, leaning back and sunning her face during a rare break in the clouds. "Yes. So, I did become a writer, at least. Just not a novelist."

"It's never too late, you know," he offered lightly.

Phoebe sighed. "I don't feel like I'd be able to focus the way I used to. My brain is ... Well, everything's different since the experiments."

And since I got my head bashed in by Jordan Cole in his office before he assaulted me, she thought, then shrugged it away.

"Like ... it's hard for me to stare at a computer screen for a long time now without getting a migraine. That sort of thing. I'm not ... right." She tapped her right temple and made a silly face then, sticking out her tongue.

She could tell that Ronan was fighting an internal battle between offering her therapeutic suggestions and simply lending an ear. He opted for the latter. "Does that make you sad?"

Phoebe found herself genuinely surprised (and somewhat frustrated) that he'd taken the heartfelt route. He was proving more difficult to redirect than she'd expected—a journalist's worst nightmare. Earlier, he'd had no issue speaking about himself to her and been easily re-directed towards other topics. Now, though, he was being so ... *attentive*.

"Sad?" she echoed, considering it for a moment before shaking her head. "No, I don't think so. I mean, you can't be sad for long about the things you can't change." She shrugged then and added casually, "I've got plenty of other things to be sad about, anyways."

She hoped like hell that he wouldn't ask her what those things might be. Her list was far too long to want to get into right then.

"You could still write one, you know. A novel. There are writing alternatives you could try, like dictation and—"

"I know that," Phoebe said, pushing back and looking him directly in the eye. "You still haven't answered *my* question, though."

Ronan leaned back into the Adirondack, which put him in a fairly deep recline. It also reduced their ability to watch for Wraiths, which Phoebe found interesting, even as she joined him in the pose.

"Hmm ... I think very young me would have liked to be a dog trainer or something," he said at last, "but that's probably because I really wanted a dog, and my granny Sheila was wholly resistant to the idea." He chuckled at the memory, then mimicked his grandmother's voice and tone: *"There will be no flea-ridden beasts in your bed!"*

"Did you end up getting a dog in the end?" Phoebe asked softly, touching his arm again, this time pressing her fingertips against him for a moment longer than before.

"Eventually." Ronan seemed relaxed and unbothered by the touch. "A little border collie cross called Grace. She was my best friend," he said simply. "She was rescued from one of the many unfortunate farms across Ireland that didn't, and still don't, follow humane breeding and care practices for such a clever and high-energy breed. When she came home with me, she was emaciated, but I nursed her back to health, and we were best friends for nearly fifteen years. Her death remains one of the toughest moments in my living memory."

"I'm so sorry."

"I still miss her ... Is that silly?"

"Not silly at all," Phoebe said, openly gripping his arm this time, trying to subliminally assign her compassion and comfort to his validation and perceived need for her. "It sounds like it was maybe the first step in your medical journey. Nursing her back to health, and all that. What a gift she was to you."

Ronan smiled in fond reminiscence. "She really was."

"Would you like a dog now?" she asked, leaving her hand where it was.

He shrugged slightly. "I'd love to slow down enough to have a dog again ... someday."

"What kind?"

"*Ehm* ... It depends really."

Haunting voices started echoing near the shoreline then, causing the hair on the back of Phoebe's neck to stand up, even as Ronan whispered hoarsely, "Look!"

She let go of his arm and looked towards the dock.

CHAPTER 15

RONAN

BESIDE RONAN, PHOEBE'S BODY WENT FROM CASUAL TO ALERT IN A single heartbeat. Their shoulders pressed together as they jostled for better vantage points. Her warmth against him was steadying, just as her compassion towards him about his childhood dog had been only moments earlier.

And then, there they were: six fully robed and hooded Wraiths, stalking slowly towards the dock. Behind them, they dragged what appeared to be two black body bags.

"That's them, alright ... *Jesus, Mary, and Joseph,*" he muttered, reminding himself of Dom and immediately wishing that the great Celt had joined them on this mission. They could use him right about now.

This was serious.

On the wind, Ronan detected the Wraiths' putrid scent as it wafted towards their hiding place beyond the bushes on the deck. He'd been surrounded by the rank stench of Wraiths for the entirety of his time spent beneath Cassius's thumb, doing his experiments, and while he'd grown accustomed to it, interestingly enough, the reek had not decreased in intensity even as Ronan's body had slowly succumbed to the infection of their decaying magic—despite fighting against the actual transformation. In moments of clarity, he'd occasionally wondered if the Wraiths just lived with smelling awful, but it was more likely that they lost their sense of smell somewhere along the way, just as they lost their natural voices.

"Shit!" Phoebe said, gagging loudly. "Some of them must be super old."

"Shhh!" Ronan's laugh was bracketed by a full-body shudder. "Julia used to get so sick when she smelled the old ones that she'd actually vomit."

"I don't doubt it. This is"—she gagged violently—"something else. I don't remember it being *this* bad in captivity."

Ronan smirked at her with a sidelong look. "You're telling me Nyx didn't smell bad up close? You *were* very much 'up his business,' after all."

"No. Not like this." She glared at him through her long lashes. "Asshole."

"You can sometimes guess their age by how they dress," he said, ignoring her barb. "Nyx is young compared to these ones ... He still showed his face."

"I *know* that. Remember? I used to live with them?"

"Of course."

A huge black Zodiac, at *least* eight metres long and not dissimilar to those used by police on Canadian lakes during boating season, approached the dock where the six Wraiths were awaiting its arrival, milling about like horseflies at a beach picnic. Two Wraiths were on board, manning the vessel. When they got close to shore, the one steering turned it around slowly and backed up alongside the dock, the deep keel scraping softly against the ground in the shallow waters of low tide. The engines shut off, and the two newly arrived Wraiths disembarked to join the other six.

Ronan sighed darkly. He and Phoebe were now outnumbered four to one.

Not the best odds.

He picked up his satellite phone and tried to get through to Lennie, but it didn't seem to be working. *Strange.* "Looks like we're on our own."

"Oh good. Just how I like it," she said wryly.

Together, they left their hiding place on the deck, crept past the last outcropping of bushes, and headed towards the water, keeping low as they rounded several large boulders to approach the dock from its northern side, keeping it between them and the Zodiac.

Ronan was leading the way. He silently signalled to Phoebe that they would *cross* the short (though completely exposed) rocky stretch next in order to hide *beneath* the dock.

Thank the goddess the tide's out, he thought, not fancying the idea of swimming today. Phoebe frowned in what must have been confusion as, the next moment, she quickly strode past him, only to be stopped short by his hand, which shot out and grabbed her arm almost violently—definitely too hard, as Phoebe released a whimper, which he felt deep within his pelvis.

"Wait!" he whispered fiercely, then quickly reached inside his jacket and procured a small linen pouch, which he held out to her. "To silence our footsteps."

They'd come this far, after all. They might as well try to listen to what the bastards were going on about.

She stared at the pouch, her eyes widening. "Is it safe ... *for me?*"

"I believe so. It's not mood altering, if that's what you're wondering, or cognitively disruptive. It'll just dampen any sounds."

"Alright," she mumbled, understandably hesitant.

Thanks to this Druidic implement and a bit of luck—and probably also the muffling hoods that the Wraiths wore as they hissed to each other in their strange, deadened voices—Ronan and Phoebe managed to crunch their way across the rocks to the exposed pilings beneath the dock without being heard.

Then they crouched down together beneath it to listen.

"How many survived the most recent trial?" one Wraith asked.

"Three," another grunted. *"These two were weaker than the others. We'll throw them overboard once we're out in deep water."*

Their voices sounded even more distorted than usual as they echoed across the gently lapping water.

"There's two more on the ship," said a third Wraith. *"We can replace these ones and bring them back with us."*

And then a terrifying hiss rent the air. *"They were supposed to arrive intact!"*

Ronan noticed Phoebe's breath slow as her trapped magic began to thrum. He could feel it in his chest as clearly as if he were standing beside a loudspeaker, vibrating wildly with a pulsing beat.

"Are you alright?" he whispered.

"Never better." She turned to look at him with a dark gleam in her eyes that had him stepping back a bit.

He swallowed hard. "Good."

Phoebe reserved the right to get her vengeance wherever she could. She deserved it. Thankfully, there was an unspoken agreement among the generally very diplomatic Druidic Order: if a kill or raid was deeply personal to one of their number, the others would do everything they could to make it happen—"it" being the successful deliverance of violent and just retribution.

This obviously flew in the face of everything they stood for, but the fact remained that the Druids' best battles occurred when they harnessed their anger with a sense of justice and empowerment. The Druids might be essentially ethical, but they also didn't shy away from a bit of bloodletting. A caveat to all of that, though, was a consideration of the odds. Today, the odds were definitely not in their favour.

Phoebe crept closer to the edge of their hiding place, leaving Ronan no choice but to follow.

"*Phoebe*," he hissed. "They'll *see* you!"

She ignored him.

Ronan pulled out yet another pouch and shook a portion of its contents onto Phoebe, and then the rest onto himself, sending up the subtle scent of cardamom and black pepper.

Up ahead of him, Phoebe paused and sniffed the air, her shoulders stiffening. Then she turned slowly and looked at Ronan as he caught up to her.

"Don't worry. This one doesn't elicit any sort of feelings either. It just keeps the Wraiths from noticing us."

"How?" she asked in a low voice, and he noticed her pupils were fully dilated.

Ronan realized then that they were officially way past overdue for their meeting with Imogen. "I can't explain it here, but I doubt you'll be affected." He swallowed hard again. "Much."

Between her concerns about the pouches and her own system's agitation around the Wraiths—both neurological and magical—Phoebe seemed to be feeling a bit ... *off*.

"That's not the same as being sure, Ronan."

"It basically camouflages us. That's all."

So far, neither of the pouches he'd selected were intended to be mind-altering, merely illusionary.

Without warning, two body bags were tossed unceremoniously from the deck above them and into the Zodiac, one after the other, each of them landing with a dull and heart-wrenching thump in front of the last row of seats. The Wraiths then started making their way down the ramp and climbing into the front of the boat.

Ronan listened to their shuffling footsteps for a few moments before suddenly looking around, his eyes widening in concern and confusion. Phoebe was no longer at his side. For a moment, he thought that his new batch of magic was working too well, affecting him as well as the Wraiths, but then he saw a flash of blonde hair near the water's edge as Phoebe leapt up and into the very back of the Zodiac, quickly covering herself with a loose black tarp.

Instinct took over then, and Ronan rushed to follow her, his heart pounding in his chest, narrowly avoiding being seen by a cloaked Wraith who jumped directly into the centre of the Zodiac even as he was climbing into the back. Breathing heavily and thanking the Goddess once again, he quickly joined Phoebe beneath the tarp.

The Zodiac's twin engines were located directly behind their hiding place, and once they were powered up again, with the vessel pulling away from the dock, their volume allowed Ronan to hiss fairly loudly into Phoebe's ear without concern of being overheard, even if the camouflaging magic should fail suddenly, "What the fuck do you think you're doing?!"

"They said there's a ship with more captives! I can't just leave them."

If Phoebe wanted to continue working with the Druidic Order, she definitely had much more to learn about the Order's methods. Of course, at this rate, this mission might end up being her last.

"You're no help to them *or* us if you're *dead!*" Ronan spat, quickly realizing that this entire mission had been sheer lunacy on his part. What had been intended as a training and recon expedition was swiftly becoming risky as hell. She had just placed both of them in grave danger, and he wasn't willing to die for Phoebe's impulsive antics. Not today.

"You didn't have to come," she said, her tone resigned yet somehow focused as well. The magic inside her seemed to be pulsing now ... thrumming with intention.

Squirming closer to her as the boat picked up speed and made the tarp ripple above him, he gripped it tight to keep it still as he wrapped her up in a tarp-laden bearhug. "We're partners ... I'm not going to just abandon you."

"So, we *are* partners," Phoebe said, the heat of her breath tickling his neck and sending a shiver running up his spine.

He had to hand it to her. She was just brave and stupid enough to fit in perfectly with the rest of the Order's members. Not that he was going to tell her that, of course, and certainly not while they were travelling as stowaways on a Wraith-driven boat to some unknown destination off the coast of eastern Vancouver Island.

"How long do the effects of this pouch last? The one that keeps them from noticing us—"

"Thirty minutes, more or less." He knew it was likely more like sixty, but he didn't want to put any ideas into her head.

Phoebe shifted uncomfortably, her knee digging into his thigh. "It really doesn't seem to be an exact art."

"Maybe if we *survive* this," he said through gritted teeth as they rearranged their limbs, "you can learn more about the pouches and devise methods for perfecting them yourself."

"Science has never been my strong suit."

"Then you might consider keeping your criticisms to yourself," he hissed, his lips grazing the soft skin at her jawline.

She snorted. "Anyway, if the boat doesn't stop before that time is up, I say we just hop up, kill the bastards, and drive ourselves back to shore."

"You're pretty confident in our ability to take down eight Wraiths."

"I know my strengths," she said, her self-assurance stirring something within him. Ronan liked that she was confident, but her impulsivity was a problem. It may have been bravado, but he wondered what kind of Wielder she would truly be once the trapped magic inside her was finally released.

Assuming that it *could* be.

Still, he felt certain that she'd be able to kick his ass someday—with the right training, of course.

As the Zodiac's motors slowed, jostling their bodies together under the tarp, Ronan braced himself, forming a protective cage around Phoebe's curled body with his own, inadvertently burying his face in her hair and finding the scent of her utterly intoxicating.

Given the choice, this wouldn't be the worst place to die.

Then he remembered the two dead and discarded bodies that lay just beyond the row of seats in front of them. He knew that they had to be freshly dead, as there was no smell of human decay coming from them.

The aged Wraiths began to talk again in their eerie timbre—the sound of decaying tongues and vocal cords, only functional at all because of retained magic. During the time Ronan had spent under Cassius's thumb, when he had the rare opportunity to conduct his own chosen work, he'd once been able to dissect several of the younger Wraiths' mouths and throats before they'd disintegrated entirely.

It had been fascinating.

Distant and less magically affected voices called out from somewhere far above them then. It seemed they had arrived at the referenced ship left anchored far offshore. Judging by the volume of the screeching seagulls overhead, it was likely a fishing trawler.

"Stay still until they're gone." His voice was so low that it was barely audible. "Then we can follow."

"You mean we're *not* going to steal the Zodiac and head straight back?"

Ronan let out a sigh, knowing that cooler minds likely *would* choose that option. But something about being hidden beneath a tarp in the back of a Zodiac in the cold, dark Pacific Ocean had ignited a fire in him. Initially, he'd been angry with Phoebe, of course, and really would have just turned the thing around and headed back to shore. Now, though, he felt ... *invigorated.*

"We've come this far," he said quietly. "Why don't we have a little poke around, and *then* steal the boat and drive straight back."

He could feel Phoebe's body shake as she silently laughed beneath him.

She was all in.

Once the Zodiac reached its destination, Ronan and Phoebe didn't have to stay hidden for long. The Wraiths quickly tossed the two dead bodies overboard—with Ronan's silent blessing going with them—then climbed into the ship's stern. Ronan checked the time. They had maybe ten or fifteen minutes more of magical camouflage before they'd need to come up with a different plan, and another ten before they would officially be in deep shit.

He'd only brought so many pouches with them; the ones he already used had contained rare ingredients and took ages to prepare. Phoebe had no idea he'd just dusted them with products worth tens of thousands if sold in the magical world. If they managed to make it out alive today, he'd need to do a better job of clarifying such details.

He finally flipped the tarp back and pushed himself up from the cold deck of the Zodiac.

Phoebe rose to her feet, her cheeks red and her hair tousled. "That was fun."

"Indeed," Ronan said, smirking.

The Zodiac appeared securely tied to the new vessel. He had been correct in assuming that it was an active fishing trawler. At about twenty-five metres long, it wasn't massive (as far as trawlers were considered) but large enough to remain on the water for extended periods. He took note of the full-displacement hull, with its deep storage capacity visible from their vantage on the water—perfect for storing food, fuel, caught fish ... or *people*.

"Who goes first?" Phoebe asked.

"Me." He reached into his pocket for the satellite phone and handed it to her. Luckily, it had been enclosed in a waterproof case before they'd first set out on this trip. "If anything goes wrong or if something happens to me, you get your ass back to this boat and get to shore. Then call Lennie and get yourself out of here."

A strange look crossed her face for a moment. Then she nodded slowly in agreement and stowed the phone safely in her jacket pocket. "Alright."

"Good. Let's go."

The only way aboard the trawler seemed to be via its largely rusted-out stern ramp—a chute designed for dragging large fishing nets aboard. Ronan climbed up carefully, noting the general disrepair of the vessel, with Phoebe following noiselessly behind him, the residual magic from the first pouch still silencing their footsteps.

Ronan slowed as they neared the working deck, listening for any disturbances. He heard nothing, but he knew that the Wraiths also had methods for controlling how their environments were perceived. Just because he couldn't hear anyone didn't mean they weren't there.

He popped his head up above the stern to check and found the deck empty. The Wraiths must have gone down below almost immediately upon boarding, or perhaps up to the pilot house.

"They must be inside," he whispered. The cries of the gulls were even louder from this vantage point, with the remnants of an earlier catch still holding their attention, the stink of fish guts lingering despite the presence of the Wraiths.

"Do you think these guys are tied to the plant-growing operation?" she asked. "Like ... with the fish fertilizer?"

"I doubt it," he said seriously. "Feels more like a coincidence to me."

Phoebe's expression was skeptical, her journalistic brain always primed to connect such dots. "The two groups couldn't be working together?"

He shrugged a bit vaguely. "Not since Cassius's demise. I mean, different groups *do* work together sometimes, but we don't think these ones are—Lennie's found no connection between the groups whatsoever. And unlike Nyx or the warehouse Wraiths, *these* bastards are old, like ... three or four hundred years old. They were forged under *his* rule, which means they still wouldn't take kindly to young upstarts making moves like that. Realistically, they'd be more likely to kill the plant-growing group than join them."

Ronan knew this all too well. The ancient ones had always given him the most trouble during his experiments. They had been Cassius's biggest threats and had never willingly sacrificed themselves to be harvested for the killing smoke like so many others had.

Phoebe peered around nervously, seemingly scanning the nets, ropes, and assorted fishing paraphernalia littering the deck ... and finding no other humans (or Wraiths) present. "Is it just me, or is it *super* weird there's no one around out here?"

"It is," Ronan said and started sneaking forward. "Let's poke around a bit."

Looking up, he noted that the door to the pilot house was shut tight. Inside, he assumed, at least one or two Wraiths were navigating the ship, with possibly several more on the top deck. This was no small vessel and had plenty of room for an entire legion of Wraiths to hide in.

As a rule, Ronan always assumed that there was a Wraith present in every hidey hole. And as the trawler was bigger than he'd anticipated, he was beginning to think they'd miscalculated their odds.

"Should we take a look inside?" Phoebe said, gesturing towards a door that led to the boat's interior.

He checked his watch. They had another ten minutes, at most, before they would become easily detectable once again. "Yes, but quickly. I'm guessing they're in the main saloon."

"Daggers out?"

"*Daggers out.*" He unsheathed his blade and looked at it for a moment. Long and light, it was one of his favourites and especially effective in slicing through thick cloaks and straight to the heart of things.

He reached out for the door handle. Turning it carefully, he opened the door, allowing them to make out several magically affected voices speaking from somewhere below them.

Together, they crept down several steps and started looking around. There was a large communal space to their left, fully equipped with couches and several tables, both littered with stacks of yellowed papers and battered tomes. To their right was a galley. Of course, Wraiths didn't exactly eat, so the communal kitchen had been relegated to some sort of storage space to contain still more evidence of their misdoings.

Ronan noted several rusted and bloodied knives in the galley sink, along with broken glass and empty vials, and realized that the aged Wraiths must be "living" on board.

Suddenly, the voices grew louder, emanating from a still deeper level of the fishing vessel.

"Down there," Phoebe mouthed, pointing her dagger towards the entrance of another stairwell.

Ronan tried (and failed) to ignore how much the thrill of this mission with Phoebe was arousing him. Suddenly realizing he was a very disturbed man but riding the feeling nonetheless, he led the way down the steep flight of stairs as the voices grew progressively louder.

At the back of the next level down was a large engine room, and opposite it, towards the front of the ship, was a narrow passageway lined with cabins, along with what Ronan assumed to be an access hatch for the trawler's blast freezers. The ceiling was quite low, but they managed to duck their heads and creep forward without too much difficulty.

A moment later, they were able to pinpoint their targets' location, in a cabin further down the hall, from the sound of their voices, one of which sounded unimpressed to say the least.

"You mean to tell me that these *two have died as well?"* one of them growled furiously. *"That we have lost* four *potentials today!?"*

"I told you this was folly!" a second voice scoffed. *"We* cannot *create more Wraiths without the ritual!"*

The rage in the first voice only deepened in response. *"That 'ritual' was a lie! ... A lie created by Cassius in order to keep our numbers more manageable for his own purposes! And now, just like him, that lie is dead!"*

Ronan's mouth went dry, and his heart started beating out a violent staccato against his ribs. It couldn't be true. Could it? Surely, the second speaker had been right to dismiss such a possibility. If they ever managed to start creating Wraiths *without* the ritual ... He shuddered at the thought.

"But it's not working!" a third voice hissed.

"It will work. We will have the numbers."

Ronan looked to his right, and in another dim cabin nearby, he spotted the bodies of two more dead women, which had been unceremoniously discarded atop a disgusting-looking bed. Unfortunately, Phoebe noticed the corpses at the same moment he did and gasped loudly. It was never easy to see a dead body, let alone the bodies of two young women—girls, really—who'd clearly been manipulated and damaged beyond repair.

He shushed her quickly. "Shhh! We only have so long before the pouch wears—"

"What was that?" hissed a menacing voice.

Ronan grabbed Phoebe's sleeve, intending to pull her backwards and out of the narrow passageway entirely. "We have to go."

She, however, remained rooted to the spot, staring wildly at the broken women. "This ... this has to stop."

Ronan pulled at her arm again, this time more forcefully. "I agree, but we're outnumbered and isolated! We need to get off this fucking boat! Now!"

She either didn't hear him or didn't care. Instead, she strode forward down the passageway to where the Wraiths were gathered—all eight of them.

"You!" the closest Wraith cried, spying Phoebe and lunging for her instantly; clearly, the pouch's magic had now worn off.

In the narrow quarters, it was impossible to discern who and what was where, leaving Ronan standing helplessly behind her for the moment. As the beast reached for her, Phoebe dropped low and forced her dagger upward with two hands. Ronan, meanwhile, delivered a punishing blow to the same Wraith from over her shoulder.

The Wraith collapsed in a billowing pile of filthy black linen, disintegrating almost immediately into ashes on the floor. *That fucker was old.*

"We have to get above deck," Ronan shouted, and this time, she listened to him.

Together, they sprinted back up the stairs and rushed through the saloon towards the working deck, Phoebe close on Ronan's heels.

Suddenly, she slid to a stop in front of a pile of papers and began frantically grabbing them up.

"We have to get out of here!" Ronan yelled. "There's no time!"

"But we came all the way here!" she said, her eyes wide. "There could be useful—"

A flash of red-hot Wraith magic streaked towards them from across the saloon, slamming into one of the stacks of papers and igniting it. Phoebe dropped the stack she was holding to the worn carpet at her feet and leapt towards Ronan near the exterior door, even as the carpet burst into flames.

"I didn't know they could do *that!*" she shouted, looking over her shoulder as she slid out onto the deck. The weather had turned on them, with the earlier misty drizzle having worsened into heavy rain now being whipped around by a violent wind that was growing stronger by the minute.

"They can do lots of things!" Ronan yelled back, almost panting for breath as he backed hurriedly away from the saloon door, trying to cover Phoebe. "But I'm not keen to see any of them right now."

The seven remaining Wraiths charged out from a different entrance then, their sickles raised and dark magic crackling.

"There's nowhere to go," said a massive and sneering Wraith, its voice carrying strangely on the gusting wind. *"You're trapped here."*

"Oh gee, thanks, Captain Obvious," Phoebe quipped, bracing

herself on deck with her feet spread wide and her dagger held out in front of her.

Ronan didn't know if she was really this fearless or just stoking herself up, but either way, he liked it.

Fighting back to back, the next several moments were just a blur of blades, cloaks, and death for Ronan and Phoebe. Together, they efficiently dispatched four of the Wraiths, Ronan's finely honed magic crackling through him in a strange sort of harmony with the wild vibration of Phoebe's magic at his back. She might not be an effective Wielder yet, but she was one hell of a fighter.

"To your left!" she shouted.

Ronan's dagger clattered across the deck as a heavy blow suddenly knocked him sideways into a pile of nets. If he were to get tangled in them, he knew that he'd be *royally* fucked.

Phoebe was engaged in her own battle, this time with an uncloaked Wraith—the ship's captain, presumably—leaving Ronan on his own with the giant Wraith who'd knocked him down now looming menacingly over him.

"I remember you," the Wraith said then, grinding his heavy boot into Ronan's chest and pinning him down. *"Oh yes. I know exactly who* you *are ... Druid doctor."*

Ronan had no access to his backpack, which was trapped below him at present, and no weapons within reach. He tried to resource whatever magic he could from within himself, to at least free himself from the pressure of the ancient Wraith's boot on his chest, but it was no use. The bastard was ancient and powerful as hell.

"Funny," Ronan said, gasping for air as he attempted to roll out from under the Wraith's weight. "I don't remember you at all."

"You will now!" the Wraith snarled, grinning hideously at him. *"I serve the Hounds of Hell! And soon they will raise an army of us so vast, no Wielder will remain who is not one of us."*

Ronan felt the air leaving his lungs, and his veins popping out in his neck, as he desperately searched the area around himself with his hands, desperate to find something with which he might strike back.

"Ronan!" Phoebe screamed, getting his attention as she kicked a loose metal rod in his direction—a pipe of sorts.

Images of the violently ruined bodies in the cabin below rushed back through his mind, kindling his rage, as his reaching fingers wrapped around the pipe. Then drawing on every ounce of fury, and all the sourced magic left within him, he managed to dislodge the Wraith's foot and knock him away. Then he launched himself sharply upwards in a rising handspring, flying up from his back and onto his feet, and faced off with the Wraith once again, the metal pipe braced firmly in a two-handed grip.

Any concerns he'd had about his own survival vanished. He was going to kill this fucker dead, no matter the cost. Any Wraith that was hellbent on forcing Wielders into the darkness with them could not be suffered to live even a moment longer. He bared his teeth and prepared to attack.

His adversary seemed unimpressed. *"The time of the Wraith has come—"*

Ronan leapt forward in a high arc, raising the pipe high above his head and ramming the end of it violently into the spot where he presumed the Wraith's neck to be. Then using his own weight and momentum as leverage, he yanked down on it, wrenching it away even as his feet landed back on the deck.

The Wraith wailed loudly.

Phoebe arrived at his side then, holding his dagger out to him. "I assume you want this kill." Her eyes were fully black now with the exhilaration of battle.

"I do," Ronan said quietly as he accepted the weapon and finished the job.

Seconds later, his huge opponent disintegrated into dust at his feet, just as rolling black smoke started billowing heavily outwards from the now-blazing trawler's interior. Then from the top deck, several more Wraiths appeared, stepping outside and directly into the heightening squall, their robes flailing wildly in the driving wind and rain, their hoods yanked roughly out of place to expose the ancient horrors beneath.

"Let's go!" Ronan shouted over the gale-force winds, grabbing Phoebe by the hand and rushing with her towards the vessel's stern.

It was now or never. They needed to make their escape.

CHAPTER 16
RONAN

"*Fuck!*"

The Zodiac was their only means of escape, assuming they didn't want to swim the countless kilometres back to land in the ice-cold Pacific. But even though it had once been firmly affixed to the trawler's side, the mooring lines had since come undone in the squall.

Ronan peered down into the frigid water, knowing he would have to jump in but hesitating. Exposure alone would kill them if they didn't successfully recapture the smaller boat quickly. The ocean was churning violently; staying on board and battling things out on the trawler might have actually offered them better odds of survival if not for the fact that it was currently ablaze.

Without warning, Phoebe leaped from the trawler into the icy water. Ronan watched in horror as she (somehow) managed the sudden shocking cold and immediately started swimming towards the Zodiac. He didn't think he breathed once as he watched her struggle along that choppy surface above unfathomable depths and finally haul herself on board the Zodiac with considerable effort. Then she quickly started its engine.

For a split second, Ronan thought she meant to leave him behind.

Then she started frantically signalling for him to jump as well, shouting unheard words until he realized what she was pointing at—behind him, three hooded Wraiths were now approaching from previously unnoticed hidey-holes (as predicted). At any moment, they would be crawling all over him like sand fleas on a beach carcass.

It seemed that he and Phoebe had severely underestimated how many Wraiths were on this boat.

Phoebe steered the Zodiac towards him, and Ronan knew the time for hesitation had passed. He could afford it no longer. He jumped feet-first into the icy water, the sudden submersion beyond cold. The shocking impact was painful and robbed him of his breath even after he bobbed up to the surface. Stunned and gasping for air, he floated there for several seconds, unable to fathom how Phoebe had managed to jump in the water and swim towards the boat without becoming disoriented.

Eventually, he felt two hands gripping him by the armpits and trying to haul him up onto the Zodiac's deck.

"We need to g-go!" she screamed into his ear, her voice breaking slightly. "Help me!"

Ronan finally came to his senses and kicked his legs to help.

Once she'd managed to get him into the boat, she shook her head and rested her hands heavily on her knees.

Still feeling breathless, he looked up at her. "You ... are an idiot."

"I could say the same for you," she said, her wet hair sticking limply to the sides of her face. "We need to get to dry land."

"Do you know how to drive one of these?"

"I'll figure it out."

Despite his better judgement, Ronan believed her.

They had been back on dry land and heading back down the gravel logging road for about forty-five minutes before Ronan finally managed to get through to Lennie.

"You rat bastard, Lennie! Answer your fucking—"

"Ronan," Lennie snapped, cutting him off.

"Christ, man! Where have you been?" Ronan shouted as he swerved the Range Rover one-handed around a series of massive potholes on the gravel road.

"I could ask you the same question. You've been out of service for hours." The bastard had no idea what they'd just endured.

"We've just uncovered some unbelievably sinister shit, Lennie, out in the Pacific." Ronan lowered his voice as Phoebe readjusted herself on the passenger seat beside him. "We were lucky to even make it back to shore. I don't want to talk about it over the phone, but we need to gather the inner circle as soon as possible."

Phoebe had been so exhausted by the time they'd dragged themselves from the Zodiac and jogged back to the Range Rover that she could barely climb in once Ronan had unlocked the doors. It had been a miracle that they'd made it back to the vehicle unseen. The saltwater and mud would have been hard enough to try to explain, let alone the blood on their faces.

It had also been a miracle that Ronan still had his backpack.

"Are you out of danger now?" Lennie asked, sounding genuinely concerned.

"I'm far enough down the road now that I don't think we have a tail ..." Ronan wasn't entirely sure that meant they were out of *danger*, of course, but their odds of survival had improved significantly from two hours before.

"Excellent. Are you injured?"

"We'll survive. I sustained a significant gash to my forearm, but it's wrapped well enough for now." He looked down at his arm as he swerved the SUV past yet another massive gap in the road. The storm was swiftly turning the gravel into quicksand. "I also took my usual herbal drought to warm up. I'm not sure we would have made it otherwise."

Ronan had *also* taken a small dose of Bloodsbane to keep himself focused as they sped down the road, but Lennie didn't require that level of detail.

"Dare I ask why you would have needed to warm yourself up?"

"It's a long story."

"Right. And Phoebe?"

"She's okay." He glanced over to her, curled up beneath the wool blanket he usually kept in the back seat. She suddenly looked so small. "I gave her the same tonic to warm up, and now she's sleeping everything off. It seems, in the aftermath, that high-level physical exertion mixes unfavourably with the trapped magic inside her."

"Hmm ... We'll probably want to make a note of that in her application to the Order."

Lennie was right, but for some reason, Ronan didn't want points marked against her for this. "She didn't show any signs of fatigue during the fight. Only once we'd found safety."

"You know, it's interesting—"

"Do you feel like *now* is the time to discuss this?" Ronan whispered into his phone.

"No, I'm serious. It *is* interesting. You'll recall Sean used to have a fair bit of fatigue after battles sometimes, and Graham too, but that was because they were often dabbling in darker magics—holding onto it longer than they should sometimes when they were making bombs and the like."

"The additional elixir I gave her should allow her to sleep for a few hours," Ronan said, ignoring Lennie's observation. Phoebe's mouth was slightly open in sleep, allowing the tiniest trickle of drool to consider dripping down to her chin. "She'll be fine when she wakes up."

"Is she aware you've given her the elixir?"

"What kind of man do you take me for?"

"A stupid one," Lennie said. "You weren't supposed to board any vessels! Let alone nearly drown yourselves in the ocean."

"Yes, well, it was unavoidable. And anyway, who says we almost drowned?"

Lennie scoffed, ignoring his question. "So much for a training mission."

Their primary objective had been to observe and document proof of suspected Wraith activity on the coast—not to almost get themselves killed. Realistically, this sort of mission had been far beneath Ronan's station in the Order, but he and Lennie had agreed it would be a good opportunity to show Phoebe the different sorts of jobs that Druids took part in on a regular basis. Just because Phoebe was paired with Ronan now, it didn't mean she wouldn't be paired with someone of lower standing in the future.

Unfortunately, the entire endeavour had been a fucking disaster.

"Indeed," Ronan replied through gritted teeth. "So, what should we do next? I have time-sensitive information that needs debriefing."

"Can you make it to Dom and Julia's in Victoria? We can connect a secure call from there."

Ronan's jaw ticked. "They don't want to be involved in any of this anymore, Lennie. Not at this level."

"I know that. But they've agreed to act as a safe house before. You need to get somewhere protected and take care of your arm."

How the bastard knew Ronan's arm was much worse than he was letting on stood as a perfect testament to how well they truly knew each other.

"Yes, but those circumstances didn't include taking in Order members who are being potentially followed by Wraiths!" Ronan said, his voice raising slightly. Phoebe stirred beside him but didn't wake up. When he spoke again, it was in a harsh whisper. "This isn't temporary boarding we're needing. It's safe harbour!"

Dom and Julia had been through enough in their many lifetimes already. They didn't need this. Not to mention the fact that Ronan wasn't entirely sure he was ready to introduce Phoebe to his best friends and chosen family. Not yet.

What if her trapped magic is in some way a threat to them?

He was rationalizing, of course, though the logic of this was undeniable and *would* explain the hesitation he was feeling.

Lennie continued, blatantly ignoring Ronan's protests. "We need to discuss whatever the fuck happened today ... and what it was that you found. And before you launch into another futile petition for leniency, this isn't up for discussion! Even if you *did* uncover something significant today, Ronan, you've been making reckless choices, and you know it."

Ronan's anger surged then. "Don't try to pull fucking rank on me, Lennie."

"I'm not pulling rank. I'm merely keeping up my end of our pact."

When Ronan had been in recovery following his time with Cassius, he and Lennie had forged a private pact that should Ronan ever again succumb to the madness he'd once fallen victim to, Lennie would intervene ... using forceful measures to prevent further harm, just as he'd done previously. Despite Lennie's current attitude towards him, Ronan knew that the Brit truly did not want to have to play jailer again.

Ronan's anger deflated like a leaky balloon. "Fine."

"Good. I'll notify Dom and Julia. If they have an issue with it, I'll call you back. Otherwise, your job right now is to get yourself and Phoebe safely to Victoria."

Ronan had spent quite a bit of time in Victoria since Cassius's demise. In fact, he'd lived temporarily with Dom and Julia on more than one occasion. For all intents and purposes, their home was his as well. *They* certainly saw it as such.

"How long have they owned their house?" Phoebe asked as they wound their way through the Garden City.

"Well, it took a little while to find something that met their needs. Even for a centuries-old Celtic prince, the property market on the West Coast is a bit difficult to tap into," Ronan said with a smile. "They settled on a gorgeous and very private oceanfront property in Cadboro Bay, which is close to the university for Dom."

"Oh, is he a professor?"

"No, not right now. He's currently a student, actually."

Phoebe looked perplexed. "Why? What could he possibly need to go back to school for? Isn't he, like, a billion years old?"

He shrugged. "Dom gets bored. While Julia carries on her efforts to bring the Witches together, he's mostly just at home with their daughter."

"Ah, I see."

"What makes it intriguing is that he no longer has any concrete memories of his former lives, which makes for an interesting educational experience when he takes a class that his ancient subconscious ends up having a particular knack for. Julia thinks it's cheating, but he's of the firm opinion that there's no way for him to know what he already knows."

"So, he doesn't have a major then?"

Ronan let out a hearty guffaw. "No ... and he doesn't want to have one either."

Phoebe smiled. "And what do you think? Is it cheating?"

"I think he's a big silly boy."

Ronan thought she would laugh, but several beats passed before Phoebe responded in a voice that suddenly seemed a bit wary. "It sounds like they've found a really *normal* life ... And I mean that in the nicest way possible."

"You're not wrong, but sometimes I think it gets to them. Still, they also have Ayla to keep them on their toes. Boredom doesn't last for long in the O'Brien household."

At the O'Briens' Victoria home, Ronan was now sitting in front of his laptop, one leg crossed over the other, peering exhaustedly at the screen. Practically the moment they had arrived in Victoria, following a nearly four-hour drive, he and Phoebe had been shuffled into an online meeting. The scheduling of this (allegedly) had something to do with time zones, though Ronan sensed it was more likely due to a collective intent to rein him in before he made still more impulsive decisions.

Unfortunately, it meant the conversation was a real trial by fire for Phoebe.

"So, what you're telling us is that you've uncovered a whole new branch of the Wraith underworld?" Thomas asked in the heavy scouse accent from his side of the world. "I mean, if they're talking about moving away from their roots—and *the ritual*—this is a massive deviation from the norm!"

For the past several thousand years, and long since deviating from the Druids, the Wraiths had shrouded their sacred rite even more closely than their decaying bodies. Even Ronan, who had "cohabitated" with countless Wraiths while at Cassius's Gloucestershire estate—many of whom had even undergone the ritual under the same roof—had never been privy to how it all worked. It was just that "sacred" to them.

"It is," said Peggy, sounding increasingly concerned. "If the Wraiths no longer value the ritual of transformation, and find some way around it, it means that whatever element of consent was once needed to join their ranks—coerced or not—would be gone."

Thomas and Peggy were both career Druids, who had joined them on this video call from Peggy's place in Cornwall, where Thomas also resided much of the time. Years ago, she'd taken him on as a surrogate son, despite his being only slightly younger than Julia, and had been training him ever since.

"It sure seems like it," Ronan said, feigning a calmness he didn't feel. "The bastards apparently call themselves the Hounds of Hell, if you can imagine."

"Still," Peggy said, "getting on that boat at all was a reckless decision, Ronan. The numbers weren't on your side."

If there was anyone who might make Ronan second-guess the quality of his choices, it was Peggy. She'd been more than a mentor to him over the years; she was a dear friend. Clearly, Lennie had brought her into this meeting for a reason.

"It was my idea," Phoebe suddenly volunteered from where she was sitting curled up on a nearby couch, still feeling chilled from their dip in the Pacific.

Ronan frowned. "There's no need, Phoebe—"

"No, I'm serious! It was my idea. Don't blame Ronan for trying to keep me out of trouble. I have a vendetta against those fucks, and sometimes it's hard to contain myself."

Ronan tried (and failed) to keep the heat from creeping up his neck.

On the laptop's screen, he saw Lennie purse his lips. "Thanks, Phoebe. Though as you're only in training, and Ronan is your mentor, the responsibility for that still lies with him."

Dom pinched the bridge of his nose with one hand and waved a bit dismissively towards Lennie with the other. "Regardless of all that, we — or, rather, *you* will need to send a team out there ASAP."

"Already on it," Lennie said. "Amos, Amelia, and most of the Vancouver Island branch are already on their way."

Dom rolled his shoulders back several times in a calming gesture that Ronan was very familiar with. He knew that the great Celt was struggling to manage the natural draw he felt towards leadership. Once the World Ruler, always the World Ruler, it seemed.

Lennie wasn't done. "Can you finish reporting your findings, please? In detail?"

And Ronan obliged.

Sparks popped and freshly chopped wood crackled as Ronan's best friend leaned back in his armchair beside the fireplace. No matter how many times Ronan had visited the great Celt, he was always staggered at first by the sheer magnitude of the man—both physically and energetically.

He was a king in every sense of the word.

Dom's hair was longer these days, its tousled blond waves now resembling a lion's mane more than a golden crown. Of course, that was when he wore it down. Usually, like today, he wore it pulled into a messy bun at the back of his head, which made for quite the pairing with his thick beard ...

The handsome bastard.

A vast sheepskin had been tossed over the back of Dom's chair, adding to his ruggedness as he reclined there. Fast asleep on the floor to his right was Nuala, his new dog. She was distantly related to their late Wolfhound Oisín, and Dom had taken a special trip to Ireland last spring just to bring her home.

He'd been in love with her ever since.

Dom reached down and casually scratched behind her ears. "I'm really sorry that Julia couldn't make it back here for the meeting. We'd only just arrived up Island, to visit Eleanor, Tim, and the kids, when Lennie called asking to use our house as a muster point."

"Ugh, I'm sorry, Dom. I told him not to bother you with this."

"Oh, no, don't mistake me. It's no problem. He just gave us zero notice. So, we made the call for me to rip back down without them and meet you here." He offered Ronan an easy shrug. "Though you could have used the house regardless of our presence, of course."

Ronan settled back into the plush leather couch. Dom's "Study 2.0" was even more "him" than his original one in Ireland—where he still owned a massive estate and castle, only with slightly fewer weapons than this one and a *much* bigger TV.

"I completely understand, Dom. It's asking too much to expect little Ayla to arrive there, and then just turn right around and come back home."

"Exactly. You can imagine she gave me the gears, though," Dom said, adding in a voice as tiny as the great Celt could muster, *"Why does Daddy have to leave?"* then dramatically clutching his chest. "Break my heart!"

Ayla was the only human, other than Julia, who could freeze Dom in his tracks with a single look, let alone a pleading question like that. The man was a brute force only tameable by the (even more) powerful women in his life.

"Julia sends her regards, though," Dom said. "We didn't tell Ayla that you would be here, or she would have threatened mutiny."

"Far too confusing for her," Ronan said, nodding. He was Ayla's godfather and loved that kiddo like she was his very own. "I'll plan to come back and visit in a few weeks ... I mean, if that works for you."

"You know you're always welcome here, Ronan. Ayla will be thrilled."

Ronan took a contented sip of his whisky, feeling comfortable and safe. "I know."

"So, how have things been?" Dom asked, pointing towards the doorway with his chin, beyond which Phoebe was sleeping things off in a guest room.

Ronan knew what he was really asking him and to whom he was referring. "*Ehm* ... it's been complicated."

"How so?" Dom set his empty drink down and tented his long fingers.

"Phoebe's good. A natural fit for the Order. It won't take much in the way of training to bring her up to speed."

Dom cocked an eyebrow at him. "Maybe some *taming* though?"

Ronan snorted. "Don't even hint at that, Domhnall. I can't go there."

His best friend knew that Ronan was a sucker for women who required a certain level of "handling" to get close to.

What could Ronan say? He liked a challenge.

"As far as I can tell," Dom said, "Phoebe has a complicated past—even beyond the experimentation she underwent—so that's something that will need to be taken into consideration."

Ronan leaned back comfortably. "I can't think of anyone in the Order's modern history who *hasn't* arrived without considerable baggage. The job appeals to a fairly certain type of human, after all."

"Well, if the shoe fits," Dom said, his bearded mouth pulling upwards into a cheeky and all too familiar grin. "When I met you, you were a complete mess."

Ronan laughed. "I still am."

"I don't know about that ..." Dom seemed to ponder this for a moment. "Still, I know that Lennie called this meeting to pre-empt any potential interventions being needed. I mean, Peggy's presence alone should have done that if nothing else."

Ronan nodded, then watched as Dom stood up and walked casually over to a sideboard dotted with several whisky bottles and amber-filled decanters. He held up two fingers horizontally, glancing at Ronan, who held up three in reply. He needed a stiffer drink than two fingers would have to offer.

"If anything," Ronan said, "I think I see a bit of myself in her. She's absolutely relentless when she's following a lead."

"Do you think it's healthy for you to work closely with someone like that?" Dom asked, handing him his drink.

Ronan took a sip of it and shrugged. "I'm unsure. Sometimes, I think it's exactly the type of colleague I need. She forces me to keep my head in the game ... and if I've been guilty of anything over the past several years, it's complacency."

"I don't agree."

Ronan frowned and took another sip. "I haven't been happy in the job for quite some time. Not really. But missions with Phoebe remind me of the old days with you ... and Sean and Graham. It reminds me why I landed in the Order in the first place: to make a difference."

"And what really happened on the boat? Did she lead the way ... with you following?"

Ronan shook his head. "Not really. But you can't tell Lennie. He's meeting with her this week to discuss her application to the Order."

"Oh, Lennie already knows, I'm sure. The way she stood up for you—"

"Yeah, yeah. That's actually something I wanted to ask you about. Why the hell do you think she did that?" He leaned forward and rested his elbows on his knees. "I'm at a loss."

"Isn't it obvious?"

Ronan groaned. He'd been worried that Dom would say that. "She's not like that though! ... In fact, she's made it pretty damn clear that she isn't looking for a relationship of any sort. I think she'd rather continue to fuck Ian, to be honest. Seems to scratch whatever itch she's feeling."

"None of that indicates that she lacks feelings for *you*. Even if those are simply feelings of strong loyalty."

"Are you trying to talk me out of working with her?"

"Quite the contrary, actually."

Ronan set his drink down and ran both hands through his hair. "*Fuck.*"

"Right," Dom said, smirking briefly before growing serious. "You're aware that you've got a very personal problem on your hands?"

"I know. But how can I tell her now? After she's already gotten to *know* me?"

He knew that Phoebe desperately wanted to uncover what exactly had happened to her in captivity and why ... not to mention how the hell to get the trapped magic *out of her* without killing herself in the process. Informing her of the role he himself had played in those experiments was not an idea he relished. And in any case, Ronan sensed that there was something Phoebe wasn't telling him either.

Too many secrets for us both.

"I get it," Dom said simply. "There is a time and place for total honesty. But I'd do it soon if I were you. One way or another, she *is* going to find out. You know that."

Ronan sighed in resignation. "She's just so desperate to get the magic out of her," he said quietly. "But I swear to the *Goddess* ... I just can't figure out how to help her do that."

"You don't recall anything about it in the Codex?" Dom asked, matching his friend's hushed tone.

Ronan slumped back in his seat. "Nothing that won't kill her before reaching the trapped magic inside."

"*Shite*," Dom said, then threw back the remaining contents of his glass.

"Indeed."

"So, what did you think of Dom?" Ronan asked Phoebe somewhat tentatively as he parked his Range Rover on the ferry.

On the one hand, he'd always known what Phoebe would think of Dom—the bastard was as magnetic as a meteorite. You just *had* to like the guy. On the other hand, Ronan worried that Phoebe might be finding the whole "Dom and Julia" situation she'd recently learned about too overwhelming to handle. Too *big*. Too unreal ...

When she didn't answer right away, he backpedalled a bit. "Or rather, what was your first impression of him?"

Phoebe looked up from her phone finally. She'd spent the last half hour saying very little, distractedly swiping through listings from an online vintage-clothing shop. "Dom? He seems really nice."

Ronan turned off the engine and looked over at her in the

passenger seat. They'd arrived at the docks just moments too late and had missed the previous ferry crossing. So, for the past hour and a half, they'd been forced to sit quietly together, bored and awaiting its return. Usually, Phoebe kept herself (and others) entertained with her chatter in that sort of situation, but she'd been unusually quiet ever since leaving Bamfield.

Were his Druidic implements (again) affecting her more than they should? He didn't think he'd given her that much of the sedative.

"He's nice, yes," Ronan parroted. "But did you ... I guess what I'm asking is ..."

Phoebe set her phone down. "Are you wondering whether it's hard for me to imagine that gigantic hunk of a man travelling repeatedly through time for the past thousand years, chasing the love of his life and being hunted by an evil Sorcerer?"

Ronan didn't think she meant "hunk" in the attractive sense but rather more in reference to his ... enormity. But he supposed it could have been both. Although he'd always been a massive physical presence, over the past several years, Dom had somehow bulked up even more.

He nodded slowly. "Yes, that's exactly what I'm asking, I suppose."

She pondered this for a long moment. "Yeah, it's a bit hard to imagine."

Ronan's heart sank.

For some reason, he'd really wanted Phoebe to like Dom—to see in him what he always had. Dom, Julia, and Ayla were his family, after all. If someone were going to be in his life long term, in any capacity, they would need to fit into that same space with ease. He was even more than okay with admitting that this was non-negotiable for him.

"But after everything I've been through," she continued after a moment, "I suppose I could get used to the idea."

"That's fair," Ronan said, allowing himself to hope. "If it makes you feel any better, I had a hard time believing him too at first. Especially about his feelings for Julia ... The idea of voluntarily tethering yourself to someone else for countless lifetimes ... Well, let's just say I had some difficulty wrapping my head around that one."

"Don't you believe in love?"

"Me? Sure, but I just couldn't quite imagine a love like that. Or it having formed so quickly either. They were only teenagers when they met for the first time and barely knew each other before Julia's grandmother sent her off into the future. Domhnall, being the ever-loving hero that he is, chased after her blindly—actually enlisting ancient Druids to tether them using a rib bone from her dead mother if you can imagine such a thing."

He went on to explain to her that the Druids no longer engaged in those sorts of actions. That sort of bone magic just wasn't in their modern repertoire. And of course, due to the largely oral nature of that ancient and heavily guarded practice, Ronan doubted the modern Druids could successfully reenact it even if they tried.

Phoebe chuckled. "You do realize how crazy that all sounds, right?"

Ronan laughed along with her, running his hands through his hair. "Oh yes. I definitely know."

"Think about it though ... If they were teenagers at the time, regardless of the era, that's probably exactly why they were able to throw themselves at each other so recklessly. Young love is always wild like that."

Ronan reflected on his own love life. Sure, he'd had lovers through the years, from his early twenties onward. But there had never been anyone he'd thought of as "the one"—someone as much his best friend as his sexual companion who made him feel whole. Complete. At one time, he'd thought that he and Lindsey might have grown into a love like that, but they'd never got in step with each other. And their fights had been horrendous ...

"What are you thinking about?" Phoebe asked.

The way she looked at him then made Ronan squirm. "Just thinking about my own life. I won't go into the gory details, but I've never been a particularly romantic man. Or more accurately, I'm not great at getting it *right* ... at least over the long term."

"Do you want my opinion?" Phoebe asked. Her face was unreadable, and Ronan wasn't sure if she was about to offer him kindness and advice or just start making fun of him.

Hopefully not all three at once.

"Sure."

"I don't think that love has to be romantic. In fact, I don't think it should be ... not really. I mean, sure, in the beginning, there's all the tension and confusion, which I think is what people imagine when they think of the romantic stage of dating, but I've always sort of hated that." She laughed introspectively. "I suppose that's why I've never settled down into a monogamous relationship. I find the early stages of dating almost unbearable."

Curiosity got the better of him then. "What makes it unbearable? Surely, if you're into non-monogamy, you could find like-minded—"

Her sudden chuckling silenced him as she shook her head. "No, that's not what I mean. It's not that I'm against any of that stuff. I just think ... It's just how I am. I've always found social connections sort of ... complicated. People can be so fucking unclear with their intentions, and I find it tiresome."

Ronan fidgeted for several seconds before collecting his wallet from where he'd tucked it into the console to avoid sitting on it and developing back strain. In truth, he wasn't exactly sure what to say to Phoebe right now and was just trying to keep his hands busy. He wanted to tell her that he liked interacting with her. He liked it quite a bit, actually. He also wanted to say that despite what she'd just said, he'd never seen any evidence of social discomfort between her and anyone else.

Frankly, she always seemed like the life of the party. But of course, he didn't say that and kept it to himself. Unfortunately, his surprise and confusion must have shown on his face.

"See?" she said with a soft laugh, returning her attention to her phone. "Even *you* have no idea what to do with me."

"That's not true," he said, although it was. "I'm just hungry. I'm going to go grab some food in the canteen area. Did you want to come?"

She smirked. "No, but I'd love some chicken strips and French fries."

CHAPTER 17

PHOEBE

PHOEBE WAS SURPRISED AT HOW RELIEVED SHE FELT WHEN SHE AND Ronan finally arrived back at the Druid safe house. The place had grown on her. After their escape from the trawler, they'd spent the night (and most of the following day) at Dom's house, though she remembered little of it. She'd slept through almost the entire visit, minus the video conference with Lennie and the rest of their inner circle of Druids. By the time Ronan finally woke her up to leave, she'd lost track of what day it was.

Even now, she felt like absolute dogshit and wanted to sleep forever.

"I do wonder if it wasn't the sedative I gave you that's having adverse effects," Ronan said, as he unlocked the front door and led her inside. "And if it is, I'm very sorry about that. You don't seem to process Druidic implements the same way others do."

He scratched his head as Phoebe yawned for what felt like the hundredth time in the past hour. "Maybe. I've never handled any medication very well, though," she said, "especially painkillers and sedatives. Even cough medicine makes me feel weird as hell."

"Hmm ..."

Phoebe swayed on the spot ever so slightly, and Ronan caught her by the arm before she could even think to hide her increasing weakness. "I'm worried about you, Phoebe."

She could tell he meant it (and was probably right to be worried) but shrugged. "I think I just need a good night's sleep in my own bed."

"Is it alright if I check on you before I go to bed?" He looked at his watch. "Should be in about an hour. I've got a few emails to send before then. I'm worried about how deep you might sleep with the sedative draught still in your system."

"Sure," she said, yawning wide, "but don't wake me up."

Normally, she'd need a more *targeted* distraction after an excursion like this to help her sleep—someone like Ian. Or maybe a bottle of whisky. But she legitimately felt exhausted and wanted to be alone.

Ronan nodded, unzipping his laptop from its case. "Goodnight, Phoebe."

She climbed the steps towards her bedroom. The single flight of stairs proved a momentous challenge. What the hell was going on? She hadn't experienced fatigue like this since she'd first escaped captivity. Mercifully, she made it to her queen-sized bed before the inner turmoil had a chance to take over.

She'd spent the majority of the days and weeks following the explosion at the lab sleeping everything off, bouncing between park benches and any hidden refuge she could find. She'd been damn lucky that it was summertime and that, somehow, she'd had the innate sense to hide. She had a vague recollection of stealing some clothing from an unlocked van, along with a blanket, and eating discarded meals from dumpsters behind several restaurants.

Though, she still could not recall exactly how she'd re-entered civilization from the rubble of such an isolated lab—let alone how she'd escaped in the first place. The moments leading to her freedom were a blur, as were the days that followed.

Mercifully, after several weeks (or so she'd assumed), Phoebe had managed to rouse herself enough to stumble into a women's shelter—still patently unaware of what day or month it was—and was able to find some sort of peace and proper rest.

At least for a time.

From what she'd been able to find out afterwards while researching at the public library—going through newspaper clippings and the like—her disappearance (more than a year earlier by that point) had barely made the news beyond a reference to her previous employer having hired a new lead journalist, offering no explanation for why Phoebe had been replaced.

Digging deeper, she'd discovered that the Wraiths had spread carefully crafted lies to everyone connected to her, ensuring that everyone knew she had fallen into hard times while following a disturbing lead into organized crime in British Columbia and their dangerous drug-trafficking and supply practices ... and in the process had started using herself. The sad part was that no one seemed to have even *thought* to dispute this. Phoebe knew that she had burned a lot of bridges in the months leading up to her abduction. Her obsessive focus on work, coupled with routine burnout, meant that she'd had little time left for maintaining healthy personal connections, but still ... she hadn't realized it had gotten quite *that* bad.

The Wraiths had been clever, knowing that the efforts of pulling off such extensive misdirection would be far better in the long run than having another missing person's case show up on the local authority's radar. And it had worked; Phoebe had essentially disappeared off the map for twelve months without anyone ever looking into it.

She rolled onto her side, curling her body inward and tucking her wrists under her chin like a little shrimp. She tried not to feel lonely—a familiar emotion she thought she'd come to terms with long ago. And yet, she'd be lying if she said that some small kernel of her being didn't long for Ronan's company. He'd probably make fun of her for sleeping all curled up like this, but even that might feel nice at the moment.

Phoebe had no close family or relatives on the West Coast—or at least, none she could call for help who'd actually show up and give a shit about her issues. She allegedly had a cousin somewhere in North Van, but she'd not seen them since a family reunion back in the nineties. Her parents were both gone now—which was a long story she preferred not to think about—she had no siblings, and the few friends she did have had apparently believed the Wraiths' story.

Phoebe hadn't been in the best place mentally when she'd first been captured, and after her long imprisonment, she'd been absent—and completely unreachable—for long enough that her bank account was now frozen, her credit cards had been locked, and her lease had expired. So, of course, her beautiful East Van apartment and everything inside of it had since fallen into the hands of her landlords, Sherry and Ivan. They'd been thoughtful and compassionate enough to go through her things and put anything they deemed potentially sentimental into a single storage bin for her in case she ever returned. But the rest they'd sold, donated, or just kept for themselves.

Phoebe was sure they'd pawned some of her jewellery, but she couldn't fault them for it. After all, she had owed them money for all the rent that went unpaid while she was gone. When she'd awkwardly collected the bin one rainy afternoon, she found that they'd left it outside on the stoop with a note: *"For Phoebe."* They clearly hadn't expected her to actually pick it up and hadn't wanted to waste their time.

The Wraiths certainly didn't care about her things, friends, or livelihood either ... but they *had* cared about keeping anyone from looking too closely around the last place she'd been seen and the story she'd been researching at Spectre Fidelities Corp, the shadow conglomerate led by none other than Jordan Cole.

At least she'd somehow managed to kill the fucker.

And so, when she emerged from captivity, she'd gone along with this line of thinking too. It made more sense than going to the authorities to tell them that she'd been captured by Wraiths. *"You know? The magical bad guys?"* That was a sure way to get herself either recaptured, which was the last thing she wanted, or institutionalized.

No, she'd needed to figure out if and how the trapped magic might be removed from her body. And to find out what had happened on her last day in captivity.

In her dreams, she had vague flashes of there being a strange surge of power ... of her walking down a long hallway wearing a hospital gown ... and then an explosion. She remembered the crushing weight of rubble all around her. And sometimes, on nights when she felt particularly frail and vulnerable, she could even hear the screams of the other captives as they died excruciating deaths.

Phoebe hated the memory of that more than all the rest. The pain in their voices ... the absolute fucking waste and loss of it all. She hated the Wraiths, who, in their cruelty and desperation for power, had stripped the right to choose away from her in every way but one.

So, she would destroy every last Wraith who even thought about coming between her and her freedom again.

She was going to win back her life ... even if it killed her.

Thirty-two hours later.

Phoebe looked out the window from her new favourite armchair in the front living room of the safe house. It was a sort of plush, navy blue rectangular thing that almost reminded her of a dog bed. *She* certainly found it easy to curl up in. Outside, it was a cool yet unseasonably sunny January day. At her side was an empty plate of what had once been eggs, bacon, and toast. She'd polished it off (rather enthusiastically) ten minutes earlier.

She felt settled for the first time in a very long time.

Sleep, as she'd suspected, had drastically improved her condition. However, the length of that sleep had been concerning, at least for Ronan.

The Druid doctor, true to form, had dutifully checked on her throughout the night and well into the following day. It wasn't that she'd been incoherent, just that she'd never woken up feeling rested.

And so, she'd kept going back to sleep.

More than once, Ronan had opted to just stay there in her room with her for a while, working on his computer or reading case notes. She'd even caught him reading a pulpy crime novel in the chair in the corner—the type of book they kept turning into limited series on British television.

"Is that one any good?" she'd asked blearily, without any sense of what time it might be.

He'd tipped his glasses down and stared at her for several moments, assessing her. *"Sadly, no."*

"But you'll finish it?"

"Yes."

"You know you can just DNF books if you don't like them. No one will kill you." She'd yawned then, rolling over. *"Life is too short, and there are too many good books out there to read something you don't like."*

"DNF?" he'd asked, but she'd felt the clutches of sleep dragging her back down before she could reply.

This morning, she'd snagged the book in question from his nightstand when she had used the upstairs bathroom. He had already chided her about entering his room without his permission, though he let it slide because of her weakened condition. And she was reading it now, keeping his bookmark stuck between the pages about halfway through. The story was pretty gritty—a fast-paced thriller about a police officer and a scientist who somehow end up in Switzerland on a heist, which she didn't necessarily hate. However, the book also failed to keep her attention.

Ronan entered the living room then, carrying two large cups of coffee. He was dressed surprisingly casual this morning, in loose grey sweatpants and a black t-shirt. He was also barefoot, to her surprise, and she caught herself admiring his feet.

"I hope breakfast hit the spot?" he asked.

He'd initially suggested she try something milder, like oatmeal, but she'd eaten so much of it in captivity that the idea of spooning even a morsel of the stuff into her mouth again made her gag. In the end, he'd reluctantly agreed to make her a greasy breakfast. *"If this upsets your stomach, don't say I didn't warn you."*

Thankfully, the heavy meal had been exactly what she'd needed. "It was *perfect*."

"I brought you another coffee," he said, setting it down beside her plate. "Two cream and a spoon of sugar, correct?"

Phoebe was unsure why Ronan continued to care for her to so

attentively. She was up at last and feeling a lot better now. Then she frowned, realizing that he was working up to something.

"I'd like to take you to see Imogen this afternoon. Is that okay?"

She had suspected this conversation would be coming sooner rather than later, though she might have liked another day to pull herself together before it did. "Yeah, alright."

"We can meet and have dinner with her afterward if you feel up for it. I owe her a meal, anyway."

Phoebe immediately found herself wondering about the nature of their relationship. He spoke about Imogen with a familiar fondness, but she couldn't tell if that was because they were friends or because they had once been lovers.

She reminded herself that she didn't care.

And so, just before three o'clock that afternoon, Phoebe climbed into Ronan's Range Rover, and they drove to False Creek. While she'd initially been *extremely* resistant to any form of testing, it was becoming clearer by the day that she could use any help she could get.

Sleeping for thirty-two hours wasn't exactly normal.

Imogen lived high up in a large, glass-framed condo, apparently subsidized by whatever research company she worked for as a botanist. For some reason, Phoebe had assumed the Druid would work for the government, with the Ministry of Agriculture or Fisheries and Oceans. Surely, it would be helpful to have Druids working in government, after all, but Imogen worked privately, which meant she received some serious job perks.

"Do most Druids maintain regular jobs outside of the Order?"

"Many but not all," Ronan said, pulling up to the large black door of an underground parking garage. "It's another one of those 'it depends' situations. Sometimes, it's out of necessity, as in they work to pay their bills. And then there are situations like mine. I take on casual work at the hospital because I have expensive tastes, and the Order only provides so much in terms of spending money."

"And, let me guess, Ian doesn't work outside the Order."

"No, he doesn't."

She snorted. "Wouldn't want to look like a freeloader."

He rolled his eyes. "Anyways, sometimes it's also out of need, such as us *needing* a Druid planted in some organization specifically to gather information. Or to hold power and access in certain realms. Like Lennie for example," Ronan said, pulling his phone out to text Imogen and let her know they were outside. Seconds later, the door to the parking garage lifted open.

"Would you like to be working more frequently as a doctor now?" she asked, genuinely curious. "I mean ... if you could?"

"Not right now, no. I do miss it sometimes, but I think after everything ..." He let that thought trail off. "I'm sure I'll go back to it with more purpose someday."

Phoebe knew she'd recently told him she didn't give a fuck about his personal challenges, but that wasn't necessarily true. She hated that he continued to lie to her about his early involvement with the Wraith experiments—and about having elected to work with Cassius in the first place. But she also didn't like the idea that he'd clearly suffered over the years too, especially during his own time with the Wraiths. As far as she knew, he'd also played a *huge* part in eventually defeating Cassius.

On the balance, she'd come to truly believe that Ronan was more good than bad.

He parked his SUV familiarly in a guest parking spot.

"I take it you've been here before?" she asked.

"Yes," Ronan said simply and left it at that. Clearly, he wasn't planning to divulge any more about his relationship with Imogen than he'd already shared.

"Alright," she said a bit sharply as she started gathering her things. She had no idea why she cared anyway ... She *didn't* care.

"She's a good friend," he said then, either reading her mind or just trying to allay her fears. The more time they spent together, the more he seemed to anticipate her needs.

She was still on the fence about whether she liked this or not.

They climbed into the elevator together and rode it up to the tenth floor where Imogen lived. Phoebe adjusted her thinning hair in the elevator mirror, grimacing at the memory of the chunks of hair swirling at her feet in the shower that morning, as Ronan checked his phone for emails. Soon, the doors opened, and Ronan led the way down the hallway, with Phoebe following several paces behind.

Grief settled heavily upon her then, realizing just how badly she missed having her own apartment—a place that was hers alone. Ronan's earlier comments about some Druids not working had struck a nerve with her, making her realize that it wasn't likely she'd ever be able to manage a "regular job" again after the injuries she'd received and the trauma she'd experienced.

Becoming a Druid might be her only chance for a comfortable life, assuming the magic trapped within her didn't kill her first. With each passing day, she felt less sure that she could keep it under control.

Ronan knocked three times on Imogen's door, and they were soon welcomed inside by a short, kind-looking woman, who appeared to be older than her but younger than Ronan. Phoebe towered over her, of course, but she was accustomed to being taller than most women.

"Hi, Phoebe! I'm Imogen," she said, extending her hand.

Phoebe accepted it and shook it briefly before tucking her hands back into the sleeves of her oversized sweatshirt and crossing her arms. She didn't know why she felt so protective of herself at the moment when there were probably no two safer people with whom to discuss her wellness.

She reminded herself that she *wanted* this to work.

"I've boiled a kettle for some tea, but I can also make coffee if you'd prefer." Imogen gestured towards her polished-granite kitchen island, where a colourful teapot sat beside a glass French press.

"Phoebe prefers coffee," Ronan said, turning to her. "Would you like some?"

She nodded, appreciating the continued attentiveness. "Yes, please."

Imogen's place was lovely. It was sunny and bright, with low comfortable furniture and, as expected, plenty of potted plants. She also had a knack for selecting unique artwork, with each wall adorned with what looked like original pieces thoughtfully tucked between the tendrils and variegated leaves of Imogen's indoor jungle.

"Do you paint?" Phoebe asked, her voice breaking. She swallowed back an unexpected sob, recalling the countless hours she used to spend behind an easel—yet another light-filled fragment of her life she'd lost to the Wraiths and their torture.

Neither Druid seemed to notice her discomfort.

"Goddess, no," Imogen said, chuckling to herself. "But I have friends who do. As well as friends who like to buy me artwork." She beamed at Ronan.

"I tend to owe Imogen a lot of favours," he said, laughing. "And big ones too, for calling her at odd hours and asking her to dive into situations she perhaps doesn't want to be in."

Phoebe felt suddenly embarrassed. "Oh ... I hope I'm not an inconvenience today."

Imogen smacked Ronan on the arm. "Look! You made her feel bad!" She took Phoebe's hands into her own much smaller ones. "You are no inconvenience, Phoebe. Besides, what we're doing here today is part of my job description with the Order ..." Imogen paused then, her brows furrowing, and Phoebe assumed that she was attempting to sense the magic trapped inside of her. "I'm very curious about you."

Ronan led Phoebe to the living room while Imogen prepared their coffees. He unzipped his laptop bag and retrieved his computer and the same small stack of files he seemed to carry with him everywhere —the files pertaining to Phoebe. He'd also brought his aged leather medical bag, which he now placed on the carpeted floor beside him.

"What exactly *do* you keep in there?" Phoebe asked. "You've never actually shown me." She was intrigued by the contents of his bag and didn't mind redirecting attention away from herself.

"Pouches, medicaments, and the like ... and my gun."

"Your *gun?!*"

"Sometimes you need the non-magical option," he said, failing to hide the cheeky smirk lifting one corner of his mouth.

"Ronan guards that one with his life," Imogen said, setting their coffees down on wicker coasters on the coffee table. "He doesn't even let me poke around in it."

"Because it's proprietary?" Phoebe asked, curious about what could be so private.

Imogen smiled. "Because its contents are nearly priceless. At least in the magical world."

"What do you mean?" Phoebe reached for her coffee, allowing its scent to invigorate her as it always did.

"She means to say that the value of our pouches and tinctures are essentially priceless due to either the cost or the rarity of their ingredients. And yes, also because of the proprietary nature of how they're created."

Phoebe wondered just how much each pouch Ronan had thrown had actually cost them and how much *she'd* cost him simply by being by his side on recent missions.

"Can I ask you a question, Phoebe?" Imogen said, cupping her own coffee with both hands.

"Sure."

"What exactly *were* you looking for after the explosion when you were visiting all of those Wraith establishments. Ronan has told me that you were hoping to find out more about what was done to you, as well as what happened on that day, but I'd like to hear it in your own words."

Phoebe thought for a few moments. She wasn't sure how much she wanted to divulge to Imogen. Although the woman was friendly, if a bit frank, she was also a stranger. "I'd really like to get the magic out of me if I can."

Imogen nodded, her expression thoughtful.

Sipping his coffee, his eyes darting back and forth between Phoebe and Imogen, Ronan seemed happy just to watch and wait.

"Well," Imogen said, "I think my biggest question, when considering your health and the adverse effects some of the pouches seem to have on you, isn't so much what happened or how to reverse it—though those are also important, of course—but rather how much magic actually resides within you."

Ronan let out a soft whistle through his teeth.

Imogen smirked at him. "I sense that wasn't top of your list, Ronan?"

He set his coffee cup down and ran his hands through his hair. "No, it wasn't. I've just been oscillating between how they did it and how to undo it."

Or how about the effect on my physical body? Phoebe wondered.

"I have a suspicion that the *volume* of the magic is the reason for most of the complications," Imogen said, leaning back. "Can I ask you another question, Phoebe?"

She nodded.

"We know that they either directly injected the magic or used an IV drip with regularity, but did they actually *force* their magic into you? And if so, how much? Can you recall?"

"No ... not really. I remember it was ... happening for quite a while, though ... being restrained there as they—" She started hyperventilating as images of her early days in captivity started flashing before her eyes.

Ronan slid closer to her on the couch and gently stroked her back, just as he'd done in the motel room in Bamfield. "Shh, it's alright, Phoebe. You aren't there anymore. You're safe here." After another several minutes of his soothing tone and touch, she felt both the trapped magic and her own racing thoughts begin to settle.

"I'm so sorry," Imogen said, looking concerned, though not guilty at all.

"It's alright. It happens sometimes."

Ronan piped up then. "I believe that particular dataset is part of the approximately thirty percent of the facility's files that are still missing, despite our best efforts to gather them."

"Which explains why it hasn't been on the top of your mind," Imogen acknowledged. "But it *is* a question that will need to be answered down the line."

Phoebe breathed a sigh of relief, thankful that the pair of scientists didn't opt to speculate any further without the entirety of the dataset in hand. Realistically, just how much magic had been packed into her was something they might never know. Not fully, at least.

She wasn't lying about barely remembering.

Ronan left his arm behind her as they settled back on the couch—more than likely to continue projecting a sense of safety to her—but to her surprise, she found that she liked it. Imogen was eyeing them both with curiosity when a strange rattling sound could be heard coming from a hallway further inside the condo.

"Ah, yes," she said. "So ... that's the other curiosity we need to address today."

"What do you mean?" Ronan asked, glancing at her and then back towards the hallway.

Phoebe, meanwhile, was feeling a strange pull coming from somewhere behind her sternum. She placed her hand on her chest. "What *is* that?"

Imogen rose, her expression grave. "There's something I need to show you both."

Together, they walked about halfway down the hallway to a locked door, which had been further sealed with what looked like duct tape and some other extremely sticky substance that Phoebe recognized as tree sap upon closer inspection. It smelled like turpentine.

"So ... this is my guest room."

"Looks more like an unwanted-guest room," Phoebe said dryly and noticed the corner of Ronan's mouth twitch slightly.

"The sample you gave me of that strange vine, Ronan?" Imogen said. "Well, I propagated it. And now it's gotten out of hand."

"You propagated it in your condo?" Ronan was shocked.

She rolled her eyes. "Well, it wasn't like I was going to do it at work! Plus, I've got it completely under control. The room is basically a magically sealed container now, though I do have to feed the container every few days. The plants are constantly draining the magic from it and trying to escape."

Imogen was saying all this as though it were completely normal.

"How do you feed it?" Ronan asked, his eyes wide.

"I gather magic into myself, like we always do, and then transfer it into the container."

Ronan's tone was swiftly growing colder. More dangerous. "How did you *make* the container, Imogen?"

Her own eyes widened then. "What do you mean?"

"What ... incantation ... did you use?" he asked through gritted teeth.

Phoebe had no idea why Ronan was getting so agitated but assumed it had to do with the various secrets that she knew he was harbouring.

"I didn't use *any* incantation. I used mould."

Ronan's jaw dropped. "Mould?!"

"Yes, Ronan. Mould. Before I narrowed my scope to botany for my post-doctorate, I was a microbiologist. I worked in a lab for several years, studying radiotrophic fungi—mould, specifically—and the Wraiths' developments with this plant got me thinking ... What if I encouraged a strain of mould to eat magic too?"

"You've lost me," Phoebe said, fascinated but confused.

"Simply put, radiotrophic fungi grow towards radiation, instead of away from it, and then process and store it using melanin. Sort of like how most plants will grow towards the sunlight, using chlorophyll to process that light into energy."

"Melanin," Phoebe said. "Like what's in our skin?"

"The very same."

"Wow." She looked at Imogen in wonder.

"Indeed. The Wraiths have developed what appears to be a pea and nightshade hybrid, which is quite unusual in and of itself. But more importantly, this specific hybrid seems to grow towards *magic* ... consuming, processing, and storing it."

Phoebe fought back a chuckle, realizing that Imogen had seemed just as perplexed by the hybridization the Wraiths had achieved as she herself was at the idea of them having some sort of internal mechanism for eating magic. She realized then that the Druid was growing on her.

"*Now* she tells us," Ronan said wryly.

Imogen shot him a look. "I was getting there!"

"So, let me get this straight," he said, puzzling it all together. "The mould you're using to keep the plant in check seeks out magic and eats it. And the hybrid *plant* the Wraiths came up with grows towards magic, rather than light, then both consumes *and* contains it. Right?"

"Right," Phoebe answered for Imogen, confident now that she was following. "But then why doesn't the plant just drain the magic from the mould and escape?"

"It's the melanin," Imogen explained casually, as if this made perfect and obvious sense. "Once the mould has ingested the magic and stored it, it's no longer of a type that the plant can access to feed on because it was processed in such a different way internally." She shrugged then and added, "And vice versa, of course."

Ronan and Phoebe just stared at her, so she continued. "At Chernobyl, they uncovered a mould called *Cladosporium sphaerospermum*, among a number of others, growing on and around the reactor and even in the extremely radioactive water at the core. Growing in *unbelievably* inhospitable conditions. Fascinating stuff. But I mean, really, when you think about it, the earth used to tolerate a lot more radiation than that, particularly during the Early Cretaceous Period."

Imogen paused briefly, sighing at her own rambling thoughts before returning abruptly to the matter at hand. "Basically, the plants and the mould are now at a sort of ... magical standoff if you will. Like pressing two matching magnetic poles together."

Ronan was astounded. "And you figured all of this out in the last week and a half?"

She snorted in amusement. "Well, I *am* a genius, Ronan. Isn't that why you keep me around?"

Phoebe pressed her hand against her sternum as the feeling of her magic being tugged at intensified. "So, you said you've been feeding it ..." She was beginning to sweat from the tension in her chest. "If I'm understanding you correctly, the plants don't discriminate when it comes to what types of magic they consume in general ... as long as they can actually access and store it?"

"That's right."

"But what about *decaying* magic, like what the Wraiths have?"

Like I have.

Ronan nodded, looking impressed with her line of questioning. Phoebe's brain seemed to be lighting up in ways it hadn't in months—years even. She was genuinely curious now and desperate to ask questions and learn everything she could. Unfortunately, she didn't think her body could take remaining in such close proximity to the plant *or* mould for much longer.

Imogen gestured at the sealant around the door. "I've sealed the room a couple of different ways as you can see, just in case either of them somehow gets the upper hand and tries to escape." She shrugged a bit awkwardly at the notion. "And of course, I've also been periodically pruning and burning them both back."

"How have you had time to actually work?" Phoebe asked.

"I took some holiday time. This is far too interesting to miss out on." She rubbed her hands together excitedly.

"And you're not worried that they'll both turn on you at once?"

"My bosses or my captives?" Imogen asked, raising an eyebrow at her, before shrugging again. "My bosses owe me," she said simply. Then she nodded at the sealed door. "One of them is just a non-sentient plant, despite its rapid growth, and the other is a flat black mould. I don't think I'm in any danger when it comes to either their speed or their ability to escape containment."

"So how do you actually care for them?" Phoebe asked, quickly realizing that many people found themselves in Imogen's debt quite regularly.

"Every few days, I have to go in there and feed them. Like today for example. That's the rattling you're hearing. They're hungry."

"They're that powerful?" Ronan asked.

"The plant runs out of held magic slower than the mould, which causes it to sort of ... *shiver*."

"How big are they?"

"Big." She sighed. "Like, big, big ... Do you—"

"Wait!" Phoebe said, cutting her off and reaching towards the locked door, wincing as her chest pounded. "Can either of you explain what I'm feeling in my chest right now?"

"What do you mean?" Imogen asked.

Ronan turned towards Phoebe and began scanning her from head to toe. "How long has this been going on?"

"Since we got here. It's worse the closer we get to the plants. Or maybe it's the mould. I don't know."

"Let's get Phoebe back to the living room," Imogen suggested.

They moved back to the living room together, where Ronan unzipped his medical bag and retrieved his stethoscope. He listened to her heart, and then her lungs, front and back. Everything appeared to be in order. He took her pulse, and it was normal too.

Phoebe's body had immediately relaxed as he went through a

routine so ingrained in him it came as second nature ... something she found unexpectedly soothing. In fact, almost everything about Ronan's nature—his particularity, his stubbornness, and even how he kept his vehicle so infuriatingly tidy—left her feeling safer and more stable than anyone else had in recent memory.

Or perhaps, he simply had exemplary bedside manner.

Once Ronan was satisfied that Phoebe wasn't about to die, he tried to refocus, looking back at Imogen. "So, why do you think the Wraiths have been developing magic-stealing plants?"

"You mean other than to steal magic?" Phoebe mumbled lamely, trying and failing to lighten the mood with humour.

Imogen just swallowed hard and looked at Ronan. "I have absolutely no idea."

CHAPTER 18

PHOEBE

PHOEBE SAT BEFORE A BLACKENED LAPTOP SCREEN IN THE DINING room of the Druid safe house, waiting not-so-patiently for Lennie to join the video call. She drummed her long fingers on the antique tabletop and popped her gum noisily. She knew better than to be chewing gum—her jaw popped at the best times (not mention her teeth felt extra sensitive these days, yet another side effect of the Wraith magic), and gum was no help—but she was nervous, and the spiced cinnamon flavour seemed to ground her.

Through a wood-framed doorway, she could see Ronan seated in the nearby living room, pouring over a stack of documents in a light-brown file folder. His (admittedly) fashionable tortoiseshell glasses were giving him an air of subdued confidence. He had his left leg crossed over his right knee and was wearing a pair of wool slacks and a soft, grey t-shirt that exposed his biceps and muscular forearms. The dress shirt he'd been wearing over the tee was now slung over a wing-back chair nearby.

It was all very "on brand" for the Druid doctor.

"He's late," Phoebe said, her attention shifting between the clock on the computer screen and Ronan.

"I can tell." Ronan said, not looking up from whatever the hell he was so engrossed in. At Phoebe's audible release of breath, he lifted his blue eyes. "He'll be there. Just be patient."

Her video call with Lennie had been arranged for this morning specifically to work within the Brit's schedule. Lennie often worked unusual hours at his "other job"—which Ronan had briefly described as "working for an international intelligence agency" before interrogating her for hours on end—and of course, there was also the time difference between Vancouver and wherever he currently was in England.

She tapped her blue pen loudly against the tabletop before setting it down. "Where exactly does Lennie live in England?"

"He maintains a flat in London, though he's rarely there. I'm not entirely sure where he's calling from this morning, though."

"I see," she said, storing that information for later. Lennie's vast network could prove extremely useful should she ever gain access to it, though if he was MI6 as she suspected ...

She leaned back in the creaky wooden chair with another loud sigh.

"He might be at Dom's estate," Ronan added, his eyes still on his paper.

Phoebe had learned that, during their final fight against Cassius, Dom and Julia's home in the Irish countryside had been used as a stronghold for their cause. Following his defeat, Dom and Julia had relocated to Victoria, on Vancouver Island. And now, their home served as a work centre for travelling Druids, and nothing more.

"Gotcha. Do you *maintain a flat* anywhere?" Her question was innocent enough, though she did tease his accent for extra levity. Ronan still kept many aspects of his life private, which, under normal circumstances, might not be such a big deal. But in Phoebe's current reality, any and all information could end up being priceless currency at the right moment. "Aside from your room here, I mean?"

"I briefly owned a condo downtown but sold it a few years back. I was never there and didn't want to deal with the hassle of renters. Not in Vancouver, anyway."

That piqued her curiosity. "Do you have renters elsewhere?"

"I do."

She could have sworn that a smirk danced at the corner of Ronan's mouth before he clicked open a sleek silver pen and began hastily scribbling down some notes on the paper in front of him. She wondered if it was work for the Druidic Order or the hospital. She knew that, somehow, the workaholic Druid still managed a few shifts at the hospital each month on top of his other duties, just to *keep himself fresh*.

Well, that and to pay for his expensive tastes.

"Okay, mystery man," she teased. "Am I allowed to know where?"

He let out a long sigh though his nose and closed the file folder, placing it on his knee and looking over at her in the nearby dining room.

"I'm sorry I keep interrupting you," Phoebe said, smirking. She couldn't help herself; she'd always been a *"yapper."*

Ronan's eyes narrowed, though not unkindly. "Why are you so curious about where everyone lives this morning?"

"Well, if I'm going to join the Druid network formally, I'd like to know more about the people I'll be working with."

"It's not much of a secret network if we know everything about each other. Especially our private locations."

She waved this off. "Lennie knows everything."

"It's Lennie's job to know everything."

"Right, right. But I mean ... I assume working closely with *you* will be ongoing."

Ronan raised his eyebrows. "We'll see about that ..."

Phoebe's heart pounded momentarily before his stern expression gave way to a cheeky grin.

"You bastard! You already know what Lennie will say, don't you?"

Ronan shrugged innocently and collected his things. "I'm off to a short consult at the hospital. Lennie will fill you in on everything." Then he paused and winked at her. "I'm looking forward to working with you."

Phoebe's heart fluttered unexpectedly. She opened her mouth to spit back a cheeky retort just as her screen lit up and Lennie's face appeared. When she looked back to the living room, Ronan was gone.

"Hi, Lennie," she said, cheeks flushed unexpectedly pink.

"Hello, Phoebe."

She shifted in her chair, crossing and uncrossing her ankles as she waited.

"So, I suppose ..." Lennie began and then paused, his lips pursing slightly. "Well, as you know, today's call is about formally opening the door, as it were, for you to join the Order officially."

She nodded. "Alright."

"Well, obviously, that position is yours, Phoebe ... if you'd like it."

Her body stilled.

She'd learned long ago to listen to her body's responses whenever an opportunity was presented to her, before trusting her own thoughts, which were always far too convoluted. However, with the volatile magics now trapped within her, she was curious how that process might go. She closed her eyes, placed her hand on her heart, and asked herself if this was what she wanted.

Yes, she thought. *Yes, it must be ...*

She opened her eyes and looked at Lennie, who apparently hadn't been finished.

"But ..."

Phoebe blinked stupidly at him. "But?"

"Well, if I'm completely honest, Phoebe, I sense that you might actually be better suited to the Order of the Knaves."

"Okay ... are you a Knave?"

"I'm many things ... but yes. I was born to Druid parents and continue working with the Druids. But at my core, I'm a Knave."

Phoebe leaned back in her chair, her mind going a mile a minute now. "How would *you* classify the difference between Knaves and Druids? I can't seem to get a straight answer from anyone. They all say, 'You just need to meet one.'"

"Well, I think it's pretty specific to the individual ... but for many, it comes down to a discussion of ethics."

"Ethics?" She laughed. "Are you suggesting that I'd make a good Knave because I'm unethical?"

Lennie snorted. "Well, I'm not *not* saying that."

Somehow, Phoebe knew he wasn't actually criticizing her but naming her as kindred to himself. "So, do the Knaves work for the Druids?"

"Alongside them. The relationship is collaborative in nature, and there are several like me who straddle both sides. As I've said, my parents were Druids—" He stopped himself abruptly and asked, "Did Ronan tell you about this?"

"No, he didn't."

"Okay, well ... The long and the short of it is that my parents died on a Druidic mission when I was a teenager and ... well, I never really meshed properly with the Druids after that. Not fully."

Phoebe considered what she knew about Amos and Amelia, and how their parents' deaths seemed to have only solidified their allegiance to the Order.

"Oh, wow, Lennie ... I'm sorry for your loss."

"It was a long time ago."

"Still ... It sucks losing your parents at a young age." Phoebe knew that feeling well but preferred not to dwell on it. "So, why do you still work for the Druids if you don't always see eye to eye?" She had to know.

He laughed brightly then—a full-belly, mirthful sound that Phoebe didn't think the overly serious Brit had in him. "I don't believe I've ever seen fully eye to eye with anyone in my life, Phoebe. If I refused to work with anyone who wasn't completely on my side, I would be working alone forever."

Phoebe also knew that reality all too well.

"The simplest explanation I can give you is that the Druidic Order is more organized and less divided into factions than the Knaves are. The Knaves operate more in ... I guess you could call them 'camps.'"

She still couldn't even understand the organizational structure of the Druids. If the Knaves were even more chaotic than that ... She shook her head slightly.

"So, where's your camp?"

"I don't currently have one." A flicker of sadness crossed Lennie's face before he steeled himself again. "But that's nothing new for me. I like working with the Druids because even though I am very much a lone wolf by nature, it allows me to connect with other humans regularly." He shrugged. "Perhaps that sounds foolish, but they provide me with some semblance of a family—something I've never found easy to come by elsewhere."

Lennie had been right; they had more in common than she'd initially thought.

"One of the reasons I supported Ronan's bid for you to join the Order," he continued, "is because I think you're a bit like me. We are both rather ... nonconformist."

Phoebe smiled. "You can say that again."

"It's not bad. Or at least, I don't think it is. But we need to be wise and allow ourselves a sense of community. Otherwise ... the world can grow very dark very quickly."

Phoebe was surprised to get this level of vulnerability and introspection from him, but then again, like often recognized like.

They were kindred.

"If you'll oblige me," he said, looking directly at her through the screen, "I'd like to be honest with you. I know what you're capable of ... what specific skills you carry. I looked into your research, as you suggested that I do during the initial interview."

Phoebe schooled her features. "Oh? And?"

"Well, I think you're not so different from many other journalists, investigators ... spies—"

"I'm not a spy."

"But you could be if you wanted to. I'm aware of the articles you wrote comparing pickup artists and CEOs ... and your research into neuro-linguistic programming and the power of hypnosis ..."

So, they were getting to the heart of it now.

"Are you going to tell Ronan?" she asked, her expression serious.

"That depends on you."

Phoebe felt red creeping up her neck. "I'd rather if you didn't."

He thought about this for a moment before responding. "I'm sure you've already guessed that I'm similarly trained in those areas.

Though, in my case, that training was offered by a governmental body." He laughed darkly. "Which somehow feels much worse. You though ... Well, I assume you're wholly self-taught."

"I am."

"To be clear, I don't hold any of this against you. I'm fairly immune to such manipulations, which is why I wanted to speak to you privately, without Ronan being present. So, we could talk straight."

"I don't use it against Ronan if I can help it," she offered.

"But sometimes it's subconscious, especially under duress." His expression was unreadable now. "You can agree, I'm sure, that it's not entirely possible to completely shut that skillset off once you've integrated it into your system."

She saw no point in lying. "I don't disagree."

"Right, well ... A word of caution. Dr. Ronan Gallagher is not someone I would personally mess with. Other than Domhnall—who I'm fairly certain could physically crush me to a pulp before I even had a chance to fight back—Ronan is the only other Druid in this network that I wouldn't 'fuck with,' as it were. He has an edge to him that ... well, it's an edge that the rest of us do not have. If you can believe such a thing."

"I'm starting to think I can."

"Excellent. So ... sooner or later, I advise you to tell him. I can only hold onto what I've uncovered about your ... *areas of interest* for so long before I'll have to inform the Order."

"Why can't you just keep it a secret?"

"The Order doesn't work like that, Phoebe. All secrets eventually find themselves rustled out, regardless of attempts to suppress them. It's simply the nature of the beast. I can keep it a secret for a time. But ..."

"But what?"

"Well, pardon my bluntness, but you might choose to use this skillset to your advantage within the Order. Or with the Knaves, which as I stated earlier, might be better suited to accommodate your unique set of skills."

"I see."

"My other job prohibits me from embarking on too many Druidic missions these days. All too often, I'm locked up behind various computer screens. But out in the field, I am expertly trained in espionage and, just like you, in the art of seduction."

"So, you're saying I should let them know what I'm capable of?"

"I'm saying you could teach them—the Druids—what you know."

Phoebe laughed darkly at that. "Like any of them would listen to me."

"From what I'm told, you've already made quite an example of Ian. Perhaps you could take that experience and demonstrate how much you've been capable of within only weeks of entering the Vancouver safe house."

Phoebe's back went up at this. "And just what exactly do you think I've been *capable of?*"

Lennie stared at her. "Only you know for sure. But personally, I've never seen Ian Braithwaite be nice to *anyone* for more than a few days. He's a jackass at the best of times. But he seems to like you quite a bit ... and he's been on his best behaviour too." He raised a cheeky eyebrow. "Ronan was about this close"—he pinched his thumb and forefinger together—"to kicking Ian out before he found you and brought you back to the safe house."

"Maybe Ian just likes me."

"Maybe," Lennie said, fighting back a smirk. "But I'm not convinced that Ian likes anyone."

She'd only been using Ian to bring herself both pleasure and much needed distraction. She'd had no idea she'd been bringing him to heel simultaneously. *Apparently, I've got a magic pussy,* she thought a bit sarcastically.

Phoebe couldn't help but wonder if that was why Ronan had been so awkwardly tight-lipped about her interactions with Ian, rather than being jealous as she'd assumed he would be. To her surprise, her heart sank a bit at the thought. She would have liked the idea of Ronan being jealous of someone else holding her. Fucking her. Needing her ...

She would be lying if the idea of Ronan actively pursuing her didn't give her a bit of a rush. She could only imagine how doggedly he'd chase a woman he was crazy about while still maintaining his "cool." In another life, Phoebe might have even had a lot of fun with it; she'd already established how much she enjoyed teasing the shit out of him.

"So, let's just say I accept your offer. What comes next? Do I continue to work with Ronan, or will you pair me with someone else?"

Phoebe realized then that she was asking this question not only because she didn't want to lose the chance to search Ronan's personal files—something she was ashamed to admit that she'd lost sight of—but because she didn't want to lose the chance at having more time with Ronan himself.

Since Lennie had already stripped her bare about her past life, she figured she might as well offer some truth. "I like working with Ronan."

"Good. And I don't see any reason why you couldn't continue training under him, at least for the time being. As much as your trip to Bamfield went against protocol, no one can deny that you make a good team. In fact, from what he's told me, you made an exceptional one. In combat at least."

Phoebe blushed.

"Not to mention the fact that you standing up for him in the meeting spoke volumes about the type of bond that's forming between you two. To be partners in the field ... Well, you have to be willing to go to bat for one another. The last field partner who had that sort of bond with Ronan was Dom, and I assume you've been read into the history around all of that."

"But Dom wasn't really a Druid, was he? Ronan said he was more of an honorary Druid."

"Well, an honorary Druid, perhaps. But Dom is also an 'otherworldly prince' and led us to defeat Cassius in one of the wildest battles any of us has fought in our lives." His eyes seemed suddenly far away, as though he were fondly reminiscing about the bliss of a life-altering war.

"Dom is a legend," he continued. "And he and Ronan made an incredible team. They still do when Dom decides that he's willing to fight."

Phoebe's brows furrowed. "Do you think he's wrong to choose a quiet life instead?"

"Not at all. I just think that Julia's arrival in Ronan's life, and in Dom's, fucked with him in a meaningful way ... even if they *are* his chosen family. Ronan has been attempting to claw his way towards his truest self, and happiness, ever since."

Phoebe looked intently at Lennie, who seemed to be debating saying something more. Finally, he cleared his throat.

"Look, Phoebe ... I do have one request."

"Oh? Shoot."

"Ronan has been through a lot. And it's made him ... Well, he's got some personal leanings ... psychological proclivities that require his closest friends—Dom and myself, specifically—to keep an eye on him."

Phoebe bit her lip. Was this a setup to force her to admit that she knew about Ronan's past role as Cassius's pet scientist, or merely a plea for her understanding and a call for compassion towards the Druid doctor?

"What do you mean?" she asked innocently.

Lennie grew suddenly serious, and when he responded, there was a pointedness to his words that was impossible to miss. "What I'm saying, Phoebe, is that Ronan has people looking out for him."

At this, she felt a sharp jolt deep in her belly, which had nothing to do with the trapped magic. "I see."

"Please don't take this the wrong way, but if you fuck with him ... we *will* know. And we will do something about it."

In the end, Phoebe accepted her new position with the Druidic Order without further discussion.

Following her video call with Lennie, Phoebe realized that she was now completely alone in the safe house. The temptation to blast music, dance around completely naked, and make a general mess was trumped only by the niggling realization that this might be her only chance for a long time to unearth Ronan's personal files ... the ones that she still suspected contained the whole truth of whether he actually possessed the skills to free her from her torment, which he might be too ashamed to actually admit to her.

She didn't believe that Ronan's involvement in Cassius's experiments reflected hidden malice in the Druid doctor. She'd overheard too many snide and degrading comments about him from her captors to think otherwise. Instead, she saw it as being symptomatic of someone who was prone to obsession and the consequences of such pursuits, if only because she shared that trait and ... like recognized like.

She also knew how dangerous this quality was. How utterly destructive. Her thoughts travelled to a place she preferred to avoid ...

Phoebe's family of origin had disintegrated into such a skeletal existence through the years—largely due to her parents' combined obsession with their respective jobs and avoidance of each other—that by the time Phoebe had reached high school, she'd effectively become an orphan. And so, when they'd died in a boating accident in her twenties while on a vacation to "save their marriage" (a routine that stretched back as far as she could remember) ... well, Phoebe was already accustomed to the disasters born of unhealthy habits.

She shut the laptop and strolled from the dining room into the kitchen. She could hear the buzz of an electrical appliance somewhere nearby—the fridge, she assumed—and it got under her skin. So, she climbed the stairs to the second floor, pausing in front of Ian's empty room, which was a complete disaster. She'd never really noticed before what a slob Ian was. In fact, the way he treated his space—which she now knew was offered to him free of charge by the Druids in exchange for his services—bordered on disrespectful. Man-child he might be, but he was also *extremely* hot. What a conundrum.

Phoebe flicked on his light and crossed the room, heading to a wooden box in the top drawer of his dresser, where she knew he kept his stash. She helped herself to a joint. He wouldn't notice, and she could certainly use the chill right about now. Then she turned off the light and quietly shut his door.

Next, she peered into Ronan's room, which was the picture of cleanliness. Phoebe knew damn well that neither mess nor tidiness were sole indicators of one's mental states; people were far more complex than that. But something about Ronan's room perfectly reflected the calm sense of order she'd come to appreciate about him. And now was her chance to enter his space and have a look around.

She knew that he ordinarily locked his door, so this glimpse into his room meant that he was likely nearby. But something—other than the obvious risk of being caught—held her back. Was it guilt? Simply exhaustion, perhaps?

She turned on the spot and looked behind herself into her new bedroom, which, in her opinion, was *just right*. It was a little sloppy, sure. But she'd already started making touches of her own to bring some personality into the space. She'd recently brought a vase upstairs from the kitchen and filled it with some sprigs of eucalyptus, which she'd found growing unchecked in the backyard. She'd also scrounged up a few rocks, shells, and crystals that had been lying around the house and lined them up along her windowsill. A striped wool blanket that had been relegated to the back of the couch downstairs now adorned the armchair in the corner. Her bed was unmade, and some clothes were strewn about, making it look like a college dorm room. But still, it was starting to feel like home ... for now, at least.

Someone cleared their throat behind her, making her jump and spin around. Ronan was standing there, about two feet away and wearing the same pair of well-tailored slacks as before, though he had his dress shirt back on and had topped off the outfit with a dark-blue, button-down cardigan.

"What are you doing?" he asked, a cool edge to his voice.

Phoebe had learned long ago that a partial truth was always better than an outright lie. "If you must know, I was comparing our rooms. Yours is so tidy."

He chuckled. "I noticed you've been adding some personal touches to yours."

She cocked an eyebrow at him. "So, you've been comparing our rooms as well."

"Not comparing. Just noticing. I like that you're making yourself at home. I take it you've accepted Lennie's offer?"

"I have." She felt an unexpected and gnawing need for his approval. "Does that please you?"

Ronan's nostrils flared. "It does."

Phoebe hadn't expected her need for approval to arouse him somehow, nor did she know that the tone of an entire room (or in this case, hallway) could shift so suddenly; the sudden onset of sexual tension between them was beyond palpable.

Ronan seemed to be thinking similar thoughts, even as he flexed his thighs where he stood and cleared his throat again. Phoebe watched him, seemingly frozen in place, and licked her lips, her eyes flicking between his face and the stack of files he was currently white-knuckling across his chest.

Phoebe's cheeks flushed as the magic within her calmed somewhat, making room for a much more wicked desire to rise to the surface. Her heart pounded. She knew that somewhere in that big, silly, complex brain of his, Ronan was feeling it too. And maybe it was exactly what they both needed ...

Fuck it.

"What are you up to now?" she asked in a breathy tone.

"Imogen emailed her findings from our visit yesterday." Ronan's voice was strangely even. Impossibly controlled. "I was going to cross-check her thoughts with what I've already gathered and sort out what other information we might still need to collect."

Phoebe stepped towards him, reaching out her hand and opening her palm to expose the joint she'd retrieved only a few minutes earlier. "I took this from Ian's room. I was going to smoke it and watch a movie maybe. You're welcome to join me instead of reading all of that." She nodded towards his stack of papers.

He blinked hard several times, effectively snapping himself from his stupor. "*Ehm* ... No, thank you, Phoebe. This is important, and I'd like to get on top of it while it's still fresh."

With that, he breezed past her into his bedroom and shut his door, the lock making an audible click.

Phoebe remained where she was for several moments before slowly walking into her bedroom, cracking the window, and lighting up. Her heart was still racing.

Well, that was new.

CHAPTER 19

RONAN

RONAN WOKE UP DRENCHED IN SWEAT FROM A VIOLENT NIGHTMARE, one of the worst ones he'd had in months. Years, perhaps. However, instead of fighting his usual demons—most commonly Cassius (and on rare occasions, demented versions of himself)—in this dream, he'd come face to face with Phoebe. But in an altered form.

A *demonic* form.

In the dream, Ronan stood alone in a generic hotel hallway. But instead of it having a defined end, the hall seemed to go on forever in both directions. Above him, artificial lights were flickering ... very much like they would in a horror movie.

Jewel-toned beetles skittered over his boots, seemingly having come from his room, the door of which stood ajar just ahead of him. Inside was a swampy forest, along with his medical bag and several other personal items, including a teddy bear from his childhood and a photograph of his granny Sheila. Long tendrils of vines, ferns, and other foliage crept past the threshold of the room like a spreading green infection. The air inside the room pulsated for several seconds before the door suddenly slammed shut with a echoing *"Bang!"*

Ronan turned slowly on the spot to face the room across from his, his instincts screaming at him that this was the place he'd been looking for. He'd been tasked by the Druidic Order to locate the mysterious woman ... and keep her safe. He looked down at his empty hands. He'd arrived to apprehend one of the most powerful women alive without any weapons.

His blood pulsed through his veins like cold honey as he forced his limbs to cooperate with his intention: getting inside. Sluggishly, he knocked on the closed door to Phoebe's room.

She didn't answer.

"Phoebe?" he called, trying to keep the fear from his voice. It sounded strange. Far away.

"*Phoebe!*" he shouted.

Soon, and much to his relief, he heard shuffling from behind the door. She was in there but seemed to either be patently ignoring him or unable to hear him. The images began screeching through his mind so violently then that he wasn't sure he could ever forget them.

The door might be shut, but it wasn't locked.

It swung inward, creaking open.

The lights continued flickering ominously as Ronan crossed the threshold of the dim hotel room. He looked down and noticed that he was up to his ankles in dark water. He sloshed forward, his pace slowing further as the water thickened to the consistency of molasses.

He could see someone sitting near the window ... Phoebe, presumably.

"What are you doing over there?" he asked, suddenly transported right next to her. She was gripping her chest, and blood was pouring from every orifice in her head, her ears and nose ... her beautiful and terrifying mouth ... "Phoebe, you need help—"

"Do you truly think you can help me, Dr. Gallagher?" Her words were slow and thickened with coagulating blood. She gurgled slightly and flashed her sharp teeth.

"I don't know how ... I swear."

She growled menacingly before snapping her wretched jaws at him. "Yes, you do! Don't lie to me!"

Ronan raised his hands and began backing towards the hallway. The wild plants from his room had grown into that space, though, and now barred the doorway. Black mould crept forward in a vast swath of darkness across the ceiling.

"The plants listen to me ..." she murmured, crawling closer to him, her broken body clicking and popping like some demented, quadrupedal zombie. "The earth listens to me ... Even the mould listens to me ..."

Ronan looked down to see that the hotel carpet underfoot had turned into rich, black earth that rose up then, rumbling and rolling ... and swiftly burying him alive.

Demon Phoebe crawled closer and crouched down on top of him, pinning him between her demonic body and the enveloping earth below.

"Do you believe I should be *allowed to exist?*" she hissed, drawing so near that the blood from her lips dripped onto his face and into his mouth. "You know I'm an abomination ... Druid." She sank several long nails into his chest then as he screamed in agony. "I'm something that should not exist." She sank her long teeth into his neck and drank from him. "Only you can save me ..."

The next time Ronan woke up, early the next morning, his face was planted on his desk. He'd been unable to get back to sleep following his wretched nightmare, so he'd stopped trying and, instead, redoubled his already overzealous efforts to wade through Phoebe's medical notes, old and new, as well as Imogen's recent findings about the plants and her observations about Phoebe. The fact that Imogen's lengthy email had arrived only moments before Ronan had run into Phoebe in the upstairs hallway last night had likely impacted his frenzy to rule out anything and everything they might be missing ... and fuelled his nightmare as well.

He'd needed to remove such thoughts from his head and focus on what was truly important. And as a result, he'd compiled a nearly exhaustive list of the information he believed they still needed to find —information on what exactly happened to Phoebe during her capture and intake and what had happened on the day of the explosion, the two sets of details effectively bookending Phoebe's experience in captivity.

He still hadn't managed to run any meaningful diagnostic tests on Phoebe either. The conversation at Imogen's condo, about the plant and mould propagation, had obviously been their priority at the time ... but he worried that he was still missing something that even a rudimentary medical exam might expose.

Before he'd dozed off again reviewing her notes, Ronan had also arrived at a new theory that he wasn't entirely ready to share with anyone yet. He looked down at his notebook, reviewing his scrawled notes from hours earlier:

Re: Imogen's experiment
What if Phoebe's body is "the mould" and the trapped magic is "the plants"?
Does Phoebe feed the mould or the plants in any way?
And if so, is it conscious or subconscious?

This thought worried him considerably because it meant that no incantation, potion, or pouch would be able to effectively remove the trapped magic. It seemed that only Phoebe could influence the magic that now resided within her ... and she was both traumatized and utterly untrained as a Wielder. How would they coax it out of her? If doing so was even possible.

She was both a bomb and its detonator.

He picked up his cell phone and called Lennie.

"We need more information," he blurted out as soon as Lennie picked up. "Where are the rest of the files? Where is the next target? I feel like we've exhausted all our West Coast options. And south of the border—"

"Hold it right there, Ronan," Lennie said, his interruption punctuated by the clacking of keys as he continued typing fiercely at his computer on his end of the call. "I can sense you're feeling restless, but you need to breathe for a second. I can't keep up."

"Restless?" Ronan thought for a moment, then sighed. "I suppose I am. I had a nightmare last night that, while completely unrealistic, has stirred up some intense feelings in me."

"Can I ask what it was about?"

Ronan relayed the gist of his dream to Lennie, who just listened quietly, periodically typing something in the background. "That's interesting," he said when Ronan was done. "What do you think it means?"

"I think it means we need more information!" Ronan said impatiently; he was unbelievably overtired and in a foul mood.

When Lennie spoke again, his tone was stern. "Well, as you are aware, based on the computer files and logbooks we've managed to retrieve since the explosion, we're still missing about thirty percent of the research documentation from the facility. It's possible that the files we need were inadvertently destroyed on that day, but it's also possible that they were saved and relocated somehow."

Ronan felt his blood pressure rise. "I know this already, Len. What are you trying to say?"

"What I'm saying is that if I knew where the fucking documents were, you'd be the first to know!"

"Yes, but—"

"I understand you're anxious to solve this, Ronan. But you also have to understand that, right now, we only know what we know. You can trust that I'm working on it though."

"Sorry ... Of course, you're right."

Lennie's voice lightened then. "Thank you. In the meantime, I do have a lead you might wish to follow. I've just received intel that several truckloads of those plants are being transported east even as we speak."

"Really?" Ronan asked, surprised. From what he'd seen of the plants, there was a genuine risk that the transport trucks would be overcome by them before ever arriving at their intended destination. "How far east are we talking?"

"Not far. The waybill listed a delivery just beyond the Rockies ..." Ronan could hear Lennie typing feverishly on his computer from his current location across the pond. "There's major Wraith activity in Calgary, Alberta, and it's increasing daily. It might be worth looking into that location for facility files while you're there; though, so far, we don't think the two groups are connected. If nothing else though, it's somewhere we haven't already looked.

"It's worth a shot," Ronan said, scratching his beard.

"The primary goal for the mission," Lennie clarified, "will be to find anything that might explain what the Wraiths are planning to achieve with the plants."

"How soon can you get us out there?"

"Is this afternoon too soon?"

"I'll manage, as long as Phoebe is game." He doubted he would get any more sleep before then, but what else was new?

"Affirmative. I'll email you travel directives shortly. But hey," Lennie added, his voice growing soft, "are you doing alright, mate? You sound ... tired."

"Yes, I'm fine. Thanks for asking though. I think ..."

"You think what?"

"Ah, it's nothing ... You're right. I just need some action. Thanks a million, Lennie. I'll watch for your email."

"Cheers."

Ronan shut his eyes, pinching the bridge of his long nose.

This couldn't be an obsession, he reassured himself, since his focus was tied directly to his worry for Phoebe's wellbeing. He cared one hell of a lot more than two shits about the enigmatic woman.

The meeting with Imogen had brought up an important question for him though: exactly how much magic *was* trapped inside of Phoebe? And how had the Wraiths managed to trap it there? From what he'd been able to infer, it was a fuck-ton of magic, but that wasn't exactly a useful unit of measurement, and it certainly didn't bring him any closer to figuring out how they had done it or how he could even begin to help her.

In his nightmare, *Demon Phoebe* had accused him of being the only one who could cure and save her, believing he was withholding information. And he couldn't help but wonder if she had been right. With that dream, was Ronan's subconscious pushing him towards knowledge that already lived inside of him?

Deep down, he knew that was patently false. The only person applying pressure on Ronan specifically to solve Phoebe's mystery was himself. And regardless, the magic that had once been contained within the Codex would be useless here. It was inherently destructive and would either trap the magic inside of her even worse, or it would end Phoebe's physical body.

Following a series of unfortunate events leading to his final demise, the Sorcerer Cassius *had* developed a modality to trap Wraith magic within Bearers. But Ronan was confident, though not wholly certain, that the Wraiths would not have known about that particular spell since Cassius had guarded the Codex with his life.

There had only been one Bearer in history able to hold—and contain—Wraith magic without disastrous effects: Julia. The rest had faced insanity at nearly every turn. And to the best of Ronan's knowledge, the same experiment had never been even attempted on a Wielder.

So, how exactly had the Wraiths managed it?

From personal experience, he knew that a person exposed to the Wraiths' dark and decaying magic for extended periods of time would be infected by it. But how did they manage to trap so much of it inside of Phoebe without killing her? Or even worse, turning her into a Wraith herself?

The answer, he surmised, lay buried somewhere deep inside of Phoebe ... who had proven to be both a singularity and an anomaly.

Ronan stretched his legs out on his bed and opened his laptop. He was soon going to be joining his therapist, Eunice, on a video call. He'd long resisted therapy, not believing it necessary for someone like him. He already knew all too well how the human mind worked. How people worked.

How *he* worked.

But then, several years ago, he'd lost control of his obsession to understand both Wraith composition and the *Codex Druidicus*, coming face to face with the undeniable fact that he was just as susceptible to mental-health challenges as anyone else.

And likely even more so.

Her smiling face appeared on his screen then. "Hello, Ronan!"

Eunice was in her late fifties, with stylishly cropped hair, and wore a different pair of dangly earrings each time they met. Today, she was wearing a set comprised of golden suns and silver moons, which somehow reminded him of Phoebe.

Ronan smiled back. "Hello, Eunice. How are you today?"

"Well, it's a bit embarrassing, but I spent most of yesterday at the vet with my dog. He got into my laundry and ate some of my underwear, which required an emergency intervention to clear the blockage, the little shit." She paused and chuckled wryly. "Oh god. Oversharing. Sorry, that was unprofessional."

Ronan laughed, but his heart went out to the pup. "Is he alright now?"

She scoffed at his concern. "Yes. He's fine. This isn't the first time he's done that. He's become a rather expensive rescue dog if I'm honest. He's just lucky he's so cute."

Ronan thought of Gracie and how much he'd like to get another dog. And then, strangely, he thought of Phoebe, and how he might want to talk to Eunice today about some of the things he was struggling with ...

"So, what do you want to focus on today?" she asked kindly, recapturing his attention. "Your email only said that you sensed it was time to reconnect."

Ronan realized that, initially, he'd hoped to share with her the fact that his panic attacks had been returning as of late and that he was feeling a pull towards his old obsessive tendencies—ones he knew were wholly unhealthy for him. Instead, he realized that he really wanted to talk about Phoebe.

"Well, most of what we've worked on over the past few years has been sort of functional ... about my work or coping skills. My flashbacks." Eunice knew that Ronan had served in the military and was a doctor. "But another area that we've never really touched upon is relationships."

Eunice tilted her head inquisitively. "Do you mean the interpersonal ones ... or romantic?"

"Romantic," he said, clearing his throat. "I've not had the best track record."

She nodded. "Well, it's not easy to maintain balance when you're often in high-stress situations. Presumably, your field of work has had an impact on that."

"It has, but it's more than that ..." Ronan honestly wasn't sure where to start.

"Can I ask what best describes your sexual orientation?" she asked then. "I don't want to misstep as we discuss this, and we've only briefly touched on it in our past sessions ..."

Up until this point, Ronan had mostly leaned on Eunice to help him manage job stress and his obsessive tendencies and need for control.

"Heterosexual."

"Thanks. And so, do you spend time with women casually? And how best do you like to spend that time with women if you do?"

Ronan leaned back against the wall, propping up his pillows behind him. "Well, I have plenty of platonic friendships with women, and those relationships are sound."

"And what about sexual relationships? Do you find yourself drawn towards casual hookups, or are you more of the wait-until-dating type? How would you describe yourself?"

Ronan smirked, pulling off his glasses. "What do *you* think?"

Eunice chuckled. "Ronan, I'm not paid nearly enough to make those sorts of assumptions."

He sighed. "The long and the short of it is that I have no trouble maintaining healthy friendships and no difficulty finding myself in consensual sexual encounters either."

"But ...?"

"But as soon as the partnership grows into something more than friends, or more intimate than casual sex, I feel like I get all ... confused? Maybe that sounds silly, but it's like one minute, I'm finding myself attentive to their needs and quite content with that, and the next, I'm shutting them out over something stupid. And then when they call me out on the behaviour ... I get angry. Well ... maybe more frustrated than angry, but still ..." He felt like he was rambling.

Eunice cleared her throat. "So, what I think I hear you saying is that you find yourself engaging in a sort of push and pull with partners? Is that correct?"

"I suppose so."

"And what is usually the breaking point for these relationships?"

He ran his hands through his hair. "Like the reasons they cite for having ended things or ...?"

"In your words ..."

"Most often it's that I'm unable—or maybe unwilling, I don't know —to be intimate and vulnerable with them the way they'd like. They want me to open up more and let my real self out. And I just ..." Eunice waited patiently. "I just ... can't."

She looked genuinely sympathetic, which made Ronan squirm. "And am I correct to assume that you *want* to engage in that way?"

Ronan pondered her question. *Did* he want that? He'd been single for most of his adult life but, generally, not alone. He had many good friends, particularly within the Druidic Order, who "filled his cup," as it were, both socially and emotionally. On the other hand, he'd only experienced a handful of serious relationships ... nothing that had last for more than a few years.

The same confusion came up when he thought of answering her question honestly. "I honestly don't know anymore."

"Okay, let me phrase that differently. Is there someone, right now, making you consider entering into a long-term relationship, someone with whom you might like to explore these deeper connections?"

Ronan suddenly regretted bringing this subject up. "*Ehm* ... Specifically, right now, I'm having a similar sort of confusion about someone I work with. But before you suggest that it might be an ethics issue, there isn't. How can I put this?" He looked up at the ceiling, reminding himself that Eunice understood and respected the strict privacy required for his work, despite not knowing the specifics. After a moment, he continued. "The professional position that she and I share can be shared by romantic partners and historically has been on occasion. It's not the case as a rule, but it's not uncommon either."

"It sounds like you are struggling with the decision of whether or not you want to engage in an intimate relationship with her or keep it platonic."

"No, that's not quite it," he said. "It's that this person, she ..."

Eunice waited again.

"I think ..." Ronan grimaced. "Hypothetically speaking, if I *were* to engage in something ... more with her, I'd be terrified of fucking it up. It's— *She's* complicated."

"Aren't we all?" Eunice offered sagely.

"More than that, though, the nature of the job itself makes things quite thorny all on its own." As much as he liked Eunice, Ronan knew that he needed to find himself a therapist within the Order; it was unbelievably challenging to tiptoe around sensitive subjects this much while still showing up authentically to do the work.

"And has she expressed an interest in taking things beyond the level of co-workers?"

"Co-workers" was not a word Ronan would have used to describe their relationship. "Not explicitly, no. But I feel like I need to get my head around all of *this*," he gestured at himself, "before I consider anything serious with anyone else."

He was in no place with his otherworldly mission to dig deeper with someone romantically right now. Besides, where the hell would he find the time?

They chatted for a while about his past relationships—about how his relationship with Lindsey (another Druid) had been the closest he'd ever come to settling down in a way that felt *hopeful*. Someone he might have even considered getting a dog with ...

Again, Ronan's mind wandered to Phoebe.

Eunice listened intently as he shared details with her about the final argument he'd had with Lindsey, in which she'd given him one last ultimatum after far more chances than he deserved, telling him that if he didn't get his shit together, she would leave him.

Ronan had *not* gotten his shit together.

"I'm still not entirely sure what happened," he said. "She wanted kids, but I don't think that was really the main issue."

"And do you want children?"

"No, but at the time, I suppose that I might have. The whole thing was just so fucking *confusing* though."

Eunice considered this. "You've brought up your confusion a few times now, and I'm curious ... When you think of the sort of confusion you experience in relationships, I wonder if you can remember any other times or circumstances in your life, possibly when you were much younger, when you might have felt that same way. Is that something you could comfortably try to do right now?"

Ronan could think of about fifty different examples of feeling that same way throughout his life. "I can, and it is."

She smiled. "Good. You don't have to tell me about the specific instance, but I'm curious where you feel it in your body?"

He closed his eyes and let out a slow breath, trying to bring himself fully into such a moment and considering the sensation. "In my throat." He opened his eyes. "It kind of feels like when I want to cry."

"When you *want* to cry," she parroted. "Do you cry often?"

"No. But I'm not immune to it," he chuckled (rather avoidantly).

"What happens when you place your hands on your throat and try to breathe through the feeling."

Ronan did as he was told and thought of what it might be like to engage in a deeper relationship with Phoebe. He felt ... *afraid*. But also ... a little soothed for having admitted that to himself. "It feels like fear, I suppose."

Eunice smiled kindly, then looked at her watch with seeming reluctance. Their time had flown by. "Can I ask you something? Something that I want you to think about between now and our next session."

"Sure," Ronan said, yawning, exhausted as usual by the therapy session, not to mention his recent lack of proper sleep.

"I want you to consider whether you think your fear around the possibility of entering into a deeper relationship with your co-worker centres around a fear of things going wrong ... or a fear of things going *right?*"

The ominous voices of the Otherworld shouted in his mind then: *"We have always rewarded surrender over sacrifice, Ronan."*

CHAPTER 20

RONAN

It was mid-afternoon when Ronan and Phoebe arrived in Calgary from Vancouver. The flight from YVR to YYC had been quick, though not without its hiccups. Phoebe had dumped her sugary, and nearly half-full, iced latte onto Ronan's lap as they'd sat side by side on the narrow plane. Of course, she'd laughed this off, but he had been less than enthused.

"Easy for you to laugh, Phoebe. You're not the one covered in caramel syrup!"

"I'm so sorry," she said, blinking back mirthful tears, then sobering at the look on his face. *"Actually, though, I'm really sorry."*

"It's fine," he'd grumbled. *"I brought other pants with me."*

Crossing the Rockies, they'd hit major turbulence. With fear-widened eyes, Phoebe had gripped Ronan's hand so tightly that it hurt. He'd gripped her hand right back though, until the skies and Phoebe had both settled. Despite the outward show of confidence she always portrayed, there was also a sort of unassuming innocence about her.

From experience, Ronan knew that Phoebe was a woman who could hold her own, both in a fight and in life in general, but her hidden softness had somehow triggered his instinctive protectiveness; he hated the idea of anyone taking advantage of her.

Her softness. Her kindness. Her authenticity.

Ronan had spent the remainder of the flight fighting a flurry of emotions—ones he knew all too fucking well that he shouldn't be battling about the gorgeous woman sitting beside him. He'd also considered Eunice's question about fear and decided that it was far more complicated than distilling it down to any single emotion or impulse.

Not only was Phoebe his adopted partner in the Druidic network—not that partnerships didn't regularly turn into romances in their world—but she was also interwoven far too closely with his own sordid past. If she knew the hand he had played in all of this—in all that had happened to her—well, there was no way even a working relationship could survive that sort of bomb, let alone a romantic one.

The real mission here was to get the damned magic out of her or, at the very least, slow whatever appeared to be happening. Even at a glance, Phoebe's hair seemed thinner than when he'd first met her, not to mention the dark circles under her eyes that rarely relented. She was sick and getting sicker ... and he was no closer to understanding why.

Ronan would just have to appreciate what time they did have together. Whatever else might come would come regardless.

Nearing the end of the flight, he tapped her on the shoulder, and she pulled down her noise-cancelling headphones. He was pretty sure she'd been listening to a podcast about cults as she gazed out the window.

"I have a bit of a random question," he said, a hint of playfulness in his voice. "But you like those, I think."

"I do indeed," she said with a smile. "Shoot."

He shifted his body ever so slightly to face her more directly. "If you could pick anywhere in the world to visit right now—like, if this plane could just magically take us there—where would you go?"

He watched as Phoebe bit her lip, pondering this as she looked at him with narrowed eyes, likely questioning whether or not there was catch of some sort. But then she let out a long sigh.

"Ireland."

His eyebrows shot up. "*Really!?*"

"Don't get all self-important about it. I've wanted to visit there since long before you came along. As far as I know, I'm at least a quarter Irish, with that arm of my family coming over several generations back. The other side is Dutch, I think. I'm not totally clear."

"Have you had your ancestry or genetics done?"

"Not intentionally. Though I imagine *they* did it."

At this, Ronan's smile had faltered. "*Hmm* ..."

"What?"

"Oh, it's nothing." He folded his hands on his lap and bit back burning regret for having opened this (or any) can of worms with her. "But you know, I could actually take you to Ireland someday, assuming you wanted that. In fact, there's a strong possibility we'll end up there anyway with the Druid network, assuming you stick around long enough."

He blushed as she smirked at him rather cheekily.

"Would you *like* me to stick around?"

"Depends on a few things."

"I'll bet," she snorted sarcastically. "Alright then ... So, where in the world would *you* want to go?"

Just then, the pilot's muffled voice came over the intercom, announcing that their arrival in Calgary was looming and that they were about to land in the tail end of a snowstorm.

Realizing that his answer to her question was not a destination at all and that, really, he just wanted to spend time at her side, without fear, he opted to ignore it, pointing out the window at the wall of white beyond.

"I hope you packed your winter coat."

Their cab dropped them outside a generic airport hotel.

"Lennie's such a *prick*," Ronan muttered under his breath as they unloaded their luggage and paid the cab driver.

"Why?"

"Because he's booked us at a hotel that's the exact *opposite* of the kind I requested."

Phoebe pulled her jacket closely around her as they stalked towards the hotel's front sliding doors. "Is he mad at you?"

"Probably, though I couldn't say why."

"What sort of hotel *do* you prefer?" she asked. Ronan raised his eyebrows knowingly, and she laughed. "Let me guess: no less than four stars?"

It didn't take a genius to know that Ronan had a disproportionately high standard for his vehicles and accommodations, despite being deeply connected to the earth and all growing things.

"I'm a creature of comfort," he said, nearly slipping on the snowy pavement. "Whenever I can be, at least."

"Fair enough."

Ronan regained his footing and led Phoebe inside the low-star hotel. Lennie, at least, had booked them two separate rooms this time, though they *were* conjoined.

"I don't sleepwalk," Phoebe said with a wink as they exited the elevator on the ninth floor. "At least, I don't think I do. But I can't be held accountable for what I might do if your door is left unlocked."

Their banter was growing increasingly flirtatious, which was dangerous territory. "Oh, really?" he said. "I'll tell you what, at the moment, I'd like to take a nap—"

"Okay, old man."

"—and have a shower," he finished, shoving her playfully to one side as they stood shoulder to shoulder in the hall outside their two rooms. "I have to wash your bloody coffee off my thighs. But when I'm done, I'll knock on your door, and then we can maybe have room service or something before heading out. If not, then I'll meet you in the lobby for eight. Okay?"

She grinned mischievously while biting her lip, no doubt holding back whatever sassy retort was currently sitting on her tongue. "Sounds perfect."

Ronan slid into his mundane room and (somehow) resisted dialling Lennie to chew him out; the whole conjoined rooms thing was actually proving interesting.

Two hours later, Ronan had showered and changed into his only pair of blue jeans (a costly Japanese denim) and a tailored black button-down shirt. For the life of him, he'd not been able to find the only western-ish shirt he owned—a light-blue chambray shirt with subtly detailed front pockets. He hadn't worn it for a few years, but it was designer.

He'd resisted taking a nap, opting instead to catch up on any last-minute details from Lennie's brief. He turned the lock and opened his interior door, pausing momentarily before rapping on the adjoining door to Phoebe's room.

Seconds later, she opened her inner door.

"Howdy, Ronan!" she said, popping a chestnut-brown cowboy hat onto her beachy blonde locks and grinning ear to ear. "What do you think?"

Ronan gaped at her.

Phoebe turned and quite literally strutted a quick runway loop through her room. She was wearing a white crop top and a pair of blue jeans that looked like they'd been painted on. On her feet, she wore cowboy boots that only reached her ankles. Cowboy booties?

According to Phoebe, she was very familiar with these sorts of "country" haunts, and he had to admit he believed her in this outfit. Seemingly unaware of his uncouth behaviour, staring openly at her, Phoebe rifled through her backpack and pulled out a buttery leather belt followed by a light-blue chambray shirt, which if he wasn't mistaken belonged to him.

"Phoebe—"

"I found this in a closet at the Vancouver house before we left."

He watched in near disbelief as she pulled the shirt on over her crop top, tying it at her waist, which carved out her sumptuous figure even more than usual. "That's *mine*."

She smirked. "That's funny. It was *your* closet? We're pretty much the same size."

Ronan took stock. She'd now snatched his book from his bedside table and a shirt from his closet. He could have sworn that his door was locked this time, as was his standing practice. Had she picked the lock? Or was he just careless? He shook his head, which was still (mercifully) hat-free. Phoebe had already teased him several times that he was being a spoil sport for not dressing the part on this mission.

But on that point, he'd been *firm.*

"Are you completely sure you won't wear the hat?" she asked, yet again, twirling a strand of hair through her long fingers.

He groaned. "Absolutely *not.*"

She pouted. "Wear it for me?"

"Fuck off already about the hat, Phoebe," he said, though not unkindly. "I've already said no."

"You're a spoil sport." She stuck out her tongue.

"I'm an Irish Druid-doctor ... patently *not* a cowboy."

"Exactly. That's what makes it fun!"

Someone like Dom—a literal ancient Celtic prince—would have *gladly* donned the cowboy hat. The bastard would have looked like a million dollars in it too and probably won some bullshit prize for being the biggest, best-est, cutest country boy ever.

"*No.*"

"You'll have women falling all over you."

Ronan was growing irritated now. "That's not the point of this mission."

She momentarily locked her stare on his before releasing him with a low snort. Bending at the waist, she slid an index finger into her boot, presumably to adjust her sock.

The look she'd given him had definitely been feisty. He shook his head. "Where did you find those boots, anyway? Aren't your feet like a size fifteen?"

"Ten and a half, asshole," she replied easily, standing and now swiping clear lip gloss across her naturally pink lips. "And I thrifted them."

He shook his head, impressed. "Another disguise?"

"Nope," she said, turning on her cowboy-booted heel and heading for the door. "I just have a soft spot for country music. It's kind of swoon-y."

"Well, I'm far from swoon-y."

She didn't look back as she stepped into the hall ahead of him. "You look fine."

He grabbed his key card and followed her with a huff. "Let's go, then."

Ronan trailed several paces behind Phoebe as they approached the bar's entrance. The plan was to enter separately this time. If she got into trouble, he'd cut ahead and support her, but it was important that they built their skills as a team not only working together but in tandem.

People were out in droves, anticipating some big-name rodeo star who was in town and rumoured to be arriving at the bar later that evening, and being generally obnoxious. It was a perfect cover.

Naturally, Phoebe had been concerned about entering the Wraith-owned establishment on her own, but Ronan could feel himself being pulled towards her, even in the growing crowd. Ever since fighting back to back with Phoebe on the trawler, when he'd been able to feel her magical presence without seeing her, he'd been curious if they could hone that connection into something useful.

During their taxi ride from the hotel, he'd told her, *"What you'll need to do is see if you can feel me behind you ... or more accurately, my essence."* Their driver had been listening to the radio, so Ronan had been fairly certain they were in the clear, but one couldn't be too careful. So, he had spoken in a near whisper. *"See if you can sense me as I move through the bar too. It would be good to determine at what distance the feeling starts to fade."*

Phoebe, for her part, had been skeptical. *"If you're sure ..."*

A connection like that was rare in partnerships within the Order, though not unheard of. And it wasn't always romantic, either. Sean and Graham—the Druid pair who'd died at the hands of Cassius mere weeks before his final demise—had worked together for so many years that their magic almost seemed to work in tandem, each seemingly speaking some unknown but magical tongue to the other. Amos and

Amelia's twin bond had helped them survive on more than one occasion and was one of the main reasons they continued to work together, rather than with other Order members. It kept them safe.

Ronan thought that, if he and Phoebe did indeed share some exceptional connection (sexual tension notwithstanding), they would be foolish not to develop it.

"It's not common what I'm picking up on, but I'd like to use this mission as a chance to explore it," he'd said.

And now, he found himself waiting in line outside the entrance and watching Phoebe chatting with the bouncer up ahead—or, more accurately, loudly flirting with him. She tossed her head back, laughing wildly at whatever he'd just said, even while doing this sort of hip-wriggle thing that had captured the staring eyes of Ronan and every other man within twenty metres.

He tried not to feel jealous.

Thankfully, the bouncer didn't appear to be a Wraith, though he'd been fooled before, especially with Wraiths in their early stages of degradation. After a few moments, Phoebe slipped into the bar. And the line kept moving, though painfully slow. When Ronan finally reached the front of it though, he wasn't welcomed inside.

"Sorry, friend. We're at capacity. You'll have to wait until a few more people leave."

He probably should have worn the damn cowboy hat, although he'd never admit that to Phoebe.

When he finally entered the bar nearly twenty-five minutes later, Ronan closed his eyes and attempted to feel her presence, sensing her out on the dance floor already. Then he opened his eyes and checked the accuracy. Looking around, he was almost immediately greeted by the sight of Phoebe on the dance floor, doing the two-step in the arms of a big man wearing an even bigger hat. She said something into the man's ear that made him laugh as they continued dancing their way across the floor.

Ronan realized that he was grinding his teeth as he watched this display. Even now, appreciative eyes from all over the bar were being drawn to her like wasps to a watermelon.

When Phoebe put "it" on, no one could resist her.

And yet, as much as he hated the effect that she was having on everyone—including *him*—he had to remember their mission. They needed to get into the back room and access any potentially relevant files they might find there, and attempt to track down the place where the plants had been stored upon their arrival at this building. He knew they were around here somewhere as Lennie had been tracking them throughout their entire trip. Even if Ronan couldn't find where the plants were stored at present, Phoebe might be able to feel them, at least based on her reaction to the plants back at Imogen's place.

Phoebe finished her dance and left her partner standing stupidly on the dance floor, looking forlorn. Her eyes immediately tracked to Ronan as she walked towards the bar, pointing discreetly towards the ceiling.

Ronan looked up.

He hadn't even noticed how high the ceilings were. He'd been too busy watching Phoebe dance the two-step with some raunchy ranch hand. But there they were, the vines, dangling down from high in the rafters in all their bright-green glory. Interestingly, the white buds that he'd spotted on the plants at the rave were in bloom on these vines, their bell-shaped flowers opening wide ... and seeming to be reaching for the patrons below.

That settled it. The Wraiths were definitely using the plants to (somehow) collect magic from unassuming Wielders in the crowd, just as they'd done at the rave. Imogen was working on a theory regarding nitrogen fixation in the hybrid plants—only with *magic* instead of nitrogen. But what were they planning to *do* with the plants afterward? Would they then grind them down to be used in some sort of pouch or tincture?

Surely an organic compound like the vines would be meant for consumption ...

The Order had been correct to send him and Phoebe to check on the plants; they would need to keep a close watch if they were to discern what *exactly* the Wraiths were up to.

Ronan walked smoothly towards the bar about four seats from where Phoebe stood and ordered himself a beer. The bartender smiled at him. She was gorgeous, with long, shiny black hair, and had a sort of goth-meets-country thing going on, which Ronan found intriguing.

"First time here?" she asked, but Ronan was suddenly distracted.

Down the bar, Phoebe was somehow already doing shots with a handsome bartender and three other boot-wearing "gentlemen."

He felt his nose scrunching up. Was it just him or did the bar stink of horny cowboy?

"What gave me away?" he asked the bartender as he finally returned his attention her way. Unfortunately, she'd already moved on to another group further up the line. That suited him just fine. He wasn't there to flirt unless it would somehow gain him swift entry into the back room.

That was more *Phoebe's* style anyway.

Her target was the owner-operator of this fine country establishment: a Wraith called Trent. Upon hearing his name, Phoebe had been delighted, saying, *"It's so normal!"* By the look of things, she was already working her magic to draw him out from the back room. The bartender who'd been taking shots with her had since slipped into the back room and returned with a man who matched Lennie's description.

Trent was tall—*so* tall that Phoebe seemed wholly dwarfed by him as Ronan watched her look way up at him, her eyes wide. Ronan knew that he needed to hurry. The Druid doctor stepped back from the bar and, sipping his beer, casually made his way towards the rear door through which Trent the Wraith had recently emerged. It was currently unguarded, at least on this side, so he figured it was now or never. All Ronan required was thirty to sixty seconds at Trent's personal computer, with a specialized USB key that Lennie had provided him. Then he'd be out of there.

For all intents and purposes, this mission was similar to each of the efforts he'd made while trying to catch up to Phoebe, but seemingly simpler. All they were looking for here was documentation that might help shed some light on what they were doing with the plants.

Quick as a flash, he slipped through the doorway and hurried down a short, nondescript hallway towards the spot Lennie had marked for them on the building's blueprints. The hall was mercifully empty, and soon, he was slipping into Trent's office and coming face to face with an entire wall of CCTV screens and a standard desktop computer sitting on a desk before it.

Over the past several years, Ronan had noticed a trend among the "establishment Wraiths"—those Wraiths who owned and operated nightclubs, bars, and the like as fronts for their shadowy operations and as the perfect setup for watching women dance.

Creeps.

Ronan reached into his pocket, sorting past several bundles of cords until he found the USB itself, then pulled it out and quickly plugged it in. Then he waited, watching the various screens. Phoebe was smack in the middle of the dance floor now with Trent the Wraith and his goons.

If he was honest, it was unbelievably uncomfortable for him, watching her out there, playing distraction. It had been all too easy for her to lure the bar's owner out of his office. But was it the trapped magic they were so attracted to or simply Phoebe herself?

When the download was complete, he slid the USB back into his front pocket and then quickly emerged from the back room unnoticed. The general atmosphere of the bar had intensified during his short absence—the music was louder and the people were drunker. He instantly homed in on Phoebe, who was still dancing with Trent the Wraith and his friends.

Ronan attempted to flag her attention to let her know he'd collected what they needed, but she appeared to be having far too much fun with the burly country boys. So, he settled for brooding in the corner, watching as she tossed her head back, singing (shouting) out song lyrics, much to the pleasure of all those around her. Someone delivered another round of shots to the group, and she accepted hers easily.

Ronan casually snatched a beer off a distracted server's tray and took a long swig.

Before long, Trent the Wraith was dancing with Phoebe so tightly that the fucker could probably have slipped his dick into the pocket of her jeans if they'd been looser. Ronan watched as the Wraith spread his broad palm across her lower back, pulling her closer still into their dance and jostling her left and right.

Heat rose to Ronan's cheeks, and he felt the animal within him start to stir ... and growl.

Ronan *was* the jealous type, and whether it was the atmosphere of drunken debauchery surrounding them or the fact that Trent the Wraith very likely had his filthy, decaying erection pressed against Phoebe's waist ... something in him snapped.

Thinking on his feet, he dumped the remainder of his beer onto a nearby point-of-sale system, knowing that if Trent the Wraith was any sort of real manager, he would have to quickly move to deal with any potentially lost income on one of their busiest nights of the year.

Or at the very least, stop dancing long enough to give someone else hell about it.

Ronan watched and waited as the bartender with the sleek black hair discovered the damage to their system. "For fuck's sake! Seriously?" she said, looking around and catching Ronan's eye momentarily.

He shrugged at her, then watched in satisfaction as she stormed out onto the dance floor and tapped Trent the Wraith on the shoulder. He looked instantly irritated and began negotiating with the woman. Her body language was clear, though, and he eventually peeled himself from Phoebe's side.

Ronan couldn't tell if Phoebe was relieved or not. Her cheeks were flushed pink, and she looked slightly disoriented by Trent's sudden departure. If Ronan didn't know better, he would have guessed that Phoebe had enjoyed dancing with the bastard. Her eyes flickered guiltily towards the bar then, where she expected to find Ronan waiting for her but found nothing.

He'd already stepped back into the shadows, watching and waiting.

She tried again to locate him, her brows furrowing as she searched the room with her eyes. Ronan realized then that she was looking very uncomfortable now, as following Trent's departure from the dance floor, several of his cronies moved in on her.

"Not on my fucking watch," Ronan said, his jaw tight, and then headed in her direction, stealing a cowboy hat directly from the head of someone he passed and placing it atop his own. *I'm a regular klepto-*

maniac this evening, he thought as he pressed onwards through the crowd.

As he stepped up to the group, Phoebe registered his arrival with a mixture of surprise and delight. "Nice hat!"

"*Don't*," he said firmly.

Trent's cronies were visibly pissed about Ronan's arrival, but the look he shot them in return, as he grabbed Phoebe's hips and pulled them to his own, was one of pure danger. She slipped into his arms with unexpected ease.

"I was beginning to worry you wouldn't rescue me," she said breathlessly into his ear, sounding relieved.

Hearing this didn't help Ronan's mood. She shouldn't have had to feel relief over being "rescued" by him on a mission that he'd designed for them both. It felt like failure. Overcome with raw animal instinct now, his voice dropped to a low growl. "You seemed to be enjoying yourself just fine."

She rolled her eyes, but the gravitational force between them was undeniably more intense than everything else in the room combined. "I did my part, Ronan. Did you do *yours?*"

"Of course, I did. Quick and dirty."

She snorted.

He fought hard to keep his tone from becoming nasty in response, but it was surprisingly difficult, especially considering how thrilled he should have been to have her in his arms.

"You were dancing so close with Trent the *Wraith* that I'm surprised he didn't knock you up mid-verse."

A new look flickered across her face then, but she quickly schooled her features into a stoic mask before he could figure out if it was anger, hurt, or something else altogether.

"Didn't they teach you how reproduction works in medical school?"

"Yeah, they did. Which explains my surprise," he replied impulsively, still growling into her ear. Ronan was being a jerk, and he knew it.

Her eyes widened then as she searched his face. "What's wrong with you?"

"Nothing. I'm just glad you're here with *me* now."

She stared at him for another long moment, then shook her head. "Do you know how to dance to this?"

"Of course, I do." And he did.

Ronan might not like country music, but he'd been on the earth long enough to know how to dance to almost any type of music—one of the perks of pushing fifty, he supposed.

And so, they danced.

As Brooks and Dunn's cover of "My Maria" played and he led her through a rousing two-step, singing along to every word, Ronan could tell that she was shocked.

Perhaps an explanation is in order ...

"I remember the summer this song came out. I was on leave and travelling around Canada, and it was on the radio a lot. This was back when I was twenty."

"Then I would have been ..." She frowned a bit, as though working on the math.

"*Eight* years old," Ronan finished for her, a little too quickly. He had calculated their twelve-year age gap much earlier in their interactions than he would ever care to admit.

She didn't seem to notice the surprising readiness of his answer. "So, how does that make you feel? My age, I mean."

"I'm fine. Why?"

"Nothing. You *are* old, though."

He laughed in surprise, then pulled her closer as a slow number began.

No longer quite so high above their heads, tendrils of the strange hybrid plants continued coiling down from the ceiling, inching ever closer to where Phoebe and Ronan stood ... almost seeming to be reaching for them. *But were they dangerous?*

Ronan didn't have a chance to consider further, his attention instead helplessly drawn to the woman in his arms; Phoebe seemed almost transported as they continued dancing. He could still feel her magic, though it had been slowly cooling from a raging boil to a gentle simmer ever since he'd first pulled her into his arms, pressing one hand against the small of her back. He wanted to believe that he was having this effect on her—making her feel protected in his arms—but at the same time, he couldn't help but wonder if their close proximity to the magic-starved plants overhead might have had something to do with it.

"Do you think it's us the plants are drawn to?" she asked then.

"I think it's *you* they're attracted to, Phoebe," he said, tucking a loose strand of hair behind her ear and then gently cupping her cheek. When he felt her press her cheek against his palm like a cat, practically purring, he swallowed hard.

Then she blinked at him. "You really don't see it, do you?"

"See what?" he asked, but she just shook her head and remained silent. Although he was reluctant to break the spell between them, he knew that it was time. "We should leave soon ..."

"I know. But this has been nice. You should take me out again sometime."

"Maybe sometime ... yeah," he said quietly. Ronan suddenly felt like a sixteen-year-old again, with his long-time crush finally agreeing to go out with him. "I'd like that," he whispered, unsure if she actually heard him.

CHAPTER 21

PHOEBE

PHOEBE SHOULD HAVE KNOWN THAT THE NIGHT BEFORE HAD BEEN too good to be true. When Ronan had stormed out onto the dance floor like a burly, pissed-off, salt-and-pepper Irish cowboy, she'd felt her entire world flip on its axis. He had surprised her. Simple as that.

Trent the Wraith had been intimidating, sure, but at the very least, he'd known how to dance, which was impressive for a half-dead piece of rotting garbage—not that she'd ever admit that to Ronan. Trent's buddies, however, had been downright scary as they'd started closing in on her. And so, Ronan's arrival in that moment of dawning uncertainty had been *more* than welcome.

She had landed herself in a bit of a pickle, so his "rescuing" her had only made sense. But still ... the way he'd looked at the encroaching Wraiths after appearing in their midst had been formidable.

Dangerous, really.

Keeping her safe was just part of his job ... So, why had she felt like her heart was going to burst when he'd pulled her into his arms? Why had she felt a truly cartoon-level *swoon* spread through her body when he'd growled into her ear following her jab about his stolen cowboy hat?

Ronan had been a complete bastard to her at first, verbally at least. But she was swiftly discovering that whenever the Druid doctor got mean, it was because he was grappling with complicated emotions that he didn't know how to process. Frankly, it was a good thing that she wouldn't—couldn't—allow herself to ever fall for him. He was a piece of work for sure, in more ways than one, which was a trait she'd always found problematically attractive.

It wasn't her responsibility to sort out anyone's shit but her own. She knew that ... even if she did find Ronan quite physically attractive —the Doc was hot, what more could she say?

By the time they'd returned to the hotel, any warmth between them had disappeared like a forgotten cup of coffee, cooling and needing to be reheated too many times to be palatable any longer. She had said goodnight to him in the hallway, retreated into her room, and fallen into bed—though not before raiding the mini-bar. And perhaps unsurprisingly, she'd woken up with an absolutely *raging* hangover.

Phoebe slid into the booth across from Ronan. She'd been impulsively tempted to scootch in beside him on the same bench, simply to see how he might react, but less-impulsive thoughts had prevailed in the end. The fact was that her body ached, and she was feeling somewhat dizzy from the previous night's events—and not just from the alcohol either. Their evening at the bar had left her with the same strange feeling she'd experienced while at Imogen's apartment—something she hoped to discuss with Ronan over breakfast.

"How did you sleep?" he asked mildly, stirring cream into his coffee.

"I'm sorry ..." she said with a playful smile. "Is Dr. Ronan Gallagher drinking coffee with *cream* this morning?"

He looked somewhat affronted. "I have cream in my coffee sometimes."

"No, you don't. *You're* hungover."

He stirred several more times before placing the teaspoon down on a paper napkin. "I had less than two beers. It's you who got deep into the drink," he said bluntly.

Phoebe felt her body tense. Last night on the dance floor with him had felt so good. It had perhaps been impulsive, but she could have sworn he'd enjoyed himself too. So, why was she getting the cold shoulder this morning? Had they tried to fly too close to the sun?

Ronan slid a breakfast menu towards her without even looking up from his phone. He seemed to be reading the news on its small screen.

Fine, she thought. *You want to act like a petulant child? Two can play that game.*

She reached into her sunflower backpack and pulled out Ronan's chambray shirt. "*Here*."

"I don't need that back."

"You said it was yours."

"Well, I don't want it."

"Oh, *I bet*."

He jerked his head up to look at her, the coolness of his façade starting to crack slightly. "What's that supposed to mean?"

She sighed heavily through her nose. "Why are you being combative?"

"I'm not."

"You are," she said, feeling the heat rising. "I'm sorry I took it, okay? I shouldn't have."

Ronan huffed, then reached across the table and grabbed the shirt. She tightened her grip on it.

"For fuck's sake, Phoebe! *Grow up!*"

Phoebe's cheeks were entirely crimson now, betraying her upset ... which pissed her off even further. She was so sick of Ronan's constant waffling. One minute, he was storming across the dance floor, possessive and disarming, and the next, he was rejecting her over a borrowed fucking shirt.

Phoebe knew damn well he had to be feeling equally as strange as she was this morning—no doubt due to the influence of those strange plants dangling above them last night. But if he wanted to act like a big man-baby, he was welcome to it. She sure as shit wasn't going to share her observations with him now.

She finally released the shirt and stormed off to wait outside for their taxi to the airport without breakfast.

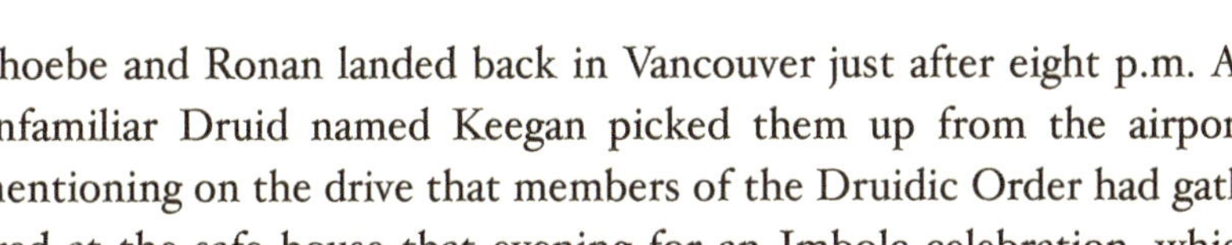

Phoebe and Ronan landed back in Vancouver just after eight p.m. An unfamiliar Druid named Keegan picked them up from the airport, mentioning on the drive that members of the Druidic Order had gathered at the safe house that evening for an Imbolc celebration, which had included a candlelit dinner with a bit of ceremony. Keegan told them that he'd missed the earlier revelries too but was looking forward to the party that would surely follow.

He also made reference to Lennie being in town, which was a detail Ronan had failed to mention to her. When she called him on this, he just shrugged.

"I don't know, Phoebe," he said, looking both miserable and exhausted. "I guess I just forgot to mention it." Then his attention was diverted to another (apparently) *extremely* important email on his phone.

"How many people are expected at this party?" she asked Keegan, who was blissfully unaware of the sheer volume of human tension he'd loaded into his vehicle when he'd picked them up.

"Around fifteen or twenty, I think," he said pleasantly. "The Vancouver house always gets a decent turnout for the quarterly fire festivals."

Keegan was somewhere in his twenties with brown skin, a well-kept beard, and longer hair, which he'd pulled into a bun at the back of his neck. He was dressed in subdued Gorpcore and smelled faintly like woodsmoke: earthy and rooted. His presence had been instantly calming to her, despite the black cloud of tension that was today's Ronan.

"Cool!" she replied with seeming enthusiasm. "It'll be nice to meet more of the locals!"

Phoebe wasn't actually thrilled with the idea of stepping off a plane and almost immediately into a party with barely a minute to transition from travel mode. But of course, she wasn't going to let Ronan know that.

"It's so great to finally meet you in person, Lennie!" Phoebe said, clinking her glass against his. He was drinking a vodka soda, while she was sipping on something she'd classify as a kitchen-grade margarita, more of which was being blended by a Druid named Emily as they spoke.

Lennie nodded at her. "Likewise."

Phoebe licked some crushed salt from the rim of her glass, then beamed at him, liking his look. About as tall as she was and quite attractive, he reminded her of a somewhat older Harry Styles, though with narrower features. Where Lennie differed from Harry, though, was in his short-cropped hair and that he was dressed entirely in black. Nothing about him screamed "computer genius," but he was *all* super-spy.

"How long are you here for, Lennie? Are you staying in the house?"

"Yes, I'm in the room Amos usually uses. I'll be here off and on for the next week. Then I have some Knave business to attend to south of the border. Friends to visit. You know how it is." He winked at her.

Ronan was watching their interaction with rapt curiosity from across the kitchen, and Phoebe wondered if he was surprised by their familiarity. Perhaps the Druid-turned-Knave had yet to relay to Ronan the details of their extended conversation following her invitation to join the Order. She wondered if that also meant he hadn't yet told Ronan about her *"specific set of skills."*

"Well, it's nice to have some new faces around," she said, brushing a long strand of hair back behind her ear. She could feel Ronan tracking the movement with his eyes. "It's been just me and Ronan for the last little bit."

Just then, Amos and Amelia entered the room with Ian.

"Oh good! You're back!" Lennie said brightly, turning his attention towards the twins and ushering them into the dining room to discuss whatever Order business was most pressing. Evidently, the Druids took zero issue with mixing business with pleasure.

Suddenly, Ronan drew close to her and angled himself so that he blocked her view of Ian, who was busy loudly greeting another Druid Phoebe was unfamiliar with.

Liza? Or is it Laura? Something like that ...

"I didn't realize you and Lennie were so *chummy*," Ronan said quietly.

The way he'd said the word *"chummy"* agitated her. "Is that a problem?"

"Fuck no!" Ronan laughed, the familiar sound lacking its usual underlying kindness. "And really, I'm not surprised. You two are actually *quite* similar. Don't know why I didn't see it before."

He stepped closer then, his heady smell of cedar (this time lacking lime cordial) engulfing her. It was too much.

"Am I missing something?" she asked pointedly.

"No. Just an observation. You have a way with people that I've always found perplexing. After the trip to Calgary, though, I think I'm finally starting to get it."

Phoebe stared at him for several seconds, her lip twitching. Finally, she said, "Bite me, Druid. Go analyze someone else's behaviour ... Or maybe you should take a look in the mirror first."

Phoebe had known that Ronan was sleep deprived even leading up to their foray to Calgary. And by the time they landed back in Vancouver, he looked like he'd been hit by a bus. Taking that into consideration, she had to admit that this party really had been very poorly timed.

She actually might have even felt sorry for him if he wasn't being so rude to her.

Shoving her compassion for Ronan down like a bad pill, Phoebe sought out Lennie, finding him sitting alone in the dining room, pouring over information from several mobile phones and a nondescript black laptop.

She cleared her throat to announce her presence, then asked, "Did you tell Ronan?"

Lennie looked up. "Oh. Hello, Phoebe." He looked perplexed. "Did I tell him what?"

His posh accent suddenly annoyed her. "*You know what!*" she hissed. "About *me!*"

"No. Not in so many words. Sometime in the coming days, I was planning on outlining your previous work experience to some of the ..." He paused briefly, looking for the word and waving his hand around vaguely in the air. "The *inner circle*, I suppose you'd call it. As well as how it might benefit the Order in the long run to tap into it as a resource."

She groaned. "*Fuck*."

"It's not personal, Phoebe. And besides, I did tell you I was going to have to tell them."

Phoebe gritted her teeth. "I know you did."

She truly felt no ill will towards Lennie. She would have done the same thing if she were in his position and likely actually would one day. Hell, she had done it countless times before when she was active in the field, doing whatever she'd needed to do to chase down a lead.

The truth took no prisoners.

And indeed, this skillset of hers—the ability to subtly manipulate someone's perception of both her and their surroundings—could be considered either an asset or a liability, depending on who you asked. Lennie certainly saw it as an asset, which she appreciated. It had also aided her career trajectory greatly on more than one occasion.

Still, she wasn't entirely sure Ronan would feel the same.

As though sensing her concerns, Lennie said, "Domhnall will be here for the next day or two, so the timing is right for Ronan to learn about it. Dom tends to provide the needed balance that Ronan and I lack on our own."

Phoebe hadn't seen Dom yet, but that didn't mean he wasn't lurking around somewhere; the house was filling up quickly. She looked towards the kitchen, where she'd left Ronan standing beside the sink. "Then do you have any idea why Ronan is being such a prick to me tonight? Beyond his usual mood swings, that is."

"Well, we had a disagreement about certain actions he took in Calgary, and I *may* have mentioned that he should watch more closely how you move through this party tonight ... that he might learn a thing or two from you. Find some inspiration if you will."

"I thought the mission went off pretty smoothly and was a success. It wasn't even particularly high stakes."

"You did fine, Phoebe. It was Ronan who was ... emotional."

"I see ..."

"You must understand that my comments to him were made in support of you, Phoebe. I want him to appreciate that you bring other assets to the Order, even though you may not be able to Wield magic effectively."

"*Yet*," she said defensively, knowing that this wasn't her fault.

She'd been minding her damn business—okay, not *actually*; before the Wraiths had captured her, she'd been a pathological snoop—living her life, completely unaware that she was a Wielder, let alone that she was also some sort of abnormality in the world of magic. She'd always been a rule breaker but had never anticipated it escalating into something like *this*. She understood that Wielding was genetic, so any knowledge or secret—had even a flicker of it existed—would have died with her parents.

"Indeed." Lennie took a thoughtful sip of his drink. "We have many things to discuss this week, namely all that you and Ronan uncovered at the rave, as well as on the boat in Bamfield. As you're aware, our current objective is to figure out what the various Wraith groups are up to in the absence of Cassius."

Phoebe felt her blood run cold; she'd been trying to avoid thinking about what she'd seen on that boat or what forced Wraith conversions could mean for Wielders everywhere. She'd lived that horror in her own way already and had no intention of allowing others to share a similar fate.

She realized then that she was swiftly becoming radicalized as a Druid.

She steeled herself. "Don't you think it's a bit ... *flimsy* of the Druids to continue chasing the Wraiths without any real intention of ever getting ahead of them? What's the point of always being several steps behind?"

"You're not wrong," he conceded. "It *is* critical that we get ahead of them, which is the purpose of our meeting this week. While it's not entirely a revelation that they're growing more sophisticated in their methodology, it still brings up more questions than answers about what precisely the Wraiths are hoping to accomplish or create ... based on their most recent experiments on both people and plants."

"Right. Good." She looked at Lennie for a moment, then nodded, gesturing towards his assorted phones and the laptop. "Well, I'll leave you to it then."

He nodded back at her, then drink in hand, returned to whatever it was he'd been focusing on.

Phoebe left him to his work and prowled back into the kitchen, an unsettling anger simmering deep and slow in her belly. Was it the Wraith magic, acting up in accordance with her mood, or simply discomfort at the thought of Ronan soon finding out just exactly what she was capable of ... even *without* the use of magic.

Across the kitchen, Ronan was now chatting with Keegan and some others who'd gathered around the table and were shuffling what appeared to be a mixture of rune stones and Rummikub tiles. Phoebe was not into table games, especially ones that already existed as "lore" within a group unless she led the charge; she'd always found integrating into established social dynamics difficult.

"Ah, Phoebe, there you are," Ronan said, clearly attempting to play nice with her. "Care to join us? We invented this game a while back—"

His mouth clamped shut as Ian walked into the kitchen behind her. She could smell him before she saw him; he absolutely reeked of weed—as he often did. It was a habit she'd personally benefited from only one night: the tattooed Druid maintained the juiciest rhythm when he was high, seemingly able to fuck for hours on end. Steady and deep.

His arrival in the kitchen was truly divine timing as well because she needed to get the fuck out of there. Pun intended.

"Oh, no thanks," she lied, feigning a smile. "I'm not really into games."

The others didn't seem to notice that she was absolutely seething as she looked at Ronan, and he at her. The worst part was that she didn't even entirely understand why they were feuding. She just knew that, for the past several days, he'd been so hot and cold to her that she was just about at a breaking point.

Phoebe detected his narrowing eyes just before he slid a mask of serenity over his features and shrugged. "Suit yourself."

Gritting her teeth in frustration, she turned smoothly to Ian, who was leaning casually against the kitchen counter, about to peel an apple with a very sharp-looking knife. She placed her palm against his broad chest, leaned in, and whispered, "I need to get laid tonight."

In the end, simple honesty trumped artful seduction.

Magic fucking pussy indeed ...

"I can tell," Ian said with a low laugh that he probably thought was sexy. "You look seriously hot tonight, Pheebs. I like this shirt on you."

It *was* one of her most flattering tops, draping just right across her full chest. "Oh, this old thing?" She fluttered her lashes dramatically, unsure if Ian could tell that she was in a foul mood and just looking to use him as a distraction ... but not particularly caring either way.

"My last mission *was* a shit show," he said, placing his hands on her hips and staring at her hungrily. "I wouldn't mind forgetting it."

"I'd like to forget a lot of things right now too," Phoebe said, nibbling softly on her bottom lip and feeling the heat of Ronan's stare on the back of her neck.

Ian grinned. "Then I'm your man."

Without another word, he took her hand and led her out of the kitchen towards the stairs. The tension and the roiling magic in her body were nearly unbearable when she and Ronan were at odds. This seemed to be becoming a routine occurrence for them, particularly when they were in conflict. And she'd never had particularly good emotional regulation skills. Unfortunately—or not, depending on who one asked—on their way to the stairs, she and Ian passed Dom in the safe-house entranceway as he arrived for the party.

While Ronan's best friend greeted Phoebe with a neutral sort of kindness (and Ian with a curt nod), Phoebe also detected what she thought might be a hint of concern in his expression ... and disappointment. Clearly, Ronan had spoken to Dom about her ... to the extent that Dom apparently felt called to pass judgement on her for going upstairs with Ian.

Her body, her choice. They could all go fuck themselves as far as she was concerned.

And yet, for whatever symbiotic, magical process was attempting to bind her to Ronan—as they'd been testing at the country bar—each step upwards felt like scalding disinfectant. She told herself that this was for the best. Phoebe had no time or energy to navigate the Druid doctor's ever-shifting moods. This dance of hot and cold with him would surely burn her out entirely if she weren't careful. If she didn't stop it in its tracks.

And anyway, by all rights, Ian was a better-than-average lay. He hadn't asked too much of her the first time and didn't appear to have any unexpected kinks she wasn't into. That was probably for the best too, as she doubted he'd be even vaguely competent in a discussion about safety and consent. Simply put, Ian was a workhorse in the sack, often eager to fuck two or three times before crashing for the night.

And then again in the morning, as if to prove the point.

Once in his room, Phoebe pulled off her top, revealing her full breasts to Ian, who grinned like an idiot as usual. "Still the best tits I've ever seen, *Pheebs*. Ten-out-of-ten. *Eleven even*."

She snorted. "Thanks for the high score, dumbass."

Ian laughed, unsheathing his cock from his loose jeans, more than ready to deliver her some much-needed relief. He reached over to his drawer for a condom while she patiently waited, biting her nails and realizing that she really needed a manicure.

"Do you like living here, Ian?"

"No, not really. But the rent is free, and it works for when I'm in between missions on the West Coast."

"That *is* a serious perk."

"Can I tell you something, though?" he asked, his inhibitions clearly low at present. "Sometimes, I stay here just to piss off Ronan. He can't stand it when I'm around, which cracks me up."

She laughed too, though it felt bitter, harshly spiteful, and acidic in her belly. Ian really was oblivious to everything that went on around him.

Lucky bastard.

Phoebe stirred at around midnight to find Ian's cock pressing against her. They'd passed out a while ago, bleary and blissed from having fucked each other's brains out once already. Ian had no interest in foreplay or oral sex; he simply wanted to get it in, which suited her just fine.

Besides, she saved that sort of intimacy for people she felt truly connected to.

"Are you up for another round, *Pheebs?*" he asked, his voice low.

Phoebe wasn't sure she liked this nickname; it was overly familiar considering that he knew next to nothing about her. She pushed down the feeling. "Only if you are."

Ian quickly unwrapped another condom, and the smell of latex and lube filled Phoebe's nostrils. A few moments later, he set to work once more, and she moaned deliciously in response, attempting to lose herself in the sensations. Above her, Ian grunted loudly, rutting with renewed intensity.

That was the thing about Ian, and why she kept coming back for more: he was like the fucking Energizer Bunny.

In the hall beyond them, however, Phoebe could have sworn she heard a low voice: *"Christ, you weren't exaggerating about them."*

"Goodnight," she heard Ronan say to someone then, his tone cold.

"Goodnight, brother," the first voice muttered.

Phoebe paused for a moment, an unexpected and deep-seated jealousy pooling in her belly. Ronan had his own people—people who loved him desperately. So, why the hell would he need her? She was a fool to think he could ever need *anything* from her.

"Everything okay, *Pheebs?*"

"Everything's *great.*"

Calgary, Alberta, 1:07 a.m.

The loading bay door clattered open as three hulking Wraiths stood shoulder to shoulder, peering out into the unusually balmy winter night. A large transport unit had just arrived with a second shipment of vining plants from B.C. ... many hours later than expected.

The truck's driver climbed out and trudged to the bay door, red-faced and road-worn as he hollered to the Wraiths, "Sorry, fellas! I would have been here sooner, but those Chinook winds were brutal on the highway this afternoon—passed several rigs jack-knifed along the way, thought I better not take my chances rushing here." He added, breathing heavily, "Precious cargo and all."

The driver was not a Wraith but a non-magic user they'd come to rely on for discreet delivery runs between the two locations in B.C. and Alberta—not because he was inherently reliable but because he was in considerable debt with the Wraith currently receiving the illicit shipment.

Money (or the lack thereof) had the potential to move mountains, especially in the world of modern Wraiths.

"I appreciate your discretion ..." Trent said coolly, arms crossed and flanked by his two main cronies. It was hard to discern which of the three was the eldest since none had started showing any signs of degeneration. Not yet. "Were you stopped anywhere?"

It was little more than a ten-hour drive between locations (inclement weather notwithstanding), yet the shipment still risked falling prey to commercial vehicle inspections. Trent and the rest of their modern faction preferred not to draw attention to themselves if they could help it—not least because it was becoming increasingly difficult by the day to hide dead bodies.

"No, but I know how to get around that, of course," the driver said proudly; he clearly sought praise, which he wouldn't get. Several beats passed as the wind gusted forcibly, causing the driver to retreat and shield his face. "So ... do you want to inspect the contents before I leave the trailer here for the night? I haven't opened it, of course, as instructed."

They'd been cautious about transporting plant matter between provinces without a permit—the vines were undocumented and undoubtedly invasive, and should they be set loose into any ecosystem, they would cause irreparable damage—not that they cared about conservation, but it would lead back to the Wraiths and their current endeavour: cultivating a plant species that could collect and contain magic from unassuming Wielders.

Phase two would include processing the flowers into a consumable drought, which was scheduled to begin in several weeks once enough of the vines matured between the two locations at the Surrey warehouse and the Calgary bars. This second shipment of vines was intended for Trent's satellite bar—a new establishment whose raucous nighttime patronage he was eager to take advantage of and a perfect location to experiment with accelerated propagation.

"Make it quick," Trent said, swiftly descending the four concrete steps into the alleyway. The other two Wraiths silently followed suit.

With the warmer weather, they could wait until dawn to unload the cargo, when more of their faction was set to arrive, but it remained in Trent's best interest to ensure the contents had arrived unscathed. The driver diligently unlocked and swung open the latch at the bottom of the liftgate, allowing the mechanized door to raise and expose the cargo hold.

And then shit hit the fan.

All at once, the lush green tendrils surged from the back of the truck, finally released from their confinement after so many hours on the road. Though non-sentient, the vines somehow appeared to be judiciously reaching towards the closest source of magic: Trent and the two Wraiths.

They weren't supposed to be attracted to Wraith magic ... and yet ...

"Why the hell did they pack so many of them in there?" the second Wraith shouted as he and the third Wraith climbed back into the loading bay.

Trent's body froze where he stood, boots buried deep in the snow; amidst the chaos, a lifeless body had also fallen from the cargo hold at the feet of the driver.

"Jesus Christ, you didn't tell me there was somebody in there!" the driver shouted, staggering back and stumbling onto his ass in a snowbank.

"It's ... a Wraith," Trent said numbly, ignoring the driver's shock. It appeared their kind was now just as susceptible to being magically asphyxiated by the vines as other Wielders were ... which was a massive problem.

Just then, blinding LED headlights came around the corner, spotlighting everything between the loading bay and the transport truck. An unfamiliar black SUV had arrived on-site and abruptly cut its lights.

Trent, the two Wraiths, and the driver watched warily as a looming, heavily cloaked figure exited the back seat, slipping through the snow like a dark spectre on the wind.

At last, Trent regained his senses. "Who the hell are you?"

"I'm here to take over this operation," Levi said, his magically enchanted voice travelling through the blustering wind like a knife. *"Didn't you get the memo?"*

"The fuck you are!" Trent shouted, but he was no match for Levi's ancient prowess.

In one swift move, Levi—aptly named after Leviathan, a grand admiral of hell—lunged for Trent, a gleaming silver sickle raised high above his head. He slashed down at a speed unprecedented for a body carrying so much bulk, severing Trent cleanly in two.

Levi looked up to the two Wraiths standing in the loading bay several feet above, mouths gaping open. Under his studded, booted foot, he was actively crushing the truck driver's throat.

"You have two options for how we are going to move forward. Choose wisely," the primal Wraith said, his menacing voice carrying on the wind and into the night.

CHAPTER 22

RONAN

Clearly, both Ian and Phoebe used avoidance to cope with life's stressors in the Druidic Order: drugs, alcohol, and sometimes gratuitous sex. It wasn't uncommon in their sect—and was even more common among the Knaves, their not-so-distant kin—but it was far from sustainable.

Members of the Order needed to develop their mental strength to last for as long as Ronan had.

In truth, it had been far too long since he'd actually gotten laid. And hearing Phoebe and Ian go at it yet again this morning had been almost enough to make him march into their room and stop them ... or worse, demand to take Ian's place. Lennie would likely have encouraged him to just join them and then congratulated him for it—the Brit was keen on group sex—but that wasn't Ronan's style.

He had his own kinks.

Through sheer mental grit, however, and perhaps pride, Ronan had resisted the urge to either interrupt the pair or "rub one out" in the shower (out of frustration). As he turned off the water, he sighed deeply. He knew this wouldn't be the first time today he'd be forced to call his imagination to heel after picturing Phoebe panting and moaning in the sheets below him.

He probably should feel ashamed of himself for even considering any of that. That *wasn't* the reason the Otherworld had returned him to this world after all. He knew that he was far from finished cleaning up the horrible mess he'd made of things years earlier—which had hurt *so* many people and continued to do so—and as such, it simply didn't matter that his attraction to the woman was undeniable. He knew that she wasn't for him.

Ronan towelled off and stretched slowly in front of the mirror. He might be getting older, but in his opinion, he still looked pretty damn good for forty-seven. He ran and worked out regularly, ate well, and took good care of his appearance. Excellent care, actually. His ego was very much intact, and he knew that he was evolving, for all intents and purposes, into a *"silver fox."*

Phoebe saw it too. He knew she did.

And yet ... Ronan exited the bathroom and strutted down the hallway like some young buck, towel hanging low on his hips. He already knew that doing this would (or at least should) embarrass him deeply in hindsight, but something about Ian just brought out the worst in him.

Every goddamn time.

Ian's door cracked open, and while he'd hoped to run into Phoebe and goad her with his near nakedness, instead, he came face to face with Ian. Beyond the man's muscular and tattooed form, Ronan could see several condoms and their torn wrappers littered across the floor like wrapping paper on Christmas morning.

"Morning, *Doc*," said a grinning Ian, his cock looking heavy in his tight-fitting boxer briefs ... like he'd been using the damn thing all night.

For him to come out into the hallway dressed like that, showing off his fuck-sore dick, was more than taunting. It was a personal affront to Ronan.

"Be very careful what you say next, Ian. Or it might be your last mission operating out of this house."

Ian rolled his eyes, stretching his almost-naked body. "You haven't kicked me out of the Order yet ... because you know damn well that I deliver ... whether you like me or not."

Ronan had (unfortunately) gone on countless missions with Ian over the years, and indeed, the Druid was an excellent fighter. More than excellent actually, further evidenced by his powerful physique, which was now on full display.

It was in every other area of the job that Ronan found him lacking.

"Your paperwork is overdue," he snapped. "And you're already on your last warning."

Ian rolled his eyes again. "I'm not gonna get kicked out of the house just for fucking your ops partner all night, Ronan, and you know it. I'll get the paperwork done."

Ronan shoved past him, allowing his towel to slip further as he passed the open doorway across the hall, beyond which Phoebe was still lounging in bed. He had no idea why he was acting half his age, but he knew it was absurd.

And then Ian moved just enough to whisper into his ear, "What did you do to her this time, Ronan? She was so desperate to forget her last mission with you that she practically dragged me upstairs by the dick."

And there was the Ian Braithwaite he knew so well and loathed so much. The bastard either couldn't fathom how unbelievably inappropriate that was, or he had a death wish.

Ronan bet on the latter and swiftly levelled a punch straight into Ian's nose.

Blood splatted, and Ian shrieked.

"*Argh!* ... What the *fuck!?*" Ian lunged at Ronan in retaliation, just as Dom descended from his room on the third floor, easily separating the two men with his massive frame.

"Don't you fucking *dare* talk about her like that again!" Ronan snapped at him over Dom's shoulder.

Dom's hands clenched into fists, evidently prepared to defend his best friend without explanation. "You'll get out of here, Ian, if you know what's good for you."

"Fuck you guys!" Ian spat through the blood, then spun and stormed off towards the bathroom.

"Don't talk about me like what?" Phoebe asked, now standing in the doorway to Ian's room wearing only his t-shirt ... and some of his blood, which had apparently splattered down her thighs as he'd spun away from the punch.

Ronan swallowed hard. *She saw the whole thing.*

Dom nodded awkwardly to Phoebe. "I'll let you two sort this out," he said, then headed downstairs to breakfast and to Lennie, whom Ronan assumed would hear all about what had transpired.

"What was it, Ronan?" Phoebe demanded. "What did he say?"

"Nothing. I've already told you that you're better than this."

She raised her eyebrows. "Better than *what*, Ronan? You keep saying that, but I don't see *you* offering me any brilliant alternatives!" She looked him up and down then, apparently utterly unimpressed.

Ronan resisted the urge to lash out, not having the energy for another fight with her right then, especially not if it might end up inspiring her to have even more sex with Ian. Instead, he stalked off into his room without another word, locking the door behind him.

"Ronan, we need to talk," Lennie said dryly.

"About what?" Ronan grumbled. He, Dom, and Lennie had gathered around the safe house's dining-room table. Scattered around them were books, papers, and several laptops that Lennie had been working on moments before.

"About *whom* actually. Phoebe."

"If you're going to get on me about punching Ian, the bastard had it coming."

"No, not that." Lennie fought back a smirk. "Though Dom thinks we should have Ian reassigned to a different location, and I agree. Not that either of us think Ian and Phoebe's new dynamic is *technically* a problem, of course ... Do you?"

"It's none of my business," Ronan grumbled stubbornly, knowing that Lennie was intentionally goading him.

"Right. Well, we are a touch concerned about how their interactions might be ... affecting your judgement. That is, we want to offer Phoebe the best chance at integrating into the Order, and conflict in the safe house between two established Order members isn't exactly ... conducive to that."

Ronan glared at Lennie, who seemed just as pompous as ever. "Ian's a prick. He's always been a prick."

Dom snorted in agreement. "Here, here."

"Indeed," Lennie said. "So, it's decided."

Ronan thought about how Phoebe had looked last night, dragging Ian from the kitchen, and the simpering look Ian had thrown back at Ronan over his shoulder. At the thought of it, even now, he felt heat rising to his cheeks.

The bastard needed to go. It was long overdue in fact.

Lennie cracked on. "Anyways, now that we have that sorted, I've got some updates on Phoebe's past and what might have brought her to the Wraiths in the first place."

"Oh?" Ronan asked, glancing towards the stairs. "Shouldn't she be here for this conversation then?"

"No, actually." Lennie pulled out one of the pouches the Druids used to mute their conversations for outside listeners. "She really shouldn't."

Ronan raised his eyebrows, but Dom put up a hand, silently stilling his best friend.

"We already knew that she was an investigative journalist," Lennie said, "but it's taken us some time to chase down all of the leads she was working on right before she was captured."

"What do you mean?"

"Her landlord had already gutted and re-rented her apartment, so we were unable to inspect the physical premises and—"

"Of course, they gutted and rented her apartment," Ronan interrupted impatiently. "She was in captivity for nearly twelve months!"

"Yes, but that means the only physical traces of her past life that remain are what she carries on her person," Lennie said pretentiously. "Amos relayed to us that this is only a duffle bag and a small backpack. From what we can tell, the Wraiths planted a story about her so that anyone she knew would believe she'd developed a substance-abuse disorder and disappeared."

Ronan was again reminded of how little Phoebe had left to her name and how much she'd lost because of the Wraiths. Her home, her identity ... *everything*.

"And for all intents and purposes," Lennie continued, "that was true, minus her using drugs, of course. Records, or lack thereof, indicate she's been unhoused since surviving the lab explosion." He frowned. "As far as I can tell, the safe house here is her first secure residence in the last eighteen months."

Ronan shifted uncomfortably in his seat.

What Phoebe had been through since her capture was almost unimaginable. And yet here Ronan was, pissed at her because she'd snatched his shirt and had (consensual) sex with another adult a handful of times.

He'd let himself lose sight of the bigger picture.

Dom released a long breath. "Though the memories of my re-births aren't clear anymore, I can say with certainty that to emerge from utter *nothingness* and claw your way back into the world alone, and then to secure food and lodgings without any sort of financial means at your disposal ... Well, she's likely no longer averse to lying or stealing."

He trusted his friend's intentions. Ronan could easily recall Dom's stories of emerging from his passage through the Otherworld completely naked and alone. Each time, it had been terrifying even for the strapping and mentally prepared Celt.

And yet Ronan's back still went up in her defence. "What are you getting at, Dom?"

"I'm saying she's a survivor, Ronan. And likely *incredibly* intelligent too. It's no small feat to pull off what she's managed for herself over the past six months, especially in the modern era."

"Tell me something I don't already know," Ronan said, sighing loudly and leaning back in his chair. "Phoebe's far cleverer than anyone gives her credit for ... myself included a lot of the time."

"And that's all well and good," Lennie said grimly, "but there are bad people after her, and not just the Wraiths either. If she were to be spotted by any one of them, she would be in grave danger. Over the course of her career, she developed a reputation for sticking her nose in places she shouldn't, and all for the sake of getting the story."

"Well, that's not changed, has it?" Ronan said, shrugging. "Besides, that was her job. Chasing leads where others wouldn't was just part of the gig."

Lennie nodded. "Yes, but I believe she may have infiltrated a serious crime ring before being taken by the Wraiths and was posing as someone else—"

"*Sasha*," Ronan interjected.

"And *allegedly*," Lennie continued, ignoring the interruption, "she even resorted to poison on more than one occasion."

Dom started to laugh. Hard. "You're not implying she's KGB, are you?"

Lennie threw his hands up, exasperated by the pair of them now. "They're called the FSB these days, and no. I've already looked into that. And she's not affiliated with the mob either."

"What then?" Ronan asked as Dom continued laughing.

Lennie glared at the big Celt.

"Sorry, sorry," Dom said, offering Lennie his best good-boy grin, knowing that he and Ronan both had a terrible habit of interrupting him. "We're listening."

The Brit sighed. "It appears that over the course of her career, Phoebe developed a particular set of skills that, on many occasions, allowed her to 'get the story,' as it were."

"What do you mean?" Dom asked, sobering now.

Ronan was puzzled too.

"From what I've unearthed so far," Lennie explained, "I believe she was chasing a lead and became so heavily invested that she ended up rubbing shoulders—and likely other parts of her body—with some very *unsavoury* characters."

Ronan leaned back in his chair. Even more than his words, Lennie's posh accent and biting condescension were truly pissing him off now. "Fine, but ... why does *any* of this matter?"

Dom answered for him. "It matters because he thinks *yer girl* Phoebe is even more cunning and dangerous than any of us initially thought." He shrugged and added amenably, "Not that that's a bad thing."

Ronan glared at Dom. "She's not *my* girl."

"Right," Dom said, stretching his arms up and back behind his head. Apparently, the ancient bastard felt in no way intimidated by Ronan's glare. "And *I'm* not the son of Brian Boru."

"Most people would think you're touched in the head for believing that you *are*," Ronan said haughtily.

Dom laughed again. "Doesn't mean it's not true."

"Gentlemen, please," Lennie said sternly. "Apparently, one of Phoebe's targets found out that she was going to expose them. Which *is* a bad thing, as these are the kind of people who kill for that sort of thing ... which Phoebe likely knew. And yet she went for it regardless."

That fact sobered Ronan and Dom both.

"Simply put," Lennie said, "throughout her career, Phoebe has developed a set of skills not so dissimilar to my own ... which means it's highly likely she's been strategically using the Druids ever since we first brought her in, and possibly even before. The fact that she so often showed up where you did, Ronan, but was somehow never caught is also something to consider."

Ronan's jaw ticked as he felt his blood pressure rise. Was it possible that Phoebe had been manipulating him from the start? And if she had been ... did it even matter?

He considered what he knew about the studies on head trauma in military veterans, particularly those involved in reckless behaviour post-injury, and how it was difficult to determine the magnitude of the impulsiveness in these patients because they were likely already predisposed to that behaviour beforehand, at least to some degree.

Lennie clearly sensed Ronan's spiralling ruminations. "Before you jump to conclusions, Ronan, or *anger*, I believe we could use this to *our* advantage. I've already discussed it with her, and she's admitted to honing those skills she's utilized in the past to get her needs met ever since. That said, I don't believe she's done this out of any sort of malicious intent but rather simply necessity. Like Dom said earlier, she's a *survivor*."

Dom nodded in support of this statement.

Ronan wanted to argue with this and ask what could *possibly* necessitate her manipulating people to that degree, but he bit his tongue, knowing it would just be his own insecurity talking. Ultimately, he knew Phoebe. While she didn't always make the right choices, he'd never gotten any sense that she was driven by an intent to harm others.

Quite the opposite, actually.

Just like him.

Ronan ended his meeting with Dom and Lennie, though reluctantly. He missed spending time with the two of them alone, fighting and laughing like brothers. However, Dom needed to catch the ferry back to Julia and Ayla before bedtime; one night away was enough to make him almost frantic to return home. And of course, in the coming days, Lennie would have business to attend to with the Knaves south of the border, for which he needed to prepare.

Dom was standing by the front door now, running his hands through his hair, his expression flickering between concern and delight. "I suppose now is as good a time as any to tell you that Julia ... well, she's pregnant again. She's been sicker than a dog, so I really do need to get back."

Ronan beamed at his best friend and gripped his shoulders firmly. "You don't waste any time, brother."

Dom sighed dreamily. "Well, Julia's made it abundantly clear that two babes are her limit. And I have to say that I agree. Ayla is—"

"Don't you *dare* speak a word against my goddaughter!"

Dom laughed. "She's got the best parts of her mum and, if I'm completely honest, the most difficult parts of me. Not to mention that she's already got a pretty good handle on her magic. The other evening, she locked me out of the bathroom when it was time to brush her teeth. Julia was out grabbing some groceries, and I had to wait until she got home to get back inside."

"Couldn't you have knocked the door down?"

"Sure, but I can't demolish my house every time one of those women is mad at me. The house would be in ruins!"

Ronan laughed heartily. "Fair enough."

"I'm in trouble if this next babe is a Bearer," he said, grinning like a madman.

Ronan didn't disagree. Ayla was as smart as a whip but also got into trouble with her parents at regular intervals—and with other children at playgroup. At only two and a half, she was already mastering autonomy.

He smiled fondly, thinking of her, before growing serious. "Does Ayla know her mom is pregnant?"

"No, not yet. Julia wants to wait until she's out of the woods. She's about seven weeks along now and feeling fucking awful."

Guilt tightened in Ronan's chest. "You didn't *need* to come over this weekend."

"I wasn't going to, actually. No offence. But Julia insisted. She was right, of course. You did need backup ... as evidenced by coming to blows with fucking Ian—" Dom broke out laughing then, as Ronan had just muttered the words *"Fucking Ian"* in perfect unison with him. Then Ronan joined in Dom's laughter, the two men leaning helplessly against each other in shared merriment.

"Honestly, Ronan?" Dom said finally, tears of laughter making his eyes sparkle a bit. "Being a father? ... I've never been so happy in my life. Or at least, not that I remember, but I can feel it, you know? This is *it* for me. All I've ever wanted."

Dom had elected to have the memories of his previous lives basically erased when Cassius had finally been defeated—a choice gifted to him by the Otherworld—choosing to live out the rest this life with Julia without carrying the weight of his countless traumas. And he had never regretted it. Indeed, a life of simple fatherhood suited Dom in every possible way. In fact, Ronan was pretty sure that Dom liked parenting *considerably* more than Julia did, even though she still was a wonderful mother.

"Tell Julia I'm sorry for dragging you into this mess."

Dom grew serious then and chewed his lip for several moments. "Ronan, I'm going to tell you something, and you better promise not be a bastard about it."

Ronan snorted. "You and I both know I don't make those sorts of promises, even with you."

Dom nodded, his expression softening along with his voice. "Look, brother, I think you need to be careful with Phoebe, and not because of everything Lennie just shared about her past."

Ronan cocked one eyebrow at him in challenge. "Oh? And what makes you say that?"

His best friend's face grew suddenly stony. "I'm serious, Ronan. There's something between you and Phoebe. I can tell by the way you're acting. You're all ... *muddled.* And fucking jumpy too. I think she's causing you both stress and worry, which you need to keep an eye on."

Ronan snorted, but Dom ignored him.

"That said, regardless of whether you have actual *feelings* for the woman or not, I'm not convinced that you can just step out of her path either."

Ronan shifted uneasily as the hair on the back of his neck stood at attention.

"Forgive my reaching, brother, but my experience in the Otherworld has given me a good sense of these things." Dom scratched his beard for a moment, choosing his words carefully. "I believe this might actually be another reason you were sent back—beyond your mission with the Codex magic and stealing the spear from Cassius. If you try to separate from her before you've done whatever you're intended to do, I'm afraid something terrible might happen."

"Well, that's ... *fucking* ominous," Ronan said, his stomach suddenly swooping about inside him like a swallow in an old barn. The sensation was so intense he actually swayed a bit on the spot. Dom reached out and steadied Ronan for several moments as he breathed slowly and consciously through his nose.

Air in, air out ...

"What do I do?" Ronan whispered at last, looking to his most cherished friend with widened eyes.

Dom pursed his lips briefly before answering. "I think you continue on ... *carefully*."

Ronan blinked several times before bursting into tension-releasing laughter. "That's completely *useless* advice, you idiot."

Dom laughed too, even as Ronan leaned in and pulled him into a long hug.

"I'm always here if you need me," Dom said.

"I know."

Ronan saw Dom off, waving as he headed down the driveway, then returned inside to find the main floor empty but for Lennie, who was neck deep in paperwork and clacking away on one of his many laptops. The pounding beats of EDM were leaking out from his not-so-noise-cancelling headphones.

"Lennie, have you seen Phoebe?"

The Druid-turned-Knave didn't respond. So, Ronan reached out, tapping him on the back and making him jump. "What!?"

"I was just going to ask if you've seen Phoebe."

"No, I haven't. She's not my respons—"

"Never mind," Ronan said quickly, with a wave of his hand, and returned to the entranceway, leaving Lennie to his hyper-focusing. Then he climbed the stairs to the second floor and Phoebe's room.

Which was empty.

"Phoebe?" he called as his heart began to pound in his chest.

He pulled out his phone to text her on the cell she'd been supplied with by the Druids:

Where are you?

He elected *not* to include any of his rabbling, stream-of-consciousness thoughts in that moment, which would have included accusatory statements about how irresponsible she was for not having told him where she was going. She had his number, after all. He figured that keeping it brief was better, since technically, she *was* allowed to leave whenever she wanted.

Phoebe replied quickly:

Thrifting. I don't like any of my clothes.

...

Three dots started blinking on the screen as she typed, then stopped, and then started again:

Want to come and help me pick out some outfits?

Ronan resisted responding with anger. If what Lennie had said was true, and she was in danger from some organized crime jerks, as well as the Wraiths, she shouldn't exactly be walking about the city without backup. Even though picking out outfits with a woman like Phoebe was sure to be ... *stimulating*, he resisted reading anything into the flippant-yet-flirty tone of her text and settled on the simplest message he could muster in reply:

Send me your location.

Please.

CHAPTER 23

PHOEBE

Several hours earlier.

Shivering, Phoebe finished a shorter shower than she'd intended and turned off the water. Ronan and Ian had left her only about five minute's worth of hot water, forcing her to wash her hair in an icy cold stream.

Assholes.

The second-floor bathroom smelled like earthy camphor soap, with a subtle tang of blood. The latter scent belonged to Ian (whom she'd passed earlier when he'd left the bathroom, glowering). Meanwhile, the earthy soap scent was so distinctly Ronan that she'd almost aborted the shower altogether.

It felt impossible to find a moment without Ronan infiltrating her mind ... or her senses. Meanwhile, she was keen to forget absolutely everything about Ian Braithwaite. She had no interest in bringing him to heel or whatever the fuck Lennie had insinuated she'd done.

In the morning light, it all felt just so ... *sour*.

Phoebe softly towelled her aching body. Between the mission with Ronan, the flight home, and the physicality of her night (and morning) with Ian, she was sore. Not to mention the fact that the magic inside her was acting up, thrumming ferociously any time she stayed still for more than a moment. She needed to keep moving. Fighting. *Fucking.* Whatever it took to stay focused on the task ahead.

The volatile trapped magics threatened to take over whenever she was too idle for too long.

Phoebe brushed her teeth quickly, gagging on the combo of bleeding gums and weird baking-soda toothpaste the Druids seemed to prefer, and eyed herself in the mirror. She had bags under her eyes—oversized luggage, really—and her skin was splotchy from the shower's changing temperatures. There had once been a time when she'd embarked on full-fledged skincare routines. *Expensive* routines. She used to love nothing more than to spend an entire weekend scoring deals on thrifted outfits while spilling oodles of cash on unnecessary body treatments—skin, hair, and nails—the lot of it.

Now, she looked down at her brittle nails and sighed.

The trapped magic was breaking her down a little more every day.

Phoebe exited the bathroom to find the second floor empty. No doubt Ronan had gone to speak with Dom and Lennie, his "comrades in arms," about his having punched Ian. She was glad when she managed to avoid Ian, who was in his room as she strode by. As much as she liked fucking him, she had no interest in getting attached.

Phoebe slipped into her bedroom and shut the door, padding barefoot to her mostly empty closet. She wondered if she could slip out for just a few hours on her own and do some shopping, maybe get a few more throw pillows and some clothes. A lamp or two. She had no intention of abandoning the Druids though. She'd come to terms with the fact that she needed them as much as they needed her.

In fact, she likely needed them more—a truth that didn't sit well with her. But as it was, she was stuck.

She slipped on her only pair of jeans and shrugged on an oversized T-shirt. In an ideal world, she would have styled the outfit with an interesting jacket, a belt, and some cute boots, but this would have to do. She still had several rolls of cash at the bottom of her backpack, which meant that she would hopefully return from her shopping trip with a few new items, assuming she made it out the door before someone sidelined her for whatever ridiculous reason.

Phoebe tiptoed from her room and down the stairs, heading to the front door. In the entranceway, she discovered the safe house eerily quiet—the sort of unnatural stillness that meant the Druids had deployed one of their magical pouches to influence the atmosphere. And indeed, as she peered through the narrow living room towards the conjoined dining room, she found Ronan, Lennie, and their hulking friend Dom seated at the table, talking animatedly.

And yet, she didn't hear a peep from any of them.

She'd never been into herbal crafts and so couldn't imagine taking the leap and learning to make pouches of her own. Then again, since they were apparently nearly priceless, she might need to if ever she wanted a stash of her own. It seemed like a frivolous choice for them to use one of the pouches for today's meeting, but then again, if they were talking about *her* ...

Heat rose to her cheeks as she pulled on her Doc Martens, cursing the noisy tedium of lacing up the combat boots. But of course, it didn't matter; they wouldn't hear her anyway. Finally, she reached for the door handle and stepped out onto the front stoop, breathing in the moment of long-awaited freedom before ascending the creaky wooden steps towards the gravel driveway and then onto the pavement. Just like the rest of Vancouver, Kitsilano was close to any transit she might need. In one direction, she'd hit UBC, and in the other, she could easily slide into East Van—and her favourite shops.

To her surprise, Phoebe felt *light*.

For the first few moments on the bus, jostling back and forth, she delighted in feeling a little bit like herself again. In the months since her still inexplicable escape, she'd found it difficult to enjoy much of anything. Where once she'd delighted in the spontaneous laughter of children or even the inconvenient-yet-exhilarating thrill of being caught in the rain without a raincoat, now the entire world had somehow blurred and faded into the background.

Everything had felt dull, and she'd felt incredibly numb.

She'd chalked it up to the lingering damage to her body and mind from life in captivity. In truth, she'd not expected to feel vibrancy around her ever again. But now that she was working with the Druids —with *Ronan* and the others—everything seemed a little bit brighter. Even if she *had* made a few rash decisions along the way.

Today was a new day. It had to be.

Phoebe hopped off the bus and wandered peacefully down Commercial Drive, giving herself permission to just maybe allow a little more colour to return to her world.

Two hours into her adventure, Phoebe stood in line at one of her favourite coffee shops, mindlessly listening to the music and the conversations around her when a firm hand pressed onto the small of her back.

"You're either very foolish or so desperate for independence that you'd risk your life for a latte."

She whirled on the spot. "Ronan! You came!"

Ronan stood before her, dressed simply in dark khakis and a wool sweater. He tucked the arm of his sunglasses into his collar then, and Phoebe noticed that the knuckles on his right hand were swollen.

"You left the safe house," he said then, his tone even. His expression looked serious, but his eyes remained somewhat light. Was he at least *trying* to be reasonable?

"In my defence, the coffee here is *really* good," Phoebe said, grinning naughtily. Then she shrugged. "Besides, you were busy. I would have invited you otherwise."

"Liar."

"Me? Never."

His grip tightened on her arm as she attempted to pull away. "You frightened me, Phoebe, disappearing like that without notice."

Her heart pounded. "I'm allowed to leave, aren't I?"

Ronan's jaw flexed almost imperceptibly. "Yes, but—"

"What? *You suddenly care about me now?*" she hissed, turning back to the counter to order her flat white. Ronan insisted on paying for her coffee while quickly ordering his own: a small dark-roast drip, black.

This only pissed Phoebe off more.

At the end of the bar, they were waiting in stony silence to pick up their coffees when Ronan finally decided to speak. "Lennie shared a little bit more about your past—the types of leads you used to chase," he said, lowering his voice, "and the type of men you used to hunt down and expose."

"So?" she challenged loudly. "I'm sure you'd agree they had it coming."

His nostrils flared. "Even still, Lennie said it was just as likely that you have non-magical enemies after you as magical ones." He leaned in so close then that she could feel his breath on her ear. "Tell me, do you think leaving alone was a wise decision?"

Phoebe began to regret her choice to invite Ronan as a shiver ran up her spine. His tone of voice was dangerous and, at the same time, somehow dizzyingly erotic. When he had texted to ask where she was, she'd been so (stupidly) excited he'd even noted her absence that she'd (impulsively) invited him to join her. And now that the asshole actually *had*, it seemed she had no choice but to face the consequences.

"I'm fine," she said, taking a short step away from him. "My dagger is in my backpack. You know I can handle myself."

"Clearly." He grabbed his coffee and strode moodily towards the door.

Phoebe rolled her eyes before scooping up the large flat white with her name on it. She smiled kindly at the barista. "Hey, thanks a lot!" Then she turned to follow Ronan out of the coffee shop.

They walked in stony silence towards Phoebe's next thrift destination. The sky was grey but, so far, rain-free. She watched as Ronan took a sip of his coffee and burnt his tongue, swore, and then went back for another sip. She bit back a laugh. He glowered at her, but Phoebe could sense at least a hint of playfulness there ... a ghost of a smile. It wasn't the first time she had noticed the effect her laughter had on him.

"Can you please stop being grumpy now?" Phoebe asked as they wandered into one of her all-time favourite thrift shops. "You've had me cooped up for ages, and I was going stir crazy! Besides, what do you want me to say?"

"Nothing." His Dublin accent was more clipped than normal. "In any case, I've actually been meaning to offer to buy you a new wardrobe."

"What?" she said, staring at him from between a rack of men's jeans and another of suit jackets. "Why?"

"Well, it's just, I know you don't have a lot, and—"

"You're confusing the hell out of me, Druid," she said, shaking her head.

"I really don't mind. Stipends from the Druids won't cover a lot in the way of personal items." He dipped his head closer to her then. "Just let me do this for you, Phoebe. Please."

The look on his face was so desperate that she almost believed he genuinely wanted to make her happy. *Almost.* Ronan was developing a bit of a toxic pattern with her.

"If this is your way of apologizing, I could get used to it. Maybe ..."

Ronan relaxed a touch as they began browsing the racks together. "I'd prefer to take you shopping somewhere downtown."

Phoebe knew that Ronan had *expensive* taste. "Oh, come on," she said, piling several pilled wool sweaters into his arms. "This is *way* more fun."

Ronan sneezed. "I don't know if my sinuses agree."

She smirked. It seemed *Mr. Perfect* was allergic to dust ... just like a normal human. "Just a few more minutes, please?"

"Go on then," he said with an amused look.

She shook her head again in near amazement. Had Dr. Ronan Gallagher just smiled at her ... *sweetly?*

In fact, Phoebe could have sworn that, in spite of everything—including his sniffles—he was legitimately enjoying himself. Or at least, he was enjoying *her* enjoying herself, which with Ronan was probably the same thing. "Thank you!"

As she wasn't only an avid thrifty but a picky one as well, in the end, Phoebe only found four garments she was satisfied with, along with a dark-blue glass coffee mug painted with yellow celestial-style suns and moons that just screamed the early 2000s, though in the best possible way.

"This is for you," she said, pressing the mug into Ronan's hand.

"For me? *Why?*"

"I'm not sure. I just feel like you need it."

"I need a lot of things, Phoebe, but I'm not sure if—"

"Don't hurt my feelings," she said, frowning.

He sighed. "Alright."

Back at the safe house following their thrift adventure, Phoebe listened for the back door's familiar snap before rising from her comfy perch on the couch. Dom had already left. Lennie was headed south as of ten minutes ago. And Ronan had just headed out for a run.

Meanwhile, Ian was nowhere to be found.

That meant that not only had Phoebe just been gifted solitude in the safe house—a miracle in itself—but should she choose to take advantage of it, she'd also gained access to Ronan's room, and the mysterious notebooks he was determined to keep her from reading.

Despite the afternoon's (mostly) positive turn of events, with Ronan joining her for the latter half of her adventure and driving her home comfortably in his Range Rover afterward—not that she minded the bus, of course, which she'd been sure to tell him—Phoebe couldn't help but reflect on how he'd treated her over the past several weeks, and just how damn confusing it had all been. Even today, he'd come in all hot and angry, only to soften after time.

In some ways, she thought it resembled "breadcrumbing," a tactic she'd watched being employed by the PUAs she'd profiled and had been on the receiving end of herself thanks to a few ill-fated romantic interests in her own life. What better way to control someone than to string them along, giving them *just* enough so they're always hungry for more, but never *quite* committing to an actual intimate relationship.

It was mean and avoidant as hell, and it hurt a lot too.

Still, Phoebe wasn't convinced that this was what Ronan was doing. In fact, it was almost as if what he really wanted (getting closer to her) was being blocked by something else. *Some dark secret, perhaps?* That would certainly explain the chronic ebb and flow in his treatment of her; it didn't excuse the behaviour, of course, but it surely explained it.

When it came down to it, she truly wished Ronan well. He was a decent person despite his mistakes and his flaws. Sure, he was a bit of a jerk sometimes, but who wasn't? In truth, she kind of liked that about him; it made him easy to tease, which she enjoyed far more than was reasonable. If she were to compare Ronan to a dog, he'd likely be some sort of German Shepherd mix: gorgeous, wildly intelligent, but also slightly neurotic, whiny, and prone to stress—the sort of creature that makes you earn their love, but once you're in ... you're in.

If only Phoebe had that sort of time.

The fact that Ronan was so damn attractive—especially when his temper flared *just enough*—didn't help anything ...

But she just couldn't bring herself to trust him. Not entirely. And especially not when he *still* hadn't divulged his connection to the torture and experiments that had later endangered her life while in captivity for nearly twelve months ... even after the very real intimacy they'd shared. How could she trust him when, after everything they'd been through together, he still didn't deem it necessary to share *that* particular part of his past with her?

He was probably ashamed, which she could certainly understand. But what *else* might that shame be hiding from her? She found it very hard to believe that a man with his knowledge, and lived history, couldn't come up with a single solution to cure her.

At this thought, an old familiar feeling made her heart begin to pound excitedly. She lunged up the stairs, taking them two at a time as she hurried to Ronan's room, stopping outside his door and breathing heavily. Phoebe had become an investigative journalist for a reason that had never faded: her hunger for the truth, which was beating its drum again now, right along with her rapidly beating heart.

Phoebe needed to find out what else Ronan was keeping from her. There *had* to be more.

She'd worked hard to gain his trust over the past weeks, and most (if not all) of what she'd offered him of herself *was* authentic. Phoebe genuinely had his back in a fight—unable to deny the magic thrumming between them in combat—and he really *could* count on her to follow through on their missions as planned ... for the most part.

But in this, her interests had to come first. Her survival depended on uncovering some means for removing the Wraith magic from her body before it was too late.

Magic that was throbbing low and prickly even now.

"I just need twenty minutes in there," she whispered, promising herself that she would be in and out long before Ronan returned from his run—he was usually gone for at least an hour.

She let out a slow breath. "Here we go ..."

As expected, the door was locked. It was rare that Ronan didn't physically lock his door when he was away from the safe house. Having anticipated this, she reached into her hair and pulled out a pin, which she slipped into the lock. Picking it easily, she swung the door open. *Easy-peasy lemon squeezy.* Admittedly, she would have had more difficulty if he'd used magic to seal it as well as the lock, but as Phoebe lacked the ability to Wield, he'd likely not felt the need for that level of precaution at present.

Ronan's room was dim as she stepped inside. Its blinds were drawn. The bed was neatly made. And the heady scent of cedar filled her nostrils.

Though this was her first time technically breaking into Ronan's room, Phoebe had already snuck into it a couple of times before. He routinely locked his door, so she had kept close attention when he left his door ajar or an opportunity arose, first borrowing a book and then his cowboy shirt, even as she did some recon to get the lay of the land. She'd already learned that he kept nothing in his bedside-table drawers beyond the usual: old charge cords, lip balm, a sleep mask, and a new box of latex condoms. His closet was expectedly militant, with shirts, jackets, and dress pants hanging neatly, and shoeboxes carefully lined up both above and below—all of which contained shoes and nothing else.

If there was anything to be found, it would have to be in the crawl-space under the second-floor roofline—a twin to the cubby in her own bedroom, which had no internal lighting.

Prepared for this, Phoebe reached for Ronan's bedside lamp and placed it on the floor between the bed and the wall before switching it on, not wanting him to see light coming from his bedroom window should he return too soon. It was a damn shame she'd lost her penlight in the warehouse, which would have been far more discreet. Of course, she also could have used the flashlight on her phone, but as an added precaution, she'd left it downstairs, charging by the couch. She wasn't sure, but she'd gotten the distinct sense that Lennie might be able to use it to track her location—and by extension, so could Ronan.

Better safe than sorry. It's floor lamp or bust.

As soon as Phoebe pulled the crawlspace door open, her suspicions were proven correct: beyond the small door were countless legal-size boxes full of neatly organized files. She crouched down and started crawling into the small space, dragging the lamp in with her. A few feet inside, she located several low, wooden file cabinets and was surprised to discover that the drawers weren't locked. She smirked slightly. Lennie would be appalled at Ronan's piss-poor security measures, though perhaps they simply didn't expect someone within their own ranks to cross this sort of boundary.

The application process for joining the Order *had* been rather rigorous after all.

She opened the first drawer, and while she'd hoped to find medical logs or research dossiers from his time with the Sorcerer, instead she uncovered the Druid doctor's *personal journals*. Phoebe's heart pounded harder than ever. This was, without a doubt, crossing a line.

And yet, she'd made it this far ...

"*Fuck it*," she said, then reached for the stack of hidden journals.

As Phoebe flipped through the pile, she felt sweat dripping down her spine. The cover of the first completed journal was labelled *"Two Years,"* and the next, *"Eighteen Months."* They seemed to be stacked chronologically, in reverse, so she had a strong hunch about what the third volume might contain. She grabbed that one, labelled *"One Year,"* and opened it to the first page:

The anniversary of the Sorcerer's demise arrives with complex emotions. I obviously do not lament his death—in fact, I revel in it. But it serves as a constant reminder of everything that could have been … the mistakes that almost cost me everything. Today is not an easy day …

She started flipping through the pages and entries:

I still look forward to each mission with the Druids. It takes my mind off things, at least for a little while. However, sleep remains difficult … Peggy's draught has drastically improved things, but his voice still haunts me nearly every night … I fear I will never be free of it.

Ronan's writing bordered on illegible, with the stereotypes about the handwriting of doctors ringing true. Thankfully, she was skilled at deciphering messy script. And while she'd never formally studied handwriting analysis (unlike some of the PUAs she'd profiled), Phoebe could easily see that Ronan's writing became more frenetic the further back she delved into his history.

She opened another journal labelled *"Six Months,"* which began with a particularly distressed entry:

Today, I thought about dying again. The days are short, and while the darkness feels familiar, it makes for poor company. I am so desperately lonely …

Phoebe's breath caught as she delved further into the sadness (and darkness) Ronan had endured over the years, moving on to the *"Three Months"* journal:

The nightmares are getting worse, though I suspect that's more to do with the conversation I had with Domhnall last night than anything else ... It's difficult for me to move on from everything like they have—Ayla's arrival has been a wonderful distraction for them. She is a marvel. I still cannot believe they've asked me to be her godparent, I don't deserve it ... but I will endeavour to be the best one I can for that miracle of a child.

Phoebe lost all sense of time as she flipped through the pages, a downpour of thoughts, feelings, and phrases jumping off the page with every pained utterance and breaking her heart ... the confession of a man wholly tormented by past choices. The vicious repeating cycle of shame, guilt, and grief—not just at the betrayal of his friends but of himself and every oath he took—that Ronan had subjected himself to was on raw display. Whatever concern she'd ever harboured about the Druid not taking his past involvement in her eventual suffering dissolved entirely when she read the initial passage in the very first journal, with the words *"Begin Again ..."* on the cover:

Cassius is dead. I pledge to locate any and all documents about any experiments done in his name that I influenced, fostered, or otherwise had a hand in. I will not rest until the blackness I brought forth is wiped clean ... The damage my unbridled obsession has caused must be reversed ... or I will die trying.

She knew all too well the lure of obsession and the (patently absurd) willingness to greet death before facing failure. Only freaks like the two of them would go that far. Phoebe knew this.

She knew *Ronan.*

At that level of obsession, it was impossible to do anything but reach that finish line, whatever and wherever that might be. Such choices could come in many forms. Sometimes, one's motivations were good, as was the case with Ronan's vow to clean up his residual messes following Cassius's demise. But they could also turn incredibly sour, as must have been the case when he'd betrayed his own kin and crossed to the other side.

Phoebe sank back onto her heels then, clutching the final journal to her chest as her eyes welled up with tears. She realized then that there was no way he was hiding anything from her regarding the removal of the magic trapped within her. Ronan was far too obsessed with wiping his slate clean to ever *choose* to leave her in such a confounding condition.

Obsession just didn't work like that.

CHAPTER 24

RONAN

RONAN RETURNED TO THE SAFE HOUSE CARRYING A BOUQUET OF sunny yellow flowers, and with a bottle of red wine (in a paper bag) tucked under his arm. He had not actually intended to go for a run, as he'd told Phoebe, but rather to secure means of further nurturing the understanding and fragile harmony that had taken root between them that afternoon. He was keenly aware of the frequency with which he needed to dig his way back to "normal" with her, but since they were the safe house's only two inhabitants, at least for the time being, it seemed worth the effort.

Maybe he was showing his age, but he found himself wondering how long it had been since anyone had bought Phoebe flowers.

He removed his runners and peered into the living room, noting Phoebe's phone plugged in on the plushest couch by the window—her favourite couch. However, she was no longer seated there, as she'd been when he'd left thirty minutes earlier. She wasn't in the kitchen either.

Upstairs perhaps?

Ronan set the wine down on the kitchen counter before shifting the flowers into his left hand and starting up the stairs. Humming absently to himself, he checked his phone for messages with his free hand. When he reached the second-floor landing, he immediately sensed that something was off and felt his heart rate increase. Then he noticed that the door to his bedroom was cracked open, and that a stream of faint light was sneaking out from beyond it into the dim hallway. He stepped up to his previously locked bedroom and peered inside.

"What are you doing in here?" he asked quietly as he opened the door the rest of the way.

Phoebe looked up at him from the floor, her eyes wide and full of tears as she hugged something tightly to her chest. "Oh! Ronan, I ... um ..."

He took a slow step over the threshold, scarcely tempering his anger at what he'd just uncovered: Phoebe kneeling just outside the crawlspace of his room, illuminated solely by his bedside lamp, which she'd apparently dragged across the hardwood floor towards a scattered pile of journals—*his* journals.

His nostrils flared. "I asked you a question, Phoebe."

"Okay, so ... Yes. This is exactly what you think it is." She gingerly placed whatever volume she'd been prying into down on the floor, then released a torrent of word-vomit in his direction: "Basically, I got this idea in my head that you were hiding something important from me about the trapped Wraith magic. So, I thought ... What if I *quickly* went through your files while you were on your run, just to check, you know? But then I found your journals ... which I admit I shouldn't have read, but ... Oh, Ronan, everything you've been through since ..." She finally ran out of words then, or perhaps breath, and just stared into his eyes looking uncharacteristically sad ... almost desperately so.

Instinct told him that she wasn't lying. Not entirely, at least.

He'd stepped out for a run (or really, to buy her flowers), and instead of minding her own business, she'd decided to break into his room and go through his things, taking matters into her own hands and betraying his trust.

But then again, had he *really* trusted her anyway? He'd specifically locked his door before leaving, after all ... Phoebe's previous intrusions —stealing both the book and his shirt—had not been inherently harmful and likely occurred because of his carelessness. However, he *had* re-doubled his efforts to deliberately lock his door to guard his privacy.

The bouquet he carried dropped limply to the floor as his anger boiled over.

"I'm sorry—you did *what!?*" he snapped, his voice echoing harshly through the bedroom. Ronan rarely raised his voice. This didn't bode well for their already fragile relations.

Phoebe flinched, her breath quickening. "Look, I know who you are," she admitted at last. "Or rather, what you did ... your part in all of *this*." She gestured vaguely at herself. "I've known for quite some time, actually."

Although she was facing him directly, her words stabbed into his back like an ice pick.

"*Excuse* me?!" Ronan's voice cracked as he took another step towards her. "Whatever you *think* you know about me, Phoebe, you are *wrong*."

"I— Ronan, please, *please* forget I said anything! That I did this," she begged, standing shakily to face him. "It's not what you think— Or, okay, maybe it is what you think, but it's not a threat to you! *I'm* not a threat to you! You know what it's like ... Surely, you of *all people* understand why I had to do it! What it's like to need answers that badly!"

He *did* know what it was like—a fact that he'd repeatedly scrawled onto the many pages of his private journals, which she'd just snooped through. "You had absolutely *no* business going through my personal things."

"Yes, you're right."

Ronan knew that Phoebe was someone more concerned with correctness and accuracy than with being *right*—a trait they shared. As such, her words were triggering, even if that hadn't been her intention.

He gritted his teeth. "So, why did you do it then?"

"I just needed to figure out how to get the trapped magic out! That's it, Ronan. I promise. I really am sorry I read your journals. That was a mistake."

Phoebe's bottom lip quivered, diverting Ronan temporarily from his anger, its pink flesh so close now that he could *so easily* draw it in, taste the salt of her tears, and finally kiss her *at long last*. He hated how alluring she was, even when having just been caught red-handed. The pleading tone in her voice was too much. The begging ...

And then his stomach dropped as dread overtook his basest desires. If Phoebe had known about his involvement in Cassius's early experiments all along, did that mean their *entire* relationship had been built on a false foundation? Lennie had warned him that Phoebe had more than likely been manipulating the Druids from the get-go. Still, Ronan wanted to believe that *he* might be different—an exception to the rule with this mysterious and devastatingly beautiful woman.

He suddenly felt like his heart might rip in two.

Despite avoiding it like the plague, Ronan had developed *very real* feelings for Phoebe—feelings he might have even admitted to her tonight, should things have taken a different turn. He eyed the discarded flowers on the floor as panic reared its ugly head, coupled with a deep-seated fear of abandonment and rejection.

Really, hadn't she been rejecting him all along? He knew that he could never tell her how he truly felt. His hands shook as he tried (and failed) to contain his churning emotions. "I *knew* you were keeping something from us, Phoebe, and only let it slide because I thought *we* had an understanding ... I thought that I could trust you!"

"We do, and you can ..." she practically whimpered, her voice barely audible now.

Defensiveness flared as his fight response took over. "Besides the fact you've likely received second-hand knowledge about me from the fucking Wraiths, I can't even *begin* to imagine why you thought withholding that information was wise!" Ronan shouted, pointing between them aggressively. "The whole Druidic Order has been working tirelessly to unwind what's happened to *you, and no one more so* than me!"

Phoebe didn't reply, seeming almost completely frozen ... which should have been his first warning sign.

But he roared onwards. "No more *lies*, Phoebe! None of us wants this for you! Me least of all!"

At the very least, that was the truth, though it was too late.

They stood facing each other, chests heaving, their heated breath the only sound amidst the deafening silence between them.

And then Phoebe's pupils dilated, her jaw set, and she sneered at him. "*You're* ... accusing *me* ... of being a *liar?*"

Ronan's beside lamp flickered as her fury rose, the trapped magic threatening to claw its way out by any means necessary—attacking her system was far easier when she was upset.

Sensing their imminent peril at last, Ronan attempted to switch gears, raising his hands and taking several slow steps backwards towards the door. "*Ehm* ... I think we both need to calm down ... maybe take a few minutes apart and—"

"Don't you *dare* tell me to *calm down!*" Phoebe spat, her voice low and threatening. "Not after you've dressed me down like some sort of *fucking* subordinate!" She prowled towards him then like a great cat ready to strike. "*You're* the one who developed the research program that led directly to *my* torture!" she growled, pointing between them just as aggressively as he had done only moments before. "Who the fuck are *you* to blame *me* for *any of this?!*"

The lamp's bulb finally burst, shooting glass shards outwards in all directions and plunging them into darkness. Ronan quickly switched on the overhead light, even as Phoebe hissed at him just like the demon in his nightmare.

"I was going to tell you eventually," he bleated helplessly, his hands raising to brace himself against the doorframe. "It's just ... my past is very complicated, and I—"

"You what? You thought I would *hate* you for it? That I would reject you?!"

Ronan's mouth opened and closed but no sound emerged; Phoebe knew his weaknesses all too well.

"And so, what if I *did* reject you?" she continued, glaring at him. "That would be my right as the recipient of *your legacy!*"

"Okay, perhaps," he said in what he hoped was a soothing tone, "and we can certainly talk about that, but seriously, Phoebe, you need to settle yourself before—"

"You didn't even give me a chance to *try* to understand your perspective!" she yelled, and the floorboards groaned beneath her. "Not *Dr. Ronan Gallagher* ... too busy telling everyone how it is! How they should think and *feel* about *you!*"

"I was going to tell you eventually, Phoebe! I swear! But it's also *my* story to tell."

"Your *story* ..." She laughed then in bitter amusement, the sound quickly becoming harsh and rasping.

Then she faltered, swaying on the spot. And a trickle of bright blood dripped from her right nostril. Within seconds, blood was pouring down over her chin and onto the floor. She looked down at her hands, which were now shaking violently, and then back to Ronan, who winced at the look of terror in her eyes. The attack of dark magic was too much for her physical body to bear.

"What do I do?" Ronan asked helplessly.

She tucked her hands into her armpits and sank down to the floor, hugging her ribs and gripping her body tight in an attempt to contain the magic. It wasn't working. The entire house began to shudder as Ronan lowered himself to the floor as well and crawled towards her.

He hated the pain on her beautiful face—hated that she was hurting so deeply because of him. A very old wound ripped open then and started pouring out an even older and more familiar shame. The guilt he felt for what had happened to her, and all because of his own shitty life choices, was nearly unbearable. To have played such a part in it all ...

"I'm sorry, Phoebe ... I'm so sorry."

She closed her eyes as tears started trailing down her cheeks to mix with the bright blood now dripping steadily from her quivering chin. Ronan instinctually knew to pull this magically volatile woman close, more attuned to her needs than he cared to admit. So, he wrapped his arms around her as she bled and sobbed into his t-shirt ... until slowly, by the grace of the Goddess, her magic began to settle.

"Shh ..." he cooed to her, rocking her back and forth.

Ronan wanted to tell her that she was safe but didn't know if that was even vaguely true. He didn't seem to know the answer to anything anymore. The closer he got to this woman, the more confusing everything felt. Yet, how could he possibly pull away, when at this moment, he seemed to be the only person who could calm her inner darkness?

And so, Ronan held her.

The morning after discovering Phoebe in his room, Ronan finally texted Dom and Lennie in their group chat:

> Fuck, lads. I've landed in a bit of a situation. Phoebe has known about my connection to the experiments all along. We had a huge blow-up last night, and then she blew up, magically speaking. She's sleeping now, but …

Ronan wasn't sure what else to say, so he set his phone down on his bedside table and just stared up at the vaulted ceiling of his bedroom, fighting for clarity and feeling so overwhelmed that it threatened to choke the life from him.

Naturally, he'd barely slept.

Thankfully, Phoebe remained fast asleep in her own bedroom, having nearly passed out in his arms after what he (now) believed had been a near-ruinous magical outburst. Once the magic had settled, he'd tenderly helped her back to her room and into bed, where she'd immediately fallen asleep. Tucking her in, he resisted the urge to kiss her forehead before stepping from her bedroom; he'd felt utterly sick to his stomach. The effect of her trapped magic was undeniably worsening with time, and he had no fucking idea what to do about it.

The entire thing was a fucking disaster.

While he still had no answers, he'd at least managed to clean up most of the blood and broken glass from his bedroom once she'd been safely tucked into hers, though he'd likely need to look more closely today for any small glass shards he might have missed. He eyed the floor, and then the bulb-less lamp on his bedside table, then anxiously picked up his phone again, expecting Lennie to soon reply to his text and for Dom to phone shortly thereafter. Instead, it was Julia's name that popped up on the call screen a moment later.

He answered it immediately. "Julia?"

"Hi, Ronan," she said, her voice soft. "Are you alright?"

A low sob escaped his control then as he sank back into his pillows. "Yes. No ... Not really. I don't even know."

Julia was miles away, and yet Ronan could still feel her calming energy, like water trickling over smooth stones. Perhaps it was only in his mind, but perhaps not. They did share a very deep and otherworldly connection after all. Julia *had* saved his life on more than one occasion, and she'd also been there when he died ...

"You sound like you're really confused right now," she observed kindly. "Do you want solutions or support?"

Ronan couldn't help but smile. She was such a good friend and had her own share of therapy hours under her belt (an observation which also made his sorry Gen-X arse feel miles behind). "I think support to start."

"Sure," she said easily. "I'm here to listen."

And so, he told Julia the truth about what had happened after he found Phoebe in his room, give or take the more primal emotional details that he likely wouldn't have even said out loud to Dom, even after several pints.

Then the frustration set in. "The problem is ... Ugh!" He ran his free hand back through his hair, resisting the urge to start pulling it out. "The fucking *problem* is that I have feelings for her! Real ones. Like life-or-death sort of feelings ... feelings I didn't ever expect to have for ... anyone really."

Julia remained silent on the other end of the line.

"Are you judging me right now?" he asked after a moment, his feelings bordering on mortification over what he'd just shared with her.

"No." Julia let out a soft laugh, filled with kindness. "Quite the opposite, actually. I'm proud of you, Ronan. Thank you for sharing all of that with me."

"Well, proud or not, I've made a bloody mess of everything." Ronan rarely cried, and yet hot tears were now streaming down his face.

"Sounds more like *she* made a bloody mess if you ask me ... of your bedroom at least."

Ronan snorted at Julia's signature dry sense of humour, wiping his cheeks with the back of his hand. "I'll be lucky if the Druids support me in working with her anymore ... She's too volatile, and I fucked everything up by getting so angry with her."

He sighed, sitting on the edge of his bed now. "We had a good thing going, you know? And it's been a long time since I've worked with a partner and felt so much ... synergy. If you can believe it, I even bought her flowers yesterday, and—"

Julia made a sound somewhere between a squawk and a squeal. "Hold your horses, cowboy! You did what!?"

Ronan scoffed loudly. "Oh come on, Julia, it's not unusual for me to buy flowers for people I care about. How many times did I bring flowers home to you and Dom after Ayla was born?"

"That's *completely* different, Ro—"

"Look, regardless of what's happening with my emotions, there's absolutely nothing I can do about it but wait for the feeling to pass." He was beginning to regret this phone call.

"Why do you say that?"

Ronan sighed. "A lot of reasons, but largely because she's still chock-full of Wraith magic, which *clearly* needs to be the priority right now."

"*Hmm ...*"

"Phoebe isn't for me, Julia. Please."

"Maybe ... maybe not."

Ronan groaned. "Look, I've already talked to Domhnall about this. Even if I were to pursue her, the fact is that Phoebe has shown absolutely no signs of reciprocating those feelings—not in the way that I would want her to, at least, though I'm sure she'd let me fuck her to sleep if I asked her to," he added sardonically.

"*Ronan!*"

"Sorry, that was rude." He didn't actually feel that sorry. "All I meant was that she has no problem sharing her bed with *other* men, which of course, is her prerogative. And if I'm being honest, her ability to seduce assholes so easily *has* come in handy on our missions. But emotionally? She's miles away."

"Sounds familiar."

"I know, I know. And I deserve that," Ronan said, pushing himself up from the bed, stepping into the hallway, and quickly poking his head into Phoebe's room to check on her. She was still sound asleep. He stepped back into the hallway. "But Phoebe doesn't think of me like that."

How could she if she thought it was okay to break into his room, pry though his cabinets, and read his private journals?

Ronan's heart began to pound, but then Julia's laughter reeled it back in. "Well, let's not forget that not everyone's like Domhnall, openly professing their love by the side of the river after knowing someone *for all of thirty seconds!*" she said, raising her voice at the end of this sentence for her husband to overhear.

He heard Dom shout back, "*Hey, now! If I recall correctly, you liked that!*"

Julia giggled.

Ronan thought of Phoebe's shared sentiments back on the ferry, how she disliked the introductory part of dating and felt that the whole romance bit was too complicated to wade through just to get to love. He didn't think that was their problem, though. They were already friends and had bypassed many of those relationship/dating steps already.

"Can I offer you some advice?" Julia asked sincerely.

By now, Ronan had padded quietly downstairs in search for food, as all of this emotional labour had left him absolutely famished. "Sure, why not? I've no clue what to do on my own."

"Regardless of whether she returns your feelings, don't let her slip away. Not now, and not after what just happened. From what I understand about her situation—which admittedly, isn't much—Phoebe is very, very alone right now."

"So am I," Ronan argued, feeling somewhat aggravated. He opened the fridge, preparing to heat up a meal for one.

"Not nearly as alone as she is, Ronan. You've got us to call. And Lennie. And your therapist ... Who does Phoebe have?"

"Fucking Ian," Ronan muttered under his breath; the bastard had apparently taken his leftovers before his relocation from the safe house.

"Well, even if he is a complete asshole," Julia said plainly, "you can't deny that Ian is extremely attractive."

Ronan heard Dom shout something obscene in response in the background and laughed despite the shittiness of his mood.

"What I'm saying," she continued, "is that, romantic love aside, it sounds like you're her person right now. Betrayal is complicated, as you well know, but it's easier to find forgiveness from the people we care most about than you think—and you clearly care about each other."

"Isn't it *me* who should be forgiving *her* for not telling me that she's known all along?"

"Can you blame her for keeping that secret?"

Ronan's heart sank. "I don't know."

"Well, I think that's up to you and Phoebe to sort out."

Ronan gathered several eggs, some butter, a block of cheese, peppers, onions, and tomatoes from the fridge. "I actually have been working on all of that with Eunice, my therapist, and the fact is that I just don't know if I could travel down that road with Phoebe anyway. Not now ... I've been through too much over the past few years, I think. We all have."

Julia didn't reply at first, but Ronan allowed her the time she needed to gather her response.

"Well, I know better than anyone that some secrets *should* be guarded, at least until the right moment," she said sagely.

"Even when you're scared?"

"*Especially* when you're scared. Maybe she had her reasons to keep that secret, just like you did."

"Maybe. But what's the point in telling her how I feel with everything else going on?" he asked, his voice dropping to a whisper.

Ronan heard Ayla shriek for Julia in the background as he tucked the phone between his ear and shoulder and placed a colander full of veggies into the sink to wash them. Then he sighed. "Ayla needs you, Julia. You need to go. But thanks. I'll give it some thought."

They said their goodbyes, and Ronan started to methodically wash the vegetables. Then he pulled out the cutting board and began slicing them into perfectly uniform pieces. It felt good to work with his hands ... like a recalibration. Next, he cracked several eggs into a small metal bowl, poured in a splash of milk, and began whisking them together for an omelette.

As Ronan made a mental note to pick up groceries soon, he turned slowly towards the kitchen table, where the flowers he'd bought for Phoebe now sat in a simple vase. Julia's words came back to him then: *"Phoebe is very, very alone."* He'd stupidly purchased the flowers thinking that it might make Phoebe feel cared for and make himself look good by association. But what she really needed was a proper support system, with people who cared for her and looked out for her.

And probably a good therapist too.

The fact was that Phoebe needed the Druids just as much as he needed them, which had likely been evident to everyone but him. Lennie, Amos, and Amelia—even Domhnall and Julia, who didn't even live in the house—knew that she had a natural place in the Order.

And Ronan had absolutely *no* business driving her away.

Just then, the door swung open, and Phoebe entered the kitchen. "Hey, what are you cooking? I'm pretty hungry ..."

"Omelettes," Ronan said with a smile that he hoped looked more genuine than it felt.

CHAPTER 25
PHOEBE

PHOEBE WAS STANDING JUST OUTSIDE THE KITCHEN DOOR, NOT wanting to interrupt his phone conversation. Based on his gentle tone, she assumed it was Julia he was talking to. Whenever he spoke to Lennie, he was snippy, and with Dom, he was usually either laughing his ass off or throwing attitude right back at him over the line. She would have turned around and gone back to bed for a while, but she'd woken up suddenly *ravenous*.

"Even when you're scared?" she heard Ronan ask then. Several beats passed before he said in a low voice, *"Maybe. But what's the point in telling her how I feel with everything else going on?"*

Heat rushed to Phoebe's cheeks. She'd long suspected he harboured very real and very deep feelings for her. And she also lamented not being in the position to return them—no matter how enticing the prospect. Ronan was annoyingly smart, focused, and devastatingly handsome ... basically everything she'd look for in a partner if she wasn't so psychologically and emotionally bankrupt. Love just wasn't something she could afford anymore. She was too tired and too broken.

Though she'd be lying to say she wasn't flattered by the sentiment.

She slid into the kitchen once Ronan finally wrapped up his call. "Hey, what are you cooking? I'm pretty hungry ..." She saw his shoulders tighten and felt her heart sink.

"Omelettes." Ronan offered her a strained smile. Then he quickly returned his attention to his frying pan. "*Fucking Ian* took all of my Thai leftovers when he left yesterday."

Phoebe wasn't sure how to respond to that.

Ian had become a definite sore spot between them, and she knew that she was the underlying reason why he'd been reassigned. Or more accurately, how his presence there with her had been affecting her working relationship with Ronan.

"Omelettes sound great," she said evenly, "if you're cooking for two."

"I've prepped enough for both of us."

"Amazing, thanks," she said simply and sat down at the table.

Her entire body ached. So, she just sat quietly as Ronan fussed in front of the stove for several more minutes. She noticed that the flowers he'd been carrying the night before had now been placed in a vase. She assumed they'd been meant for her—another effort on his part to narrow the distance between them. And then she'd gone and broadened it into an absolute chasm.

"We didn't have any ham or anything," Ronan said, sliding half of a massive veggie omelette over to her on a plate. "And sorry, but there's not toast," he said grimly, no doubt reminded once again of Ian's final transgression. "We need groceries."

Phoebe's eyes travelled to the loaf of bread on the counter and back to Ronan. "There's bread right there."

Ronan's cheeks reddened. "Oh, *ehm* ... Well, it's just that you never eat the whole wheat bread."

Phoebe smiled shyly. That was quite the thing for him to have noticed. "I think I'll survive ... just this once."

Ronan loaded the second half of the omelette onto his plate and popped two slices of whole wheat into the toaster. He then walked to the table, sat down, placed a napkin on his lap, grabbed his fork, and looked over at her. She smiled meekly as they tucked into their breakfast together in careful silence. The omelette was delicious, hitting the spot particularly after last night's drama.

After a few mouthfuls, they both started to speak at once:

"Look, I don't—"

"Listen, I shouldn't—"

They both paused briefly. Then Ronan cleared his throat and tried again. "I don't have the capacity to fully talk things out this morning."

"Me neither."

"But soon."

"*Soon*," she agreed.

The toast popped, and Phoebe rose to grab it at the exact same moment he did. They both laughed a bit awkwardly, and she nodded at him to proceed as she retook her seat. Ronan retrieved the toast, buttered them, then returned to the table, sliding them onto her plate and sitting beside her again.

Phoebe took a bite, chewing slowly.

He raised his eyebrows and awaited her response.

She chewed some more and eventually swallowed it down. "It tastes like birdseed."

Ronan snorted. "Fair enough. Is it the sunflower seeds?"

"Definitely."

"That should be a good thing, right? Think of your sunflower backpack."

"Well, I don't eat the *flowers*," Phoebe scoffed, though she hoped he didn't miss the twinkle in her eye.

She had no idea what was "normal" between them or even what it *could* be. Were they even capable of it? They were equally complicated people, though it was a comparison that she'd preferred not to explore in depth until now, opting to keep her past to herself. Somehow, though, she sensed that now might be the right moment to change that. And of course, she *had* just read his journals. It only felt fair to reciprocate that transparency if she could.

"You know ..." she began but let the thought trail off.

"What is it?" he asked, shifting to face her.

"Okay, so this might sound morose, but I've always had this very distinct feeling that I wouldn't live very long. Or like ... not as long as everyone else."

He tilted his head with concern. "What makes you think that?"

Phoebe had many reasons to think that, though the fact that she always seemed to be either recovering from or moving through some chronic pain or discomfort or another was one of them. She'd always dealt with hypermobility issues, and her nervous system had always been incredibly sensitive, even without trapped magic battering her senseless from within.

"Well, I'm hypermobile for one, and then there's the migraines. And I'm sure you've noticed my spine."

"Scoliosis?" he offered.

"See?" Phoebe snorted. "And yes, my back feels like shit much of the time."

"But none of those are death sentences."

She sucked in her lips briefly. "No. But it adds up, you know?"

"Have you had genetic counselling or any testing done?"

"I'm not looking for medical advice."

"Sorry," he said quickly. "Habit." He reached up and scratched his beard, which had grown longer since she'd first met him, and a bit wilder. "How does that make you feel?"

Phoebe chuckled at his phrasing. "Still a bit clinical, but I'll bite." She was pleased when he laughed too. "I think I'm just resigned to it, so I don't feel much of anything. Sometimes, though, I think it makes me a little bit reckless."

He perked up. "Have you always been reckless?"

"Not really."

Ronan raised his eyebrows, and she gave him a playful smack on the arm.

"Impulsive, yes. And I still am. But not really *reckless*. That came later, in adulthood, when I was pursuing my career. The obsessive lead chasing led to some poor decisions. It *still* does ..."

Phoebe knew she didn't need to justify her choices with Ronan—not even the stupid ones she had continued to make with Ian. But she suddenly felt desperate for him to understand how much she understood him and how far she was from rejecting him for who he was.

"I know the feeling," he said, relaxing back into his seat beside her. "One of my biggest regrets is that I never learned to regulate my emotions enough to dial back obsession. Especially in the workplace. Or at least, that's what my therapist tells me. Does that make sense?"

"It makes complete sense," she said, excitement building now. "But you know how, like ... Okay, when you can just *taste* the story, that ... *information*, and it's all pulling together and—"

"It really is *such* a rush," he finished for her, smiling genuinely.

"Have you always been this way?" she asked, genuinely curious.

"My granny Sheila said I was always a busy kid. Like a-mile-a-minute sort of thing. As soon as I got an idea, I wouldn't let it go until I'd sorted it completely. Till I'd mastered it. But at the same time, my grades were absolute shite."

Phoebe knew the feeling. "Have you ever been tested for ADHD?"

"I've never really considered it."

Phoebe considered this for a minute and believed him. "I think it varies from person to person, but I've found it useful in trying to understand myself. I've always been prone to hyper-focusing, but the rest of my life always seemed to be falling apart. Late on bills, doom piles full of random shit I can't seem to put away, veggies going bad in the back of the fridge ... but I was still one *hell* of a journalist," she said finally, chuckling wistfully.

"You have ADHD?"

"What do you think?" she asked, perfectly deadpan.

He laughed again, the sound quickly becoming a tonic to her nerves. "I don't know much about the diagnostic criteria. I'm an emergency physician, after all. Deciding whether someone's bee-sting reaction warrants epinephrine is one thing, but—"

"Don't sell yourself short. I'm sure you're a fantastic ER doc."

Ronan blushed, clearly appreciating the compliment.

"Well, two things you should know then," she said simply. "First, women tend to present differently than what society tells us ADHD looks like. And second, self-diagnosis is considered acceptable within the community."

That second point seemed to bother him a bit. "Wouldn't some people just lie about having it? For an excuse or to gain attention?"

"Be real, Ronan," she said seriously. "I'm more than fine with a certain percentage of people lying if it means that the vast majority of folks who actually need proper access to supports like therapy or medication actually get them."

"Well …" he said slowly, pondering this, "I don't *disagree* … Were you on medication? Stimulants?"

"Off and on. They're controlled substances though, and I was terrible about keeping my doctor's appointments."

"You've never felt dependent on them?"

"No." She chuckled, then raised a playful eyebrow at him. "Wait. Did Lennie tell you about the lies the Wraiths planted about me when I 'went missing'?"

Ronan shook his head to deny this, but his reddening cheeks gave it away.

She decided not to focus on it. "I mean, obviously, prescribers need to be careful with that sort of thing, but for a lot of people with ADHD, the great irony is that it's honestly kind of hard to build a dependence on something when you forget to take it half the time."

He nodded thoughtfully, wondering if the Bloodsbane he relied on regularly for missions—not to mention, the amount of black coffee he drank each day—wasn't a sign of his system requiring additional stimulants to thrive. "And is that something you'd like to explore again?"

"Maybe." She shrugged. "Assuming we can ever get this damn magic out of me."

Ronan's expression grew deadly serious. He reached across the table, hesitating momentarily, then placed his hand on top of Phoebe's and looked into her eyes. "I promise you that I'm doing—and have been doing—absolutely *everything* in my power to figure this out."

"Thank you," she said quietly, swallowing hard as raw emotions began to simmer close to the surface. "I know that now."

Phoebe woke up alone in the early morning hours, tossing and turning following a wildly vivid dream. As always, in the days and nights following a magical outburst, she was plagued by nightmares and traumatic flashbacks—blurred memories of bodies, blood, dust, and rubble.

The details of this particular dreamscape had arrived in much sharper focus than ever before.

And *far* more ominously.

Up until now, Phoebe had only vague recollections of the day of the explosion, and where she must have been when everything had gone down ... but in this dream, she was front and centre, walking down the halls of the Wraiths' research facility. From somewhere overhead, she watched herself striding forward, dragging her hand along the sterile walls, with doors opening and lights flickering. She still couldn't make out the faces of the other captives but felt a distinct tang of fear as she watched herself float towards the end of the hall ... a horror story playing out in real-time.

A true nightmare.

Then the dream had shifted suddenly, and she found herself standing in front of a cave ... well, more like a deep, cavernous opening in the ground, situated at the edge of a grassy field. The hole gaped rather vaginally, if she were being honest, beckoning to her with a distinctly feminine energy. Chilling voices calling out to her then: *"Phoebe ... Phoebe ... Phoebe ..."*

Even after she woke up, the haunting sound kept ringing in her ears for *hours* like some sort of dream-induced tinnitus that just wouldn't quit. She eventually gave up trying to fall back asleep and just dragged herself from bed with a plan to head downstairs ... nightmarish headache and all.

She knew she looked dishevelled, with her hair messy and wearing only a loose T-shirt and sleep shorts, but since it was only her and Ronan at the safe house now, she just couldn't be bothered to dress up. After all, two days ago, he'd already seen her at her worst.

At the same time, though, it *was* chilly in the old house. So, she pulled on a sweatshirt and left her bedroom—noting that Ronan's door was shut tight across the hall. After using the bathroom and grimacing in the mirror at the dark circles under her eyes, she padded barefoot down the stairs, listening to the classical music that was playing somewhere on the first floor.

"Hey, Ronan," Phoebe said as she entered the living room. He was seated in his usual armchair, reading through a stack of files. She had to admit that his predictability had a soothing quality to it.

"Good morning, Phoebe," he said, removing his glasses. "How did you sleep last night?"

It was nearly ten a.m., and she appreciated that he didn't criticize her for attempting to sleep in. "Not great, but what else is new?"

Ronan grimaced. "That bad?"

"*That* bad." She sank down into her favourite spot. "If I'm going to be even remotely functional today, I think you'll have to set up an IV drip for me with espresso in the bag."

He chuckled, setting his files down and standing up. She noticed with a smile that he was sipping his coffee from the silly mug she'd given him. "How about I get you a cup to start?"

"Oh, no ... You don't have to." Phoebe hadn't meant her complaint as a request.

"I don't mind. Be right back."

She watched him as he left the room. Ronan was wearing running shoes, black outdoor pants, and a sporty T-shirt that highlighted his V-shaped back. Was he planning on going out? The day was grey, and still exhausted from her ordeal two nights ago, Phoebe wanted nothing more than to curl up in the living room for the entirety of the day and learn more about the Druids.

Ronan returned moments later and handed her a soup-bowl-sized mug of coffee. "Will this suffice?"

She nodded gratefully. "*Definitely*."

He didn't sit back down. "So, I need to step out for a few hours today. I have some errands to run, and I'd also like to take some of your blood for testing if you'll allow me."

Phoebe took her first sip of coffee. It was good. "Sure. I guess."

"Imogen has some ideas for a few things we can check for, regarding both your health and the trapped magic, so I'm eager to crack on with that as soon as possible."

"I suppose you'll need me to come with you for that?" After what had happened, she would be surprised if he was willing to leave her alone in the safe house.

"No, I don't think that will be necessary."

Phoebe didn't miss the slight flicker of his eyes towards the staircase. He was undoubtedly thinking of the stored files in his bedroom.

"Really?"

"*Really*," he said, shifting awkwardly on the balls of his feet before perching once more on the very edge of his chair. "Look, I'd appreciate if you wouldn't go through my personal journals again."

"That wasn't okay," Phoebe agreed. "I know. And I'm sorry."

He nodded gratefully. "Thank you. I appreciate that. But the rest of the files in there ... my research and other Druidic documentation you might find interesting ... Those are yours to explore if you'd like. I've pulled everything out into my room. It's unlocked, so you're welcome to it."

Phoebe's heart raced. "*Really!?*"

"*Really*, really," he replied, in a ridiculously thick Scottish accent.

Phoebe liked the subtlety of his playful side. "Didn't take you for a *Shrek* man."

He smirked. "I have no idea what you're talking about."

Ronan brought forth his medical bag then and procured the necessary implements for taking her blood. To no one's surprise, he turned out to be an excellent phlebotomist, making the blood draw quick, painless, and easy. Before Phoebe knew it, he'd placed a cotton ball in the crook of her elbow, followed by a piece of white medical tape.

"All done."

"Thanks," she said, pressing her fingers against the cotton.

"No, thank *you*," he said, smiling. "I'll be back in time for dinner. We still don't have decent groceries, so how do you feel about ordering in? I've got a craving for Greek."

Phoebe loved Greek food. "That sounds amazing."

Over the coming days, Phoebe's attention shifted from curiosity to obsession as she poured through every record of the Druids' complex history that she could get her mitts on, hoping that something might at least point her towards *a cure*. She now knew that the Druids and Wraiths shared the same origin story, long ago, but they'd split up into two factions that had gone down separate paths several thousand years ago after being forced into hiding. The Druids had formed their secret order, and the Wraiths had eventually fallen prey to Cassius's promises ... and lies.

Phoebe spent hours reviewing maps and drawings and reading through Ronan's small collection of hand-written translations of the Druids' (relatively undocumented) past. Even now, an incredible amount of Druidic lore was passed down orally—a fact she had already known from her initial dig into the Druids that had been following her after her escape from captivity—and kept as closely guarded secrets within the modern-day Order.

Almost everything important appeared to be shared solely on a need-to-know basis.

Still, Ronan's well-curated crawlspace library was a major boon to Phoebe, who finally felt properly oriented with the history of the people who'd taken her in. More than once, she kicked herself for not having simply asked Ronan about any documentation he might have in the first place.

In her defence, though, she'd been a little distracted lately.

Phoebe had particularly enjoyed the translated accounts of one Druid, who'd dubbed himself *Rory the Robust*. It had all felt sort of silly and whimsical at first, but the further she delved into Rory's notes, the more she realized how extremely fine the line was that the old Druid had walked between darkness and light. To her, his description of the Otherworld—or at least, as he'd "perceived it" during visits to sacred sites—read more like a bad acid trip than anything else.

She'd brought this up to Ronan, who had come to a similar conclusion himself.

"Oh, that old fool? Don't take him too seriously. I'm fairly certain most of his records were jotted down after dining on magic mushrooms. Have you read his

account of being made of tree bark for a whole lunar cycle?" He'd chucked then. *"I should have warned you about him."*

Rory, it seemed, was a bit too loony to be seen as fully credible.

Instead, Ronan directed Phoebe towards the musings and spiritual explorations of another Druid: a woman named Deirdre, who seemed (somewhat) more level-headed and had lived only a few hundred years ago. Her writings had a dreamlike quality to them that left Phoebe feeling wistful and sleepy. In fact, reading them often caused her to doze off, stretched out on Ronan's bed where she was reading. More than once, Ronan tucked her in following a particularly involved Deirdre deep dive, only to have Phoebe wake again hours later and be drawn right back into her work.

What drew her in more than anything were Deirdre's descriptions of the holy wells and passage caves as being the portals to the Otherworld, as well as its "feminine aspect." Phoebe would have thought it all the stuff of fiction, since myth and folklore were often used as a part of purposeful storytelling to relay information about people, seasons, and ways of the land.

About four and a half days into Phoebe's research marathon, at just past three in the morning, something of real relevance *finally* jumped at her from the page she was reading. She'd been sprawled out on Ronan's bed, toiling by lamplight through yet another stack of notes, when she came across a passage about a dream: Deirdre, just like Phoebe, had stood before an earthen cave that had called her name *"almost as if it was beckoning me home."*

Phoebe had sat up, her heart pounding as she frantically flipped through the next entry, dated several weeks later: *"I visited the cave, stepped through, and returned. I will not discuss this transcendence, for instinct beckons to secrecy ... but I can divulge that I am whole ... and I am healed."*

She'd already suspected that Deirdre suffered from various ailments, since many of her entries had referenced anti-inflammatory balms and salves. That was the main reason Ronan had her logs in the first place: first and foremost, Deirdre was a healer.

"*Ronan?!*" Phoebe shouted, hurtling from his bed, feet first.

She knew that he was still awake as she'd heard him speaking to someone on the phone from across the hall—presumably Lennie, based on the time difference between B.C. and England. Ronan hadn't actually slept in his own bedroom for days, allegedly not wishing to disturb Phoebe's "process." He'd taken her room instead, which had felt needlessly generous.

However, it was also very *Ronan*.

Several seconds later, the Druid doctor stepped into the doorway just as Phoebe slid into him with a dull *thud*. "Ah!"

"What is it? Is everything okay?" he asked, eyes wide with concern.

She braced her hands on his chest and pushed back, blinking excitedly. "Sorry, I just need your help with something. Can you tell me more about Dom and Julia's visits to the Otherworld?"

Phoebe sensed a flicker of hesitation from Ronan as he gently took her hands into his own, removing them from his chest, and led her towards the bed. She climbed atop his duvet and crossed her legs, shoving Deirdre's entry at him. Ronan scanned the page, then Phoebe jabbed her index finger on the final line, reading it aloud: *"but I can divulge that I am whole ... and I am healed."*

Then she looked at him expectedly. "See?"

Ronan's breath slowed as he looked up at her with a furrowed brow. "I do see. Yes."

Phoebe's face fell. "What?"

"*Ehm* ..." Ronan removed his glasses and started cleaning them on the hem of his shirt. "What exactly do you want to know about Dom and Julia's experiences?"

She tried her best not to be thrown off by his unexpected response. "Um ... I guess I'm just wondering if they were ever *healed* in the process?"

He cleared his throat, clearly grappling with his words. "Putting it simply, yes. But the more complex answer is that the process always involved death, or at least some similarly significant cost."

She was confused now. "It doesn't sound like Deirdre died ... or made any particular sacrifice."

"Perhaps not, though you'll notice how vague she is about everything upon her return."

Phoebe's heart sank with disappointment. "I see."

"Look, I've read that passage before too, and I understand why it might be exciting." He took her hands into his once again. They were warm, and she liked how his thumbs stroked soothing circles against her skin. "But interactions with the Otherworld are *extremely* complicated."

"I know."

"How about I connect you with Dom and Julia sometime," he said with a wink, "to interview them about their experiences?"

She rolled her eyes.

"I mean it," he continued. "I'm sure they would be more than willing to share what they know. Particularly Julia. At the very least, it might help you understand the seriousness of it all. I don't doubt that Deirdre had an ... *experience* ... but it's not the sort of magic one plays around with willy-nilly."

Phoebe still hadn't met this Witch in person, though she was clearly much beloved, at least when it came to Ronan. Still, she was growing more desperate to meet Julia by the day, especially since she'd accidentally overheard Ronan telling the woman the feelings he was grappling with.

She pulled her hands from his, looked down, and started gathering her scattered papers. "Alright." An awkward silence fell between them until Phoebe finished what she was doing, yawned, and sat back against the pillows.

Ronan cleared his throat again. "I actually have some big news. I was just about to come and tell you about it when you crashed into me." He chuckled.

Phoebe was intrigued. "Oh?"

"Lennie just called. He believes he's located the final relevant documentation from the research facility."

"No way." Her breath hitched in her chest. Her eyes felt glassy, but she was not going to cry.

"Yes, way. And guess where they are?" Ronan asked eagerly.

Phoebe stared at him blankly; she couldn't even begin to guess.

"Ireland."

CHAPTER 26

RONAN

RONAN WANTED TO BELIEVE THAT PHOEBE'S HEIGHTENED INTEREST in tapping into the Druids' rooted legacy of earthen magic throughout the ages was a good thing. Over the past week, she'd become as driven as a hound on the hunt for *anything* that might point her towards a cure. At times, it had been difficult to watch, and at other times, it was inspiring. However, when she'd arrived at the notion of visiting the Otherworld, he'd thanked the Goddess that Lennie had phoned him only seconds before with the perfect redirection of her focus: a new mission.

And really, what better place could there be to explore her burning curiosity than Ireland?

It was during their flight over the Atlantic that Ronan had been reminded of their flight to Calgary only weeks earlier, when she'd told him of her wish to visit Ireland someday ... and when he'd found himself wishing he could bring her there.

To bring her home.

As he looked out the window at the surrounding clouds, Ronan examined the synchronicity of it all, and not for the first time. Lennie had a suspicion—which was confirmed by recent intel—that the missing files from the destroyed Wraith facility had left Canada altogether and landed in the possession of one or more extremely powerful Wraiths based in Europe. One of Lennie's software applications—which had been "scraping" the internet for a match to any of the damaged documents they'd recovered from the ruins—had a hit. An underling had sloppily scanned documents, which led Lennie to a Wraith who went by the (aptly) demonic moniker "Malphas"—or *Mal*, for short. He was apparently already known to Lennie, a particularly malicious Wraith who was part of Cassius's legacy.

Ronan had to admit that it was all rather extraordinary how things had lined up.

In another life, he might even have been baffled or skeptical of the bizarre coincidence. But in this one, he was best friends with the Sovereign and the World Ruler; Julia and Dom's entire existence, and their resistance against Cassius, had been marked with chronically strange coincidences and lucky (if not unlikely) circumstances. And his and Phoebe's seemed to be as well ... though, of course, their relationship was drastically different.

Things had felt understandably strained after he'd discovered Phoebe on his bedroom floor, reading his private journals. Of course, Ronan had expected some discomfort between them after that; the conflict and confusion that had arisen within him when he'd discovered her there, plus Phoebe's magical agitation shortly after, had left them both feeling raw.

Yet, over the past week, Ronan had grown increasingly concerned about the gaping chasm between them, primarily due to Phoebe's obsessive researching. She had essentially moved into his bedroom and only left it for the occasional meal and to use the bathroom. Some days, if Ronan hadn't brought food to her, he wasn't sure she would have eaten at all.

"You want to go to *the library?*" Ronan asked, caught off guard as they collected their bags at the Dublin airport. With his backpack slung over his shoulder, he yanked his hard-sided travel case off the conveyor belt, his brows furrowing. "Like ... at Trinity, or—"

"No, no ... the *secret* library," Phoebe said, her voice dropping to a near whisper as she collected her smaller duffel bag from the belt. She already wore her sunflower backpack. "The one Deirdre references in her writings."

Having read most of Deirdre's accounts from over two hundred years ago, Ronan was unsurprised that Phoebe had been drawn to the woman's words and energy. Deirdre had often reminded him of his dear (and incredibly wise) friend Peggy, with the almost soothing way she described the Druidic relationship with nature and Wielding.

Ronan sighed. "I can take you there, Phoebe. But not today."

She stared at him with red-rimmed eyes, and he wondered when she had last slept. "Why not?"

"Because there's somewhere else I was planning to take you first, before the others arrive later this afternoon." He extended the handle on his suitcase and waved her towards the exit.

Phoebe blinked slowly. "Okay ..."

Ronan understood her gnawing hunger for a cure. Really, he did. However, it was *very* early in the morning, and they'd only just landed in Dublin following their red-eye flight. If nothing else, it was a good sign, cognitively speaking, that her ability to focus was returning. Phoebe had shared her grief and frustration that she could no longer work or research like she used to. And yet, he couldn't shake the feeling that obsession was the only thing sustaining her at present.

And he knew all too well what could happen when being fed by that sort of focus alone.

"Trust me," Ronan said, offering her a reassuring smile and a playful bump with his shoulder. "What I want to show you this morning will be worth it."

Phoebe bumped him back with a tight smile and a shrug.

The pair exited the airport then and found Dom's vintage Land Rover—the one commonly used for driving across his estate—waiting for them exactly where he'd been told it would be, with the keys tucked up underneath it precisely where Ronan had known he would find them.

Being the great Celt's best friend had its perks.

Morgan, the groundskeeper of Dom's estate and manor house in County Galway, cared quite a bit about Dom's vehicles, keeping them in tip-top shape for any occasion when someone might need to use one. All Dom had to do was ask, and Morgan would gladly deposit a vehicle anywhere—even several hours away down the M4.

"It's a bit of a drive—several hours, unfortunately—followed by a short hike in, but it's a place that's really important to my history," Ronan said as he loaded their bags into the back. The last time he'd visited the place was when he'd first returned from the dead.

Phoebe yawned. "As long as you let me nap on the way."

"Of course," he said, doubtful that she'd actually be able to sleep in the Land Rover once they hit rougher country.

For months, Ronan had debated when would be the best time to tell Phoebe about his death, his trip to the Otherworld, and his rebirth. Unlike his secret about betraying his friends and working alongside Cassius, this one felt like a quintessentially private matter. And not just because the Otherworld had sworn him to secrecy about his possession of the knowledge from the *Codex Druidicus* either. Something about dying just felt ... *personal*. He didn't know how else to explain it.

However, a few nights ago, when she'd first started questioning him about Dom and Julia's trips to the Otherworld, he'd known that it was finally time to share this final piece of himself with her.

Knowledge even of the Codex itself was considered exceedingly dangerous information that was only made available on a need-to-know basis. Of course, Julia and Dom knew all about the Codex magic that lived within him. Lennie, Peggy, and Thomas were the only Druids to know even the basics about his experiences with the Otherworld, and Stuart, Lindsay, Alanna, and Shereen were the only Knaves (and knew even less). Including himself, only ten people in total knew even a fragment of his truth.

It had always been crucial that he keep that particular secret as close to the vest as possible.

"I'm not sure if you've caught on yet," Ronan said then, laughing wryly, "but the past several years of my life have been extremely complicated. I've had ... a lot to work through."

"I know," she replied quietly from where she was standing on the far side of the vehicle, shuffling her feet a bit, and apparently *still* punishing herself for her misstep with his journals.

He ran his hand through his hair. "Well, the thing is, you really *don't* know."

Phoebe's eyes flashed pointedly at him.

"Not all of it, I mean," he added quickly. "It's nothing like the Cassius secret. This is something I've chosen to keep to myself ... something very private that I've only shared with a select few individuals. Out of an abundance of caution, I mean, not because of shame or because I didn't want *you* to know. It's just one of those things that requires specific timing, you know?"

She bit her lip. "Alright."

Together, they climbed into the vintage Land Rover. Ronan keyed the ignition, and it roared effortlessly to life. They soon exited the airport's winding maze of parking lots and thoroughfares and finally hit the road. The vehicle's suspension was just as wild as Ronan remembered, and he couldn't help but chuckle as he and Phoebe bounced around in their seats. Phoebe laughed too, which felt like a miracle, considering how things had been going over the past week.

"So, can you tell me more about where we're going?"

"I can," he said. "It's a place I first visited with my friends as a teenager ... to do secret magic."

"*Naughty*."

He chuckled. "Well, we were certainly dabbling without proper guidance. It was risky. My granny Sheila was furious when she found out I was attempting to follow in my 'useless Grandpa Murphy's footsteps.' He was a failed Druid, though really more of a drunken recluse than anything else."

"Tell me more about your grandmother. Is she still around?" Phoebe drew her knees up until her feet were on the seat with her, and wrapped her arms around them, now that they'd hit a smoother stretch of road, allowing her to tuck herself in properly at least for a time.

"No, she passed quietly a couple of years ago. She was a Wielder too, though she never practised modern Druidics the way I have. She was more ... *earthy* about it."

"Did you get to say goodbye?"

He recalled visiting Sheila in hospice following the fall of Cassius. He'd been thankful for the chance to say a proper goodbye, leaving her with a kiss on the softness of her tired hand. "I did, and there's a bit of a story to all of that, which I'll tell you once we get where we're going."

Before Ronan had died in the grove, he'd asked Peggy to relay his passing to Sheila ... once he was well and truly gone. Thankfully, though, Peggy hadn't yet done so before his return, which had saved a lot of confusion for his aged granny.

"Can I ask about your mum? It's okay if you don't want to talk about her though."

"What's there to say?" Ronan sighed wistfully. "I didn't know her. I was born in the late seventies to an 'unwed mother' and was lucky enough to be raised by my granny ... and to have a family that could both afford the pregnancy as well as conceal it. At that time, children born in my circumstances still usually ended up in orphanages or worse. Not to mention what happened to the mothers ..."

Phoebe frowned. "I've read about the Magdalene Laundries. Didn't the last one close fairly recently, like 1996 or something?"

"Correct," Ronan said, his expression growing dark.

The Magdalene Laundries had been horrific church-and-state institutions in Ireland throughout the nineteenth and twentieth centuries, housing/imprisoning unwed pregnant mothers far away from "moral society" until their babies could be born. Following the births, the babes were separated from their mothers and either adopted, boarded, or placed in industrial schools. The mothers—along with other "fallen women," including orphans, victims of assault, and disabled persons—remained in the convent/asylum and were forced to work under absolutely appalling conditions, more often than not unable to leave or return to their families. In some cases, this was meant to be penance for their immoral actions, leading to unwedded childbirth. And in other cases, this was done simply because the profoundly religious Irish state had no place for women who didn't (or couldn't) embody the grace of a "good Catholic woman."

It was a horrendously dark mark on the history of the Irish Free State.

Phoebe bit her lip, bringing her focus back onto Ronan. "So, what *did* happen to your mother?"

"Granny Sheila bought my mother a ticket to Canada to give her a fresh start. She eventually went to nursing school and started a new family, '*living a very normal and non-magical existence*,'" he added in Sheila's thick accent, "or so I've been told at least. But that's really all I know. I didn't grow up with her in my life."

"Was she young?"

"When she left Ireland? She was sixteen, but fifteen when she had me. My father—if you can call him that—was never in the picture either, beyond promising her the moon one night and leaving her in the gutter the next."

Phoebe released a puff of air. "Men really are *shit*."

"Indeed ... But I don't consider myself unlucky. My mum went on to have a better life, I'm sure. And I had Granny Sheila, who was hard but fair." He smiled fondly then. "I think she'd appreciate that description, actually."

Phoebe yawned wide, lulled by the gentle rocking of the vehicle. "She sounds like an actual saint."

"*Sheila?*" He quite literally guffawed then. "No, not really. But I have her to thank for my unyielding grit, and for that, I'm grateful."

As they continued along the M7, travelling deeper into the countryside, Ronan relayed to Phoebe more stories of his past, mostly about his time at school and what it was like growing up in Ireland through the eighties. Eventually, Phoebe nodded off, allowing him some time for reflection as they drew closer to what he now considered to be a sacred grove.

His grove.

When he'd last visited the place, Ronan had just returned from the Otherworld a changed man. Well, not entirely changed, of course. He was still Dr. Ronan Gallagher—soldier, doctor, Druid, and *lover*. Ronan chuckled then, recalling his delight when he'd arrived in the Otherworld and found that his body and perception of himself had remained intact. He was nothing if not vain.

At the time of his passing, he'd been relieved to die. Grateful, really. But then he'd spoken with the voices and been convinced (strong-armed) to return and save his friends, something he now believed reflected his truest nature. His willingness to return had turned the tides and led to Cassius's final demise. And it had also healed him in more ways than one, returning him to the living world mostly whole ... and, more importantly, *good enough*.

Despite having returned healed, though, and even after Cassius was defeated, he was still tasked with cleaning up his mess. Which wouldn't have been a problem (his roiling guilt already fuelling that quest) but for the ripe anger he felt at the fatalism of it all. The voices of the Otherworld hadn't actually offered *him* any choice—at least, not anything that might offer him freedom from his burden. And most days, he struggled to accept that he would have to just watch his life play out before him with little control.

Rewarding surrender over sacrifice, my arse ...

What kind of a reward was it to have a woman like Phoebe cross your path, only to realize that the timing was *unbelievably* wrong? The writing had been on the wall for him since the moment he'd learned of her existence. If he was being honest, that had pissed him off to no end and had been the topic of a carefully worded discussion with Eunice during the emergency session he'd booked with her before leaving for Ireland.

"You seem to have your mind set about this already, Ronan," Eunice had observed after he'd been rambling for more thirty minutes about how it could *never* work between him and Phoebe, hoping that by sharing it with her, it might help diffuse some of his anger in a safe space.

She'd studied him for a long moment before continuing. *"I'm curious where, or how, you think my support would be best targeted for the remainder of this session?"*

The way Eunice framed that question only made Ronan more frustrated. Fuming, he'd snapped at her. *"I don't know! I'm so—"*

"Angry. Yes, I can see that."

"Ugh, I'm sorry. I'm being a shit."

"It's okay," she'd said kindly. *"But what feeling do you think your anger might be covering up?"*

Ronan's brow had furrowed as he stared back at her through the computer screen. *"What do you mean?"*

"Sometimes, usually in childhood, we learn that a particular feeling isn't safe for us to experience, for one reason or another, and so we replace it with a more acceptable one ... and in your case, and for most men trapped within patriarchy, anger is one of the only 'acceptable' feelings to express openly. But that leaves no room for emotions like sadness or shame, for example, to be shared, let alone felt. So, we already know you've experienced some fear around your relationship with this co-worker, which might be fuelling the anger. But I'm curious"—she'd paused briefly to nibble on the end of her pen—*"when you think of this woman, looking beyond that surface anger, what* other *feelings come up?"*

Ronan considered this for a long moment.

Granny Sheila had run a tight ship and had little patience for emotion. And while Ronan had certainly felt a lot of anger in his teen years, he couldn't remember feeling much of anything else as he was transitioning into adulthood.

Dismissing that thought with a mental shake of his head, he tried to do as she'd asked and thought about Phoebe again, and the situation he found himself in with her. Then a different emotion came to light.

"I suppose it must be disappointment," he'd said quietly.

Eunice nodded slowly then looked pointedly into his eyes. *"And perhaps* sadness *as well?"*

Tears welled up in Ronan's eyes then as repressed grief rose to the surface.

Despite all of his efforts, the dark tendrils of the mess he'd made so long ago were still spreading ... hurting the people he cared about, along with others that he would never even get the chance to meet. *That* was why he'd been sent back from the Otherworld. *That* was the role he'd been tasked with playing. So ... Phoebe wasn't for him. Not now. And probably not ever.

Who wouldn't be sad?

"Possibly," he'd finally admitted, his voice thickened by tears.

A small bump in the road dragged Ronan out of his memories then. He looked across to the passenger seat where Phoebe was still napping, the sadness from his most recent therapy session threatening to resurface once more.

Now wasn't the time. He took several long breaths and sobered, recalling suddenly that he still needed to pay Eunice for that session—something which felt unbelievably mundane in the moment as he navigated the Land Rover towards his magical grove.

Phoebe suddenly stirred beside him, waking from her slumber and rubbing her blurry eyes. "Are we there yet?"

"Almost," he said, admiring her loveliness even now. She'd been somewhat reinvigorated by the drive, their conversation, and her cat nap, but she still looked worn out.

"Cool," she said, yawning.

"Did you know that roughly eighty percent of Ireland used to be forested?" Ronan said, gesturing at the largely open fields they were driving through and thinking of his grove, which remained hidden in a small, protected forest only a few minutes away now. "Native broadleaf trees and evergreens and large swaths of temperate rainforest too. Unfortunately, thanks to thousands of years of gradual agricultural and population growth—plus mass deforestation throughout the English colonization era and even much more recently—only one percent of it now remains."

"Deirdre talks about that in her writing," Phoebe said sadly. "It made me cry."

"It makes me cry too sometimes," he admitted. Then he pulled off the road and shifted gears, both literally and figuratively, slamming the Land Rover's sticky gearshift into park. He looked at Phoebe and gestured to a nearby path into the woods.

"We walk from here."

"Lead the way."

Ronan scooped up his backpack, which contained only his keys, his phone, a water bottle, and a large thermos that he'd had the flight attendant fill with hot water while they were still on the plane.

And his *compass*, of course.

"I'm sorry to drag you on a hike after flying all night," he said a few minutes later as he stepped over a particularly gnarly root. Ronan could already feel his body relaxing, his usual aches and pains melting away right along with the stress of city life as his Wielder's body naturally gathered up restorative magic simply by being there.

Phoebe shrugged and said nothing, seemingly unaffected by their surroundings.

So far, anyway.

One unique feature of yew forests was their darkness, and the correspondingly dense moss that blanketed the limestone and earth within them. Ronan had always loved escaping into another world—another *time*—whenever he visited these rare and sacred groves.

They walked together in peaceable silence for another ten minutes before Ronan got the first glimpse of his grove. Phoebe was leading them now, and he was curious if she would feel its pull as well, hoping that the power of the ancient woods would eventually affect her as much as it did him.

It was a *wildly* enchanted place.

"Ronan ..." she said, her voice sounding a bit strange as she suddenly stopped walking. "I don't know how to explain it, but I can *sense* that you've been here before. And someone else too ..."

"*Julia*." He could also feel her Bearer essence here. "Yeah."

She wobbled slightly on her feet, seemingly impacted by the sheer weight of the magic surrounding her. "What *is* this place?"

After taking a deep breath to prepare himself, he told Phoebe the simple truth.

And then she fainted.

CHAPTER 27

RONAN

RONAN HAD EXPECTED PHOEBE TO BE FEELING *SOMETHING* IN response to the magic of their surroundings by the time they reached his grove. But when he told her, "This is where I died," he certainly hadn't expected her to faint. Thankfully, between his quick reflexes and the mossy forest floor, she'd landed perfectly safe, cradled in Ronan's arms, though he did sustain minor damage to one of his elbows after it connected with the hidden sharpness of a stone beneath the moss. Of course, his concern for Phoebe easily overrode the painful twinges in his funny bone as he laid her gently down on the forest floor.

"Phoebe? ... Can you hear me?"

After several agonizing seconds, she started to rouse, blinking her way back to him. "Yeah ... What happened?"

Ronan sighed in relief. He'd watched Dom catch Julia countless times when she would collapse after being rocked by one of the visions that routinely haunted her, but she rarely came to quite *this* quickly.

"I think you fainted."

"Obviously," she mumbled, pressing her hands into the ground to try and sit up.

He gently placed a palm on her shoulder, keeping her down. "Stay here for a little longer, please."

"Fine," she grumbled, apparently still a brat even when barely conscious.

Ronan bit back a smirk. "Did you experience any visions while you were out?"

"Was I gone *that* long?"

"No, no. I'm just curious."

Phoebe pondered this for a few moments. "I don't think so ... but why did I faint at all?"

"Well, I did just drop a bit of a bomb on you," he said with a snort. "But my best guess? It's because of the magic here. It's very ... *unique*."

She pinched her eyes shut, grimacing. "I can tell. My head is pounding!"

Ronan suddenly worried that bringing her here had been a mistake. He opened his backpack and procured his thermos and a small fabric pouch that looked a lot like a hand-filled teabag. Somehow, he'd sensed that at least one of them might need a magical pick-me-up on their journey, though admittedly, he'd thought it would be him.

"Here ... Drink this."

Phoebe did as she was told, sipping awkwardly at first from her prone position, and then finally taking a big swig. Almost immediately, colour started returning to her cheeks. She looked both confused and delighted. "What's *in* that? It's delicious."

"Oh, a little of this, a little of that," he said, smiling at the cute look on her face before relenting slightly. "Just some herbs and spices I've found to be quite rejuvenating. If you like, you can just call it 'Ronan's Special Tea.'" Then he grinned at her. She didn't grin back.

"No."

Ronan laughed heartily at her familiar deadpan delivery even as he started helping her to slowly sit up. He hesitated several moments before actually placing his arm around her for support, and as she didn't seemed to mind its presence, he decided to go with it. It wasn't long before they were settled peacefully together, sitting comfortably in the shadowy depths of the ancient grove.

"Do you know much about yew trees?" he asked her quietly.

"A little bit. Deirdre wrote several passages about yew-tree restoration."

"That's right, yes ... But are you aware of the tree itself having long been a part of cultural folklore and myths?"

Phoebe puzzled over this briefly, then leaned forward excitedly. "Oh, wait! Doesn't one of the three Witches mention yew trees in *Macbeth?*"

"Ah, yes." Ronan smiled, gazing up through the yew boughs and breathing deeply. "*'Slips of yew silvered in the moon's eclipse.'*" He chuckled then. "But yew lore far predates Shakespeare. Long ago, the yews of Ireland and Britain were said to grow for hundreds if not thousands of years. And they were *huge* ... Interestingly, one of the iconic uses for their timber was in the production of longbows back in the medieval era. Apparently, the heartwood was especially—"

"Neat!" Phoebe exclaimed suddenly, apparently unable to suppress the outburst any longer. "Do the Druids ever *use* longbows? Or is it all swords and daggers?"

"It is neat," he said, grinning at the brightness in her eyes. "And no, not really. Though you could ask my friend Peggy more about that later today. I'm told she went through a serious archery phase back in the seventies."

Phoebe smiled. "I might just do that if we have time."

At this, Ronan was inspired to check his watch. They would need to leave soon. When they finished at the grove, he and Phoebe were expected to join Lennie and the other Druids in Dublin, and they still had several hours of driving ahead of them.

"Yew trees have the ability to form roots directly from their branches," he continued. "So, you can imagine how sprawling they used to get. It's not hard to understand why those giant yews became so deeply rooted in the culture and mythology of the local people wherever they grew."

Phoebe sighed, her expression growing tranquil now, though whether from boredom or the serenity of the place, he wasn't quite sure. She looked especially beautiful here, framed by the rusty bark and deep green of the forest—*his* forest—at the very heart of his death and rebirth.

His Adam's apple bobbed as he swallowed hard, feeling the weight of his surroundings. Then he shrugged. "Well, obviously I could go on about yews forever, but most commonly, they're associated with death and immortality, specifically in relation to the Druids. Julius Caesar even referenced it in his writings—he had bit of a morbid curiosity around the ancient Druids, in my opinion."

Ronan typically avoided thinking about Caesar since it inevitably reminded him of the Child of Rome. However, this point felt significant. "Long story short, Christianity arrived, and the original Pagan beliefs around yews were appropriated, which is why you see them planted in *so many* Christian churchyards."

"I'll take your word for it," Phoebe said, shrugging. She wasn't the religious type.

"There are even stories about the ancient yews drawing vapours from decomposing bodies near church graveyards—though it's more likely that the bodies were simply buried too shallow, and there was off-gassing," he added with a chuckle.

"*Gross.*"

"Indeed. They're also quite poisonous to humans and animals, so that's also ... *neat*." Ronan especially loved studying toxic plants and their effects on the body.

"You're such a nerd," she said, her quiet laughter carried along lightly through the enchanted air and its earthy fragrance.

Ronan allowed few people to tease him, and yet somehow, she seemed to have nearly free rein in that department. "Takes one to know one, love."

Several beats passed before Phoebe tentatively asked him, "So, the yew trees ... What do they mean to *you?*"

Ronan pondered this as he stared up at them. "Hmm ... Well, I don't think they symbolize death and immortality for me as much as the cycle of life. There is no permanency, but we *can* try ... and then try again." He was suddenly reminded of the enchanted snakes that had coiled around his body in the Otherworld nearly three years earlier—an *ouroboros*, with no beginning and no end.

"Life is a spiral," he added, shrugging.

Suddenly, the hair on his arms stood up. Phoebe was feeling it too, or at least, she seemed to be as she shifted in place beside him. Ronan sniffed the air. It no longer smelled mulchy and damp but was instead carrying the slightly chlorinated scent of ozone, not unlike the smell of lightning about to strike. Something was happening here. He frowned, suddenly uncertain if the same magic he'd experienced several years ago was coming to life once more.

The ground below them remained dry though, without the seeping groundwater that had risen up that day and engulfed his body.

And yet something had clearly just awoken inside of them both.

Ronan took Phoebe's hand in a gesture of offered safety and connection. It felt good to touch her like this. *Grounding.* Ronan had spent far too much time standing at the helm of his life all alone, and so he just allowed himself to enjoy Phoebe's companionship—or whatever it was between them—for a few moments longer.

Ever so slowly, the charged feeling started to settle again.

"So ... are you going to finally tell me why you brought me here?" Phoebe asked, sensing the break in the spell. "I mean ... besides informing me that you're actually undead and have a *major thing* for yew trees."

He clicked his tongue. "I'm not undead, Phoebe."

"Yeah, but ... you *did* come back to life. That's some serious zombie shit, Ronan!"

He pressed his free hand flat against his heart, feigning deep offence. "Isn't showing you where I died in my favourite grove enough?"

"There's always more to it with you, Druid," she said, shouldering him playfully.

He sighed. "I brought you here to tell you about what happened when I died, and why I was sent back ... You had questions about the Otherworld, specifically as it relates to healing, and I think I might be able to answer at least some them for you."

Over the next while, he carefully explained that, while conducting his experiments under Cassius's rule, his body had ultimately become so ill and ravaged from the constant daily exposure to high volumes of Wraith magic that there had been no way to recover from it. Despite his best attempts, and the efforts of his Druidic kin, there had been no way to save him in the end. His earthly body had been spent. Plain and simple.

"Would you have survived if you'd become a Wraith?"

"Possibly. But even if I'd wanted to, which I didn't, I doubt they would have allowed it." He laughed darkly at the thought.

"What do you mean?"

He grimaced. "Do you really want to know?"

"Obviously."

"Well, there are two reasons, I suppose. Firstly, during Cassius's rule, there was a sort of order to things—a way of being that he expected his Wraiths to abide. He limited the number of Wraiths created not because it was *allegedly* some sacred right that needed to be earned, as he falsely claimed, but because Cassius needed to maintain *absolute* control over the Wraiths themselves in order to maintain his own dominance as a Sorcerer."

"Was Cassius really *that* powerful?"

"Yes." Ronan shrugged. "He essentially managed all Wraith creation and destruction for centuries—roughly two thousand years, to be specific. Should any individual among their number rise too high in their ranks, that was seen as a threat, and Cassius would kill them. Although while my experiments were going on, he would donate them to my research instead, though not before their pleural fluid was drained and turned into killing smoke. The old ones were especially suitable for that job."

Phoebe's expression had grown almost grave now. "Okay ... And what's the second reason?"

"Oh." Ronan laughed humourlessly then. "Let's just say that the Wraiths at Cassius's estate *really* didn't like me."

She snorted. "I find that hard to imagine."

Ronan realized that, for possibly the first time ever, he was actually speaking freely about the experiments he'd performed and inspired without also feeling the gnawing pangs of guilt that had always accompanied it. Phoebe already knew who he was, what he'd seen, and what he'd *done*.

And she was still here.

As he drew closer to concluding his story, Ronan's relief was palpable. "Long story short, after I'd been rescued, my body continued to deteriorate, and when I realized that my final days had come, I asked Julia to bring me here. I wanted to lie down in my grove and die quietly in the shadows of my favourite trees ... in my favourite woods."

"That sounds really peaceful."

"It was."

Phoebe's brows furrowed. "Wait, where was Dom in all this?"

"Oh, we'd said our goodbyes a few hours before that. I knew Dom would have been a sobbing mess and ruined the moment," he said, chuckling fondly. "Once you get to know them both better, I swear that will make total sense."

Phoebe offered him a tight smile and nodded stiffly. "For sure."

Ronan's heart sank. He'd just (accidentally) projected Phoebe into his future—imagining her getting to know Dom and Julia more meaningfully than she likely would simply by joining the Order, but she would definitely have access to them should she remain at his side.

By her response though, she was clearly quite uncomfortable with the notion.

He cleared his throat. "*Ehm* ... Anyways, the whole point of the story is to tell you about what happened when I went to the Otherworld ... I wouldn't exactly say that it was healing for me, since I literally died, but it was still restorative in its way."

"Alright," she said, her expression encouraging him to go on.

Speaking somewhat haltingly at times, he explained to her that, while he'd welcomed death and whatever might follow at the time, when he'd arrived on the other side, the voices of the Otherworld had instead offered him a chance to return ... or more accurately, they'd strongly *suggested* that he return and save his friends, and even implanted magic inside him that would be necessary for defeating Cassius. Not only was Ronan to take on the Sorcerer, but he also had to try and reverse or repair any damage done by his obsessive pursuit of the *Codex Druidicus*, an ancient tome of dark magic that Cassius (and others) had drawn upon for evil, which had been subsequently destroyed ... though not before Ronan had memorized the text.

"... So, I'm essentially a living version of the *Codex Druidicus*," he said at last. "A book of dark magic turned human ... if you can imagine such a thing." He tilted his head slightly to one side as he considered his own words for a moment and then decided to rephrase them. "Well, not the literal book itself, obviously, but whatever's left of its essence *is* now trapped inside of me. Words are spells, though, and since I went and memorized the fucking thing ... Well, I'm kind of stuck with it now."

"Wait. What?" Phoebe looked utterly gobsmacked. "You mean that you have magic trapped inside of you too!?"

"Kind of ... though it's not really the same—"

"Pretty damned similar, Ronan!" Phoebe snapped at him, popping up to her feet and immediately starting to pace. He could feel her trapped magic, which had been calm pretty much since they'd arrived at the grove, suddenly start thrumming wildly against the restraints of her physical body.

Phoebe was starting to panic at whatever it was she thought this revelation meant ... and as such, the magic was trying to take over.

He stood up and reached for her hand, which she reluctantly allowed him to take. "Hold on, please. You haven't let me finish my story. It will all make sense soon. I promise."

Phoebe was either still extremely fragile from last week's upset, or the magic "container" of her body was starting to weaken. Ronan wished it were the former, but he had a strong suspicion that they were even shorter on time than he'd originally thought. While he'd initially likened her red-rimmed green eyes to the extensive research and lack of sleep, he couldn't deny the medical alarm bells going off within him.

She focused on her breath for several moments, then shook herself roughly, almost like a dog trying to dry itself. Ronan assumed that this was an attempt to try and activate her parasympathetic nervous system —a.k.a. the body's rest and digest response. Eunice had actually reminded him to utilize the same technique not too long ago.

Or perhaps the magic was just making her extraordinarily twitchy.

"Sorry," she said at last. "Bit of an overreaction I guess."

"It's alright. We're ... *Ehm* ..." Ronan cleared his throat loudly then —a sound that was rather jarring in the quiet grove. "We're still learning to trust each other properly. That's all."

Phoebe nodded quickly, offering him the same uncomfortable smile as before.

His heartbeat quickened. "Look, when I first returned from the Otherworld, I had this massive bundle of magic inside me that I could *only* use against Cassius or else I would die."

"Die again, you mean?"

He nodded. "The Otherworld doesn't give away anything for free. You should have heard Dom's response after *Julia* made a deal with the Otherworld! He was furious!"

"What? Why?"

"It's a long story, but she returned from *her* otherworldly visit with this enchanted amulet around her neck. Basically, she'd learned that if she didn't strip another Witch of her magic—and for the record, the evil little shit had definitely had it coming—then *Julia's* magic would be stripped instead ..." He frowned. "Or maybe she would just die ... I'm not entirely clear on that, to be honest."

"Wow ... metal," Phoebe said.

He raised an eyebrow at her. "That's one way to look at it, I suppose."

"Did *you* have any other *'prices to pay,'* or whatever, for getting to return?"

"Yes, actually. Since I now live with the burden of the Codex's knowledge, I'm also tasked with properly cleaning up my own damn mess in relation to it."

"And if you don't?"

Ronan considered that seriously for a moment. "Why wouldn't I?"

"Okay, but what about—"

"Before you ask, Phoebe. No ... There was nothing in the Codex that I can use to cure you. I truly wish there were. The fact that there isn't ..." He sighed and shook his head. *What's the point in carrying this burden when I can't even use it for something so important?*

Almost scowling in frustration, he continued. "All the Codex magic is good for is destruction. The only thing it could possibly do—aside from killing you—is to trap even *more* magic inside of you, and I'm obviously not about to do that."

Phoebe stared at him.

Ronan stared back.

"Okay ..." She swallowed hard. "I believe you."

"Thanks," he said as another wave of relief washed over him. For better or for worse, Phoebe finally knew everything.

Then he noticed her staring off almost blankly into the distance. "What is it?" he asked, following her eyeline.

"Oh, it's nothing ..." But her eyes remained fixed on some unknown place beyond the grove, almost as though she were in some sort of trance.

"Have I said something wrong? I probably could have been more sensitive ... not mentioning the idea of trapping even more magic inside you. Sorry about that."

She blinked several times. Then her eyes refocused on him. "No, no. You haven't said anything wrong. Look, I really appreciate your honesty, Ronan. I can't imagine what it's been like for you to live with this burden. Your death, being sent back ... That's a lot for anyone." She smiled gently at him then, not with pity but with something that almost looked like grief.

"I truly wish I could use it to help you, Phoebe. The fact that I can't ... It's one of my biggest sorrows." It was difficult for him to even get these words out, as his own grief started clawing its way up into his throat. Rather than forcing it down as he normally would have done, almost automatically, he instead worked to coax it the rest of the way to the surface. His Adam's apple bobbed once again as tears began to stream from his eyes.

Phoebe turned to face him and reached out to touch his face, gently wiping the salty tracks from his cheeks. "It's not your fault, you know ... what happened to me."

Ronan squeezed his eyes shut, inadvertently pressing out another cascade of tears. "Yes, it is."

"No, Ronan. It really isn't."

He couldn't speak.

"But if it helps," she continued, "please know that I forgive you anyway. I don't want this between us anymore. I want ..." She paused, biting her lip briefly, before starting again. "I want us to be okay."

"We are, aren't we?"

She shook her head a bit as though he were misunderstanding her. "No, like ... I came into your life like a fucking storm surge, and I'm not entirely sure you were prepared to batten down the hatches."

"You didn't storm—"

"I did. And you've been bailing water ever since." She laughed sadly.

"Phoebe, please. That's not true."

It *was* true, of course, but not in the negative way she'd implied.

When Ronan was with Phoebe, he had the sense that he was just beginning some incredible sea voyage ... But it also felt like he was building the boat even while simultaneously trying to push it away from shore. His feelings for her were exhilarating and terrifying in equal measure.

Phoebe stared up into the thick canopy overhead. "Do you know that when I first *met* you, I felt like I already *knew* you? It was so strange ..."

Ronan hadn't known that, but he understood.

"You just felt so *familiar*," she continued with a sigh. "And I know that makes no sense, but I guess I just want to believe that we met for a reason."

Ronan didn't disagree, though he was still at a loss for words.

Phoebe looked directly into his eyes. "You've been an incredibly important part of my journey, Ronan ... And I want to thank you for everything you've done for me."

"Of course, Phoebe," he said easily, giving her a simple shrug. "We're partners."

"I know," she replied a little too sadly for his liking. "I guess I'm just ... Well, I'm glad you came back from the Otherworld."

CHAPTER 28
RONAN

IT WAS HARD TO IMAGINE THAT JUST THAT MORNING, RONAN AND Phoebe had been seated under a yew tree on the mossy forest floor, side by side, while he told her about the time he died. He didn't know why that moment between them had struck him so profoundly; it hadn't been romantic. Not even platonic, really. It had just been honest. Perhaps it was the immense relief of releasing such a burden from his soul, but it had also felt like some sort of farewell between them—a parting between who they'd once been and who they had become during their months of forced proximity.

Ronan couldn't put his finger on it, but he knew that things would never truly be the same between him and Phoebe again. And yet, their return trip to Dublin had brought a peaceful sort of silence between them, as well as a sense of deep ease, both reflective and calm. He wasn't sure if he'd ever felt so comfortable with someone else in quiet contemplation, and he hoped she felt the same.

However, by the time they'd arrived at their destination—a local community centre which had been commandeered by the Druids several decades before—with their bodies thoroughly rattled by Dom's vintage Land Rover, the distance Ronan had been feeling between them for the past week had returned. He surmised it was likely due to the exhaustion of their travels, though, as it always did, the grove had recharged him and his magic in a way that nothing else could.

It was now three in the afternoon, and there was still much to do that day. Across the room from where Ronan sat, Phoebe stood flanking Lennie and biting her nails as they finalized the plan. In the coming days, they would need to infiltrate one of the most complex and dangerous Wraith establishments known to the Druids: Astaroth Hotel in Dublin.

He watched Lennie and Phoebe shifting their attention between several laptops, chatting animatedly. Lennie hadn't been wrong to suggest that he and Phoebe were alike. Ronan now noted that it was not only the way the two communicated that was similar—leaving slight pauses before speaking and then info-dumping all of their thoughts—but the way they moved as well seemed almost harmonized. Ronan tried not to feel jealous. After all, even though he also had come to appreciate the synchronicity he shared with Phoebe, that didn't mean he was the only person who could be expected to connect to her magic.

"Ronan?" Peggy said, giving his knee a squeeze. It seemed she'd been trying to get his attention for a few seconds.

"Oh, I'm sorry, Peg. I didn't hear you come in," he said, rising to his feet and pulling her into a warm embrace. "It's so good to see you! How are you?"

She stepped back, holding his shoulders as she took in the sight of him. "Something's different about you."

He laughed. "Well, I've barely slept in the past thirty hours."

"It's not that ..." Her eyes tracked over to Phoebe and then back to him.

"No, Peggy," Ronan said stiffly. "Don't even start."

She raised her hands innocently. "I'm not starting anything, Ronan. But I have to say that you seem more ... settled."

"I've been running a lot and going to therapy. Maybe that's it," he said sardonically.

She smacked his arm cheekily.

"We also visited my grove."

"Ah ..." she said. "I thought you seemed *lighter*."

Ronan smiled. "I missed you. How long are you here for? Will you be joining us?"

Peggy hadn't been in the field for years, but since surviving the cancer diagnosis she'd received three years previously, she had returned to at least lend moral support to local missions.

"No, not this one. I'm just here to see you."

"Did Lennie ask you to come?"

"No, no. But Thomas needed a ride from the airport," she said with a wink.

"Fine." Ronan smirked. "Keep your secrets."

She laughed heartily. "Now, show me where to find some tea."

Ronan led Peggy into the community-centre kitchen. A familiar, almost nostalgic smell greeted him—sort of dusty and metallic, mixed with old coffee and lemon cleaner.

"I'm going to be frank with you," Peggy said then, deftly plopping a teabag into the bottom of a stained ceramic cup. "Your energy ... the magic in you, whatever it is ... Well, it's reaching for *her*."

"She has that effect on a lot of people." Even now, Ronan noted, Lennie was being drawn into Phoebe's rhythm. The woman was just magnetic as hell.

Peggy poured hot water slowly over her teabag. "I'm serious."

"But how can you tell?"

Just then, Thomas joined them in the kitchen. "There you are!"

The great man had changed a lot over the years since Ronan had first met him. Back then, Thomas had been young, eager, and rather green. He'd escaped a shitty home life to find solace with the Druids, which had been very healing for him. Since then, he'd grown more spiritual. Sure, he was a powerful Wielder now, but his true strength lay in his ability to truly see people and connect with them.

When Ronan had been dying from the Wraith magic, Thomas had been an irreplaceable spiritual support. The man just had this deep sense for the old magics, and because of this, they now showed up in practically every aspect of his life.

"*Ronan*," Thomas said, pulling him into another embrace. He hugged him for a second, then held him out in front of himself by the shoulders, just as Peggy had done—though with a more serious expression. "What did you do?"

"What do you mean?"

"The Codex magic ... Have you altered it somehow?"

"No."

Thomas was clearly puzzled by something. Meanwhile, Peggy watched on, stirring a splash of milk and half a sugar cube into her tea.

Ronan groaned. "Don't start. Either of you!"

Peggy beamed at him, but Thomas remained uncharacteristically serious.

"The woman in the other room ... *Phoebe?* When I walked past her, her magic felt so ..."

"Trapped?" Ronan suggested.

"No, that's not it. I mean, I know that she does have Wraith magic trapped inside her. But her own magic feels ..." He couldn't seem to find the right word.

"What are you getting at, Thomas?" Peggy asked, not unkindly.

He took a moment to consider this, then frowned slightly. "Her magic feels extremely old ... similar to the Codex magic inside you, Ronan, but ... older even."

Ronan was stunned by this suggestion, this insight, and was suddenly furious with himself for not having thought to bring Thomas into the conversation about Phoebe months earlier. But then again, nearly everything to do with the woman had sent him into a proverbial tailspin. Thomas's intuition alone might have saved them a great deal of time that they'd wasted running around in circles trying to whittle down their theories and ruminations.

"How is that possible?" he asked Thomas then. "Do you think she's somehow siphoning the Codex magic from me?"

"Perhaps. But perhaps not."

"How delightfully cryptic," Peggy observed dryly.

"I'd have to spend some time with the both of you in closer proximity to be sure ... but it's almost like a dilution of some sort." He gestured towards Peggy, who was now tentatively lifting her beverage to her lips. "Just like milk in a cup of tea."

"Delicious ..." Peggy said then, taking a long sip.

Ronan sighed, then shook his head. "It can't be."

"I don't think it's a matter of could, should, can't, will, or won't, Ronan. It's merely an observation."

Just then, Lennie appeared in the doorway. "Whenever you're ready."

While they'd hoped to have a few days to prepare for the mission, it appeared that tonight was going to be their only option. Lennie had successfully hacked Malphas's schedule, and the Wraith was allegedly leaving on a plane *back* to Canada first thing tomorrow morning. While they could attempt to scuttle the Wraith's exit strategy, it seemed far simpler to just push their mission up a bit.

"Malphas's counterpart, Levi has—"

"Sorry," Peggy cut in. "Levi as in 'Leviathan'?"

"The very same."

"How original," she scoffed, shaking her head.

Lennie shrugged. "This Wraith group apparently enjoys demonology. Anyways, we have reason to believe that he personally transported relevant documents to this particular location." He put up an aerial map of Dublin on a projector screen then, with a red circle around the Astaroth Hotel. "It is now a well-established Wraith gathering place."

"Well-established since *when?*" Ronan asked.

"Since the last time you were there," Lennie snapped impatiently, clearly aggravated by the interruption.

Ronan rolled his eyes but couldn't help but notice Phoebe's gaze brush over him from where she was sitting beside Lennie, her expression unreadable.

Lennie forged ahead. "What matters here is that the club has become exceedingly exclusive. It's also nearly impenetrable. Assuming we manage to get in, it's likely going to be very difficult to get back out."

Amos whispered to Amelia, and she nodded. The twins had arrived an hour before, hot off their last mission in Washington State. Ronan watched as Amelia gestured towards Phoebe, who then stood up and faced them all.

Ah … no wonder she seemed so serious, Ronan thought, realizing that she was about to address the whole group.

"So," she said, "Lennie has asked me to share some of my experience with infiltrating places like these …"

Ronan flipped down the black plastic knob on an aged coffee carafe, breathing deep. He would have preferred a whisky right about then, but no one else seemed to share that sentiment. Lennie had just concluded their briefing for the upcoming mission, and the general atmosphere was one of excitement.

Which left Ronan feeling all sorts of other things.

"Mate, can I speak with you for a moment?" Lennie asked, suddenly appearing to this right.

Ronan released a long breath through his nose. "I can only imagine what about …"

Lennie didn't respond to Ronan's snark, turning away from him instead to stalk off along a hallway that ran parallel to the main community-center space. Ronan abandoned preparing his shitty coffee and silently followed him.

Along the way, he noticed Phoebe chatting with Amos and Amelia in the main area. All three of them appeared relaxed and eager for the upcoming mission. He wondered why he was the only one who seemed to be having any misgivings about the whole thing.

Lennie stood leaning against a large window that looked out onto the main road. Cars whizzed along past it as though nothing unusual or unnatural even existed in the world—no Wraiths and certainly no enigmatic women with dark magic trapped inside them.

"Are you going to be able to handle the objectives?" Lennie asked, cleaning under his fingernail with a short gold dagger. "Or do we need to find someone else for the job?"

Ronan could feel the energy coming from that blade even from where he stood. He knew it must have been forged by Wren—Lennie's Knave ex-lover, who'd been murdered by Cassius's minions several years earlier—as all her blades had a distinct hum to them that always reminded Ronan of her ... and of when she died.

"What do you mean?" he asked.

"I just want to make sure that the role Phoebe has devised for you to play will be tolerable."

Ronan's brows furrowed. "Oh, please, Lennie. I don't know what—"

"Don't," Lennie said, cutting him off, his eyes piercing as he stared at Ronan. "I saw your face when you found out what your part would be. And that I'd agreed to it. You looked like you wanted nothing more than to wring my neck."

Their plan *was* complex, involving countless moving parts and rather unconventional ... for the Druids at least, though he supposed it was nothing out of the ordinary for Lennie. Or even for Phoebe. The long and the short of it was that they intended to have the Druids employing advanced seduction tactics to win their way into the VIP lounge—real "super-spy" shit.

And Ronan was to play the part of a jealous and domineering boyfriend, giving Phoebe free rein to trick some unassuming staff member into "rescuing" her from his thrall. Meanwhile, Lennie would be using a similar tactic, and between the two of them, they hoped to breach the lounge and gain access to the private-access floor, which is where they suspected Malphas's files would be hidden.

Simple, *right?*

Ronan knew Lennie would be in his element with such tactics, and Phoebe similarly so. And while he was happy for her, truly, it also seemed to highlight, once again, just how soon he and Phoebe would likely have to part ways.

"It just wasn't what I'd expected for a final mission with her, that's all."

"What do you mean?"

Ronan sighed, running his hands back through his hair. "Once we're back in Vancouver, I'd like to request a transfer, either for myself or for Phoebe. I've told her everything, and—"

"Everything?" Lennie looked surprised.

"Everything. I even took her to my grove. That's where I told her about my death, the Otherworld, and that whole bit. And I've already given her all the information I had back at the house, and then some, about what it means to be a Druid. And what the Order is all about."

Lennie continued to stare at him, his expression calculating now. If he didn't know any better, Ronan might have thought he even detected a hint of sadness on the Brit's face.

"Don't look at me like that," Ronan said, agitated. "I've made my decision."

Indeed, on the drive back from his grove, Ronan had made peace with this decision. It was going to be uncomfortable, perhaps, but he knew it was for the best.

He'd done his part as a mentor, and she was all set to start her life as a member of the Druidic Order.

"Fine," Lennie said a bit reluctantly. "We can make the necessary arrangements once you're safely back in Vancouver."

"Thank you."

"As for tonight, you'll need to be on the top of your game. She's relying on you to play the part ... so do your part."

He would, of course. Ronan was already dreading every fucking minute of it, of course, but he'd experienced worse. Far worse, in fact, and knew that he could suck it up.

"Of course."

"She'll also need to stay with you while you're in Dublin. I don't have time to line up alternate accommodations for tonight. Sometime in the next few days though, I should be able to get one of you on a flight out."

Ronan nodded. "Fine. Thanks."

Lennie left the room without another word. Ronan heard him bump into Phoebe somewhere just beyond the door, and then the pair of them rejoined the others, presumably including Amos and Amelia, hammering out the final logistics of the mission.

In five-and-a-half hours, they would begin.

Ronan pulled out his phone and texted Domhnall:

> Are you available to chat?

Then he waited, leaning against a cool wall and appreciating that the sun was still up as they approached the vernal equinox. The inherent balance this time of year always made him feel level-headed. Through the winter, he tended to feel inexplicably drawn to the darkness … and to inward thought. Soon enough though, the days would grow longer, leading to a sort of restlessness in him once again.

Ronan's phone rang. It was Domhnall.

"Hello, Ronan," the great Celt said calmly.

Ronan suddenly felt the urge to cry. Again.

"*Domhnall*," he said sadly as he moved across the room to the door and shut it to give himself some privacy.

"Are you alright?"

"Not particularly, but I will be."

Ronan quickly filled Dom in on what had happened at the grove, as well as Lennie and Phoebe's plans for the night. Lastly, he shared his intention to break up his partnership with Phoebe in the Order.

"Don't you feel like you're rushing this decision a bit?" Dom asked, concern evident in his tone.

"No. Quite the opposite, actually."

He heard Dom sigh heavily then. "You're too old to be looking for relationship advice from me."

"But?"

"But I think you should take a few more days and consider it further. From what you've told me, and what Lennie has shared, you two make a great team."

Ronan's Adam's apple bobbed as he swallowed hard, his mouth suddenly feeling almost unbearably dry. It wasn't the thought of losing Phoebe as an ops partner that was upsetting him but of losing her as a friend. Not that they wouldn't still interact periodically within the Order, of course, but their close proximity had brought him a lot of joy as of late. Phoebe was a lot of fun to be around. And fun was something he knew he could use more of in his daily life.

"We *do* make a great team, but she can find that with others too. Watching her tonight with Lennie ... She was in her element, Domhnall. I can't provide her with that sort of mentorship, or partnership, and that's clearly where she's meant to be headed."

"Are you suggesting that she'd like to *partner* with Lennie? I've never gotten the impression that he wants another partner."

"No, no ... Not Lennie *per se.* Though she would be wise to train under him if she can."

Dom was silent for a few moments. "I trust you to follow your gut."

Ronan had no idea what the hell Dom meant by that, but just then, there was a knock at the door. It was Phoebe, and she was ready to leave.

Saying a swift goodbye to Domhnall, he hung up and moved to join her.

"Okay, Ronan, I need you to take me shopping ..."

CHAPTER 29
PHOEBE

Astaroth Hotel, 10:07 p.m.

Phoebe lowered herself onto a velvety powder-blue chaise and crossed one perfectly polished leg over the other, seductively dragging her calf halfway up her shin before leaning back to survey the room. The black strappy sandals adorning her perfectly manicured feet—the purchase of which she'd convinced Ronan was necessary to ensure both seduction and the evening's success—had been perhaps excessive, just as the designer clutch likely was, but she'd figured it was better to go too big than not big enough.

And anyway, Ronan clearly had the means to cover it.

Following their meeting at the community hall, Phoebe and Ronan had made several stops to prepare for the upcoming operation. While he'd seemed inconvenienced, citing that he would have preferred a longer turnaround time at his place, Phoebe suspected he was just eager to show her his house, which turned out to be an historic red-brick terraced property in an area called Ranelagh, which he'd apparently remodelled a little over a decade before.

After they'd brought their purchases back there to start getting ready, she'd also gotten the distinct impression that he took a specific sort of pleasure in buying luxurious things for himself, almost as much as he enjoyed purchasing them for her.

A problem for later ...

Tonight, she'd dressed for success, which in this case, meant dressing not just to impress but seduce. During her six months on the run, she'd discovered this to be quite effective in luring these Wraith assholes out of hiding ... and into her web. And tonight, there would be a great many spiders in the mix.

It was endlessly amusing how weak men—and Wraiths—fell so hard for such an obvious *femme fatale* act. And in this case, much like the tips and tricks she'd learned from studying the PUAs, sometimes the best weapon against an enemy was the most toxic one of all.

She hated to do it, but she also knew the kind of target she would be dealing with tonight.

The plan was in full operation now; it was time to climb into the belly of the beast.

The hotel lobby's posh (and rather plush) cocktail lounge reminded Phoebe of the Hotel Georgia back in Vancouver—down to having a signature scent all its own, in this case a heady jasmine with verbena that threatened to give her a migraine. What set this establishment apart, though, was that it was owned and operated by an exponentially growing branch of the greater Wraith complex.

"Christ, they *have* become civilized, haven't they?" Ronan drawled, sitting neatly in one of two buttery leather armchairs across from her. Between them on a low, round table, an oil flame candle flickered moodily.

Ronan was also dressed quite smartly, though he'd flippantly claimed the outfit to be "just some things kicking around in my closet." The *liar*. Phoebe knew for a fact that his Dublin home had been rented out until relatively recently, and she'd never seen him wear anything like it in Vancouver. That meant that anything this fancy in his possession would have been either still in storage or only recently returned to its rightful place; she *highly* doubted that he'd have had the time to have the suit pressed and readied.

This outfit had to be new; *Mr. Expensive Taste* must have a tailor on call.

"That really is a nice suit," she said, smiling knowingly. "Very James Bond."

"Just wait until you see Lennie," Ronan said casually before reaching long, capable fingers towards the cocktail menu and flipping dextrously through it. Phoebe couldn't help but fantasize about what other things those hands might be capable of.

Fuuuck ... she groaned internally.

That wasn't going to help anything. For over two months now, they'd been doing the same dance. And for all the scripted lines, formulas, and methods she'd developed over the years for ensuring that her needs were always met—whether by a juicy journalistic lead or a potential "romantic" entanglement—Phoebe had never let anyone so close to her heart.

But it couldn't be helped.

She suddenly oriented herself to Ronan like a sunflower reaching for the bluest of skies, keenly aware that his attention was decidedly *not* on her. Intellectually, she knew that his cool and uncaring affectation was part of his persona for the evening—and that hers was to be both fearful and wary of his gaze. But she rapidly found herself hungry for his attention, with her breath unwittingly short as she stole glances at his adept hands and parted lips. To others, she knew that he might seem stuck up and too serious (and admittedly, he *was* a bit stiff), but for Phoebe, he was also a light that had been keeping her from being entirely consumed by her roiling inner darkness.

Phoebe had meant what she'd said in the grove: when she'd first met him, she'd felt like she already knew him. *From another lifetime, maybe?*

Now though, she knew that they had met for a reason.

And she wanted him. Tonight. In the flesh.

She didn't know if this was because she wanted to know him, just once, in all his fullness, or because it would be the final step in shedding her old skin. But either way, she wanted him.

Desperately.

"*Hmm* ... Impressive," Ronan said as he continued studying the extensive list of available cocktails, drawing her abruptly from her thoughts.

She knew she had to pull herself together. "I never buy my own drinks. I've got a trick for that."

Ronan either didn't hear her or was patently ignoring her.

Finally, after several more moments perusing the menu, he looked up, the ghost of a smile pulling at his lips. "Said every woman everywhere ..."

His attention remained fully on Phoebe, drinking in the sight of her then so deeply that it was like he'd been without water for months and had finally been given the means to quench his thirst. Everything from her oxblood toenails to her plunging and equally sanguineous velvet wrap dress were now targets of the Druid's intense scrutiny. Eventually, his heated gaze settled somewhere between Phoebe's exposed breastbone and the cupid bow of her red-coated lips ... his attention dancing back and forth between the two as though he might just lunge across the table and tear out her jugular with his teeth at any moment.

Phoebe's heart began to pound, even as her entire pelvic floor clenched. *Fuck!*

"Not much of a trick really," he said then. "If you ask me."

"I didn't ask you," she said breathily.

Ronan laughed darkly.

Phoebe couldn't decide if she liked the way his eyes seemed to grow inkier then. Almost dangerous. She knew that she needed to regain control and fast. She slowly shrugged one shoulder. "And anyway, I haven't started the trick yet ..."

She leaned slowly towards him then, almost conspiratorially, exposing even more of her neck for him to salivate over and delicately brushing a long, golden strand of her unbound hair back behind her shoulder.

Just then, as if by magic, a server appeared to Ronan's right. He was wearing a starched white dress shirt, neatly tailored black slacks, and perfectly polished black brogues. His hair and beard were both expertly trimmed—clearly, he visited the barber regularly.

His face, however, was unremarkable ... and his entire focus was on Phoebe.

"Good evening! My name is Fionn, and I'll be your server tonight. Have you had a chance to peruse our cocktail menu?"

"Not yet," Phoebe said, smiling meekly. "I think he wanted to choose for me."

Fionn seemed to suddenly notice the presence of Ronan, who was now leaning back in his chair like fucking Hades on his goddamn throne, his legs spread just wide enough to broadcast his prowess, with his feet firmly planted on the black and white marble floor.

Phoebe shifted in her seat and slowly recrossed her legs.

Fionn's jaw twitched as his nostrils flared. "I see. Well, if I can make any suggestions ..."

It'd taken only a fraction of a second for Phoebe to recognize the sort of man that Fionn believed himself to be. All she needed now was to look just lost and needy enough, trapped beneath the thumb of her controlling "boyfriend," and Fionn would feel that he had no choice but to rescue her from such a hellish situation.

Whether intentionally or not, for the past minute or so, Ronan had been showing her a side of himself that he'd never offered before. And confused the hell out of her once again.

Staying carefully on task, she quickly raised one hand to her left face and tentatively began running her fingers along her jawline, slowing to a stop with her fingertips resting lightly just behind her ear. "That would be amazing. Thank you, *Fionn*."

"Can I start by asking what sort of drink you like? Or perhaps, what you *don't* like?" The server's eyes flickered almost imperceptibly over to Ronan before returning to Phoebe.

She tucked a strand of hair behind her ear then dropped her hand back down to her lap in apparently helpless uncertainty.

"We pride ourselves on delivering a cocktail experience that's second to none," Fionn offered. "I've personally tried every drink on this menu and even designed several of them myself. And I can honestly say that you will be embarking on a unique sensory journey with every sip."

Phoebe could sense the server's confidence growing now as he continued.

"And while I'm sure that sounds like a bold promise—"

"Actually," she interrupted timidly, intentionally slowing his roll, "I think I'm looking for something ..."

With the server's attention firmly fixed on her, she raised her fingertips back to her jawline and ear, just barely grazing her own skin. Then she allowed her eyes to dart nervously to Ronan before looking back at Fionn. "Okay, this might sound silly, but I want something that feels *exciting* and bright and ... I don't know. Exhilarating maybe? ... Does that sound stupid?"

"Not at all!" Fionn took a step closer. "So ... you're looking for a drink to liven things up?"

Her hand dropped down into her lap, though slower this time, and Fionn's eyes tracked its movement the whole way without hesitation. Then Phoebe brought the same hand up again, repeating the tentative jaw stroke. This time, she laughed brightly for a moment before tossing her head back and "inadvertently" exposing her long, graceful neck.

"Yeah, I think so. Like a drink that makes me feel like ... like I want to *break the rules*." She glanced around briefly, then looked deep into Fionn's eyes. "You know?"

The server's cheeks flushed a deep pink. "I understand ... Well, it *is* somewhat subjective, but if that's what you're looking for, I have the perfect drink in mind: an 'Unholy Trinity.' It's tequila based and somewhat spirit forward, for that nip of excitement on the first sip, but after that, the iconic blue agave harmonizes well with our custom botanical bomb."

"That's it!" she exclaimed. "*That's* what I want!"

Ronan grabbed the cocktail menu again and flipped loudly to the (gratuitous) description page before looking back up. "Don't look so impressed," he practically growled at her then. "He just quoted the menu word for word. Is that *really* what you want?"

She dropped her hand to her lap once more and nodding innocently. "Um ... I mean, yeah. That *is* what I want."

He snorted obnoxiously. "Sounds like it was written by ChatGPT ... Ridiculous."

She blinked at Ronan.

Then Fionn cleared his throat. "Right. Well, I'll tell you what ... Why don't I bring you one on the house, and you can let me know how it makes you feel?"

Phoebe looked at Fionn and nodded gratefully, her fingers trailing lightly across her throat then. "*Thanks*."

After taking a beat to bolster his patience, or perhaps something far more primal, Fionn turned to Ronan then. "And for yourself, sir? Did you want any suggest—"

"I'll have what she's having," Ronan snapped, flashing his teeth at the man.

Phoebe had never heard this tone from Ronan before. This ... possessiveness. And she wasn't entirely sure it was an act. What the fuck was happening?

"Just to be clear, your drink *won't* be on the house," Fionn said, flexing slightly and puffing out his chest.

Ronan's eyes rested heavily on Phoebe, ignoring this apparent challenge altogether. "Naturally."

"Right then. I'll return with those shortly." Fionn turned away then and strode off towards the bar.

Ronan blinked slowly, ever so slightly dialling back the intensity of his ongoing stare. "You're a *very* dangerous woman, Phoebe Ashburn."

"I know." She smirked, though inside, she was struggling to keep the effect Ronan was having on her under wraps. "Fionn is going to be our key to getting in."

Across the lounge, Phoebe watched as the man shuffled the bartender aside and began mixing the cocktails himself, knowing that she'd pegged him perfectly.

"So, did you read the menu ahead of time?" Ronan asked, drawing her attention back to him.

She winked. "*Maybe* ..."

Ronan shook his head and crossed his legs informally, with his right ankle practically resting on his left knee. Though crossing his legs more properly and politely was far more his style, she had to admit that this pose gave him a much broader stance and made him look *far* more formidable.

Together, the two of them surveyed the room discreetly as the lights around them dimmed somewhat, and the curated jazz grew louder. Across the lounge, in another dimly lit corner, Amos was seated casually with several Druids she'd only met that afternoon. And near the entrance, Amelia was leaning into one of the servers, a woman who was laughing heartily at whatever joke she'd just told.

Lennie, meanwhile, was sitting at the bar.

Although Cassius was dead, the surviving Wraiths remained on constant alert for offensive attacks from their enemies—a fact that had become plain to Phoebe since she'd started working with the Druidic Order. Even before she'd joined them, they'd been working tirelessly to try and take out each and every Wraith establishment that popped up. In her many talks with Ronan, she'd learned that, for all the generational power of Cassius, he had never allowed the Wraiths to grow into any sort of stratagem of their own.

So now they were running wild.

Trying to keep up in some sort of magical arms race, Lennie and some of the others had done their best to match their adversaries' technical advances, while the Knaves, whom she was surprisingly curious to meet, had continued on with weapons development.

So far, what the Wraiths had *not* been on the alert for, however, was a full-scale assault of the mind ... and the senses. And despite their well-oiled machinations, the Druidic Order lacked the strategic poise to really crack open the greater Wraith complex with each of its separate branches and groups continuously modernizing.

It was time for the Order to level up.

Phoebe had hated even suggesting seduction as a tactic, but she'd been certain that this would be their best approach this time. And Fionn, being the very good boy that he was, had just become living proof that she'd been right.

She watched him approach the table with two cocktails on a round black tray. He patently ignored Ronan as he set Phoebe's Unholy

Trinity down in front of her on a branded coaster, its gold writing covered almost entirely by the cocktail. Ronan's drink, however, remained sweating on Fionn's tray for just a moment longer as he petulantly watched the spectacle unfold before him.

Phoebe lifted her hand expertly, gently touching the same spot just behind her ear. And when the server's eyes tracked the movement, his pupils dilating slightly, she knew it was time to make her move.

Drawing her hand carefully away from her face and reaching for the chilled glass on his tray, she wrapped her fingers around it and brought it slowly to her lips. Then she took a long sip and let her eyes fall closed to "savour the journey." After a long moment—and an audible *mmm*—she opened her eyes and looked up at him again.

"How do you feel?" he asked.

"I think maybe ... like I *do* want to break the rules."

And then she giggled.

And Fionn laughed.

And Ronan glared.

"I'm so glad," Fionn said, his cheeks flushing brightly before he swiftly turned away and headed back towards the bar.

"What was *that?*" Ronan asked.

"It's called seduction, Ronan. That's part of the plan, remember?"

"You had him practically drooling over you. Do you honestly think that's ethical?"

"No," she said, her eyes darkening in challenge. "Do you?"

Ronan ignored this and took a sip of his drink. Then he closed his eyes and practically groaned at the flavour. "*Fuck me* ... That *is* good."

Phoebe smiled into her drink, not wanting Fionn to catch her having a good time without him. While several Druids were in on this operation, all of them attempting to gain access to the VIP lounge, Phoebe was sure that she'd be the one to break through first. She was competitive like that.

From the corner of her eye, she watched as Ronan seemed to struggle with a deluge of complicated thoughts. She knew that this mission was pushing his sense of ethics to the limit, but still ... he *had* consented to the plan.

"So," he said finally, "now that you've adopted Fionn as your lap dog ... remind me what comes next?"

Ronan knew damn well what came next, but she indulged him anyway.

Looking over to the bar where Lennie was standing, schmoozing with another bartender, she gestured in his general direction with her drink. "Lennie over there is going to make his move shortly. It's almost time to act."

"How can you tell?" he asked without turning to look.

"Because he knows even more than I do about the art of persuasion. He's some sort of super-spy."

"We don't talk about Lennie's other job," Ronan said, smirking. "First rule of Druid club."

She snorted, then hid her amusement behind her raised glass. "You *do* make me laugh," she admitted somewhat reluctantly, finishing the remainder of her cocktail.

Ronan looked a little confused by this, but they managed to chat amiably for another few minutes before the Druid doctor suddenly stiffened, evidently sensing the quiet approach of Fionn on their right.

"So, what did you think of it?" Fionn asked. "Going to rob a bank? Or maybe a little light jaywalking on your way home?"

Phoebe lifted her hand to her cheek as she giggled once more in response, which predictably restored Fionn's earlier blush.

"I really, really liked it," she said in a tone that wasn't even vaguely suggestive but had their server nearly panting anyway and subtly flexing his thighs.

Ronan stood up then, visibly disgruntled. "I'm going to use the washroom."

Phoebe knew that Ronan was just making space for her to gain access to the private lounge, yet she couldn't help but think he also wasn't appreciating having her attentions stolen by another, despite it being a critical part of their plan. She watched as the Druid strode confidently across the lounge like he owned the joint before disappearing into the hotel lobby.

That was their signal. When Ronan stepped away from Phoebe, it meant that his partner had gained some new level of potential access. For better or for worse, Fionn *had* taken the bait.

"So, look," Fionn said, wasting no time in making his move, "I know I don't even know your name, and—"

"It's Sasha."

"Nice to meet you, Sasha," he said quickly. "Okay so, I know you're here tonight with ... someone else. But this hotel actually has an exclusive VIP lounge and—" He cut himself off then, shaking his head quickly. "Sorry. What am I saying? 'Exclusive' and 'VIP' mean the same thing!"

He nervously cleared his throat to try and start again, and Phoebe had to suppress a grin. She had this man-child absolutely stumbling over himself.

"Anyways," he said then, looking like he was starting to sweat, "I'd like to take you back there and keep serving you drinks. That is ... I mean, assuming that I can spirit you away from your date. Or ... have I misread the situation?"

Phoebe looked "nervously" past him to the lobby for a moment, then back at Fionn, her hand returning to her cheek. And then to her lap. And then back up again. "You haven't misread *anything*."

Fionn released a shuddering breath and nodded. "Okay ... If it helps you to decide, I'm breaking the rules too. I'm still on the clock for another hour, but I'd be willing to ditch early if you'd come with me to the lounge." He looked over his shoulder towards the lobby. "Right now."

Clutching her purse tightly, Phoebe climbed to her feet. Thanks to the heels she was wearing, she was surprised to find herself towering over Fionn, though even without them, she likely would have been taller by a few inches.

"Why do I have a feeling I'm going to regret this," she whispered timidly to him then.

"You won't," Fionn said nervously as he reached out his hand for hers, looking like a dog who couldn't quite believe the bone he'd just stolen. "I promise."

CHAPTER 30

PHOEBE

PHOEBE FOLLOWED FIONN INTO THE POSH HOTEL'S VIP LOUNGE. IT was in this inner sanctum that they expected to find the majority of the Wraiths, perhaps even their emerging leaders—an unknown pair whom Lennie had identified as "Malphas" and "Leviathan." The intel they'd managed to gather indicated that the Wraiths never cavorted out front with the rest of their clientele, probably to keep their putrid scent from overpowering the lobby bar's dizzying "boutique" fragrance.

That shit was pungent.

Lennie arrived on the scene in the VIP section several minutes after she did. While Phoebe was still a bit uncertain about everything his "other job" might entail, it was plain to her that he was beyond adept at this part of it. He looked even more like he owned the place than Ronan had earlier, despite remaining utterly relaxed and intrinsically cool.

His dark-blue suit and starch-white shirt were perfectly tailored, with long lines and pressed seams looking crisp and sharp as he leaned against the bar, crossing one perfectly polished brogue over the other. He casually crooked his finger at the bartender to bring her to his side. Phoebe wondered in amusement if he would be ordering a shaken martini from her.

As the Brit placed his order (whatever it might have been), Phoebe watched him reach up to the collar of his shirt and casually undo the top button. He wasn't wearing a tie. He didn't need to.

To Phoebe's eyes at least, that unbuttoning had been an incredibly simple gesture. And yet she soon realized that this was about as polished as it got. That ever-so-slight unravelling of the man, so soon after arriving in the VIP lounge, worked its charm almost immediately. Heads quickly started turning his way. Within seconds, Lennie had captured the attention of everyone present.

He'd wanted to be noticed, of course, and had achieved that with something as simple as loosening his collar. Lennie was impossibly smooth, and Phoebe knew that there was a great deal that she could learn from him should she ever be given the chance.

She bit her lip, fascinated by the scene playing out at the bar—he'd apparently ordered a whisky on the rocks—even while keenly aware of Fionn's persistent gaze dogging her from her left-hand side. She kept watching Lennie for a moment longer, forcing the little man beside her to squirm uncomfortably. She knew that everything would be easier if Fionn were overly covetous and practically panting for her ... even though doing so made her skin crawl.

At last, Fionn mustered his courage and cleared his throat. "Can I get you another drink, Sasha? Everything is on the house back here."

Phoebe slowly turned towards him and tucked a strand of hair back behind her ear. Red heat crept from beneath Fionn's tightly buttoned collar, once again, continuing up into his cheeks as her gaze *finally* landed squarely on his face.

"Oh, sorry. Yes, please ... Surprise me?" she suggested, batting her eyelashes.

He nodded and swiftly left her side.

Finally ... While the server had been an easy ticket into the VIP lounge, she feared that she'd inadvertently captured herself a stage-five clinger.

Still, she had dealt with worse.

Phoebe watched Fionn approach the bar and place their order. He attempted a similar lean as Lennie's, but instead of looking like James Bond, he just looked like a wannabe and a fool. Several moments passed, and then Lennie casually sidled up beside Fionn and struck up a conversation with yet another bartender.

When Fionn finally accepted their drinks from the woman, Lennie turned swiftly, colliding with him, "accidentally" spilling the drinks down the front of the man's shirt, while staying dry as a bone himself.

It looked to Phoebe as though Lennie started apologizing then, though far from profusely. But only seconds later, as she watched, the tables turned, and Fionn began apologizing to him.

Lennie really was a master.

Once Fionn had disappeared into the back to clean up, Lennie walked towards Phoebe with a casual grace she'd never seen from him before—not that she'd seen all that much of him so far.

"*Sasha*," he said, nodding.

She chuckled. "I don't think I know your code name."

"And you're never going to," he said with a smirk, then took a slow sip of his drink.

Yep. That looks like whisky.

"Have you heard from Ronan?" she asked, surveying the room.

"Not yet. After you left, he got started on the second phase. If all goes according to plan, we shouldn't see him again until we're back outside. Though, he'll likely be able to see us."

Ronan, along with some of the others, had been tasked with effectively putting the hotel on lockdown while Lennie and Phoebe (and any other Order members who managed to make it into the VIP lounge) focused on making their way to the off-limits private level. While Lennie was usually in charge of surveillance, the other members of the Order were equally capable of managing such tasks. Or at least they were once he'd equipped them properly according to his own standard.

This time, it was finally Lennie's turn to play spy.

Phoebe stretched her back and shifted in her heels. With them on, she was well over six feet tall, which gave her an excellent view of the entire lounge. And so far, only she and Lennie had made it inside.

Lennie leaned towards her then, smelling like whisky and something else that was unfamiliar and strangely sweet. She wondered if it was one of the Druidic pouches.

"Do you see Malphas in the corner?" he asked. "He needs to stay right there for as long as possible if we're going to get through to the off-limits level."

Phoebe reached into her clutch, pulled out a compact, and peered into it, powdering her nose as she spied the corner table over her right shoulder. Six or seven lesser-looking Wraiths sat in a crescent formation, surrounding Malphas, their leader.

"I see him."

The Wraith in question was wearing a hooded robe that looked almost regal, with a peculiar secondary collar that stuck out past his actual shoulders, making him look bigger than he was. The entire garment seemed to have been cut from heavy black velvet, which shimmered slightly when the light hit it just right, and adorned with dark-gold filigree.

As he took a sip from a heavy-looking brass goblet, the whole ensemble reminded Phoebe of a Halloween costume, which suited his demonic moniker a little *too* well. She frowned slightly then, hoping there was only alcohol in that goblet and not something more ... sinister.

"Is he using a glamour?"

"Must be," Lennie said, shifting slightly and looking convincingly bored and unimpressed with their surroundings. "And that's concerning. It takes a surplus of magic and immense control to maintain a glamour like that for very long at all. He's powerful."

"Hmm ..." Phoebe recalled Ronan having mentioned Cassius's glamour as being a constant necessity for him, allowing him to be in public without wearing a full cloak or hiding his face. "Where are the others?"

"Leviathan is over there," Lennie said, scratching his nose with one hand and gesturing subtly in the Wraith's direction with the other.

Once he'd been pointed out to her, Leviathan was hard to miss. He wore a hooded robe like Malphas, though his appeared much rougher and less regal, and its raised hood kept the majority of his face hidden in shadows, reminding Phoebe more of the other Wraiths she'd encountered in the past.

He was also enormous, which Phoebe doubted was due to any magical glamour.

"So, what do you propose?" she asked Lennie, closing her mirror and slipping it away.

Just then, Fionn returned, wearing a fresh shirt and carrying two cocktails. Anger flickered across his face when he noticed Lennie's close proximity to his date.

"I'll catch up with you later," Lennie said, taking this as his cue to duck away. Phoebe watched as the Brit strode over to a corner table and initiated yet another new conversation.

He really *was* fearless.

Phoebe made yet another mental note to definitely study with him should she ever get the chance.

Against her better judgement, Phoebe allowed Fionn to kiss her. He tasted like vodka and chewing tobacco, which made her stomach churn. They'd been chatting in a small corner booth for no more than ten minutes before he'd placed a clammy hand on her thigh. Three minutes later, he had his hands in her hair, messing it up even as he drooled all over her face like an overly excited basset hound.

Phoebe eventually halted his efforts, swallowing down a righteous gag. And for a moment, Fionn looked like he'd been kicked, but then she raised her hand delicately to her jawline and smiled sweetly at him.

He immediately relaxed.

"I just need to use the washroom," Phoebe said then, needing to keep dangling the carrot in front of him for a little bit longer if she were to gain access to the hidden upper level. If she ended things with him too soon, she would miss her mark.

Fionn looked pathetically disappointed.

She ran her thumb seductively over his lip then. "Don't worry ... I'll come *right* back."

The fool nodded stupidly.

Phoebe rose then, straightening her dress, and walked away, designer clutch in hand.

While he'd been sloppily kissing her, she'd managed to snag his security key card from his back pocket ... with relief. She'd been worried earlier that she'd have to take things to "another level" with him if he'd tucked it into a front pocket. That would have been much trickier to access while seated.

She'd also snatched his cell phone, for good measure, after he'd absentmindedly left it on the bench seat between them. And as she strode away, she could feel it weighing down her clutch, along with her own phone and her dagger—Ronan's impossibly thoughtful gift. She could only hope that Fionn wouldn't notice her thievery until it was too late to matter.

"Wait!" Fionn called after her, swiftly rising from the booth and following her into the dimly lit hallway that led to both the women's washroom and the access point for the off-limits private level they were all trying to reach.

Phoebe's heart sank. Had he noticed his things were missing already?

Thankfully, as she turned to face him, her mind racing and chest heaving, though to the hapless server, she knew her guilt and anxiety would simply translate as normal nervousness at his sudden approach. "What is it?"

"I'm going to come with you." He raised his hands quickly to forestall any argument. "Not *into* the washroom, of course. It's just ... there are individuals here tonight who ... well, let's just say that you'll be safer if I wait outside for you. That's all."

"Oh, wow! ... *Fionn!* ... How *thoughtful* of you," she said, smiling at him and tucking her hair behind her ear before turning to enter into the washroom, which was thankfully (and surprisingly) empty.

She couldn't help but wonder then if the men's washroom would have been left without a lavatory attendant for even a moment. Especially if it were located so close to such a strategically important area.

Apparently, women weren't considered threatening enough to Wraith management for them to bother with such close supervision.

Morons.

Of course, having the hallway to the women's washroom also house the access point to the private level was likely very convenient for the Wraiths when it came to grabbing victims and spiriting them away quickly. It also further explained Fionn's concern about her being in that hallway alone. While she wanted to believe that he was truly trying to protect her, it was far more likely that he'd just been worried someone *else* might drag her out of there and up onto the private level for some "fun and games" behind the scenes.

Of course, the dim and moody lighting in that hallway—and *only* in that hallway—was also sinister as fuck.

Stepping into one of the stalls, she shuddered with overt nervousness before swinging the door closed behind her and locking it, feigning a need to find some safety there in case she was somehow still being observed.

Then she pulled out her phone to check it and found that a two-word text had already come through from Ronan:

All clear.

Phoebe nodded to herself. All she had to do now was break away from Fionn's clinginess and sneak up to the private level. *Should be easy enough,* she thought, then frowned slightly. *Of course, if the key card doesn't work for some reason, I might still need him to get me through the door.*

That would take some figuring, but she had solved far more complex problems than that on almost a daily basis back in her investigative-journalism days. And without any help either.

She took several slow, shaky breaths, barely managing to quell the trapped magic within her that had been roiling frantically ever since Ronan had left her side—which had been *very* difficult to ignore despite the adrenaline of the mission. Watching him storm away from her in the lobby bar might have been hard, but she knew that what would be coming next would be even harder.

Somehow, she (and hopefully Lennie) still had to breach the most secure part of one of the most complex Wraith establishments this side of the Atlantic.

She needed to get her shit together.

Phoebe forcibly pushed down her ill-timed longing for Ronan's presence, flushed the toilet for appearance's sake, and then confidently exited the stall. She paused in front of the washroom's heavily embellished floor-to-ceiling mirror when she saw the state of her hair, which was tangled and messy now thanks to Fionn. Scowling, she quickly got to work putting it back to rights.

Any man worth their salt knew not to fuck with a woman's hair and makeup in public, and especially not when that woman looked the way she was looking tonight.

A man like Ronan would have known that ...

She gritted her teeth and looked herself in the eye as she mentally prepared to (somehow) dispatch Fionn. She fucking knew she'd regret not bringing her poison-laced lipstick. Then she steeled herself and nodded. *Okay ... It's now or never.*

As she strode confidently towards the bathroom door, Lennie suddenly backed his way in, dragging an unconscious Fionn behind him by the shoulders. When she saw that Lennie had shoved a rag into the server's mouth, she felt a light bulb go off in her head.

Chloroform! ... I knew I smelled something sweet on him.

"Sasha," Lennie said, greeting her with a curt nod as the heels of Fionn's shiny shoes dragged sloppily across the floor. Then his whole body was heaved unceremoniously into her recently vacated stall, his head banging against the toilet with a dull *"thud"* on its way down to the cold tile floor.

Barely winded by his efforts, Lennie reached smoothly into his jacket pocket and procured a syringe, which he quickly uncapped and jabbed forcibly into Fionn's neck. Then he pushed down the plunger with his thumb.

"What was *that?*" Phoebe asked, curious as hell now.

"Another sedative. We don't need him rejoining us anytime soon, though as far as I can tell, he's not a Wraith." Finished with the syringe now, Lennie walked calmly over to the yellow disposal unit for such items, affixed to the wall near the row of sinks, and deposited it inside.

"You mean he's not a Wraith *yet*," Phoebe said, both shocked and relieved by the quick progression of events. "Though he tasted just about as disgusting as one."

"I bet." Lennie grinned mischievously at her. "I assume you got his key card? I couldn't find one on him."

"Yeah, I got it." She flashed it at Lennie, matching his naughty smirk with one of her own. He seemed to really "get" all of this: the espionage, the thrill of the hunt ... the delicious seduction of complex schemes and imminent danger.

"Perfect. Let's go!"

With that, Lennie led her from the washroom and nonchalantly steered her towards the entrance to the private level ... just as three Wraiths rounded the corner from the VIP lounge at the far end of the hall.

"*Shit!*"

Without warning, Lennie grabbed Phoebe and spun her around, slamming her up against the wall and digging his face into her neck with an unexpectedly animalistic sound that she'd never imagined coming from the normally prim and proper spymaster.

She nearly laughed.

"*Sorry*," he hissed quietly, shifting his hips against her and running his hand up her thigh.

Phoebe's chest was heaving now, though not from passion or intimacy. He'd simply knocked the wind out of her. Luckily, there would be no way for their audience to realize that.

A heaving chest is a heaving chest ...

"It's fine," Phoebe whispered somewhat breathlessly as she started planning their next moves and mentally reviewing the floor plans she had worked so hard to memorize. She had no doubt that Lennie was doing the same. Assuming the stolen key card would actually work for them, once they made it through the locked door, they would need to head down the long hallway on the other side of it to the left, where there should be a short stairwell that would take them up to Malphas's personal quarters. If the missing files actually were in this building somewhere, then that was where they would find them.

Several long moments passed before the trio of Wraiths passed them by and continued onward to the locked door. Lennie grabbed Phoebe's hand as the lead one got it unlocked, though he didn't yet break their embrace. It wasn't until the last of them stepped through the wide-open door that he started pulling her after them, managing to slip the blade of his dagger between the door and its frame just before it swung fully closed, disrupting the locking mechanism, if not the electronic key-card sensor.

"We can't be sure that the little rat bastard's card will actually work," he whispered to her.

As calmly as she could, though her breath still felt terribly short, Phoebe pulled out Fionn's key card and pressed it to the sensor to find out. Its blinking red light stayed red.

She shook her head in silent judgement of Fionn. Then she gave it voice: "What a loser."

Lennie nodded. "So, we now know that there are at least three Wraiths beyond this door."

"Easy-peasy."

He smirked, then grabbed the door handle and started to pull. "Good lord!" he said with a grunt. "This thing weighs a ton!"

Phoebe wasn't sure what she'd expected to find standing in their way. An enchanted threshold? Possibly. Some sort of magic-sensitive alarm? That was a likelihood for sure. But some bomb-proof, heavy-ass door? That one hadn't made it onto her list.

"Ah ... So, *that's* why we need to be so careful about getting back out." She chewed nervously on her upper lip. The deeper they travelled into the hotel, the more fortified it seemed to become.

"Correct."

With a final full-bodied heave, Lennie finally got the door open. Then together, the James Bond look-alike and the newly minted Druidic spy crossed the threshold and headed onward to the hotel's private level.

It's even darker up here, Phoebe thought, grimacing slightly. *And smellier too.* The second floor absolutely reeked of Wraiths, and from what she could tell, there was no real lighting anywhere except for the occasional wall-mounted lantern. She found herself wondering if the bastards could actually see in the dark—something she made a mental note to ask Ronan about the next chance she got.

Lennie reached into his jacket pocket once more, this time pulling out a Druid's pouch and released its contents.

That's one of Ronan's ...

"He made me bring this," Lennie said, as if reading Phoebe's mind, "and also promise him that if we made it this far, I would use it before we actually entered Malphas's lair."

As the familiar smell of cardamom and black pepper surrounded them, a peculiar feeling welled up inside of Phoebe, coiling uneasily in her belly, although it was a very different sort of discomfort than what the trapped magics had ever inspired.

This had more to do with Ronan having given them one of the nearly priceless pouches that he usually guarded so closely ... and all to keep *her* safe. He might not be physically with them at the moment, but he was still protecting her.

Still caring for her.

"Thoughtful of him," Phoebe said quietly, then quickly brushed that same thoughtfulness away like a pesky mosquito, even as she white-knuckled the dagger Ronan had given her.

Lennie saw right through this casual display, however, and seemed about to say something when she beat him to the punch.

"Where do you think they went?" she asked, peering into the near darkness up ahead.

"Didn't Ronan lend you his compass?"

He had, of course, though she'd completely forgotten about it. He'd pressed it into her hand when they'd first arrived on-site, and she'd immediately slid the priceless magical artifact into her clutch purse, having no intention of using it. She preferred to operate in her own way. And it wasn't like he'd ever taught her to use the thing anyway. Of course, even at the time, it had not been lost on her how precious the compass was to him.

"Oh, shit ... Yeah, he did." She reached into her clutch then, fumbling a bit as she dug through her makeup, and past two cell phones, before finding the compass at the very bottom and scooping it out.

Lennie put out his hand. "Give it to me. I'll do it."

As the compass left her possession, she felt the sudden pang of its loss. Then it was sitting on Lennie's outstretched palm, and she watched as its arrow started to quickly spin. After a few tense moments, it finally slowed to a stop, pointing down the hallway and directly away from where they needed to go next.

"Perfect. I think we're clear," he said, slipping the compass into his pocket and gesturing for her to follow him.

When Ronan's compass slid from sight, she felt another strange pang of loss. She couldn't help but wonder if this was some sort of warning. *An omen maybe?*

With his back perfectly straight, and as cool as a cucumber, Lennie walked straight towards the locked door of Malphas's private living space. Following calmly behind the Brit, Phoebe took note of how different his posture was from the mission-based crouching she'd come to expect from Druids like Ronan. She was enjoying his faster pacing immensely.

"This is nice," she said, chuckling.

"It doesn't always have to be a smash and grab," Lennie said quietly. "Though I do enjoy the occasional rough-up as much as anyone else."

"Sure ... sometimes," she said as they reached the target door, then watched as he slid a specialized knife into the lock, which quickly clicked open. "But this suits me far better."

"Oh, *I know*."

Phoebe didn't have a chance to ask Lennie what he meant by that before they found themselves in Malphas's ... *inner chambers?* It was really the only way she could think of to describe it. Earlier that evening, she'd thought that the Wraith's robes had seemed almost regal, and now she understood why. The room was practically empty of furniture except for a throne-like chair; the solid, wooden podium to its right; and a massive oak desk placed across the room in front of a heavily curtained bank of windows.

"*Jackpot*," Lennie said easily and stepped forward.

Alone atop the desk sat a massive and double-locked black briefcase, practically begging to be stolen by the Druids.

"Wait!" The trapped magic inside of Phoebe was reacting violently to its presence, and she lurched on the spot, struggling to bite back sudden panic. "Um ... give me the compass first."

Lennie slowed and looked back at her, then reached into his pocket to retrieve it before handing it back to her. "What is it, Phoebe?" he asked, looking at her with one eyebrow raised.

"I don't know, I just ... I think it's worth checking. They wouldn't just leave the briefcase there like this, would they? So unprotected?"

"Fair enough," Lennie said, watching as she placed it in the palm of her hand and held it out in front of her.

While he and the others apparently used the compass to detect potential foes—usually Wraiths—Phoebe wasn't sure if the compass would work *with* the magic that was trapped inside her or *against* it. Admittedly, she was terrified of what she might discover by using it ... but somehow, with the briefcase just sitting there in front of them like that, she knew that she should at least try to check things out first.

The compass's needle remained still. Practically frozen.

"Okay ..." Phoebe said, her jaw muscles quivering slightly. Then almost feeling like she was going into shock, she took a deep breath and repeated herself, though with more certainty this time. "It's okay."

Lennie nodded and strode slowly and silently towards the desk. Then he spent almost a minute fussing with the briefcase, trying to open it, but he had no luck. "It's not working," he said, scratching his chin.

She watched him try his knife, as well as several other tools that he'd retrieved from hidden recesses in his jacket—some magical and some practical—but not one of them worked.

He finally tried to lift it, only to find that it had been affixed somehow to the desk ... with seeming permanence. "Well, I suppose that explains why it isn't being more heavily guarded."

"Can we just bust it open here?" she asked, approaching cautiously.

"I'd really prefer to confirm that it contains what we're actually looking for first," he said with a reluctant grimace. "Rather than a bomb or something."

Still, they both knew that time was quickly ticking away.

"Let me try," Phoebe said finally.

Lennie stepped back with a skeptical look. "Suit yourself. We've got about five minutes," he added, checking his watch, which Phoebe suddenly noticed was a vintage Cartier.

Fancy ass.

She nodded then, moving to stand in front of the briefcase. "Got it."

Moving slow, and very carefully, she reached for the small brass latches, which were indeed locked. As she touched them though, she closed her eyes for she could feel the trapped Wraith magic inside of her trying to lash out ... violently. She instinctively worked to suppress it but then had an idea.

Since this is a Wraith briefcase, maybe I can access my trapped Wraith magic just enough to get it open ...

Just this thought was enough to trigger a flash of memory.

"It seems that her body can absorb and store even the darkest of magics," said a timeworn voice that Phoebe heard often while in captivity. "Fascinating."

"Indeed," hissed another voice, this one less familiar. "But what does it mean?"

"Unclear ... but she's been able to take in the magic of both Malphas and Leviathan with ease ... and those are two of the oldest of our entire legion."

Phoebe shook herself back to the present and felt herself begin to tremble as she imagined the magics of such evil creatures being trapped inside of her—the *Hounds of Hell* were part of it. She gasped, her thoughts swirling momentarily before she took several deep breaths and pulled herself together for the sake of the greater mission. Then she reached for the locks once more.

This time, they clicked open easily.

"Holy fuck!" Lennie exclaimed more loudly than was probably prudent. "How did you do that!?"

Phoebe gulped. "I tried to picture the Wraith magic that's trapped inside of me, and ... it just opened."

This was an oversimplification of what she'd just experienced, of course, but she wasn't entirely sure it was safe to tell Lennie that. Not yet anyway. And certainly not without first putting together the final pieces of the puzzle regarding what had truly happened to her on the day of the explosion.

Lennie's eyes grew wide, but he said nothing more. Instead, he immediately began to rifle through the now-exposed documents before him.

They'd done it. Phoebe could hardly believe it. Universe willing, this single briefcase would contain the last bits of information they'd need to finally start decoding her perplexing existence. Or perhaps "enigmatic" would be a better word. She wasn't sure really, but that was what Ronan had been calling it from the very beginning.

As Lennie briefly paused his rifling to send off a quick message to the others on his phone, confirming that "Phase Three" was now in full effect, Phoebe noticed a USB stick protruding from a poorly sealed manila envelope at the very bottom of the briefcase—no doubt having been jostled partially free during its transport to the hotel—as well as the printed label on its side: Patient #87.

Her heart almost stopped. Keeping her eye on Lennie, who was still furiously pounding away on his phone, she carefully slid her red-painted fingertips towards it and slipped it into her hand.

"Do we have everything we need?" she asked as soon as he put his phone back into his pocket.

"Here's hoping." Lennie nodded then and snapped the briefcase closed.

"Let's go."

Approaching Ronan's house, 2:07 a.m.

Phoebe and Ronan were in good spirits. The entire mission had been such a success that even too-cool-for-school Lennie seemed stoked when he'd called to check in with them on their drive back.

"It's been a while since we've had a mission of this magnitude go off without any injury or loss of life on our side," he was saying now (via speakerphone). "I think we can consider it a triumph in that regard alone. Of course, we won't really know if it's a true success until we go through the files, but that doesn't mean we can't be pleased with ourselves for now!"

"I'd have to agree," Ronan replied calmly, though he was smiling too.

"Alright. Goodnight, you two. We'll debrief in the morning."

"Goodnight, Lennie."

Ronan ended the call then and continued directing his Audi effortlessly through his home neighbourhood of Ranelagh. Phoebe was glad that he'd decided to just leave Dom's vintage Land Rover parked on the side of the road earlier. The Audi's ride was much smoother and more comfortable for her, especially since she could still feel both the trapped magic and the evening's adrenaline surging through her.

"Are you alright?" Ronan asked, noting how quiet she was.

"I think so," she answered, not wanting to volunteer the truth about the turmoil she was struggling to contain. Something felt different now, after tonight's mission. She felt ... brittle. "You know I always need a bit of time to come down after these adventures of ours."

"Of course. Nights like these can certainly get the adrenaline flowing," Ronan said agreeably. "Plus, I can sense the trapped magic from here." He reached across the console then and let his hand almost hover above hers, barely touching it. "It feels especially jagged at the moment."

Phoebe shuddered involuntarily. Even the gentlest touch from Ronan triggered a dizzying contradiction of sensations, quelling the roiling magic even as her own nervous system lit up like a fucking Christmas tree.

"You're not wrong," she said simply. "Being around that many Wraiths ... Well, the magic always seems to start screaming to be let out."

"Well, it's certainly not supposed to be kept inside of you. We know that much for sure."

"No shit, Sherlock!" she said, laughing loudly in an attempt to bring them back closer to normal. *Since when does Ronan try to make small talk?*

When he didn't join in with the laughter, she started to worry that the strange and swiftly shifting tension between them would be the end of her.

"I really appreciate that you took my plan seriously tonight."

Ronan seemed to bristle slightly at this. "Why wouldn't I?"

She shrugged.

"You did really well this evening," he said.

"I know I did," she said, smirking smugly at him as he slowed the vehicle down in front of his house and turned into his laid-brick driveway.

This finally made him laugh, although his amusement didn't quite reach his eyes. Instead, there was a softness there that she didn't recognize. "Welcome home, Phoebe."

Something about his expression, or maybe his words, kicked a familiar nervousness into high gear once more, making it even harder for Phoebe to push down the new and troubling awareness of the connection she shared with both Levi and Malphas—a connection that had allowed her to access their trapped magic to open the briefcase. She'd briefly considered explaining this to Ronan but decided against it. He would surely freak out that she'd come so close tonight to actually brushing shoulders with two Wraiths who were directly connected with her containment at the lab. If not more.

There would just have to be yet another secret between them ... at least for the time being.

Swallowing hard, she suddenly blurted out, "Do you think anyone followed us?"

Seeming jarred by the sudden inquiry, his shoulders dropped at bit. "No, I don't think so. We pulled it off as well as could be hoped for. Better really ... which gave us more than enough time to leave the hotel without a trace and just return to our normal lives."

She frowned slightly at the hint of sarcasm in his tone now but didn't really think too much of it. She had too much on her mind. She had no doubt that there would be consequences once the Wraiths realized what they'd done tonight. They wouldn't take that sort of infiltration lying down for very long.

They climbed out of the Audi, and Ronan locked it with an electronic *"chirp"* before leading her over the decorative brick patterns of the driveway and towards his front door.

She could have sworn she felt the ghost of his hand on her lower back as she passed through the threshold, but when she'd smiled and looked back, he was easily two or three steps behind her. Phoebe realized then that she actually didn't hate the idea of him helping her through doorways. In fact, the closer he stayed to her, the calmer she felt.

Almost safe.

But for some reason, by the time they got inside and closed the door, Ronan's celebratory mood from earlier had turned cold. Quickly removing his jacket, he turned away from her, turned on some lights, and headed off down the hall.

"I'll be in the den ... pouring myself a drink."

He didn't bother offering her anything.

CHAPTER 31

RONAN

"So, Ronan," Phoebe said a short time later, her voice low and sultry as she stepped into the den, "I was thinking—"

"No," Ronan said shortly, dragging his eyes slowly up from the depths of his whisky glass to meet Phoebe's gaze. She looked utterly exquisite in the dim light from the crackling fire, with just the perfect amount of softness hugging her bones as she stood in front of him, all long lines and soft curves ...

Phoebe's breath hitched. "Pardon?"

Sitting in his favourite armchair, he shifted somewhat haughtily, crossing one leg over the other to hide his increasingly traitorous cock. "I said no, Phoebe. You *do* know what that word means I assume?"

His proactive refusal still lingered in the air like an icy sting despite the warmth of the den ... and the rising heat between them. They couldn't do this. Couldn't *be* this.

It was a disaster waiting to happen.

"How can you *possibly* know what I was about to suggest?" she asked, biting her sumptuous lower lip.

He looked down into the amber-coloured liquid at the bottom of his glass and started swirling it around in a vain attempt to regain some control ... and stop whatever this was in its tracks. "Because I know you, Phoebe."

When they'd returned to his house, still riding the adrenaline high from tonight's mission—and with Phoebe still wearing those goddamned strappy heels and red-velvet, figure-hugging dress, which he wanted to tear off her with his fucking teeth—he'd naively expected things to simmer down once they'd both gotten settled in for the night.

After all, not even twenty-four hours earlier, they had settled themselves peacefully down beside each other beneath the yew trees at his special grove, and he'd laid bare all of his deepest truths for her consideration. He'd spoken at length of his death and the Codex and the fact that there was no way its magic could help her. And she'd accepted all of that with grace. However, any time something he said seemed to imply some interest on his part in sharing a future with her, or possibly becoming *more* than just partners, it had been met with overt discomfort.

It was clear that Phoebe didn't really want him. Not in the way that Ronan needed her to at least.

And so, while the operation she and Lennie had designed for the night had unfortunately involved Ronan playing the part of a jealous boyfriend, which had been brutally hard and effortless all at once, he hoped it would be the last hoop he'd have to jump through before he could start phasing himself out of her life.

As soon as they returned to Vancouver, he intended to hold Lennie to his somewhat reluctant promise to arrange a transfer for one of them or the other.

Ronan knew he had no choice. He needed to put some distance between himself and Phoebe and took solace in the fact that, in many ways, he had already "saved" her just by getting her safely settled within the Order's protective folds, where she would receive ongoing care.

It was as good an outcome as he could have hoped for after all she'd endured ... and all that he had done.

"I made out with Fionn, you know," Phoebe said then, dragging her long fingers across the spines of countless novels and other artifacts that were stacked messily throughout his den. There hadn't been time to unpack properly since he'd moved his things out of storage and back into his house—the Druids he'd enlisted to help had done their best in time for their arrival, but it still lacked Ronan's personal touches. "And Lennie too. He pushed me up against a wall and pressed himself against me."

Ronan gritted his teeth, knowing that Phoebe was just trying to bait him, and not being particularly subtle about it either. Fionn was a disgusting little shit, of course, and Lennie had obviously been playing his role for the sake of the mission.

"And you're telling me this why? I'm too tired tonight for any more games, Phoebe."

She rolled her eyes and continued stroking the spines of his many books.

Grinding his teeth now, he stood up, poured himself another drink, and stoked the fire ... all in a haze of barely repressed emotion. Meanwhile, Phoebe continued to drift silently around his den in her high heels, her long hair still somewhat mussed by the evening's activities.

Then he sat back down, taking deep breaths.

As planned, tonight's mission had kicked off with "seduction tactics" aimed at the unassuming server Fionn—by Phoebe's design, of course. However, while she might have been "acting," Ronan's contributions to the role-playing had been (almost) completely honest. The two of them might not have been a domineering boyfriend and a meek, trapped girlfriend, but the way he'd been utterly devouring her with his eyes had been entirely real.

And he'd enjoyed it immensely.

Without even breaking character, he'd been able to let his eyes openly linger wherever they landed ... and though they enjoyed taking in every part of her, they'd lingered on her long supple neck far more often than anywhere else. Between the mission itself, and his recent decision to finally let her go, he was finally able to stop resisting such gazes for fear of being caught. His heart had raced, and his cock had hardened as he'd drunk her in for as long as it lasted.

And what had made it sweeter still was that she'd been watching him the whole time.

He closed his eyes for a long moment and took a deep breath. No. The feelings he'd been grappling with tonight were not even remotely "a game." Tonight, he'd brushed up against a feeling that had been left to germinate for too long, one far beyond any other feelings he'd noted between them thus far, platonic *or* romantic.

He knew that what he'd felt for her that night had been a deep and likely unquenchable *need*—like a vampire lusting after blood—and he suspected that if he were to let this seed grow into anything more, he would never be able to pull himself away.

Even if she broke his heart ... assuming she hadn't already.

Several more minutes passed as Phoebe very slowly stiffened, jutting out her chin in a way that had become achingly familiar to him by this point.

"Alright, Ronan. If you know me so well, then what was I about to suggest?"

He sighed loudly, debating an answer that he knew was cruel and belittling but very well might be his only means of stopping this insanity before it was too late. "You were wanting to fuck me tonight to escape the reality of the job and to 'cope with the stress of it all,'" he added, complete with air quotes. "Just like you used to do with—"

"*Don't* bring Ian into this," she said quickly, interrupting him before he could do so. "It's *never* been about him."

Anger simmered behind her eyes. Anger and magic.

Ronan knew he needed to tread carefully. "I'm not bringing him into anything."

He absolutely was.

Phoebe scoffed, then, like a bored or disgruntled cat, knocked one of his books off its shelf and onto the floor. Then she knocked down another ... and another.

"Stop that," he growled.

"Why?"

"Because you're obviously just trying to piss me off right now."

Phoebe just stood there for a long moment, seemingly waiting for something. But when she reached for another book to displace, Ronan found himself suddenly on his feet, grabbing her wrist as his frustration flared, though cooling to an almost instant simmer at the flash of sincere alarm that appeared on her face.

"Don't," he said through still-gritted teeth, quickly releasing her. "Please."

Phoebe let her hand drop to her side and stepped away from the bookshelf.

"Look, Phoebe ..." He sighed. "While I understand the purpose and mechanisms of your mission tactics earlier, and have even used them myself plenty of times before ... I'm still saying no to *this*." He gestured back and forth between them.

"To this?" she repeated almost silently, her eyes darkening with a betrayal he knew all too well.

This was the perfect moment to tell her how he really felt. For a moment at least, he could see it with perfect clarity. Then his longstanding fear of rejection gripped him violently once again, and he shook his head forcefully and stepped back.

"Look, I'm just not interested in fucking you and forgetting about it tomorrow!" he snapped. *It doesn't work like that for me. Not when it comes to you.* "Someone needs to draw the line in the sand where it needs to be drawn, and I'm doing that right now! For both our sakes!"

Phoebe staggered back several steps, although he knew she wasn't drunk.

Realizing then the extent of the hurt and embarrassment he'd just inflicted on her, along with goddess only knew what else, he felt almost sick. But his determination remained.

This is a fucking nightmare.

"You're such bastard, Ronan."

"Perhaps," he said, defensively, his nostrils flaring. "But at least I'm a bastard who knows better."

Her eyes welled up with tears as she looked away. "Right ... You know better."

Ronan was a bloody fool. He knew that, but it didn't change anything.

He watched as Phoebe reached down and undid her heels, slowly stepping down from them and settling each sore foot on the floor, shaking her head. She often complained about uncomfortable shoes but insisted on wearing them anyway, claiming that more practical ones would give away her intention of making a fast getaway.

She could definitely run now though ... if she wanted to.

"I really *am* sorry," Ronan said finally, a noticeable hint of pleading in his tone. He hadn't *wanted* to hurt her. In fact, he loathed the idea of causing Phoebe any pain at all. And yet, here he was, shamefully pushing her away and hurting her deeply in the process, singlehandedly placing the final nail in the coffin of their relationship ... dead on arrival.

"Right," Phoebe said then, reaching into her clutch to get his compass and return it, setting it down gently on a nearby shelf. "Thanks for lending me that." Then she left the den without even looking at him again, calling coldly back over her shoulder. "Goodnight ... Ronan."

The way she said his name this time made him feel sicker still. *She hates me.*

"Phoebe," he called out beseechingly to her as he watched her retreat from him down the hallway. "Look ... We just can't *do* this! It's ... It's hard enough to know where the missions end and real life begins! Can you imagine if—"

"It's fine," she called back then, apparently having heard enough. "I'm sorry for misreading the situation. For misreading ... us." Her voice sounded strange.

Distant.

Ronan watched, through the open door of the den, as she continued walking away from him, presumably heading towards his guest bedroom, where she'd deposited her suitcase earlier in the day when they'd first arrived there to start getting ready for the evening.

When he'd first brought her home.

"Phoebe, wait!"

But she was already gone.

"For fuck's sake ..." Ronan rubbed his free hand roughly across the top of his head, messing his hair even without realizing it.

Why isn't she fighting back?

He squeezed his eyes shut briefly, as though suddenly hearing the foolishness of his own thoughts. Then he shook his head. Perhaps the better question was why he had let her walk away in the first place. Why he'd basically given her no choice at all.

This woman—this brilliant, powerful, and unfathomably sexy woman—had just practically offered herself up to him on a silver platter. And sure, Phoebe had fucked up royally on several occasions—breaking into his room and reading his most private journals, not least of all. And yes, she was more than irresistible enough to sidetrack him from the path he knew very well he was supposed to be on, but she'd also shown him the utter depths of herself, her specialness, her kindness ...

It was suddenly hard to breathe, as panic started to bubble up in his chest at the realization that this might just have been their only chance. If Dom were here, he would probably have cuffed him on the side of the head, which would be exactly what he deserved, and say, *"Grow the fuck up and go after her, Ronan! She's perfect for you!"*

But Dom wasn't here. So, at forty-seven, and all on his own, it looked like Ronan would finally have to grow up. He hastily poured himself another whisky and knocked it back, letting the alcohol burn down his throat like an elixir. Then he coughed, set his glass down loudly, and walked over to where Phoebe had set down his compass. Grabbing it and sliding it into his pocket, he straightened himself and took off down the hallway, arriving at her closed door within seconds and just staring at it for a long moment.

Taking in this last (physical) barrier between them, Ronan noticed several long, black scuff marks along the doorframe, no doubt from its most recent tenant's hasty exit. He'd rented out his beloved house for the past several years—while he'd been busy researching Wraiths and helping to kill the evilest Sorcerer of the age—always assuming he would return someday with plenty of notice. However, when Phoebe had mentioned visiting Ireland someday, he'd impulsively emailed his tenants and offered them a considerable sum of money to move out sooner than local tenancy protections allowed.

He'd been dying to bring Phoebe home since the first moment he'd laid eyes on her.

Ronan took several deep breaths before knocking. "Open up ... *please*."

"It's not locked," Phoebe eventually said, sounding strangely distant. Almost ... disconnected.

Ronan's hands started to shake as his anxiety rose.

Phoebe clearly wasn't going fight him on his rejection anymore, which was both frustrating at the moment and unexpectedly invigorating. He wondered if he could really learn a new way to approach the subject of intimacy with this woman. Was there even room for it? Eunice's words rang through his mind then: *"What if you're afraid of it going* right?"

"So ... does that mean I can come in?" he asked tentatively.

"Yes, Ronan. You can come in."

He was relieved to hear the disdain in her voice when she said his name had faded slightly, though there was still a hint of something else there he couldn't quite unravel. Pushing the door inward, Ronan's eyes grew wide as he was greeted by the sight of Phoebe standing on the far side of the guest-room bed ... spectacularly naked.

How had she stripped so quickly?

He couldn't look away. She was *perfection.* "Phoebe ..."

"I was just looking for my pyjamas," she said, her ordinarily honeyed tones cooled by the distance he'd created between them. "I swear I packed them."

Ronan noted that her dress had been cast aside onto a corner chair, along with her new shoes and designer clutch. He wanted to buy her more beautiful things one day, should she ever let him. His urge to spoil this woman was definitely bordering on inappropriate.

"*Ehm* ... I can come back," he suggested, though leaving was the absolute last thing he wanted to do.

Phoebe didn't bother trying to cover herself, though she did avoid his gaze as she continued rooting around through her duffel, clearly agitated at the apparent fruitlessness of the search. "*Where are they!?*" She scowled at the duffel. Though she was still seemingly unbothered by his presence, she did acknowledge it enough to finally respond to his suggestion.

"No, no ... It's fine, just ... give me a second."

"As long as you're sure ..." Ronan forced himself to look away as he entered the room, awkwardly rounding the corner of the bed.

Phoebe's phone, a hair clip, some crumpled papers, a half-chewed pack of gum, and a small black USB stick were on the bedside table. On the floor, her duffel was wide open, its contents all askew and spilling everywhere as she tore her way through it. Ronan usually hated needless mess, yet somehow, Phoebe's disarray in his guest room only amplified his ache to make things right between them. He desperately wanted her to feel at home here ... and to stay for a good long while.

He was losing his ever-loving mind over this woman.

Exasperated, Phoebe sighed loudly as she pulled her hair back into a messy ponytail with a silly, oversized scrunchie, exposing still more skin for Ronan to covet.

He watched shamelessly as she bent from the waist and started digging through the duffel again, lithe hamstrings fully stretched as her knees remained locked in place. She had a bad habit of bending over like this, which was surely a leading cause for her ongoing back pain. Although he felt guilty about it, Ronan resisted telling her as much for fear she would stop doing it in front of him.

A low moan slipped from somewhere deep in his chest. "Phoebe ..."

"What? It's not like you've never seen me naked before," she said, interrupting his hedonistic reveries. "Or my ass, at least. Remember that time you stitched me up? You're a doctor, right? And a body is a body."

It sure as shit wasn't.

Ronan shifted awkwardly on the spot, wondering how Phoebe could be so hyper-logical right then when all he could think about was what it might take to get her to turn her ass just slightly further to the—

"Aha!" Phoebe suddenly exclaimed, having finally located her missing pyjamas. He recognized the pair of navy-blue sleep shorts, since more than once, he'd shamelessly lusted over the shape of her ass in them over breakfast.

"Goddess give me strength," he muttered.

"What did you just say?"

"Nothing. It's—"

"Come on, Ronan. You're here for a reason. What do you want?"

"What do I ... *want?*"

Ronan was desperately struggling to think clearly as she pulled on the shorts, apparently forgetting to put on underwear first. Or maybe she didn't wear them for sleeping? He knew that was supposed to be healthier for women but ...

He was suddenly desperate to find out her motives behind this choice, even as his heart pounded loudly in his chest, sending blood straight to his cock. It was official: he'd gone completely feral.

"Ronan? ... I asked you a question." Looking slightly annoyed, Phoebe nibbled on her bottom lip as she held the pyjama top up between them and worked to turn it right-side out. Her nipples were pert and her breasts exquisite.

Ronan's head was spinning.

He knew that passion was just the beginning of what they would experience together should the floodgates ever finally open. Was she genuinely this oblivious to his gaze or merely sick and tired of constantly trying to unmix his signals?

He wouldn't blame her for the latter.

If he were being honest, Ronan had been flirting with her off and on since they'd first met, feeding her the tastiest breadcrumbs of his desire but never delivering more. He liked the attention she gave him in return for his care. In that way, he'd been just as much of a manipulator as she was. And all because he couldn't make sense of his own damn feelings. He had originally thought it was his secrets standing between them, but in the end, it was just more of his own bullshit.

And now, Phoebe seemed downright disinterested in his attention, and not in a way he would have previously anticipated. She wasn't "negging" him. She'd just gone numb. It was often said that the opposite of love was apathy, and right now, Phoebe appeared utterly indifferent to his presence—a notion that agitated something deep and angry within him: the crushing fear of losing her for good and having it be all his fault.

"Stop this."

"Stop *what*, Ronan?" she asked, keeping her focus on the buttons of her twisted nightshirt.

"Whatever it is that you're doing." He gestured vaguely towards her. "Shutting down and just ... standing there like that—"

"I can't really help it. These buttons are all—"

"Just stop it, alright!?" he growled, the wild beast inside of him unable to stand it any longer. "I'm here to talk about us."

"Us?" She scoffed. "There is no us."

Ronan reached for the shirt in her clutches and grabbed one corner of it, stilling her. "That's a lie, and you know it."

Phoebe finally met his gaze. "Is it, though? You made the same thing pretty clear not five minutes ago." She looked back down at the shirt in their hands. "And besides, I heard what you said to Lennie at the hall. After this mission, you're planning on reassigning me."

He felt that like a punch in his gut and swallowed hard. "Phoebe, I ..." He let his shaking voice trail off briefly. Then he cleared his throat, and he tried again. "Why are you doing this? Please, just ... Ugh! ... Just be reasonable!"

"I am being reasonable," she said, her voice cracking slightly. "And you were right. We can't do this ... What I *don't* know, Ronan, is why you're so angry with *me* about it. I didn't do anything wrong tonight, except misread you, apparently, and now I feel like ..." A strange look flitted across her features, and she shook her head. "Never mind."

"What is it?"

"I just need to get this magic out of me, Ronan!" she said, with a frustrated stomp of her foot and bunching of her pyjama top for emphasis.

He felt suddenly and painfully desperate as he freed the shirt from her clutches. "Then let me try to *help*."

She offered him an almost pitying smile then. "I wish you could."

Ronan dropped the pyjama top to the floor. It was now or never. "Enough! Okay? I need you, Phoebe. I need you desperately!" He closed the distance between them in two quick steps, then he gently cupped her chin in his hands, parting her lips with a gentle drag of his thumb. "It kills me to think about losing you ... It makes me feel ... *terrified.*"

"Lose me?" she rasped, eyes wide.

Ronan pulled her closer—so close he could feel her pebbled nipples through his buttoned shirt. He could also feel the trapped magic swirling dangerously within the fragile container of her body, but this time, he welcomed the sensation, wanting every last piece of her.

"Yes." He looked deep into her eyes. "What if I told you that I want this ... want *us* to mean something more than I even thought possible in this lifetime. What we have ... it means everything to me." His breath felt heavy as his chest rose and fell against hers. "*You* mean everything to me, Phoebe."

She breathed in tandem with him for a long moment as time stood still.

And then her perfect lips split into a naughty grin. "Really, Ronan? ... *Everything?*"

It was a bratty taunt, and immediately recognizing the return of the Phoebe he'd fallen in love with, he smiled dangerously at her. "What? You don't believe me?"

She shrugged then, as if to say, *"I'll believe it when I see it."*

She knew damn well that Ronan lived for a challenge, and more than enticed by this wordless challenge, he steered her back towards the nearest wall, planting one arm above them even as he pushed his pelvis into hers. His hard length strained against his pants and pressed into her lower belly.

Then he kissed her fiercely, and time stood still.

He would never forget the warmth of her mouth in that moment, the way her lips felt pressed against his as their tongues explored each other for the first time.

Phoebe Ashburn was the sun Ronan rose to greet each morning, and if he had it his way, she would soon be the moon he worshipped every night.

He caressed her curves, peppering increasingly amorous kisses across her cheek towards her ear. He suckled at her earlobe briefly for good measure before continuing his kisses down her neck ... *I will never get enough of this woman.*

"Is this okay?"

"Yes ..."

"And this?" He trailed his fingers up her thigh.

Her breath hitched. "Y-yes."

"And what about this?" He snaked his hand up the bottom of her sleep shorts, and she nodded in affirmation. "I meant what I said"—he slid his fingers towards her entrance, and eager for more, she let out a small whimper, which he let himself savour briefly—"you mean everything to me." He cupped her sex then, teasing her clit with his thumb moving in small circles until she was grinding feverishly against him. *"Everything."*

"Ronan ..." Phoebe's chest rose and fell, pressing against him and letting him go with each gasping breath.

Both his breath and his balls grew heavy with anticipation. "Yes?"

"If you don't stop fucking around and make me come in the next five minutes, I'm going to stab you with that fancy dagger you gave me." She nodded towards the chair in the corner. "It's just over there in my clutch."

Ronan reared back, abruptly pausing all efforts. "Is that a *threat*, Miss Ashburn?"

"You know what? ... It is."

He let out a sudden bark of laughter as all the tension left his body, replaced only a moment later with an even more desperate need. "Good goddess, Phoebe ... Do you know how long I've wanted you?"

"No offence, but I'm pretty sure you've been horny for me ever since you first introduced yourself to me at Nyx's club in Seattle," she said cheekily.

She was absolutely correct.

Ronan released her then, stepped away, and began unbuttoning his shirt. His adoring gaze never leaving her perfect figure. If anything, it only sharpened. "Take off those bottoms and climb onto the bed ... please."

CHAPTER 32

RONAN

RONAN UNTUCKED HIS DRESS SHIRT, UNBUTTONING IT AS HE STARED greedily at Phoebe, now sprawled succulently atop his guest bed and showcasing the parts of herself he'd yet to memorize up close. There would be plenty of time for that, of course, now that he finally had her alone and wanting.

"Very nice," he said.

It pleased him that she'd removed her pyjama bottoms so swiftly, as it was in her nature to fight back when bossed around. Phoebe really wanted that orgasm.

"What now?" she asked, a hint of excitement in her voice. Her blonde locks spilled messily around her, making her look like an absolute goddess.

He arched an eyebrow at her as he began to unbuckle his belt. "Will you touch yourself for me as I undress? ... I want to get a sense of what turns you on." Ronan felt strongly that this was something he should ask for rather than demand.

She gazed meaningfully at him, then focused on her assigned task, her right breast pressing against her bicep as she touched herself. "Like this?"

Ronan had expected Phoebe to look at least a little bit nervous, but she was all long legs, soft curves, and confidence, leaving him almost purring. *"Good girl ..."*

Phoebe's breath hitched; apparently, she liked such praise.

He couldn't help but wonder what might happen once he'd had the chance to learn more about what she liked—worshipping her like the goddess she was and pleasuring her in every way he could think of. He had a feeling that making Phoebe come was about to evolve into his newest obsession.

Ronan's balls ached at the sight of her hand working amidst those golden-brown curls.

"Yes, just like that," he said, his voice low and gravelly.

He'd always enjoyed putting his partner's orgasms at the forefront ... finding bliss in watching them coming again and again under his spell. And when it was finally his turn, his orgasms were spectacular. However, this woman had such a chokehold on Ronan he wasn't sure he was going to be able to hold out for long.

"Speak up, Ronan," she said teasingly. "I can't hear you." Phoebe might enjoy being taken care of, but she was also begging to be tamed in the process.

"You're a *brat*," Ronan said, sliding his shirt off before letting his pants fall to the floor, leaving him standing before her in only his boxer briefs.

"I know." She paused what she was doing to eye him appreciatively.

"I didn't tell you to stop," he said, but fuck did he like how distracted she seemed at the sight of his body.

Ronan's nostrils flared as he lowered both hands to the mattress and began crawling towards her, relishing the exquisite body before him. Then he dropped down onto his forearms and prepared to lick and kiss his way up her thighs.

Phoebe was ready for him. "*Please ...*"

"Honey pot indeed," he purred, breathing in the scent of her. "I bet you taste delicious."

"You'll have to let me know ..."

She did.

And before long, Ronan had her moaning into the pillows as he licked and sucked ... sending her into an absolute frenzy. Phoebe bucked hard as he slid a finger inside of her ... and then another.

With each move he made, he was uncovering her pleasure points. "Does this feel okay?"

"*Shut up*," she growled, too heavily invested in the pleasure he was delivering for banter. She was close now.

Alright then. Ronan grinned, then reapplied himself to what he was doing with a low, vibrating chuckle that seemed to do the trick.

Within seconds, Phoebe was riding his fingers for all she was worth, even as the enthusiastic efforts of his mouth brought her all the way to climax, the shuddering waves of her pleasure crashing against his face. He kept it buried there, lapping, licking, and groaning into her as she finished.

"If I ever get the choice again," he murmured against her, "this is where I want to die ... right here between your legs."

"I have to say ... I'd be okay with that too," she managed to say between panting breaths. "Fuck ... You're *really* good at that!"

He smirked into her succulent warmth, working to catch his own breath. "I know."

Utterly content now, Phoebe swatted playfully at his head and laughed. It was the sweetest sound in the world.

Ronan gave her a little nip on the inner thigh and popped his head up at last. "And you were wrong, by the way. I've only been thinking about doing this since I stitched your arse back together in that alley beside the dumpster."

"Oh really? And what *were* you thinking about when you first saw me then?" she asked, still working to fully regain her breath.

"Mostly, I was thinking about how much of a damn fool you were, Phoebe Ashburn."

She grinned and nudged him gently on the shoulder with her foot. "Fuck off."

He tumbled dramatically backward until he was standing at the foot of the bed, then placed one hand over his heart. "You wound me!"

Phoebe rolled her eyes.

Ronan removed his boxer briefs then and kicked them to one side. His cock was fully erect. He stroked it with his left hand as he faced her, and then with his right. She looked at him hungrily, an expression he liked on her even more than he'd expected.

And he'd expected to like it a lot.

"But after *that* thought," he added, smirking, "I admit the thought of fucking you may, or may not, have crossed my mind."

"I *knew* it!" She practically cackled then, making him grin.

"What about you? What did you think of me?"

"Not telling," she said, her playful tone taking on a sultry edge. "A girl has to have *some* secrets."

"Fine," Ronan said, deciding not to press her on it. As his cock was already leaking pre-cum, banter and games would have to wait for another round. He needed to be inside her. Now.

"Just one second," he practically growled as he remembered something. "I need to grab a condom."

With that, he hustled from the guest room, slipped silently into the cool dimness of his own bedroom, and started digging around frantically in his suitcase for the fresh box of condoms he'd bought before leaving Vancouver. Then, mission accomplished, he hurried back.

"Alright," Ronan said breathlessly as he strode back into the guest room. He stopped in his tracks, staggered yet again by the loveliness awaiting him. Phoebe was perfection.

She was everything.

Just as he was raising the condom wrapper to his teeth to open it, Phoebe spoke up and froze him in place with her words: "I can't get pregnant. Or at least, I don't think I can. It's never really come up, but since the Wraiths trapped their magic inside of me, I've stopped having periods. So, you don't have to worry about *that* anyway."

He still didn't move. Even off the top of his head, Ronan could think of dozens of reasons why this might be a bad idea. The main one, of course, being that Phoebe could legitimately still be ovulating, even right now, despite everything she'd endured. He hadn't made it far enough into her medical analysis to start considering her reproductive health.

"Have you been tested recently?" he asked, his mouth suddenly feeling very dry.

She blushed. "No. But it's only been—"

"Don't you dare say his name!" Ronan said quickly before taking several deep breaths to calm himself. The last person in the world he wanted to think about right now was Ian *fucking* Braithwaite.

"Alright," Phoebe said a bit sourly, her patience clearly being tested now. "All I wanted to say was that I always made him wrap up, but that ... I'm okay if you don't want to."

Ronan knew better than to agree too quickly. "Are you *absolutely* sure?"

"Please, Ronan ... I need you inside of me."

That was all he had needed to hear.

In fact, it was almost too much for him to hear. He tossed the condom away and rejoined her on the bed, wrapping her up and kissing her ferociously. She responded with equal vigour.

Ronan knew that his record with serious relationships wasn't very good, but he sensed he could be better with Phoebe. He sensed he could be different with her ... or die trying.

Their earlier mission was still echoing around them, shrouding Phoebe in mystery like the super-spy she'd become, the scent of her perfume mixing enticingly with the lingering fragrance of "Unholy Trinity" and feigned passion ...

Ronan growled low in his throat, fully intending to wipe the memory of Ian, Fionn, and even Lennie's hands from both her skin and memory forever.

Phoebe lay back as he braced himself above her, rubbing his tip against her at first, and then gradually sliding inside. He was by no means small, yet she seemed endlessly open to him, taking more of his cock inside with each steady pump.

"Good Goddess, Phoebe ..." he groaned, his jaw slackening at the sight of her below him as he worked himself into a frenzy. "You are fucking *unbelievable*."

"No, you ... are ..." Phoebe whimpered, her hips rising to meet his.

When he finally sheathed himself fully inside of her, she moaned in relief—an almost guttural sound that Ronan felt all the way to the base of his cock and instantly supplanting her earlier laughter as the sweetest sound he'd ever heard.

"Does *that* feel okay?" he asked unnecessarily.

Phoebe nipped him lightly on his neck, and he laughed, falling in line with the rhythm of her body. Again and again, Ronan thrust himself into her, the movement of their bodies escalating in tandem with their shared desire. Before long, Phoebe was moaning into his neck and biting down hard on his shoulder as she came.

"You *are* a good girl," he panted, taking in the wonder of her writhing in ecstasy.

Eventually, when Phoebe had recovered enough, they switched positions. On top now, she looked down at Ronan, her eyes dark with pleasure, and slid down onto him.

"How are you even real?" Ronan asked, awed by the sight of her full breasts above him.

Phoebe pressed her palms into his pecs, digging her nails into his clavicles and nearly drawing blood as she pulled herself closer to him with each descent as though she could never get close enough. Ronan drew breath sharply through his teeth at her ferocity, but the pain was more than welcome. Without it, he feared he might have left the earth entirely.

"What if I'm not real?" she said then, grinning impishly before tossing her head back, an almost feral moan teasing its way past her kiss-swollen lips.

Ronan could only stare up at her in awe.

As Phoebe rocked back and forth, crying out in ecstasy above him, there was something unmistakably otherworldly in her voice that sent chills down his spine, sending a spark of power through his entire body ... a spark of *life*.

He'd long suspected there was something different about Phoebe. She was too much of an enigma even for his brain to fathom. But now he *knew* that she was something else.

What that might be didn't even matter. Ronan was hers, plain and simple. He was most definitely never going to be the same after tonight. And he was also tremendously close to coming.

Hooking his arm around her waist then, Ronan shifted Phoebe onto her back once more and watched as her golden hair pooled around her face like sunlight. She looked into his eyes—into his *soul*—as he began driving into her, desperate to be as close to her as possible. He might have been taken by her beauty at first, and who wouldn't have been? But now, he knew there was *nothing* that he wouldn't do for this woman ... this magnificent creature who was all for him.

Panting as he continued pounding into her with wild abandon, his long-suppressed emotions suddenly found a voice: "I want to ... give you everything, Phoebe ... I want to *be* everything ... for you ... I love you."

Phoebe moaned as the two of them raced closer and closer to climax, kissing and clawing at him even as her back bowed in pleasure. She got there first, arching and pulsing beneath him and driving him to near madness.

"Is ceol mo chroí thú," he rasped, spilling his seed and joining her in completion.

You are the music of my heart.

Ronan brushed a strand of Phoebe's tousled hair over her shoulder where she lay facing him, naked and fast asleep in his king-size bed. His stomach grumbled loudly then, and he peered at the nearby clock. It was nearly noon.

Last night, after their first rapturous round of lovemaking had left them wanting more, they'd relocated to his bedroom ... where he'd promised her they would have more room for their "activities." He'd been particularly eager to have them take advantage of his luxury ensuite shower—which he'd used shamelessly in the past to impress nocturnal visitors. He and Phoebe hadn't made it that far though.

Expecting more time focusing solely on Phoebe's pleasure, Ronan had been surprised when they'd instead once again slipped almost immediately into their own uniquely passionate coupling, which had blown his mind yet again ... and then again.

Each time, it was almost as if Phoebe was calling him into herself, drawing him nearer and nearer with each kiss, each thrust, each moan ... Ronan had never felt so vulnerable with anyone in his entire life, utterly raw and exposed, as though she were drawing out his very soul and intertwining it with her own as she took him to the very edge ...

And over it.

Again and again.

Phoebe had eventually passed out, ever so sweetly, in his arms—something Ronan hadn't anticipated liking *quite* as much as he did. Wrapping himself around her protectively then, he'd breathed her in, relishing how safe she must feel with him to be able to sleep so soundly in his presence. For someone who'd been on the run for so many months after been held in such harsh captivity ... and only *after* having spent years obsessively pursuing her journalism career ... Ronan knew the significance of this moment of peace between them, and within themselves, as well as what it would mean for them both to be able to slow down ... together.

He'd occasionally gotten a glimpse of this possibility with her—like in that bed with her in Bamfield and on the dance floor in Calgary—but nothing could have prepared him for this. Of course, this brought a whole host of emotions welling up from deep inside him, the strongest ones being fear and guilt. Could he actually love her the way she needed him to? Would she reciprocate?

Could she reciprocate?

He would have to trust her to lead the way because the plain and simple truth was that he would do anything for this woman. Whatever she asked for, whatever she needed, he would move mountains to make it happen.

Unfortunately, at some point last night, those hopeful and revelatory feelings had been quickly replaced by concern as her peaceful sleep was suddenly darkened by a nightmare. As her muscles twitched and tensed, her lovely features tightening distressingly, he began to whisper to her in the darkness, trying to soothe her with gentle touches and soft whispers, willing her to settle back into her dreamless slumber. It had been uncomfortable to witness, and he truly hated the helplessness he'd felt. And then she'd let out a string of unfamiliar and ancient-sounding words before calling out to him in the darkness. *"Ronan ... Ronan ..."*

He'd been taken aback, her voice reminding him strangely of the voices from the Otherworld, but he'd managed to shake off the feeling and focus on the present, knowing in that moment that he was exactly where he was meant to be.

"I've got you," he'd whispered. "You're safe with me."

And he'd meant it.

That had been hours earlier, of course. Now that she was finally sleeping peacefully again, he couldn't help but stare at her in the late-morning sunlight, taking in every freckle, blemish, dip, and curve. He smiled a bit crookedly, knowing that his own body bore the unmistakable marks of her clawing passion. It turned out that Phoebe was a handsy sort of lover, which he found stupidly attractive. Her seemingly desperate need for him was the best compliment he'd ever received and had left him utterly enthralled as she'd moved above him, weaving what might have been literal magic around them like he'd never experienced in this life ... or anywhere else.

His entire body had felt euphoric. Transcendent.

But now, here on earth, he couldn't help but feel concerned at the lingering furrow in her brow and the dark circles under her eyes, still noticeable even after several hours of sleep. Ronan let out a long sigh before turning a bit roughly onto his back. He'd barely slept last night and wasn't sure if he'd be able to again anytime soon.

Phoebe roused at his commotion, groaning audibly as she pulled one of the plush pillows up over her head. "Fuck off, Ronan. I'm sleeping."

He chuckled. "Sorry, sunshine."

Phoebe peered out from under the pillow, and when she spoke again, there was a low, almost feline rumble in her voice. "What did you just call me?"

"Sunshine? Is that too obvious? I can think of a different pet name if you'd prefer."

A ghost of a smile pulled at the corner of her mouth. "So, I'm a pet, huh?"

"You know what I mean," he said, rolling back onto his side to look at her. He couldn't help but feel excited that she was awake again ... just so he could talk to her.

"I think I like it," she said, beaming as brightly at him as her namesake. "I'm just surprised is all."

He sat up. "What do you mean?"

She opened her mouth to speak but then stopped herself as her racing thoughts made themselves known in her expression.

"What is it, Phoebe?" Concern burned in Ronan's belly, but he violently pushed it down.

"It's nothing. I'm just going to have to think of a better name for you."

Hearing this, he relaxed again, letting out a deep breath that he hadn't realized he'd been holding. "I'm sure you'll come up with something."

Phoebe tucked the pillow back under her head and settled down with the soft sunlight from the window dappling her pale skin. Then she yawned. "I'm sorry if I disturbed your sleep last night. I ... Sometimes I have wild dreams. Not all the time, but when I'm really exhausted, they tend to creep up on me."

"I didn't notice," he said, though he wasn't sure why he'd felt the need to lie about it.

She rolled her eyes, not believing him for a second.

For the next little while, they chatted about nothing much at all. This was one of the things he loved most about Phoebe. When she was relaxed, incredible (and often incredibly random) things spilled from her mouth. She was brilliant.

Eventually, they just settled into a comfortable silence for a time.

Then he looked over at her again. "I think I'd like to go have a shower. Will you join me?" he asked a bit tentatively. He hated to interrupt the peace of the moment, but he also found himself with an almost aching need to fuck her in the shower.

He was positively besotted by this woman.

Phoebe smiled at him, but it looked somewhat distant this time. “Um … If it’s all the same to you, I might get cleaned up on my own.”

His heart sank.

“It’s nothing personal,” she said quickly, perhaps seeing his disappointment. “I just … This has been wonderful, honestly. But it’s also … a lot to process.” She laughed almost musically before reaching for his hand. “I’m really happy, though. Truly. I just need a few minutes to get my head sorted. I’m … Well, I’m pretty used to being on my own as you well know.” Her smile faded a bit. “You understand, right?”

Ronan didn’t like the pleading tone in her voice. “Of course, I understand,” he said, nodding and squeezing her hand in reassurance—though whether that reassurance was for her or for him remained to be seen.

Respecting her wishes, Ronan climbed out of bed without any argument and strode off towards his own bathroom, closing the door behind him with the intention of taking his time and giving her the space she’d requested to gather her thoughts.

And she’d been right to ask for it. Since they’d returned from the mission last night, a lot had happened. Who wouldn’t need time to process that?

Everything was different now.

Ronan turned the tap on in his shower and watched as its three showerheads sprang to life, spraying out hot water from several different directions. He had a feeling Phoebe would have really enjoyed this shower, or at the very least, she would have loved teasing him about his geeky need for such a luxury.

Ronan wondered then if she loved him too. He certainly hadn’t forgotten that he’d said those words to her last night. Rather than dwell on the question, though, and knowing that they had a lot of talking to do over the coming days, he climbed into the shower and let the hot water do its work.

Ronan took his time towelling off and getting dressed before stepping out into the hallway. He could hear the shower running in the guest bathroom and hoped that he hadn't used up all of the hot water. Though he supposed that if he had, she surely would have been giving him shit by now.

Awkward and unsure what to do with himself, Ronan noticed that the door to the guest bedroom had been left open a crack. He wondered if she'd yet taken the time to unpack but bit back his curiosity and anxiety before they could get the better of him. It would definitely take some time for them to settle into their new life together. Right?

And yet ...

Pushing open the door to the guest room, Ronan noted that Phoebe had made the bed at some point since they'd gotten up, which struck him as unusual. Frowning slightly, he cautiously entered the room. It was sparsely decorated at present, with all of his good artwork still packed away in storage. When he reached the far side of the bed, he found that Phoebe's duffel bag had been zipped neatly shut and crammed under the bedframe. Her red dress, designer clutch, and heels were no longer in a crumpled pile on the chair but laid out rather neatly on it instead.

Meanwhile, Phoebe's sunflower backpack was nowhere to be seen.

"Phoebe!?" he shouted, his panic rising as he at last noticed the crisp piece of paper that had been left on the bedside table, neatly folded—a note that hadn't been there the night before.

He unfolded the letter with shaking hands.

Ronan,

Please know how sorry I am for what I'm about to do ... I do have a good reason, though I know you'll never trust me again. I only hope that someday you will understand.

Ronan's breath caught in his throat as the room started to spin, and his head began pounding in time with his heart. He sank heavily to the floor and kept reading.

I enjoyed every moment with you last night. Every breath, every touch ... it meant the world to me. Truly. It was the best night of my life.

Nothing has been lost. Thank you for loving me.

I love you too,

Phoebe

Ronan re-read the letter several times, desperately scanning it for any hint of why she would do this to him ... especially now. He'd resisted his feelings for her for months before finally giving into them at long last.

And now she was gone?

She can't have been gone for more than ten minutes. Fifteen tops.

With his heart still pounding, he scrambled to his feet and raced to the kitchen to find his cell phone and call for backup.

"Lennie?" he said in a raw-sounding voice the moment the call was answered.

"Ronan?" the Brit asked, sounding both surprised and confused. "What's going on?"

The Druid doctor's head was spinning. "Phoebe's gone!"

"What do you mean gone? Are you sure she isn't just out for a—"

"Lennie!" Ronan roared to silence him. "She's gone!"

"Why? What happened?"

"I don't know ..." Hot tears streamed down Ronan's face as he dropped down onto a nearby chair, still grappling with that same question. "I didn't ... I thought she was having a shower! And then she—"

"What?" Lennie cut in. "Did she climb out of the fucking bathroom window? Wait ... Did something change about your arrangement?"

"Does it matter?"

"Yes, it fucking matters, Ronan!" Lennie was clearly growing aggravated now. "Why else would she have run?"

Ronan felt himself bristle as he rose to his feet. "She left less than ten minutes ago," he snapped, ignoring the question. "I can only assume that she's on foot, or perhaps in a cab. I'm getting dressed now—"

"Aha!" Lennie shouted. *The smug bastard.*

"Just listen," Ronan said then, hating the vulnerably in his tone but not fighting it. "We have to find her, Lennie. Alright? And not just because of the trapped magic. It's ... She's ... I need her, Lennie." He shook his head then, frustrated at himself for stumbling over his words and hedging his bets. "I love her ..."

"Say no more, brother," Lennie said, sobering at last. "I'm on it."

Ronan sighed in relief now that the Knave was on board. "I'm going to head out on foot in case she's still nearby, and then once we have an idea of which direction she's headed, I'll get in my car." He looked outside and saw that his Audi was still parked in his small, private driveway.

Lennie groaned. "Blimey, Ronan, we need a better plan than that."

Ronan jerked his boots onto his feet, tying them hastily before scooping up his keys and storming off towards the front door. "Just call me when you have more details!"

A moment later, he was slamming the door behind him. The air outside was cool and threatening rain. That wasn't unusual for the area, but something about the air felt differently charged ... almost electric. He knew then that Phoebe still had to be close. He could still sense her essence in the air.

"Phoebe!" he called out, her name almost painful on his lips.

And then he noticed that Dom's Land Rover was missing from where they'd parked it down the street.

He immediately dialled Lennie back. "She's taken the SUV. Dom's Land Rover."

"Well, the good news is that all of Domhnall's vehicles have a tracking beacon." Ronan could hear him clacking away at his computer keyboard for a few seconds before they fell silent again. "Damn. But the bad news is she's disabled it."

Cursing silently, Ronan ran for his Audi. "I've got my compass. That'll have to do for now."

He climbed in, started the ignition, and quickly headed out to find her ... though only the Goddess knew where she might be.

CHAPTER 33

PHOEBE

PHOEBE HATED HERSELF FOR WHAT SHE'D JUST DONE, AND WHAT SHE was about to do as well, but she had no choice. She needed to get the Wraiths' dark magic out of her once and for all. And if that meant she could never return to this world again, which it very well might ... well, that was a sacrifice she was willing to make if it meant protecting the people she loved.

Phoebe had always known better than to fall for Ronan. And yet there she was.

With her eyes brimming with tears, she turned the ignition of Dom's antique Land Rover. It roared to life with a loose, rattling sound that hadn't been there when they'd driven to the grove yesterday morning. She could only hope like hell that she would make it to her destination without any breakdowns—literal or figurative. She might be a journalist, a fledgling Druid, a spy, a lover, and even a betrayer, but she was no mechanic.

Before pulling out of the driveway, she'd disabled the vehicle's tracking device, which had been hidden under the dashboard. Thanks to a loose antenna that had given away its location, she'd found it in all of five seconds, ripping it out easily and throwing it out the window for good measure. She didn't want Ronan following her where she was going.

No one could ...

Finally, she took off down the road without even looking back. The old-ass SUV wasn't easy to maneuver, but she would manage it until she got close enough to continue on foot. For a time, she shifted through the gears almost robotically as the streets of Ronan's neighbourhood blurred past the windows. Thankfully, the Land Rover was a manual right-hand drive, which for her was a lot like riding a bicycle. Back in high school, she'd a boyfriend with an imported Subaru with the same specs that she'd occasionally driven ... generally after he'd downed too much cheap vodka at a house party and needed to get home before curfew. He'd been just the first of many in her long line of shitty exes, all of whom had asked more of her than was fair.

Truthfully, Phoebe had spent most of her youth at the mercy and whims of others—masking hard and hoping desperately to fit in with whatever group seemed the most appealing at the time—until she'd finally burnt out in her late twenties and abandoned social expectations altogether. Some people started accusing her of being antisocial then, of course, but she'd come to see it as "prioritizing herself" ... and of course, her *work*. Phoebe had discovered that she and her sensitive nervous system were far healthier living as a lone wolf than as a sheep.

She'd been pleasantly surprised that Lennie had understood this about her, and even appreciated it, though mainly because he'd recognized in her a kindred spirit. Phoebe only needed a small group of friends to be happy—and she'd found that in the Druids, though this was a fact she'd come to appreciate far too late.

She tried and failed to bite back yet another sob. Then she lost it.

"Fuck, fuck, *fuck!*" she yelled in frustration, beating her hands against the steering wheel for a few furious seconds before being interrupted by an alert from the GPS system on Fionn's phone, which was the one she'd punched her destination into. It was now directing her still further away from the people she cared for ... and from the Druid doctor she'd come to realize, only after leaving him, was on track to becoming the love of her life.

She signalled her way into a thick stream of traffic as she gradually worked her way out of Dublin, eventually crossing what appeared to be a ring road and ultimately merging onto the M4, heading northwest.

She'd left most of her things back in Ronan's south-side flat, choosing to bring only the essentials with her in her sunflower backpack. She had actually hoped to "borrow" his compass for this journey, as it would surely have come in handy when trying to locate the cave she was heading for, but it had been nowhere to be found while he was in the shower, and she'd been running out of time.

As if of its own accord, Phoebe's mind wandered to her memory of Ronan's naked body—lean and lovely with a perfect smattering of body hair atop well-toned muscles. Those lengthy runs of his had made him almost deceptively strong and given him seriously impressive stamina. Simply put, the Druid doctor was smoking hot. And not surprisingly, an outrageously deft lover.

But what had struck Phoebe the most was how he'd seemed capable of transforming the jagged energy of her trapped magic, which always felt calmer when she was around him. When they were together like they had been last night, though, it was almost like Ronan had been gathering it all into himself with every thrust into her body, before returning it to her with its edges all smooth and surfaces polished.

She hadn't told him that this morning, though. There had been no point. What she was planning still wasn't a cure by any means, but she was out of options. Out of time. She'd made the choice to cross into the Otherworld before they'd even touched down in Dublin. It was simply a matter of *when*.

Though, even with this knowledge, she'd be lying if she said his intention to reassign her after this mission hadn't stung. *A lot.*

The only solace she could find was in finally trusting that Ronan really would have removed the trapped magic by now if he could have discovered a way to do so. He was the smartest person she'd ever known, and yet ... even he hadn't found such a way.

Following the stress (and excitement) of their recent missions, the trapped magic had thrashed within her so wildly that Phoebe had sensed even then that it would soon become impossible to contain. Now though, after everything that had happened yesterday, not to mention last night, she could feel that intensity increasing exponentially again ... just as it used to in captivity whenever she tried to fight it or push back.

There was no way to know how long she could continue on like this. And after watching the lost security tapes from the USB stick she'd stolen on the mission yesterday, she could no longer deny the fact that she was a danger to everyone around her.

A literal time bomb waiting to explode.

She'd correctly guessed what the USB had contained when she'd first seen *Patient #87* printed on its label, but she'd needed to confirm her suspicions. And so, while Ronan had been climbing into the shower, Phoebe had gotten up and quickly slipped the USB into his laptop and hopped onto the guest domain. On opening it, she discovered it contained countless hours of raw footage that had been recorded during the various experiments on her, all neatly organized in a series of neatly compressed files that had somehow survived the explosion at the facility and been spirited away by the Wraiths.

Choosing the last file in the list, dated July 17, 2023, she clicked it open and fast-forwarded through the video right to the end, watching in horror as her younger self efficiently wiped out each and every Wraith from the facility—something of which she'd had no recollection at all until that moment. She kept watching as, following the Wraiths' defeat, Patient #87 collapsed to the floor, writhing in pain.

And then the screen had gone abruptly dark.

Ronan's den had then started to spin, her stomach churning as the partially unpacked boxes and artifacts around her began to blur. Lurching towards a nearby garbage pail, she'd proceeded to dry heave over it for nearly a minute.

Her worse nightmare had come true.

Over the past six months, her dreams had slowly been revealing more and more of what had happened on that day. The rubble, the bodies ... But she finally had the full story now. Phoebe had been the only survivor for a reason: it was *she* who had caused the explosion, destroying everything with some sort of uncontrollable burst of trapped magic, the explosion murdering every innocent victim of the Wraiths in that facility ... except for herself.

It had been her fault. And surely, it would only be a matter of time before the "container" cracked again, destroying her this time, and likely Ronan and the other Druids as well.

Her hands had trembled as she'd reached out and shut Ronan's laptop, leaving the USB inserted so that he would find it eventually, along with the stored evidence of her wrongdoings on that fateful day. She would never hide such a thing, but neither did she have it in her to face his scrutiny, or even worse, his unconditional support. No one else deserved to be hurt simply because of her own continued existence. And certainly not because of her own inability to contain that inner darkness.

Still barrelling down the M4, Phoebe suddenly found herself letting out a cathartic, keening wail of grief, even as she practically flattened the accelerator to the floor ... sending vibrations of complaint from the Land Rover right up through her boot.

About an hour and a half further along the road, Phoebe finally stopped crying. The volatile magic, along with her own crushing heartbreak, had curated an ache in her chest that was so profound by this point that she could barely think straight. She needed to calm down or she knew she'd never make it to where she was going.

Her body was nearly at its limit, making her wonder if her love-making with Ronan might become her penultimate act. At the thought of her time with him, Phoebe shuddered involuntarily. She could still feel the ghosts of his hands trailing softly over her body, the brush of his seductive whispers against her lips and down her neck ... the warmth of that very same mouth devouring her most sensitive places and driving her to pure ecstasy. Once again, she was taken aback by the intensity of Ronan's gaze as she'd arched above him, weaving a sort of magic around them that was as yet unknown to her, though she understood it intuitively as proof that Ronan had been made just for her.

Stubborn and passionate in equal measure, the Druid doctor was Phoebe's equal in every way. And he loved her, a fact that she now knew and trusted all the way to her core ... to her very bones.

And of course, up until about ninety minutes ago, Ronan had finally trusted her as well.

She could only hope that he would someday understand.

After a solid week of obsessive research at the safe house in Vancouver—coupled with the unexpectedly emotional conversation with Ronan at the grove upon their arrival to Ireland—she had finally come to the conclusion that the only way to remove the trapped Wraith magic would be to cross the threshold to the Otherworld—into the cauldron, as it were—and hope like hell that whatever—or *whomever*—she met on the other side would be willing to help her.

Phoebe needed to let herself die ... just as Ronan had once done.

If everything went according to plan, and *only* if it went according to plan, she hoped that she might just be lucky enough to return someday, completely free of Wraith magic, and ready to build the life of her dreams within the Druidic order ... and with Ronan.

Time passed slowly as Phoebe completed the final leg of her journey and eventually broke free from the haze of loss.

"Your destination is on your right," said the GPS voice from Fionn's phone.

Phoebe parked and locked Dom's SUV, thoughtfully tucking the keys in the same spot from which Ronan had retrieved them at the airport. Then she took a deep breath and let it out slowly. She had made it.

She left her sunflower backpack on the driver's seat, unsure why she'd brought it along in the first place. It had been mostly empty anyway, containing only her wallet and Fionn's phone, which she planned on destroying shortly. Perhaps the backpack had served as a symbol of the life she was going to be leaving behind—an authentic piece of herself that might prove she'd actually been here at all on this earthly plain where she'd once loved and lost.

She grinned like a lunatic as she violently smashed the stolen phone with a massive rock on the side of the road, sending chunks of plastic, ceramics, glass, and rare earth metals flying out in every direction. Then she just stood there for a moment, facing a grassy field and spotting a small copse of trees in the distance.

The wind seemed to whisper her name then: *"Phoebe ... Phoebe ... Phoebe ..."*

And she suddenly found herself smiling broadly ... almost giggling in fact.

Sure, it had been incredibly satisfying to destroy Fionn's phone like that. But something else was bringing her an unexpected lightness ... as though she would soon find the peace she'd been chasing for so long.

It's this place, she thought. *It feels right.*

She took a deep breath and nodded to herself as she started walking. The day was surprisingly cool, and the sky overhead was overcast and dappled with shadow and light. Her nose soon began to run, the sensation making her feel incredibly alive as she left the road and started across the field at a quick jog.

Originally, she'd hoped to take a trip to the Druids' (secret) library in order to ratify this plan and confirm the location of the cave she was seeking, but it was too late for that now. Even though the ancient Druid Deirdre hadn't referenced exactly which cave had been her particular route to the Otherworld, let alone where it might be located, Phoebe had been able to cross reference several of her earlier entries with existing maps, along with important landmarks across the country to narrow this down.

And this had to be the place. She could feel it.

She smiled peacefully as she traversed the damp field, trudging over rocks and around the ruins of several rock walls that she wasn't able to scramble over.

"Phoebe ... Phoebe ... Phoebe ..." the wind called again.

She was wondering if the weather was about to change when the hair on her arms suddenly stood on end, immediately answering her own question. She could smell ozone. She frowned slightly. *And something else too ...*

It seemed very similar to the scent she'd caught at Ronan's special grove, as though an electrical storm were brewing, but as far as she knew, thunderstorms weren't all that common in Ireland—especially not in March.

She had to be almost there ...

She thought of Ronan again, keenly aware that the Druid doctor would be hot on her heels by now. There was no chance in hell he'd just let her walk away from him—not after what they'd both finally admitted to one another. Phoebe could see him now, rallying the troops and exploding outward, hot on the hunt for *"fucking Phoebe Ashburn,"* the woman who was determined to break his heart.

She wanted to believe that once cooler heads had prevailed, and Ronan had really thought things through, he would understand what had led her to this decision. She wished she could have explained it to him, but it had been impossible to convey in writing. Not to mention that, by the time she'd stopped dry heaving, she'd been nearly out of time. A person could only shower for *so* long after all. And so, she had written down the only two things that really mattered: that she loved him and that she was sorry.

She'd left out the part about her body being too close to death already to push her luck any further.

And indeed, despite her uplifted spirits, the closer she got to the copse of trees, the weaker she felt physically. Within only the first few minutes of her jog from the road, she'd stumbled several times, forcing her to slow down as her body grew more feeble with every passing minute.

Phoebe wiped her brow, and then her nose, which was now seeping bright-red blood from both nostrils.

She wasn't sure she could make it another hour, let alone another day.

"Phoebe ... Phoebe ... Phoebe ..." cried the wind.

The world around her dimmed then.

Where she'd expected to hear birdsong, especially with such lush countryside tumbling out around her in every direction, everything had grown silent and still. Even Phoebe herself was walking soundlessly now as she followed the pull of the cave, marching closer and closer to her end even as the mist started rising around her ankles.

If Ronan did manage to follow her line of thought—and realize that she was about to surrender herself to the unknown—she trusted that he would actually check for her first at his yew grove, giving her time to do what needed to be done elsewhere. As lovely as his grove had been, its energy had been decidedly masculine. Even Deirdre had described trees and groves as being symbolically phallic, and Phoebe couldn't disagree.

No. She needed to visit a wholly feminine place ... one leading directly into the womb of the earth.

As Phoebe reached her destination at last and stared straight into the mouth of the passage cave, the whispering wind began to wail.

"Phoebe ... Phoebe ... Phoebe ..."

CHAPTER 34

RONAN

One hour earlier.

Ronan punched the gas. Hard. He was all alone in his Audi and heading northwest to Goddess knew where, relying on the directives of his enchanted compass, as well as a hell of a lot of intuition and hope. Thankfully, his best friend was keeping him company now via speakerphone from Canada. Ronan hated how far away Dom was right now but was grateful that the great Celt had waded in for support, even though he and Julia were no longer particularly active in the Order.

The dilemma Ronan had found himself in being an obvious exception.

"And she gave you absolutely *no* indication of where she was going?" Dom asked. "Or why? ... Something isn't adding up."

Lennie had handed him off to Dom so that he could focus on searching for traces of Phoebe's movements. *"She's left her phone behind at your place too!"* Lennie had told him just a few minutes into the chase. Then he'd sworn loudly and immediately sent Amos and Amelia over to Ronan's place to look for more clues.

Stupidly, Ronan had gotten into his car without slowing down for even five minutes to look for clues that might have pointed him to wherever Phoebe was actually headed. Or explained why she had left at all. The note she'd left for him—and the fact she had said she loved him—had sent him flying after her like a crazy person.

He was being incredibly impulsive yet again, and it showed. But then again, when had Ronan ever been able to keep his head when it came to Phoebe Ashburn?

"I know that, Dom, but there was nothing." Ronan had racked his brain for the last hour trying to figure out where she might be heading, and why, but had come up short. "We did sleep together last night," he admitted a bit reluctantly then.

"Come on, Ronan," Dom teased. "You can't be *that* bad a ride."

While he appreciated Dom's attempt at levity, Ronan was struggling to find the humour. "That's just it, though ... I'm not. And it wasn't ... And anyway, *she* was the one who initiated it. I actually tried to turn her away ... mostly because I'm a fucking coward," he added, remembering how much time he'd wasted by resisting her for so long, and fully aware of how fucking stupid he'd been to try and deter her advances for even a second.

He shook his head and tried to focus. "But then we talked, and it finally made sense for us ..." A sudden memory of her from the previous night flashed behind his eyes, with her spreading herself below him as he'd driven himself into her, giving him everything she had to offer, even while taking all of him in turn.

He cleared his throat and tried to focus on the here and now. "All I'm saying is it's not because of that."

"You know I'm just ribbing you," Dom said, sobering quickly. "She must have had a good reason to leave then if the sex was that earth-shattering for you both."

"What makes you think—"

"I can hear it in your voice. Not to mention your immediate actions the moment you'd discovered she was gone. It's not like you to rush into things like you did, with no plan or preparation at all. It's out of character ... for you."

Ronan made a somewhat dangerous maneuver to get between a large transport truck and a minivan, causing the former to blare its horn loudly. "Are you saying I'm acting like you instead?"

Dom chucked affectionately. "I was actually saying, brother, that I know *you* ... but then again, if the shoe fits."

"Oh, fuck off, Domhnall."

The great Celt laughed, proving a soothing presence for Ronan once again, just as he had been throughout their friendship. And he was grateful.

"The only thing I can think of right now," Ronan said, "is that she uncovered something during the mission last night, or maybe only found this morning, that panicked her and made her run. It has to be something like that. The only thing that motivates her to make rash decisions like that is fear."

Pot, meet kettle, he thought. He could practically hear Dom's brain working from all the way in Canada and waited silently for him to respond.

"Lennie filled me in this morning on what went down with the mission last night," Dom said finally, "and about the briefcase you retrieved. Could Phoebe have seen anything upsetting in those files?"

Lennie had yet to officially confirm that they had finally managed to secure all of the information from the destroyed facility. It had been less than eight hours since the mission had concluded, after all, and there simply hadn't been enough time for him to go through all the data yet. But still ...

"I don't see how." Ronan thought back over the previous evening's mission and the evening that had followed, searching for anything out of place from the time they'd left the Wraith hotel until her disappearance. His pictured the way the guest room had looked when he'd followed her there last night, with her outfit strewn across the chair and a clutter of her belongings on the bedside table.

His eyes widened suddenly. There had been a USB stick among that clutter ... though it had barely registered at the time, for obvious reasons.

"Ah, shit," Dom said then, breaking him from his reverie. "Ayla's just woken up. Can I call you back?"

Calculating the eight-hour difference between Dublin and Victoria then, Ronan grimaced. It was still really early there. "Of course."

The call ended, and Ronan continued racing to the northwest, where the needle on his compass was steadily pointing from its place in his cupholder. He consciously worked to steady his breath, even as he willed Phoebe *not* to be in immediate danger.

Fifteen minutes later, a text from Lennie flashed on his phone screen:

> Ronan, can you pull over? You need to see something.

Frowning, Ronan attempted to just phone him back. Time was of the essence after all, and he couldn't waste any of it by pulling over right then. Surely, whatever the Druid-turned-Knave had to show him could be relayed to him over the phone just as easily.

Lennie didn't answer his phone. Instead, another text came through:

> I'm serious, Ronan. You're going to need to pull over and watch this.
>
> Amos and Amelia found something at your place.

Cursing, Ronan slammed on the breaks and swerved violently over onto the side of the road. Several passing cars honked loudly at him, but he ignored them all, too busy ripping his cell phone free from its dash mount. A few seconds later, a patchy video was playing on the small screen, and he held his breath.

The surveillance footage was blurry and grey, and the date in the corner identified the day in question as July 17, 2023—the same day as the explosion, and one day before the Druids had arrived on-site. A fair-haired figure in a lopsided hospital gown was stalking along an empty and clinical-looking hallway, with numbered doorways lining the walls. Even like this, Phoebe Ashburn was unmistakable. And she had clearly just had escaped her holding cell.

Ronan released his held breath past tightened lips. *"Fuck ..."*

She looked so thin, and so ... abnormal. The way she was moving felt familiar and yet ... somehow not. He watched as the Phoebe on-screen casually lifted her arms and occasionally twirling around in circles as she continued down the hall, chattering away at seemingly nothing and unlocking each door that she passed.

Strangely, none of the other test subjects had yet joined her in the artificially lit corridor.

Ronan watched in stunned silence as the surveillance video rolled on. Phoebe seemed to be almost sensing her way through the facility rather than actively looking around.

The camera cut out for several seconds then before resuming, now capturing a different section of the facility—this one a large hall where a gathering of Wraiths seemed to be waiting for her. When she entered the room, her body stiffened strangely as whatever volume of magic had been currently trapped inside her reacted to the presence of the Wraiths.

Something about the way she stood there, with her spine wildly crooked and her arms outstretched, made Ronan feel strangely nauseous. No living body should ever look like that.

Wraith after Wraith launched themselves at her then, some attacking her with magic of their own, and others wielding everything from sickles to crowbars—only to be cut down like individual blades of grass.

Phoebe was like a woman possessed. One by one, she decimated every Wraith who crossed her path, for the most part without even laying a hand on them. It was unclear whether she was sourcing this power from the trapped magic or calling on her own supressed Wielding abilities, but regardless, it was as exceptional as it was terrifying. Then suddenly everything seemed to speed up, even though the time stamp on the security footage continued ticking steadily forward in real-time.

Phoebe's body started moving impossibly fast then, taking down the remaining Wraiths as they attempted to scurry away like the cockroaches they were. And by the time her last target had disintegrated into a fetid pile of dust and sludge, she was on all fours, crawling and snapping at shadows.

The time stamp ticked on.

After a few minutes, she was lying curled up on the ground, shaking violently as blood pooled all around her ... seeping from her own tender flesh where several bones had burst forth. Ronan gasped in shock at her obvious agony as she writhed and convulsed. He longed to go to her ... to have somehow been there for her in that moment of horrific finality.

Watching her suffering, it suddenly became clear to him that the woman on the screen was just minutes, if not seconds, away from death. He shook his head in disbelief. There was no possible way that Phoebe could have survived the sort of trauma he was seeing, let alone the explosion afterward, and then just walked away unscathed. It literally wasn't possible.

Then the surveillance footage on his screen abruptly cut out, the sight of her agonized writhing washed away by sudden darkness.

The explosion ...

When Ronan's body caught up to his frozen disbelief, he opened his door, threw himself from the driver's seat, and vomited spectacularly onto the ground between his outstretched hands, his entire body heaving until there was absolutely nothing left inside him.

When the convulsions finally stopped, he reached for his phone, which he'd dropped to the floor below the steering wheel, just as a call notification from Dom's number started flashing. He answered it somewhat shakily and brought it to his ear.

"Are you there?" Julia asked, surprising him.

"Yes."

"Good."

"We're both here," Dom added in a hushed voice, probably not wanting to disturb their daughter. "Did you see the same video we just did?"

Ronan dragged himself almost blindly back into the driver's seat and leaned his head back against the headrest as he tried to gather himself. No good would come of losing it now. "I did, yes."

"I'm here too," Lennie said then, his voice sounding oddly hollow as he joined the conference call. "I have ... *so* many questions."

Since no one among them could possibly be alright after watching that video, there was no point in anyone asking if anyone else was okay. Which is probably why the next several minutes passed silently, with each of them trying to properly calibrate their shared moment of horror.

And it truly had been horrific.

"The first thing I want to know," Lennie finally said, "is what triggered the magic to take over? And why did it do so at that particular moment?"

"We're assuming that this *was* the trapped magic in action and not her own. Is there any chance it *didn't* take her over?" Dom suggested cautiously. "The Phoebe in that video didn't kill any innocents, that we could see anyway, so ... perhaps she was still capable of at least some sort of discernment."

"Perhaps," Lennie said, "but she was obviously possessed by *something*, Dom. I mean ... the way she was moving ..."

When Lennie decided to not finish the thought, or perhaps, simply had no words with which to do so, Julia spoke up. "Perhaps the two magics work in tandem somehow. The trapped magic and her own innate abilities ... like a lock and a key. I think that might make the most sense."

"She's not a Bearer though, love," Dom reminded her.

Lennie spoke up again. "Since the explosion and her escape, Phoebe has never actually shown any specific *Wielding* ability either. And according to her, she didn't even know that she *was* a magic user before the Wraiths captured her. But we— well, Ronan believes that the Wraith 'infection' is suppressing her abilities, maybe even 'consuming' the Wielding magic within her. Though, realistically, we haven't had time to test any of these theories yet."

Time had never been on their side.

Ronan was barely listening as his friends continued theorizing about how Phoebe could have decimated all of those Wraiths, with or without Wielding abilities, and even with what clearly was an inordinate amount of power trapped inside of her. He was still stuck on the fact that he'd just watched a recording of Phoebe being brutally battered from the inside and bleeding out on the floor ... surrounded by the dusty remains of the Wraiths she'd just killed.

"Right," Dom said then, agreeing with something or other and recapturing Ronan's attention. "What about the explosion then?"

"No way, Dom!" Lennie said. "Don't tell me you think that *she* caused the explosion!"

"No, you're probably right—"

Julia gasped then. "Wait ... What if *Phoebe* thinks she caused the explosion?"

No one responded to that for a long moment, though that could certainly explain Phoebe's sudden departure. Finally, Lennie asked, "Ronan, are you still there? ... What do you think? Could she have caused the explosion?"

It was a good question. Was creating an explosion of that magnitude even possible for a Wielder? Let alone one in the state Phoebe had been in?

Absolutely not.

"No," Ronan said, clearing his throat, which felt ragged from both vomit and grief. "Phoebe can't have done it. Not possible."

"Hmm ..." Dom seemed less certain. "Phoebe *is* the last thing we see before the camera cuts out. And stranger things *have* happened. From what we know, at least, there was a fuck-ton of Wraith magic trapped inside of her when it happened."

Lennie sighed. "No offence, Dom, but you're not a Wielder. And it just doesn't work like that." He paused suddenly then. "Oh shit ... Hold on a second ..."

"What is it, Lennie?" Julia asked, but the Brit didn't respond. They'd all grown accustomed to Lennie disappearing at random intervals in the middle of phone calls and eventually returning with pertinent information.

"Anyways," Julia said pointedly, hoping to steer the conversation back to a more relevant point while Lennie was otherwise occupied, "even if we don't know how Phoebe managed to take down all of those Wraiths, or whether or not she was actually tied to that explosion in some way, it's not hard to imagine how she might be feeling right now if she saw the same footage we all just watched."

"She'd be freaking the fuck out right now," Dom said.

"Well, I certainly would be," Julia agreed.

She's right, Ronan thought, looking at the time. Forty-five minutes had already elapsed since he'd first discovered that Phoebe was gone, and yet he was still no closer to locating her. Setting his phone back carefully into its holder on the dash, not wanting to inadvertently hang up on the others, he checked his mirrors and pulled back out onto the motorway just as Lennie rejoined the conversation.

"So, I've done a preliminary search through the other camera feeds at the same moment the first one went black. There was no sign of any other Wraith activity in the building at that time, except for one ..."

A moment later, Ronan's phone binged, letting him know that a texted image had just arrived: a screenshot of a dark, hooded figure entering the security office. "There is no record of this Wraith ever leaving that office again, and he didn't appear to take part in the main fight ... but if he was the one who collected the hard drives and *then* somehow left with them—"

"You think *he* might have caused the explosion," Dom said impatiently, cutting to the chase. "Do we have any idea who he might be?"

"No." Lennie coughed suddenly, then cleared his throat and continued. "Based on his general size, though, and the fact that the USB and other files were retrieved from the Astaroth Hotel, and correspond to the missing hard drives as well, it *could* actually be Leviathan himself. I don't think it's Malphas, though. He's a lot smaller and—"

"Wait a second!" Ronan said, as a realization struck him. "Wasn't Leviathan at the hotel last night? Right along with Malphas? What if he had recognized Phoebe?"

The line went silent for a long moment as the others considered this, then Dom spoke up again. "He didn't though. It sounds like she got lucky."

"No shit," Ronan said, suddenly fuming. Last night's hotel mission had been far more dangerous than they'd ever suspected. It had been reckless of him to allow Phoebe to be part of a mission of that scale, especially with so many unknowns still out there ...

Fuck! Fuck! Fuck!

"I think there's something else we need to consider," Julia said, interrupting Ronan's rage spiral. "Regardless of *how* Phoebe managed to do what we all just watched her do, the power she was drawing on was far beyond any sort of Wraith magic they could have trapped inside her. They don't have that sort of power, not even the ancient ones ..." She paused briefly, and when she continued, her voice had dropped to a whisper. "Magic that strong ... it could only come from a Sorcerer."

Ronan couldn't speak. He could barely breathe. Everything was happening both too quickly and nowhere near fast enough all at once.

He realized then that the way Phoebe had moved in that video had reminded him somehow of Cassius ... though perhaps that was simply the ease with which she was accessing the power she held. His still tender stomach clenched again. A being with magic matching that of Cassius, perhaps even surpassing it, was once again walking this earth.

And it would seem that he'd gone and fucking fallen in love with her.

When he spoke next, Ronan didn't even recognize his own voice. "What exactly do you expect me to do?"

"You need to find her," Julia said. "Speak to her. She still has the potential to stop ... whatever this is!"

Ronan's back went up defensively at this. Did they think Phoebe was about to go on some sort of killing spree? He was about to call them on this, and then he suddenly felt as though he'd just fallen off a cliff.

"*Fuck* ..."

"What is it, Ronan?" Lennie asked.

"She's ... Phoebe *is* trying to stop this! ... She's going to remove the trapped magic once and for all!" Everyone was quiet for a long, tense moment as understanding settled in.

"She's trying for the Otherworld," Dom said gravely, speaking for all of them.

Much to his surprise, at Dom's words, Ronan felt his body calm at last. For all of Phoebe's flaws, she wasn't someone who wanted to hurt others. So, if she was convinced that the trapped magic might escape again, potentially killing the people she loved—killing him—he had no doubt at all that she would do whatever it took to stop that from happening. Even if that meant somehow taking herself away to the Otherworld.

He started mentally cross referencing this theory with the latest information he'd gotten from the security footage. And something *still* wasn't adding up ...

"Ronan, are you still there?" Julia asked.

In the very next instant, all of Ronan's confusion from the past few months, about who or *what* Phoebe really was, finally distilled itself into a single moment of clarity, and he knew that he'd solved it. He just needed to confirm it.

"Lennie, I need you to check if there's a DNA match between any of the bones the Druids recovered from the site and the bloodwork I took from Phoebe last week."

Time slowed as Lennie started doing just that, leaving each member of their inner circle waiting for the results with bated breath. The five minutes that followed, listening to Lennie hammering away on his keyboard, may have been the longest of Ronan's life.

"Yes ..." Lennie said quietly then. "There's a match."

Ronan let out a long slow breath.

Phoebe's bones had been right there all along, gathered up after the explosion like so many anonymous others. She hadn't survived the explosion after all. And yet ... somehow, she had also emerged from all that destruction alive, her flesh fully intact.

Could it have been some sort of bone magic?

Ronan might not have figured that part out yet, but it was the only explanation he could come up with at present. He had long wondered how she'd managed to escape unscathed from an explosion that had levelled an entire facility. Then he'd watched that footage. He'd seen her body twist itself into something he hadn't even recognized ... battered and broken by dark magic even before the larger destruction that had hidden the truth from them all.

And it finally made sense. She *hadn't* survived. She couldn't have.

Suddenly aware of the silence from the others on the line, awaiting his response, he forced his mind back to the present and cleared his throat. "Alright. So, as soon as we end this call, I have to get Amos or Amelia on the line. I need to ask them a few questions."

"They'll be ready and waiting for your call," Lennie replied.

Ronan nodded, hitting the gas even harder now and accelerating fast. "Dom, let's assume for now that Phoebe doesn't know that she's died once already, and that she's trying to reach the Otherworld as we speak, either to pass through and be cured or just to protect us all from her. Do you think she'll have any chance at all of returning a second time? Cured or not?"

"I'm not certain," he said after a moment's consideration. "Doing so was never an issue in my experience, returning countless times over the centuries, but ..."

"But what?"

"I'm sorry, Ronan, but ... if you remember, sometimes decades would pass between my various reincarnations."

That settled it. "We need to find her," Ronan said through gritted teeth, unable to bear the thought of Phoebe disappearing into the Otherworld for even a minute, let alone decades or possibly forever.

"We need to find her *now*."

CHAPTER 35
RONAN

Ending the call with his three closest friends, and still swerving his way through the motorway's traffic, Ronan carefully lifted his compass and held it out on the palm of his hand.

"Come on ... please," he whispered, willing it to direct him to Phoebe ... to take him home. He was still travelling west, following its lead, but he sensed that if he didn't keep a close eye on it, he might miss a turnoff or something.

And it was imperative that he reach Phoebe before she transcended to the Otherworld.

She deserved to know the truth about what had happened on that horrible day—and specifically about her own apparent resurrection—before making such a life-altering (possibly life-ending) decision.

None of this was her fault.

He dialled Amelia, who picked up immediately. "Ronan, how can we help?"

The words tumbled out of him in a rush: "Phoebe died on the day of the explosion, though whether before or during the blast remains unclear. The point is, she came *back* ... possibly using bone magic, which I know sounds crazy, but—"

"*What?!*"

"That's why I've called you. Is that even possible? The bone-magic part, I mean?"

"Honestly, I don't know. If there were no Druids present ..." She paused, then started speaking rapidly to someone in the background before putting him on speakerphone.

"You think she was *resurrected* with bone magic?" Amos asked, his familiar voice sounding aghast at the notion.

"I do, yes." Ronan sighed. "I can't think of any other way that she could have marched down the mountain after an explosion like that unless something truly remarkable had happened. I know you saw that video. By the time the feed cut out, she was bleeding out, just seconds from death if she wasn't dead already."

"Yes. We saw it but—"

"Wait," Amelia said then. "Ronan, do you know anything about Phoebe's parents?"

He frowned. "All I know is that they're deceased and that she'd moved on. That's all she ever told us. Frankly, she's somewhat avoidant about discussing her past in general, and I haven't had the chance to—"

"Is there any possibility they were Druids?" Amos asked, suddenly catching on to what his twin was thinking.

"Honestly, I doubt it," Ronan said. "But ... I suppose they could have been."

He was suddenly realizing how little he still knew about Phoebe, a fact that did literally nothing to shake his resolve to move mountains if it would mean saving her life. That was his promise to her.

Amos and Amelia started speaking to each other in hushed tones on the other end of the line. And after moment, Ronan heard Amelia let out a long, slow breath.

"Okay," she said finally. "We're going to tell you something that you cannot tell *anyone* ... Do you promise?"

Ronan eyed his compass again. It was still pointing him in the same direction.

"You know I'll take it to the grave," he said, though he quickly amended his statement, "unless doing so stops me from saving Phoebe."

"Yes, of course. Okay ... Well, the oral tradition includes a belief that bone magic is an inherited trait. Amos and I have it, and so did our parents—"

"What my sister is saying is that it's not just a learned skill. Some people can just ... do it. Does that make sense?"

"None of this should make *any* sense at all," Ronan said dryly. *Get to the fucking point.* "Please, continue."

"Basically, that's how bone magic has endured into the modern era at all, considering its rarity. Sometimes it just ... happens," Amelia explained. "Otherwise, it would have been happily lost centuries ago."

And for good reason. Bone magic—which included resurrection and soul redirection—was the path of Druidics that could turn a Wielder *dark, dark*. It was believed to be one of several root causes for the Wraiths splitting from the ancient Druids all those years ago.

"Amelia and I *don't* have much of a choice," Amos said. "It actually *is* in our bones, and dumb as that sounds, it's one of those things that can be silently passed down for generations."

Ronan accepted this new information at face value, though he was struggling slightly to process it. "Alright, so ... what you're suggesting is that there's a possibility Phoebe also inherited bone magic ... assuming that's how she was even resurrected?"

Amelia sighed. "Well, we've never heard of anything like that ... but yes. It *would* be the most logical explanation."

If anyone was going to be a secretly superpowered Wielder of bone magic, it was definitely Phoebe. From the first moment he'd laid eyes on her, he'd known she was different.

She truly was a remarkable woman.

Suddenly, the compass needle shifted north. "Shit! I have to go. Thanks, you two."

"Goddess guide you," Amelia said, disconnecting the call.

Ronan signalled his way off the M4 and headed north as fast as he could, realizing then that there was only one place now that Phoebe could be heading: *Ráth Cruachan.*

The problem was that Rathcroghan had a range about six-kilometres long, with hundreds of significant sites to choose from, all of which were linked to the Neolithic, Bronze, and Iron ages. Dom's rebirth had been tied to the Neolithic site at Newgrange. The mount at Rathcroghan, the home of Queen Medb, was Neolithic.

No, that didn't track ... neither of them. Not for Phoebe.

If he really knew her at all, which he was sure that he did despite all evidence to the contrary, he was sure that she'd be drawn somewhere else ... perhaps the Cave of Cats, better known as *Oweynagat*, home of the *Morrigan*.

Fuck.

That location was on private land and far more difficult to access without a guide ... not that anything like that would stop Phoebe. She'd already stolen Dom's Land Rover, and who knew what else, to get wherever it was she was going today. Normal rules didn't apply when you were walking through this earthly realm as a fucking anomaly. And so, no blame could be assigned to her for breaking them.

He'd always assumed that this was the cave that Deirdre had (purportedly) visited so long ago, though the ancient Druid had never stated its geographical location (assuming she'd actually gone anywhere at all). Everything about Deirdre's accounts had always seemed extremely capricious to Ronan, with few roots in actual reality. But then again, after everything he'd just learned about Phoebe within the last twenty-four hours, and experienced with her for far longer, being unrooted in reality was very on-brand for her.

He needed to hurry.

Following the direction of his compass and the pull of his heart, Ronan soon turned onto a side road that wound along a rural and partially treed property. Time seemed to pass strangely for a while, and then at last, he let out a sigh of relief when he spied Dom's abandoned Land Rover parked neatly on the side of the road. Pulling up behind it, he threw his Audi into park and hopped out to inspect it.

Ronan peered inside the windows for evidence of foul play, but everything seemed intact. Phoebe's sunflower backpack was slumped on the front seat, and the doors were locked. He reached under the wheel well to discover the keys hidden in the same place Morgan had left them for him at the airport. Several feet beyond the front bumper, broken remnants of what appeared to have once been a cell phone were scattered across the road.

Ronan crouched down and took a closer look, then groaned, realizing that Phoebe had stolen Fionn's phone when he'd made one of his passes at her. Never one to miss an opportunity, she had artfully robbed the little shit of anything that might have been useful to her on the mission. Just as she'd done with the Druids ...

"Clever girl," Ronan said, the fondness in his tone colouring his frustration.

He pulled out his own cell phone then and had just sent Lennie a location pin when the air began to crack and sizzle around him, making the hair on the back of his neck stand up. He needed to move.

Ronan took off in a sprint, calling her name at the top of his voice. "Phoebe! ... *Phoebe?!*"

Though they'd never actually determined the maximum range beyond which he and Phoebe could no longer sense each other during that mission back in Calgary, which was proving to be just another example of Ronan losing track of their objectives and becoming wholly distracted by Phoebe (and in that specific case, being a complete asshole to her), his gut was still screaming that he was going the right way.

And that she was close.

Then he spotted a streak of blonde hair flowing in the wind beyond a small copse of trees in the distance. He picked up his pace, running for her as though his own life depended on reaching her in time. Because it absolutely did.

After having been sprinting full out for several minutes, his chest was heaving, his lungs fighting desperately to draw in enough oxygen to support his voice as he called out to her again, his whole body straining impossibly to make himself heard as he finally closed the distance between them.

"Is that what you've been ... hiding ... all this time?" Ronan asked as he almost stumbled to a stop a few feet away from her, gasping for breath. "The fact that ... something *happened* ... before you ever left the lab?"

Phoebe's spine straightened, though she didn't turn her head to look at him. "Everyone has secrets, Ronan."

A heavy mist was quickly moving in around them—*around Phoebe*, where she stood facing the mouth of a cave, its liminal entrance yawning open between two nondescript, moss-topped limestone slabs.

Ronan could feel it—feel *them*—calling to her: *"Phoebe ... Phoebe ... Phoebe ..."*

There was no mistaking it. This was a portal to the Otherworld.

One wrong move, and Ronan knew he might lose her forever. He took a tentative step forward, searching carefully for the right words. "It's alright ... *sunshine*," he said softly, though his determination was as strong as steel. "It doesn't matter to me what happened ... None of that matters ... I promise you."

The air around them fizzled and popped, and Ronan knew he had only seconds to stop her ... only a moment before she would step through that portal and disappear ... possibly forever.

"It matters to *me*," Phoebe said then, her voice barely audible through the rushing wind and otherworldly magic now emanating from the cave's looming depths. The mist grew thicker yet. "I can't ... I can't do that ... not again. All those people I killed ..."

She leaned forward a bit.

"Don't!" Ronan practically shrieked, his heart seeming to stop entirely in his chest as fear surged through him. *"Phoebe, please! ... Don't do this!"*

Then something much darker threatened to take hold: the residual legacy of the *Codex Druidicus* ... It was inside him still, and Ronan knew that its power could easily stop her in her tracks. It might not have had the ability to remove the magic from Phoebe, but it could still contain her.

Was that why I was given such a singular gift in the first place?

Then he heard the voices of the Otherworld calling his own name on the wind: *"Ronan ... Ronan ... Ronan ..."*

Nothing about this felt right.

He was no Sorcerer. If his time under Cassius's rule had taught him nothing else, it had taught him that.

"You didn't cause the explosion, Phoebe!" Ronan shouted then. "It wasn't your fault!"

Phoebe's posture changed fractionally upon hearing this, so he took another step towards her, his fingers now only inches from her shoulder, almost close enough to pull her back from the abyss without any magic at all.

"What do you mean?" she rasped.

"Lennie looked through the footage! Someone *else* caused the explosion ... not you. It was probably Levi or one of those other Wraith bastards, but that's not what matters right now. Just ... please let me explain."

She shook her head. "That's ... That's not true. I saw—"

"You saw yourself *die*, Phoebe!" he shouted desperately. "*That's* what you saw! The footage cut out when it did because Levi *stole* the files! And then he blew up the whole fucking building around you!"

Phoebe's voice shook. "That d-doesn't make any sense ... How am I here then?"

Ronan didn't have time to explain to her the nuances of bone magic, let alone whether or not her family line had secret Druidic origins. "Look, it's complicated, but we have some theories that I know will be proven out once we've had a chance to work through it all and think clearly ... But it wasn't you! It wasn't you, Phoebe! And right now, I need you to step away from that portal and come with me."

She was silent for a moment, giving him a glimmer of hope. And then she dashed it.

"It's too late for that ..."

A colossal spike of fear stabbed through Ronan's chest as newly minted adrenaline surged like a riptide through his veins. "What do you mean? You *literally* don't have to do this, Phoebe! I can help you! Please! We can figure this out together! We're a great team, remember?"

"I know we are," she said, her voice growing ominously distant as she continued to peer into the depths of the cave.

Ronan took another step and took her hand in his, the warmth of her skin immediately radiating through him like the dawn after a night of impossible darkness. Then his shoulders started to shake as a wash of tears blurred his vision.

"I know you must have had a damn good reason not to just tell me, Phoebe ... not to tell me about your fears ... about all of it." He blinked hard to try and clear his vision. "You could have trusted me ... You *can* trust me because I'm here for you in this ... in *everything* ... just like I promised I would be."

She was perfectly still now. "I can't, Ronan ... I can't."

The wind and mist swirled almost deafeningly around them now.

Phoebe was already leaving him.

His mind flashed to the many conversations he'd shared with Dom about his only regret at having followed Julia into the Otherworld and the future: that he had done so without her consent, which had been hugely presumptuous and even controlling in its way.

Then he quickly shook those regrets from his mind. He didn't give a fuck about them, and he was running out of time. "I've already followed you here, sunshine, to a portal at the end of the earth, and I'll follow you beyond it if you'll only ask it of me. I love you and nothing can change that, Phoebe. I'm yours for all eternity if you'll have me."

"I'm dying, Ronan, whether I stay or go," she said then, the gusting winds threatening to steal her words before they could reach him. "This has to be my choice."

And then he finally understood that the trapped magic had simply become too painful and volatile for her to endure any longer.

Her exposure to the Wraiths' darkness in captivity had eaten away at her body from the outside, just as it had done to his own body almost three years earlier, even as the container of her flesh was being eroded from within by the dark magic they'd trapped inside her. And now her physical body had reached its expiry date, yet again, and no matter how badly Ronan wanted to save her ... he knew then that she had to go.

His tears were nearly blinding as he took a stumbling step back, finally accepting that losing her was the only possible path forward if he ever wanted her to find the peace she so deserved.

This was her choice to make.

She looked over her shoulder at him then and mouthed three words he couldn't hear but understood with all his being: *"I love you."*

And then she disappeared through the portal like a wisp of smoke.

CHAPTER 36
RONAN

From the moment Ronan had laid eyes on Phoebe, it seemed he'd known that a brutal and beautiful obscurity lived inside her, though he hadn't truly understood until it was too late. Completely separate from the Wraith magic that had been slowly carving out a place for itself within her body, she'd had her *own* mysterious darkness living like a shadow inside her, coiling its way quietly through her soul and waiting for its own moment to strike.

And it had done so, piercing straight through his heart.

That darkness had undoubtedly been borne of capture and torture, grief and loss, and much like his own darkness, out of desperate loneliness as well ... though hers, of course, had also been fuelled by bone magic, a lost legacy to which she'd found herself an unwitting heir.

Unlike Ronan, though, who'd fallen victim to his own greedy obsession with the truth, which had killed him in the end, Phoebe had concluded that allowing such a darkness to fester was too much of a threat to the people she loved. A matter of life and death.

No matter what conclusions other might draw, he knew that Phoebe was no Sorcerer. No master of stolen magic. She was good and pure and had deserved absolutely none of what had happened to her.

Even if she'd been dead wrong in believing that she had caused the explosion—killing the many other innocents that had been trapped in that facility—her instincts and determination to ensure that it could never happen again now stood as testament to the kind of person she had been: a far better person than Ronan could ever hope to be.

And all he could do now was attempt to follow Phoebe's lead from the darkness and into the light.

After her passing, Ronan allowed himself to settle deeply into the fullness of his grief—collapsing to the ground at the mouth of the cave and wailing into the womb of the earth until his throat grew raw. He wanted more time with her. He needed it. And that was a loss deserving of open recognition. He screamed and cried and begged hoarsely until his tears slowed and dried on his cheeks.

"Please," he muttered at last once he was exhausted beyond all measure, "let her come back to me."

Some previous version of Ronan might have shut down completely after all of that, as the rage and agony cascaded through his psyche, reverberating through his bones and inviting him back into the icy cold he'd embraced once before.

He had finally, and openly, given Phoebe all of his love and his trust, and she'd repaid him with abandonment—or what he would surely have perceived as such at one time.

Now, though, Ronan somehow knew that what she had actually just done was something entirely different.

"You didn't deserve this ..." He was already missing her earthly presence more than he'd ever missed anything in his life. "*We* didn't deserve this ..."

But she had needed to go. Simple as that.

Slowly, the mists cleared around him, allowing the sunshine to reach him once again, instantly reminding him of Phoebe as he pushed himself slowly back up to his feet.

He had meant what he said: he loved her, and he trusted her. And he truly would have followed her into the darkness had she asked. But instead, all she'd asked of him—all she'd *ever* asked of him—was that he allow her to make her own choices. After so many months of being stripped of her autonomy, Phoebe had chosen to step into that cave ... and through that portal.

Ronan could only imagine what she'd been hoping to find in the Otherworld. Would she ask to be healed by their grace and sent back? And would that be allowed?

Only time would tell.

What he *did* know was that Phoebe Ashburn had brought out the very best in him, and he'd be damned if he didn't do everything he could to continue that legacy—both for the woman he'd once known and the one he hoped would return to him someday. *Goddess willing.*

Time passed strangely as Ronan trudged back through the fields and away from the mouth of the cave, almost as if nature's familiar cadence was somehow beating in reverse, rewinding the magic that had flowed so readily from the beyond. He felt his own Wielding magic depleting as the forces withdrew, leaving him alone this time around with the immensely heavy burden of the Codex magic and his own purpose moving forward

When he looked at his watch, he could almost not believe it. While it had felt like Phoebe had left him only moments before, he had apparently knelt there at the mouth of the cave for nearly two hours before finally beginning his trek back to his parked car, where he found Lennie standing and waiting for his return.

"Where's Phoebe?" the Brit demanded.

Ronan shook his head. There were no words.

Lennie's face fell even as his boots crunched loudly, covering the distance between them. Then he pulled Ronan towards himself. "I'm so sorry."

Ronan willingly accepted his comrade's embrace, keenly aware of the kindred grief they shared. Not only had the Druid-turned-Knave's parents been lost on a mission with the Order—orphaning Lennie before he'd even completed secondary school—but he'd also lost the love of his life to one of Cassius's darkest minions several years ago. If anyone might understand what Ronan was going through, it was Lennie.

"How long have you been waiting here?" Ronan eventually asked in a voice he barely recognized.

"About thirty minutes. Whatever magic you were dealing with wouldn't let me go beyond this point," Lennie said, gesturing to the edge of the road. "Morgan has already come and gone to collect Dom's Land Rover."

Ronan's heart thumped in his chest. "But what about—"

"I have her things there," Lennie said, gesturing towards the hood of Ronan's Audi. "I figured you'd want them, though I think it's mostly just her backpack, and it feels like it's empty."

Ronan approached his car, which was filthy with road dust and the early smatterings of rain. *So much for sunshine* ... He peered at Phoebe's abandoned sunflower backpack, which slumped lifelessly where Lennie had placed it on the hood of his car.

Phoebe really was gone.

"You didn't look through it?" Ronan asked as he picked it up.

"I didn't think you'd appreciate it if I did."

Ronan clasped Lennie's shoulder then, grounding himself. "Thanks."

Suddenly, Lennie's phone rang, and he answered quickly. "Yes, what is it?"

He stepped away as Ronan drew Phoebe's backpack up to his face. He could still smell her perfume on it. Numbly, he wondered how long he'd be able to revisit the scent of her on the rest of her belongings as well as his own.

"We have a problem," Lennie said suddenly, and Ronan's attention snapped towards him.

"Imogen is in a coma."

Ronan folded and packed a final pair of pants in preparation for his return flight to Canada later that afternoon. Lennie had booked him on an absolute milk run, citing short notice and baggage-handler strikes as barriers to finding a better option. This didn't bother Ronan as much as it usually would have; he'd already survived the longest seventy-two hours of his life since Phoebe had stepped through that portal and disappeared. And as he tried to keep moving forward, he sensed that every hour would prove equally as difficult as the last if he continued wallowing in Dublin all alone.

He had work to do in Vancouver.

It seemed that the Wraith vine specimen that Imogen had been keeping so meticulously contained with her cleverly propagated mould had won out in the end, somehow managing to make its way to her in the middle of the night when she'd been least expecting it, wrapping itself around her and sucking her nearly completely dry of Wielding magic.

Ronan had already been sent pictures of the brutal bruises and lacerations that were left around her neck and torso; it remained to be seen whether she should be considered lucky to be alive, or if the vines had damaged her far beyond the obvious physical trauma.

Ronan wasn't sure what would happen to a Wielder if they were fully drained of magic. He'd only once witnessed someone's magic being stripped from them, when Julia had forcibly removed another Bearer's magic during her own risky mission from the Otherworld. But this was different—and surely unprecedented. Wielders didn't carry magic the way Bearers did, but regardless, he needed to assess Imogen's medical situation in person before he could draw any helpful conclusions.

The vines had seemed harmless enough at the rave warehouse and at the country bar, reaching down from the ceiling and passively soaking up the wild magics around them. But once the buds had fully bloomed, it seemed that the plants grew stronger and significantly more volatile. It appeared that the Druids' initial theories that they were simply being used to collect and store Wielding magic for the Wraiths had taken a much more sinister turn while they'd been away overseas.

Choking vines ...

Something about them was still oddly familiar to Ronan, but he couldn't quite ...

Ronan's eyes widened then as he suddenly realized where he'd seen such vines before: the Otherworld!

Admittedly, that was a part of his death experience he'd since tried to forget—when the voices had begun laughing so cruelly at his expense, their melodic mirth rippling over his body even as it had somehow turned into vice-like tendrils that lifted him from the earth, nearly suffocating him, and then penetrating his mind before turning into a great snake—an ouroboros—which had held him suspended (spiritually, at least) at the very threshold of existence.

Slowly devouring him.

Ronan shook away the thought of that giant snake wrapping around him, threatening to crush his very bones, and brought himself back to the present, zipping his suitcase shut. With such big threats on the horizon and even bigger stakes, it wouldn't do to dwell.

If all went to plan, he would return back here to Dublin within the month anyway. He'd missed the home he kept here, and even without Phoebe in his life, he knew that he still had some spiritual reparations to make on native soil.

Ronan closed his bedroom door behind him then and wheeled his suitcase towards the front foyer where Amos stood waiting for him.

"Can I take anything out to the car for you?" Amos asked; Amelia was already waiting for them in the car.

The twins would be returning to the West Coast along with him. They had spent the night with one twin sleeping on his couch and the other on a makeshift bed on the floor. Ronan had dreaded trying to explain to them that he wasn't ready to open his guest room up to anyone just yet. Phoebe's bag remained stowed beneath the bed and her red-velvet dress was still draped over the chair. Thankfully, they'd anticipated this and come prepared with bedrolls and extra linens.

"Sure, if you want to take this bag out, I'll be right behind you." Ronan rolled the suitcase over to Amos before quickly turning towards his study.

He padded quietly into his den, noting his unwashed whisky glass from several nights before still gathering dust from atop the side table. He bit back a hot surge of bile and regret as he remembered just how mean he'd been to Phoebe that night. How utterly unfair and hurtful ...

He sighed and tried to focus on something else. He now knew that there would have been no way for him to save her. And he trusted in both her decision and strength in surrendering to her own destiny.

All he could do now was continue on with his own. At that very moment, he knew that the Hounds of Hell—Malphas and Leviathan—were marshalling their newly captured legions and vying for supremacy atop a horrible heap of evil. The Druids now had proof that the magical hybridized vines were far more dangerous than initially suspected. Ronan hoped like hell that he would be able to revive Imogen upon his return to Vancouver and discover what had really happened. If not, at the very least, he would need to track down her most recent findings. Luckily, Ronan knew that Imogen was a fantastic record keeper.

He had no doubt that there were still more hidden test facilities, secrets, and weapons just waiting to be exposed, doing so much harm to goddess only knew how many innocents and to an unknown end goal.

Ronan would be damned if he let that continue on his watch. And not just because the greater powers of the Otherworld had shaped his destiny for just such a purpose. He also truly cared about his fellow Druids and their future, as well as that of any other magic users likely to be caught in the crossfire.

Having witnessed Phoebe's short-lived initiation into the Druidic fold, Ronan had seen exactly how important the Order truly was, providing a place of safety, healing, and reassurance for lost and damaged magic users.

And also, providing them with purpose.

Ronan did a final agonizing sweep of his house before stepping outside onto his front step and locking the front door. Then he turned slowly to face his driveway where Amos and Amelia awaited him in a rental car. He clenched his fist as righteous anger surged through him once again at how poorly timed his "relationship" with Phoebe had been, doomed to fail from the very beginning, not only thanks to the hideous manipulation and torture of the Wraiths that had held her captive, but also due to his own stubborn unwillingness to deviate from his interpretation of the Otherworld's mission for him ... though he only recognized it as such thanks to the wisdom of his therapist.

Although it had taken him too long to identify this feeling with any clarity, within Ronan now existed an unquenchable fire to deliver painful and final retribution to Leviathan and Malphas, in particular, though they would certainly not be alone in receiving every single ounce of pain and payback they so very much deserved.

It might take me weeks, months, or even years, he thought finally, *but make no mistake, you bastards ... your time is coming ...*

EPILOGUE

MUFFLED, SNOWY SILENCE SWATHED A VAST LANDSCAPE AS DOWNY flakes floated softly against a greyscale backdrop of dense forest, looming mountains, and a seemingly endless sky. There was no colour in this place where nature (and its magic) lay in wait, pausing to catch its breath somewhere between time and space.

Air in ... Air out.

Wet snowflakes melted on her eyelashes, as not for the first time, Phoebe Ashburn wept at the sight of a miraculously open sky.

The distinctive low call of trumpeter swans bugled from somewhere high above—a species native to North America, rather than Ireland, where she'd crossed into the Otherworld. Yet even so, a flock of seven or eight black-beaked birds winged gracefully overhead, calling out to each other through the increasingly thick snowfall. This place must be Canada, or someplace resembling it, at least. Perhaps because that's where Phoebe would've wished to be buried ... had there been any bones left behind to lay to rest.

The wind picked up abruptly then, its swirling, tempestuous breath arriving with an edge so crisp it felt electric. Silver strings of magic crackled and leapt through the air, their gossamer essence glittering between each snowflake and the next.

Phoebe shivered violently before looking down at the drifting waist-deep snow that had gathered around her broken body, only to find white feathers wafting lovingly instead. A gift from the swans. With a grateful sigh, she reached out intuitively to draw them close around herself like a thick, fluffy duvet.

And she basked in the magnificence of its warmth.

As the winter squall escalated all around her, drumming itself loudly into a true whiteout, Phoebe burrowed in deep beneath her enchanted covers, the warmth of long-awaited slumber beckoning. Drawing her knees up to her chest, she curled inward around the trapped magics, safe from the storm even as her tears froze on her cheeks like sparkling jewels.

Here, she could rest and heal at last ...

Phoebe woke to hot breath and a swipe of saliva on her cheek. Gasping, she opened her eyes to discover a black-and-white dog staring her dead in the eye, its tongue lolling happily. It barked once and wagged its tail eagerly, plainly pleased that Phoebe was awake. She smiled brightly as the Border Collie began running in tight circles on the lush and vibrantly green grass. Evidently, she'd slept through the worst of the whiteout, and the world's colour had since returned with gusto.

Phoebe sat up to scratch the dog behind its ear, which it accepted only momentarily before abruptly backing up, its chest low to the ground, and starting to bark orders at her.

Bark, bark, bark!

"Do you want me to get up?"

Bark, bark, bark, bark!

Its demands were quickly becoming impatient. So, Phoebe stood up slowly, her long, slim legs feeling like a newborn foal's beneath her as she stumbled forward, her celestial body adjusting to its new environment. The dog didn't care. Apparently, there was no time to be wasted in learning to walk again, as her eager companion wagged its tail only once more before taking off in a sprint towards the distant forest.

"Wait for me!" Phoebe called out, lunging clumsily forward to follow the friendly creature.

Time and space lurched forward then, and she found herself chasing her new friend through the heart of an ash-wood forest—Oregon ash, specifically, with their long seed pods (known as samaras) identifying them clearly. *Such forests are common in the Pacific Northwest.* Their brilliant green leaves danced overhead in the warm breeze as dappled light trickled down from a distant sun, winking teasingly at Phoebe from the clear blue skies.

She smiled and glanced at the dog. "What is this place?"

The dog's only response was to snap happily at the air beside her, attempting to catch one of the helicoptering ash seeds that were cascading down to earth in spiralling waves. Utterly enchanted, Phoebe's laughter sprang from her like a spring creek and continued until tears of joy spilled from her eyes. Together with her newfound friend, she danced through the forest, casting around them a spell of pure celebration as ribbons of shimmering golden light manifested and began to swirl around them both.

Wild magics ...

Phoebe was adorned in a flowing dress that had undoubtedly been crafted by the Goddess herself, woven from pale lichen and soft green moss. Draping down from one shoulder, it was decorated with tiny white and yellow flowers, and as her unbound hair flowed wildly around her, vibrant butterflies fluttered from its depths for her overjoyed companion to chase.

Phoebe looked as radiant as the sun.

And then everything shifted unexpectedly once more, this time into vengeance-filled darkness so deep and profound that it ripped the magic from the air. Phoebe fell to her hands and knees, jarred by the hard-packed earth beneath them. Her dress was gone now, leaving her naked and suddenly alone once more.

Where has the dog gone?

The once-beautiful grove began closing in around her then, threatening to trap her within its tightening grasp. Phoebe's body, which had at last felt whole following the winter storm, began to shake violently now as the trapped, volatile magics revolted once again.

What is happening?

Phoebe leapt to her feet, running frantically from tree to tree, attempting fruitlessly to slip past their rapidly swelling trunks even while avoiding the twining branches now reaching out for her, slashing through the air. There was no escaping this grove, and as the trees pushed ever closer, threatening to suffocate her, she looked up in fear. She could no longer see the sky!

Bark, bark, bark! Bark, bark, bark!

Somewhere beyond the grove, the dog was calling anxiously, even as Phoebe shoved her fingers between the rough bark of two trunks and attempted to pry them apart with her bare hands, desperate beyond measure. Her fingertips started to bleed, the grey-brown bark shredding her tender flesh, but instead of giving way, the trunks only grew broader still, crushing her fingers between them.

Phoebe released a blood-curdling shriek of pain and horror then that filled the ever-tightening enclosure, but no sound could be heard beyond it, nor could the dog's desperate barking reach her any longer from the outside.

When the trees finally released their grasp of Phoebe's hands, revealing to her only bare bones where tender flesh had once been, time itself came to a screeching halt.

"Will you leave your bones here to rest?" asked an ominous, disembodied voice.

"Or will you wear the darkness like a crown?" asked a second.

"We know what you are capable of, Phoebe Ashburn," said yet another.

Phoebe couldn't believe what she was hearing. She swayed on the spot, looking around desperately to find the source of these chilling voices.

"What crown?!" she shouted, her throat raw. "And what could you possibly think I'm capable of? No. Wait! Better question: why would you send me back after dying in the explosion only to have me die all over again so soon? And then—"

"What becomes of a woman so infected that she cannot die?" the first voice asked suddenly.

The second voice, shrieking now, added, *"When she is too perpetual to exist even in the hidden realm?"*

"What choice does she make with her legacy of bones?" the third voice asked, its tone eerily hushed compared to the others now.

Before Phoebe could respond, countless scores of jewel-toned beetles emerged from the depths of her hair and began scuttling down her arms and all over her body, boring their way into her skin along the way and covering every inch of her frame with glittering emerald wings.

Within seconds, the rest of Phoebe's flesh was stripped away, followed by her connective tissues. And then all that remained of the enchanting woman who'd stood there only moments before was a scattered heap of bones ... as had been the case once before, when her unidentified remains had been pulled from beneath the rubble of a devastating explosion ...

Dr. Ronan Gallagher woke up, gasping for breath. In the months since Phoebe's passage to the Otherworld, he'd been plagued by recurring nightmares of her vanishing into the mouth of that cave ... and of the twisted, hauntingly demonic version of her from the uncovered video footage.

But this nightmare had somehow hit differently; it felt so fucking real—too real, in fact.

He switched on his bedside lamp, only to discover clouds of condensation forming in the air with his every panting breath. And when he looked down, he found a spray of downy white feathers scattered across the blankets.

"What in the Goddess's green—"

And then suddenly, he was choking.

Leaning forward to clear his throat and lungs, he promptly hacked up a samara pod, which dropped into his outstretched palm. He stared at it in amazement for several long seconds, and then blinking in confusion, he turned to look out his window, beyond which the early dawn of summer was threatening to break on the horizon.

This night, he knew he'd received far more than a nightmare, or even a vision. With sudden certainty, he realized that it had been nothing less than a chilling message from the Otherworld: Phoebe had not been healed after all.

But neither was she dead.

His brows furrowing in confusion, he slowly shook his head and turned his attention back to the seed pod in his hand.

So … where the fuck is she then?

The Mythic Bones Duology continues with Book Two, *Heart of the Ash Wood*.

ACKNOWLEDGMENTS

Shadow of the Yew Tree is for those readers who spent the past three years practically shouting how much they loved Ronan in the Lost Wells Trilogy. You were right! He truly did deserve his own series. I'm so glad Phoebe emerged from the rubble and found him, too. I look forward to completing *Heart of the Ash Wood* over the coming year.

Thank you to my husband, Scott, for your evergreen support. Once again, our dinner table remained decorated with my laptop, pens, and paperwork as I exorcised another book into reality. Thank you for keeping me hydrated and (mostly) sane throughout. I love you endlessly.

To my sons—thank you for the endless joy and buddy-pairing alongside me. Much of this book was written in the company of Lego builds, wooden trains, Minecraft figurines, and solar system models. Yours is the most incredible magic in the world.

Margot and Rob, all I can say is that I wish you didn't live so far away. Thank you both for being the absolute legends that you are.

To Alecia, Erin, and Fiona—we have all been through so much together over the years, and your steadfast friendship and support have been priceless. Thank you.

Thank you to Matt and Arianna for stoking my creative fire and celebrating my successes. Your belief in these magical tales has meant the world.

To Jessie, for being a gentle yet constant sounding board; to Johanna, for reminding me of the wonder all around me; and to Kristy, for making me laugh even in the darkest moments. I am one lucky woman to have friends like you.

Thanks to my beta and sensitivity readers—Whitney, Margot, Melissa, Becky, Jessie, Meg, and Kristy—your tender care has helped shape this story into what it is today. Thanks to Britt Low at Covet Design for creating yet another dream cover. To my content and copyeditor, Janet Layberry—your mentorship on yet another series has been a blessing. And to my proofreader, M. Maryann—your thorough care and attention have meant the world.

And lastly, a bouquet of gratitude to every single reader for your support.

ABOUT THE AUTHOR

Kate Gateley is an award-winning Canadian contemporary fantasy and romance author. She holds a BA in Linguistics and a BSc in Physiology from the University of Saskatchewan and is a member of the Writers' Union of Canada and the Federation of BC Writers. Her ongoing study of ancestral memory and human psychology (among other side quests) continues to inform her writing and earn her honours as an author, including two consecutive Canadian Book Club Award wins and three shortlist nominations for the novels of The Lost Wells Trilogy, from which this duology stems.

Kate currently lives, writes, and creates on a small farm in traditional, unceded Quw'utsun territory (Cowichan Bay, BC) with her wonderfully helpful husband and two amazing kids, as well as two dogs, two geese, and a whole lot of ducks and chickens. She enjoys a wide variety of hobbies, drinks a great deal of coffee, and is barefoot as often as possible.

OTHER BOOKS BY KATE GATELEY:

The Lost Wells Trilogy

Tides of the Sovereign

Mantle of the World Ruler

Severance of the Sorcerer

To contact or connect with the author, please visit:

www.kategateley.com

www.ingramcontent.com/pod-product-compliance
Lightning Source LLC
Chambersburg PA
CBHW020354310726
48979CB00015B/2587/J

* 9 7 8 1 0 6 9 4 3 4 7 1 5 *